FIRE AND SWORD

A SWORD AND SORCERY NOVEL

DYLAN DOOSE

D1568749

BOOK DESCRIPTION

FIRE AND SWORD

"An epic tale..."—*Library Journal*

A broken nation in need of a savior.

Ravaged by plague, decimated by dark magic, infiltrated by a
foreign evil seeking to dominate from within, Brynth is on
the eve of its dissolution. When all the *good* men are dead and
gone, who is to answer the call and defy what is wicked for
what is right?

A Twisted Tale of Three Unlikely Heroes.

Heretic monk turned Sorcerer, Aldous Weaver. Infamous
crusader turned fugitive, Kendrick the Cold. Aristocrat,
rogue, monster hunter, and legend in his own mind, Theron
Ward.

Three men condemned to die for their crimes find in each
other both the will and the means to survive. A dark brother-

hood with Sword and Sorcery is forged, and all monsters meek and mighty do fear the three.

"Gritty, fast-paced and compelling!"

Honorable mention in Library Journal's Indie Ebook Awards and a Shelf Unbound Magazine Notable 100!

ALSO BY DYLAN DOOSE

SWORD AND SORCERY SERIES:

Fire and Sword (Volume 1)

Catacombs of Time (Volume 2)

I Remember My First Time (A Sword and Sorcery short story; can
be read at any point in the series)

The Pyres (Volume 3)

Ice and Stone (Volume 4)

As They Burn (Volume 5)

Black Sun Moon (Volume 6)

Embers on the Wind (Volume 7)

RED HARVEST SERIES:

Crow Mountain (Volume 1)

∼

For info, excerpts, contests and more, join Dylan's Reader Group!

Website: www.DylanDooseAuthor.com

FIRE AND SWORD

e-ISBN: 9780994828309

print ISBN: 9781777324551

www.DylanDooseAuthor.com

CHAPTER ONE

THY FATHER'S WILL BE DONE

*T*he candle flickered, fighting the darkness and the damp of the stone basement where Aldous Weaver hunched over a scarred desk, quill in hand. His fingertips were stained black, black like the sucking mire of woe in the stone basement of his mind. Memories of the darkest kind clawed at the cellar door. He dipped the quill back into the ink, his eyes straining to focus as he wrote.

An honest writer is the most virtuous of heroes; one who lies is the most deplorable of all villains.

Again he dipped the quill.

Those were the most important words I had ever been told. Words that would whisper in the wind as I lay awake and wept in those long nights at the beginning, and from the shadows of my soul the words would echo back. They were the sustenance that I sipped from under the boundless burden of the truth. To write lies that cloak the veracity of what dwells in the abysmal catacombs of the soul of man is a task for politicians and rogues of equivalent wickedness. A task that is tempting with its tantalizing lure to power and control, a task the weaker man will always prefer. To write the truth, to with no more than the oil lamp of one's own honest intent crawl ever deeper into the black abyss that is human-ity, is the gravest of tasks.

These words belonged to my father. He gave them to me the night before they burned him alive.

Aldous paused for a moment to steady his trembling hand. He took a breath and blinked his burning, tired eyes. Then he returned his sword to his foe, returned the quill to the page for the thousandth time, knowing that he would have to do so a thousand times more. Frustration surged.

"Words. They are my only tool, my only weapon, yet they betray me." Aldous tossed down his quill. "Forever they betray me. This is not honesty." He glared at the parchment. "This is nothing more than a flowery illusion, masking the scent of the truth. Miserable. Bloody miserable attempt."

He needed this book, the book he would dedicate to his father, to be perfect. The whole book had to be perfect, yet after a thousand tries, the first page was still nothing.

The fire that gave him light to write his pages was the same fire that could burn them to ash and dust. When he put the edge of the parchment to the candle it caught and burned quickly. He got a glimpse of the last words—*they burned him alive*—as the flames devoured the sheet.

He remembered as a small child watching men come from far and wide, men who called his father magnificent, brilliant, a writer unsurpassed.

After they burned him, the bastards burned his books. The priests said they were the words of sorcery, and so they must be burned along with the man who wrote them.

That was all ten years ago. Mother took her own life and a seven-year-old Aldous had been given to the church to copy scripture and pray until the day he died. But every day when Father Riker was not looking, Aldous would attempt to write his first page at his desk, a desk notched in the corner from years of dragging his anxious thumbnail across the wood. Aldous liked to think it was notched the way a warrior's axe was after a thousand battles. He fought his own battles with a quill and black ink, only a faint orange glow from the candle next to him lighting his path.

As of late he'd begun to wonder if his battle at the desk was enough. Could any battle ever be won with the metaphorical sword of the quill, or were all conflicts only solved with the true iron, sharpened and made for killing?

He looked at the candle for a moment. It danced, never tiring, always dancing was that flame. Aldous thought it must have been laughing at him. It shouldn't have been laughing, though; it had no right to laugh because they were one in the same, Aldous and the flame. Always dancing for another, and never for themselves.

Aldous muttered a curse under his breath.

"Aldous." He had not heard Father Riker come down the stairs. Father Riker was as quiet as he was old, and the man was bloody ancient. The candle flame jumped in time to the stutter of Aldous' heart, as if it too were startled. *A trick of the eyes, just a flame.*

"I pray that was a prayer you just uttered." The old man's tone was uneasy, and he fidgeted with his hands as he spoke.

Aldous remembered his first sight of Father Riker, straight-backed, stern, forbidding. He had changed over the years. Every day he seemed to lose a bit of the power he once had. His cheeks had grown hollow and the loose skin of his jowls sagged, his back hunched and his shoulders caved forward. He muttered to himself and darted glances at the shadows. He was melting day by day, in sanity and in flesh.

"Oh, it was, Father Riker, it was certainly a prayer," Aldous replied, trying to sound as he thought a pious lad should sound.

"To our great God of Light, I do hope so." Father made the symbol of the Luminescent, closing his eyes and tilting

9

his head upward ever so slightly, and opening his palms to the heavens, the way one would embrace the warmth of the sun.

"Of course, Father Riker, for there is no other god to pray to." Aldous mirrored the gesture Riker had just made, all the while wondering what sunlight Father hoped to find in this dark basement.

Father Riker grumbled and walked forward to Aldous' desk so he could inspect the amount of scripture he had copied over the day and evening. Aldous was not sure of the hour, but it was most certainly late, for every other brother had long since been off to their evening prayers and then to bed. Only he and Riker were still awake.

Aldous had not copied much. He accomplished less and less each day, for he was growing restless, and in the few hours he slept, he was haunted by dreams, running from the howling wolves, hiding from the always watching ravens.

He was done being in this church basement, done copying out this indoctrinating drivel called scripture. There had been a time—not right in the beginning, but with the passage of months and years—a time where he found solace in the copying of the words, for the mundane repetition helped him take his mind from all his anger and rage. It helped cool the smoldering fire that was his soul. That time was gone, and again the fire was rising. He did not know what he needed, but it was something other than this basement and the scratching of mindless words on parchment.

Alas, there was nowhere to go. Leaving the church would mean he too would be labeled a sorcerer and suffer the same fate as his father, the same fate as his own discarded pages.

Aldous pressed the fingertips of his right hand hard into the table as he dragged his left thumbnail on the scarred edge of his desk. *Leave me alone.*

Father Riker remained.

He dragged his thumb with greater agitation, and a sharp pain bloomed. He had torn the nail, so far down it drew blood. Anger surged, at Father Riker, at himself. Heat bit at him, deep in his belly, then his chest and his hands. The surface beneath his fingers grew hot, and he jerked his fingertips away from the table.

There were four marks singed in the wood.

Something flared in him as he stared at the strange marks, a sharp flicker that burgeoned and grew.

Aldous stood and turned around to look at Father Riker, knowing he did not want the man to see the singe marks on the desk.

"Do you hear me, Aldous?" Father asked, his voice shrill. "You are worrying me, and doing so in very dark times. A hunter has been called to our great city of Norburg, for one of the Rata Plaga has been spotted crawling from a sewer in the night. And even now, outside the church, the count's men water their horses before they set out to arrest that demon, Kendrick the Cold. These are dark times, indeed, and your lack of commitment to the church does worry me."

Aldous was not sure who Kendrick the Cold was, and he doubted the rats were back, for they had disappeared four years ago with the rest of the plague. And how either of these things had anything to do with Aldous, he did not know, but he did not say so to Riker.

"There are four pages here, Brother Aldous," the priest said as he loomed over Aldous' desk and riffled through his day's work, or lack thereof. "What is it that you do all day, Aldous?"

Aldous took a step forward, meaning to pull out the fifth page he had copied. The priest took a step back and said, "You have been worrying me as of late. You have always worried me, but recently... you frighten me."

"I frighten you?" Aldous gave a harmless chuckle at this,

11

not understanding what it was he could be doing that anyone would consider frightening. Father Riker recoiled in what Aldous could now see was indeed genuine fear.

"It is true what the other brothers have told me." Riker backed away more quickly, hands coming up as if to defend himself.

Very much confused, Aldous, too, became frightened. Whatever was happening, it was escalating quickly, like a dream that could not be understood. It was as if he'd entered the scene in a pivotal moment and had not witnessed the introduction.

"What have they told you?" he asked, unable to help the menace in his tone.

"They have seen you tampering with dark energies." Father Riker's voice quivered on the last two words.

"Dark energies? I have been tired, Father Riker, that is all. Just tired. I will copy fifty pages tomorrow." Aldous tried to sound convincing, pacing after Riker, who continued to back away, uttering prayers.

"No," the priest muttered.

"A hundred, then. I swear to the God of Light, Father. One hundred pages, not a single mistake."

"It is too late for that, Brother Aldous, too late. The word 'exclusion' has been drifting around our church, and I dreaded that such a thing would need to be done, but there seems to be no other choice."

"I have done nothing wrong, Father. How can there be no other choice than branding me a heretic and forcing me into the wilderness?" he pleaded.

"The truth is in the blood. The blood of your mother. Your father," the old priest said.

The sensation Aldous had felt earlier came again, stronger, deeper. The fine hairs on his arms and the back of his neck rose as the howl of the beast shivered through him.

"You are out to see me burn," he said. "You all are. You always have been, since I came here as a boy." The words tore from him with the spite and loathing of freedom denied, with the growl of the wolf, paw caught in the snare, the hunters closing in. It came from a place beyond anger, a place where fear dies and is reborn as the fury required to live. He felt no fear now, only the kindling of rage. There would be no more reasoning. No more pleading.

His blood was boiling, really boiling. It was hurting. Burning.

The basement lit up. The lanterns on the wall ignited, the candles at the empty desks awakened, and Aldous' little candle flame kindled into an inferno. Father Riker stood frozen, mouth opening and closing in soundless terror.

In moments, all the candles melted and the many small fires crawled onto the shadow-cloaked desks of the monks who slept on in their pallets upstairs, and with a terrible craving the flames gorged themselves on the scriptures. Aldous looked around the room, horrified. As his horror grew, the fire grew with it.

Riker pointed one twisted finger and squalled, "Demon, demon... Demon!" He fell to his knees and crawled toward the stairs, blinded by smoke and fear.

Aldous, too, went down on his knees, and crawled toward Riker. "I am not a demon. This is not my doing. Please, you must believe me. I have done nothing wrong."

Riker fell back as Aldous drew near, and, like a crab, clawed and kicked his way backward. The fire closing in all around, he struggled to his feet, coughed on the smoke and stumbled, then regained his balance and clambered up the stairs. Riker looked over his shoulder once, the horror of a doom-stricken deer when it understands that there is no escaping the wolf etching his features.

Aldous went after him. "Please, I've done nothing wrong." It sounded more a threat than an appeal to innocence.

They reached the main chapel, the smoke following Aldous from the basement like a gray cape. Somewhere, a bell rang. The other monks came running.

"Flee, brothers. Flee!" Father Riker cried, in the same voice he used to preach sermons. "Aldous is a demon, a sorcerer, a fiddler of the dark arts. With nothing but his mind, he engulfed the basement and the scriptures in flame!" Despite his strong words, Riker clutched at one of the wooden pews and sagged against it as he turned toward the sound of the front doors being wrenched open. "Enter, men of the count! Enter, seekers! There is a demon within my chapel. Save me from this fiend!"

"I am no fiend!" Aldous cried, looking from the count's soldiers to the seekers to the priest, then back again.

The brothers held their distance from him, and they, too, began to yell for the count's men.

"No, it is not true! Brothers, please." Aldous begged for them to listen; he even began to weep. For all his feelings of wishing to leave this place, to never copy a page of scripture again, he was terrified at being cast out. This was the only home he had known since the death of his father. Yet they turned on him now without a second thought.

"The count's men and the seekers will have you, Aldous," Father Riker spat. "You will burn like your father, devil. I regret the day you came to this church!"

Aldous took a final step to Father Riker then. His terror faded and his rage escalated again into a terrible thing such as he had never known. He grabbed hold of the priest's wrists.

"I have done nothing wrong, and I am no devil," he yelled in the old priest's face, spittle flying from his mouth. "My father was no devil, and my mother was no devil!"

14

Father Riker screamed in agony as Aldous' spit burned his skin. Aldous looked down, and where he held Riker, the flesh was bubbling and boiling and bursting, the stink of burning skin and muscle heavy and thick. Flame engulfed the priest. Blood, plasma, and flesh dripped off the old man's bones and streamed onto the floor. He screamed and he screamed as he melted in the smoldering fire that left Aldous untouched.

Half the monks stayed and prayed for divine intervention from their absent god, and the other half ran screaming from the chapel.

The count's men swarmed through the door. Aldous stood, frozen in place. He felt as if he were outside himself, an observer to the nightmare of a play.

Five men with broad blue hats and long capes marched toward him, words pouring from their lips, eyes locked on his. Aldous felt weak, terribly weak, and collapsed to his knees. He tried to stand, but he could not, and the strange words of the blue-hats turned to a chant, louder and louder. Their eyes began to glow with a deep blue fire. They stared into him; they cooled his boiling blood. He was standing on a frozen lake. He saw a flash of a woman, black hair, pale flesh, a dress of emerald green. The ice cracked beneath him and he fell through into the black, frigid abyss. He could not see as Aldous anymore. From high up and far away he watched his limp body taken. He watched as the raven.

～

"I... I.,. I got this for you," said the boy.

The girl beamed; he beamed back.

"For me?"

"I saw it, and... and I thought of you."

"Did you buy it from the market?" she asked, concerned for the cost.

"No, I saw it in the field, outside the city. Far from here."

"Was it scary? Scary out there?"

"It was at first, but then it was exciting. It was exciting and I found the flower. I found the flower that I brought back to you." The boy blushed and looked at the floor.

The girl puckered her lips and gave him a little kiss.

～

CHAPTER TWO

THE FOREBODING MAN

*T*he axe came down and split through helm and skull and brain like it split through dry wood. Clean, fast and with a crack.

The axe came down and split through dry wood like it split through helm and skull and brain. Clean, fast and with a crack. Less spray and gore with the wood, but when one has split apart as many men as logs, the difference becomes marginal.

No matter where he was, or the job he was working, Kendrick Solomon Kelmoor always saw the bodies and the blood of his past. In the mill he brought the axe down not on wood but on men, and the smell of cedar and wood dust always turned to the smell of corpses and death. The mine had been worse; the constant clinking of pick to stone was the sound of hammer to nail as it was driven into the flesh of screaming men and women, and at times, at horrible times, into screaming children as they got spiked to crosses. And no matter where he was or the job he was working, Ken never forgot who it was who had made him into a monster.

Still worse than the mill and the mine alike had been the

kitchens. The only place as frantic and wild and drunk as the battlefield was a royal kitchen. Ken was always at the fire, turning the roasted meats, and as they sizzled and popped, so did whole families burned alive in their homes, on the stake, or crawling with their guts out through the streets. They sizzled and they popped.

Ken hadn't lasted long in the kitchens. He hadn't lasted long in the mines. And he doubted he would last much longer than his current two years at the mill, but he did what he could to reassure himself that the log he was about to split was just that. *Just a log.*

What was it that he used to tell new recruits? The ones that were just past fifteen and had never killed and never wanted to. He used to tell them, "They're nothing but rats. You and them alike are nothing but rats, but kill enough of them rats and maybe one day you can hope to become a filthy cur." He used to say it cold and calm, right before a fight. He was cold when he fought, cold when he killed; he was cold when he walked through a village of burning corpses as the flames that charred the dead and dying to ashes licked at him and quickly retreated their tongues in fear of turning to ice. Aye, a cold bastard was he. Kendrick the Cold.

"Oi! Ken, you been at the stump all bloody day. Have enough tinder there to warm the whole fuckin' city, you do." The voice of Overseer McTalish snapped Ken from his daze, his eight-hour daze. He looked over at the pile of firewood he had made and couldn't help but be amazed at the size of it.

"I ain't letting you off until you've brought all that back to the mill. Two bloody cartloads is that, and both the mill's horses are in town. You'll be pulling the cart to and fro, you will."

"Aye, I reckon I will be," said Ken.

McTalish spat on the ground and walked away back

toward the mill. Ten, maybe fifteen-minute walk. A fair bit longer pulling a cart of wood. McTalish was a small, pox-scarred weasel of a man, and six years ago Kendrick the Cold would not have given the man's order a response of words, only a stone face and a quick death. He was that man no longer, though. He was a man of peace, and he told himself that over and over for the next two and a half hours as he carted the wood back to the mill. To and fro. He told himself he was a man of peace. But the telling was easy. The believing was hard.

~

It was long past dark when Ken set out for home, but he knew Alma would still be awake, sitting by the warm hearth with a hot bowl of soup ready for him. A good lass, was Alma, a kind and sweet lass. She was more than a bit too thin and didn't have the finest features, but Ken liked her all the same. She loved him, and that pained him, for he would not marry her. Could not. Yet she stuck by him still, despite the gossip in the town and the judging glances.

Love made people endure, and Alma endured him, so he did the best he could to take good care of her, never to raise a hand, never to insult or belittle, and always to hold her in the night. He owed her that.

Every night, though, as Ken made the long walk from the mill to the little town, he wondered what sweet Alma would say or do if she ever dug up the man he was from the grave of lies he'd buried himself in. What he really was. He doubted she would endure that; nor should she. There was only one woman that could ever endure that. That woman was gone. Ken closed his eyes tight and whistled a tune to take his mind from more dark thoughts. Dark thoughts had cursed his day, and he did all he could to clear his mind for the night.

A thin stream ran all the way from the mill right down to the town. It shimmered obsidian beneath the night sky, the light of the stars and the moon making it gleam. The sound of the water running against the boulders and the stony shore soothed Ken's mind and spirit as he walked.

The lanterns were lit by the time Ken passed the town's limit. In the faint orange glow he saw a black rat scurry its way across the stones. The tiny-clawed feet bustled to get away from the approaching man. He passed the tavern at the edge of town where McTalish sat drunk on the stoop. Ken gave him a wave. McTalish grunted and belched in affirmation, or perhaps he just grunted and belched.

He reached his home near midnight. It was quiet but for the moon song of the owls and the crickets. Ken liked the little town. He liked the modest houses, the halfway-to-decent folk, and although he was not in any way a religious man, he did like the appearance of the small stone chapel with its stained glass windows and ash wood roof. It served as a centerpiece, and everyone in the town was proud of it.

Living here was a good dream from which he did not wish to wake.

A dog came up to Ken, wagging a fluffy tail, and Ken gave it a good scratch behind the ear before he took the final steps to his door. Every single time he got nice and close to his happy evening he got some nerves, his gut swayed, and his palms grew a tad moist. A man could bury his demons, bury them in the deepest pit of the soul, but they never stopped screaming and he could never go deaf enough to escape their sound.

He took a deep breath and opened the door.

There she was by the hearth, warm soup on the table, and she turned and smiled as he came in. The floor was dirt, the roof was straw, and the walls were wood. Decent wood, but definitely not stone, and the bedroom served as every room, because the house was just that, a single room. A picky man, a materialistic man, would not pay Ken's home any compliment, but Ken didn't give a damn about that.

"Oh, sweet Alma, you're a good lass. You needn't have stayed up." Ken had been saying that since they started living together, and that was about a year.

"I like to fall asleep in your arms." Alma had been responding with that for the same amount of time.

So Ken sat down and he sipped his soup and Alma laid her head on his shoulder.

"How was the mill? It was a long day. Much to do?" she asked.

"Aye, much to do and much was done. So it was a good day," he said.

For hours, though, I thought of the sea of corpses I've left in my wake. I thought of the unarmed peasants I ran through with cold steel. I thought of weeping mothers as they watched husbands and sons die, then weeping as they were raped, all in the name of the Lord of Light. All that he did not say. He only sipped his soup and stroked sweet Alma's hair, a dry ache in his eyes.

He did not weep; he finished his soup and they crawled into bed, where he gave her his like and she gave him her love. When it was done she fell asleep in his strong arms, a little smile on her lips as she drifted off into slumber. Ken was glad he could still offer someone happiness. It was a wonderful thing to give another happiness, a wonderful thing that he felt he did not deserve to give.

Ken woke to the still night and heavy rain. He thought it strange, for he did not need to relieve his bladder, and he did not wake from a dream.

There was a knocking at the door.

He turned his head. Alma stirred at his side.

There was a banging at the door.

Alma rose, a little bit of fear in her eyes.

There was a hammering at the door.

Ken knew his happy dream was over.

He looked for a moment at Alma. "I'm sorry," he whispered.

The door splintered open and Ken sprang from his bed. He reached a hand back to Alma, motioning for her to stay put.

They came into his small, humble home with perfect efficiency, for kicking in the doors of villagers and committing unspeakable deeds upon them was the greatest skill of Count Salvenius' men.

Ten men squeezed inside, swords unsheathed, crossbows drawn back, and there was likely ten more waiting outside. Ten soldiers packed shoulder to shoulder in the single room of Ken's home, a room that at times felt just barely big enough for he and Alma. One of the men winced as the sword of the man to his left nicked his ear, and another rearranged the aim of his crossbow so that if he were to need to loose a quarrel, it wouldn't penetrate the back of his comrade's skull.

"By order of the Honorable Count Salvenius," started the man in front, sword drawn and pointed inches from Ken's face. Ken disagreed with that statement. The count was far from honorable. "Kendrick Solomon Kelmoor, better known as Kendrick the Cold—"

Ken winced as Alma's frightened sobs from behind him turned to a horrified gasp.

"Ken?" Her voice cracked on the K, and the rest of his name was barely audible.

"—for desertion, for treason, and the murder in cold blood of an officer, you are under arrest." The man speaking looked a veteran, but his hand was shaking and his brow was sweating.

Ken was naked and unarmed, yet he still knew he had a bloody good chance of killing every single one of them before he died of his wounds. He would have done so six years ago. Not now, though. If he fought them now, he would be rusty and he might lose. If that happened there would be a few survivors, and they would be enraged by the loss of brothers. In their anger they would rape sweet Alma. Ken thought about those types of things now, and so he would let them take him peacefully.

He reached out a hand to hold on to Alma's, to try and comfort her. She pulled her hand away and clung to herself.

Alma's terror wrenched hard at the empty space where his heart used to be, and that pain in his eyes ached with hell's fury. For a moment he thought that if he spoke his knees would buckle and he would finally get to weep. He thought that the frightened men before him would have a laugh and go home saying that Kendrick the Cold was nothing but a sniveling coward.

Kendrick stayed silent.

"Take the woman, too," said the man in front. "She must be put on trial for aiding a fugitive. It was the count's orders to bring to justice anyone who appeared to aid the criminal."

Two men moved forward, or, rather, they inched forward as best they could in the confined space. With each little tiptoe their drawn blades shook all the more, and as the blades got closer to Ken, the men bent at the elbow and pulled the hilts toward their own bodies.

"Stand still," Kendrick commanded as he stood there naked, his manhood shrunken from the cold wind coming through the open door. "You will leave the woman be and I will come without a fight. Or you can try and take her and I will kill each and every one of you vermin that stands now in my house. I'll have a warm bath in your blood." The threat was a low, calm statement. His eyes were tired and heavy, and he cracked his neck side to side, two deep pops when his head tilted left, a high-pitched snap when it tilted right. The men up front tried to take a step back, and the men behind pressed their flanks right up to the wall.

"There are ten more men outside, criminal," the man up front said, his words sure but his hand trembling.

"They'll be slipping on your guts as they walk through the door, you craven bastard." Ken's tone remained steady, completely even. Simple conversation with strangers.

His hands hung loose at his sides. Completely relaxed. It always went like this when the violence went slithering down his spine; he just went cold. *Nice to know some things never change.*

At that, the commander of the group stepped slowly back, as did his men.

"Cover yourself, and don't try anything foolish," said the commander.

Kendrick slid on his britches and a cloth sack shirt then followed the bastards outside. There were another ten waiting, swords drawn, pikes lowered, and crossbows pulled back, ready to loose. He put his hands together before him, waiting to be bound in chains.

"Careful, lads, be real careful. We all know who this bastard is. Most of us have seen his art," came a familiar voice from one of the men. Ken turned to look and he saw a brown-bearded, scarred face that he recognized, but he could not recall the man's name. They surrounded him, pikes pressed against his skin, a crossbow right up against the back of his skull.

They chained his hands, they chained his ankles, and then they spread apart to give him a path to waddle up to the jail cart. The men used to give him such a path those years ago when he was far away in the east. When he was drenched through with the blood of his victims, they would split like that, silently watching in horror and disgust as he walked through. It took a lot to disgust a man out there; Kendrick never failed in getting it done, though. Norburg's monster, Count Salvenius' fiend, joined the ranks an orphan boy, and left them a slayer of over a thousand. *Could build a castle with all them bodies.*

Two horses were at the head of the cart, black as the night sky behind them. They were almost invisible but for their wide black eyes reflecting the flames on the men's torches, and the steam that shot from their noses in the bitingly cold air.

It felt a long walk to that cart. Every step closer, the ache in his eyes began to recede, and Alma's animalistic sobs from the house began to fade. There was no fear in him. No sadness. No rage. Just one word and one name. *Murder. Salvenius.*

~

"I will not keep you from the dark, for I cannot keep the dark from you. When night falls and the stars fade, when black clouds smother the moon, and all the lanterns of the cities burn out, when the candles have all melted and the fireflies have withered and died, from darkness you cannot hide," said the mother as she rocked her golden-haired child into sleep.

~

CHAPTER THREE

HUNTING'S A GENTLEMAN'S SPORT

The thing left a trail of thick black blood and green pus. More a stream than a trail, if Theron Ward, hunter of monsters, wanted to be precise. It was wounded and wounded horribly, but not dead.

Grimmshire was not the only town ruined by the plague. As far as Theron knew, the whole country had a piece of it. The rats came with those terrible black boils. Rats larger than dogs. In the beginning they came in swarms. Now they appeared alone or in small roving packs, as if a once powerful bond or tether that bound the group had been weakened.

Four years ago, they had come and spewed their filth into the town. Two days was all it had taken until half the town was crawling and squealing with the rats, puking up pus and bursting black boils. The other half of the town became the swarm's feast.

Those who didn't turn simply couldn't. The priests said that only the sinners turned, that the pious were protected from the plague. Theron doubted that, for he was not a pious man and he knew a thing or two about sin—sins of the flesh mostly—and he had been exposed to enough plague to wipe out a city.

Yet he had not turned.

Theron suspected something more sinister than nature, or the work of gods and devils to be the villainy incarnate that had unleashed such wickedness upon the land. He suspected something more human, or slightly more than human. Unpopular opinion, but his opinion nonetheless.

It was midday, but it was dark in the ruined town. The clouds shrouded the sun, gray and threatening, but not a drop of rain. The once green pastures were yellow as far as the eye could see. Once this had been a bustling, happy little town. Now there were just the colors of pus and piss and ash all around, beneath those suffocating gray clouds.

There came a rustling sound from the chapel, the one building in the town not entirely burned to the ground. It had been painted white when it was built, and painted black with soot and ash when death had come to its town. The stained glass windows were shattered, shards of the vibrant panes scattered round in the dirt and the yellow grass.

"How appropriate," Theron muttered to himself, as he slowly unsheathed his silver claymore from his back. It gave the singular squeal of scraping steel as it left the scabbard, and he smiled. As his blade made its sound, so did the wounded thing from within the chapel. It was in there, suffering and dying, thanks to its earlier encounter with Theron.

Deep breath. Time to finish the job. Do I lure it out? Or do I finish it off within?

Theron often faced such dilemmas on his hunts and, as he always did, he flipped a coin, a Brynthian ducat, the face of the king on one side and the dragon on the other. He flipped the coin. *Dragon.*

Theron burst through the door. His skin crawled at the

sight of it; they always made his skin crawl, though he had killed over a hundred. He could kill over a thousand and still his skin would crawl.

Theron was a beast hunter, had been for nearly a decade, but the rats had always disturbed him the most, more than any creature or demon. What made the things so terrible was not the giant, rotting buckteeth that burst from the mouth. It was not the boils or the tufts of matted fur. Not the long tail or the brutish muscles, not the naked, sagging female breasts or the male parts dangling, filthy and crusted.

It was the eyes, for the eyes remained entirely human. And so, Theron was certain that a human being was still left in there, with no control over what it had become and begging for its torment to end.

This one had been a woman once, perhaps a mother, a lover, a sister, a daughter. For a dreadful moment he pictured his own sister taking the form of the wretched thing before him.

The creature was a hulking brute of a thing, hunched over and contorted in pain, half her body covered in muscle —monstrous heaps of muscle—anatomically all wrong and grotesque. The other half was pulsating with yellow and black boils, bubbling and bleeding. Each one looked as if it had its own heartbeat as it heaved and writhed. Theron had shot it twice with his crossbow. Two bolts stuck out of the creature's chest; one was cracked and dangling and the other remained deep, blood oozing from the partially clogged holes every time it took a breath. The wounds would have killed any man in moments. He had shot the foul beast three hours earlier and nearly twenty kilometers away in the count's city of Norburg.

It was done running, though. Its breath came out heavy and in gurgling rasps, which told Theron that there was a good hole in one of its lungs. It retched and a pint of black blood poured from its—her—rotten maw.

Theron pulled down his black-brimmed hat, nice and tight so it wouldn't fall off. Then he rushed at the rat that had once been a woman—and somewhere inside still was—both hands tight on his claymore, his black coat billowing behind.

She was wounded and in a corner, and, like all beasts, that made her all the more dangerous. She squealed and charged, swinging her muscled arm at Theron, razor claws at the end. He ducked under it, but with immense speed the rat lashed out with a back swing. Theron brought down his claymore on the rotten flesh, but he only had room for a half swing, and so his blade was lodged halfway through the arm. The rat screamed and twisted away, spraying Theron with its filthy ichor.

Killing was a hard thing. Rata Plaga or not, the fetid beast still felt pain. The greatest difference for Theron between killing one of them or a man in combat was that the screams of the rats were always worse.

Deep breaths, deep breaths and ferocity until the task is done. Theron Ward, monster hunter, was a man who never flinched.

They backed away from each other. Theron retreated up the altar steps backward, looking into the human eyes of the plague rat as he did.

"Come to your peace. End your suffering, woman."

It made a sound as if to speak, but only released the squeal of a rat.

"I know that somewhere in there you hear me. You know my words. You understand me." He could see a terrible woe in her eyes, the woe that came with being the monster in one's own nightmare. The woe in a dream where one was a passenger to their own wickedness. When he stared at that singular despair, he did so with a haunting dread, a dread that, one day far from now, after years of slaying vile beasts and evil men, he too would share those eyes of woe. He swallowed that dread and carried on. "The fear is gone because you have given up on fear. You have accepted you cannot wake, that the only release is death, but there is no control and death is not yours to take. Let me give it to you."

She made a deep sound, like a sob, the sob a human makes when it sounds like an animal, and again she retched, pus oozing from her lungs and guts out between her rotting teeth.

"I will set you free," Theron yelled in a great fury, but his anger was not at the thing before him—his anger was at whatever thing had allowed it to come to be.

The beast roared, enraged that Theron had contacted the woman within, furious that he had appealed to the vessel. As the hellspawn came ripping forward, its human eyes welled with tears. Perhaps of hope, perhaps a symptom of the plague.

Theron raised his mighty silver claymore, the blade sharper than winter's bite. He leapt from the altar and brought down the sword with the strength brought on by a near decade of swinging that heavy sword, of riding, of brawling, of hunting monsters. As the honed edge of the heavy blade rent through flesh and bone, as it obliterated skull and brain, the rat screamed, Theron screamed, and together in that moment they each found peace.

～

A small stream ran just north of Grimmshire. Theron took a moment to wash the filth from his hands, for it was a nasty business cutting out a heart and putting it in a jar. It was nastier still when it was the heart of a Rata Plaga. He felt calm, as he often did after a hunt. There were always nerves in the stalking, in the chasing, and in the killing, but when it was done there was a surreal calmness. He grinned to himself as he looked into the heart within the jar, another little story in the saga of the legendary hunter Theron Ward.

He whistled a tune that his mother used to hum to him as he walked the muddy road back to Norburg. He whistled past a procession of barebacked, hooded men, known around Brynth as Doom Sayers. The cult had formed at the very beginning of the Rata Plaga, and they had been walking through mud and mire, whipping themselves, ever since. They sang some hymn or some prayer—Theron did not know—and whipped their backs bloody as they walked down the path.

Theron whistled as he passed a dead tree with strange carvings and the skeletons and fresh corpses of woodland creatures hanging from the branches. He whistled as he passed by barren farms with skeletal serfs tilling dead ground. Brynth was a nasty place, and Theron had realized early on that to deal with the nastiness sometimes it was best to squint your eyes and whistle a tune.

He reached a crossroads; from it the city of Norburg was in view, if he kept to the western path. From the northern one there came rolling a carriage, two black horses pulling and a good twenty men marching with it, all armed to the teeth.

Theron paused at the fork and stared a moment.

"Who goes there?" the man at the front of the brigade called out.

"Theron, Lord Wardbrook. I am under contract to the Honorable Count Salvenius to deal with the rat that killed a man in Norburg. This I have done," Theron called.

"Very good. At least one of Norburg's problems is bloody solved."

"One of them?" Theron asked. "Are there others?"

36

"A bloody sorcerer burned down the chapel just a week ago." The brigade was now at the fork, and they turned to go in the same direction as Theron.

"Yes, I heard about that," said Theron. He had heard about it, but he was not entirely sure he believed it.

"Are you heading back to Norburg now?" asked the leader.

"As a matter of fact, I am. Perhaps I will travel the rest of the way with you lot."

The leader blushed red. "I'm afraid not, Lord Wardbrook. We are under distinct orders to not allow anyone else, other than the King of Brynth himself, in the party with us." He nodded to the wagon. "Delicate package, you see?" The man offered a meek smile.

Theron scowled. "It's not but another quarter hour walk. I can see the front gate to the city from where I now stand."

"I'm sorry, my lord."

"Well then, what would you have me do?" When the man made no answer, Theron continued, "Are you implying that I should stand here and wait for your entourage to walk safely through the gates and only then follow?"

"I'm sorry, my lord."

Theron sighed. "You're damn well lucky I am under your count's employ. For if this situation that is now occurring were to be occurring under any other pretense, you and I would be having an issue, sir. I've dueled over far less."

"Pretense?" the man asked.

Theron gave a circular wave and then gestured them on.

～

Lower Norburg smelled of something foul. All of Norburg smelled of something foul, and in truth so did every city Theron had ever had the pleasure—or in this case, the displeasure—of visiting, but Lower Norburg's stench was in a class of its own. Four years since the Rata Plaga had mostly subsided, the majority of those susceptible had already turned, and most of those who were immune had been ripped apart and eaten by the swarm of the susceptible.

Then they just left. The swarm of human rats simply disappeared. The priests said they went back to hell. Theron doubted that, because he was still being hired to hunt them whenever they popped up and were spotted by a village or in the woods. This was the first time in four years that one had been seen in the city. It was as if it got lost on its way to somewhere else.

A grimy, soot-covered citizen looked out of a broken window of a second-story home as Theron walked down the cobbles of the main thoroughfare. Theron offered the man a smile; he always smiled at townsfolk.

Always smile at strangers, Theron. Nothing puts a wayward soul at ease like a friendly smile, his mother used to say. His mother was a strange woman, and she and Theron were not on entirely good terms, but he did still follow some of her advice. For better or worse.

The man in the window spat on his own floor and receded into the shadow.

Theron grinned and shook his head. The fellow was likely overwhelmed at having had a personal glimpse at the monster hunter Theron Ward.

He had been to Norburg many a time before the plague hit. It had been painfully overpopulated, with three or sometimes four families crammed into a single home. At all hours of the day and night, the city streets had been crammed with human traffic. Shopkeepers would be yelling the day's bargain; children would be running, their mothers hollering after them. Street urchins would be picking pockets and nabbing food from carts, city guards hot on their tails.

Theron never liked all the commotion, but this was even worse. There was only one family for every four houses now, a shopkeeper was a rare sight, and a child even rarer.

Theron felt a pinch of guilt as he looked at the miserable place—survivor's guilt, as well as the guilt of wealth. He was a wealthy young man, largely by inheritance of a fine country estate. Wardbrook, thirty kilometers north of Grimmshire, was where he called home, all twenty-two rooms and four hundred acres. Indeed, Theron was rich, and he did feel guilty, but not guilty enough to give his land and wealth away. *What could they do with it anyway? All the money in the world wouldn't fix what happened here. Their problems can't be bought away, they must be fought away.*

Theron jogged up the high steps that led to the open gate separating Lower and Upper Norburg. He walked into the lavish and abandoned the lowly. Upper Norburg was the perfect opposite to its lower counterpart. The sky was still gray, but the upper city burst with rich color and life. The noble class drank, gambled, ate, and fucked with vigor unmatched by the times before the plague. As if coming so close to death awakened a stronger desire for life within them. Or some such nonsense. To Theron they were nothing but spoiled scum, nearly as bad as the monsters he hunted. What he hated most about them was how close he was to *being* them, and that was why he had taken up the hunt.

Before seeing Honorable Count Salvenius and collecting the bounty, Theron thought it would be appropriate to retire to his rooms at the inn, have a hot bath, and change in to something more courtly than his gore-drenched overcoat and hat.

He walked through the door of the inn, and without looking at its keeper, a grouchy old lady whose name Theron had forgotten, said, "Bath—hot, please, very hot. Soup as well, with meat preferably. I know you have it. Some bread also. Something heavy. I'm very hungry." He was halfway up the stairs when he was done delivering his demands to the innkeeper, then he turned to look at the woman for a moment. She was old, fat, and scowling. He smiled at her as wide as he could with his perfectly straight white teeth.

The grouchy lady scowled all the more at Theron's smile, as if she was anticipating what his final request would be.

"And if you don't mind, could you send up that servant girl. Uhm... Caroline? Yes, indeed, Caroline was her name. I must talk to her... about the manner in which... she makes the bed?"

"Will that be all, Master Ward?" The innkeeper snarled, her face all wrinkled and mean.

"Yes, that would be splendid, thank you." Theron bounded up the rest of the steps terribly excited for a hot bath, a hot meal, and a fiery Caroline. He had paid the innkeeper four times the standard fee for his stay, so although she was a foul old bat, she was willing to please.

Theron had seen the bruises on the lovely Caroline's arms, no doubt inflicted by the goblin-ess under whom she was employed. It was his duty to always save the damsel in distress from any beast—in this case, it was a very human beast. He wasn't quite sure yet how his current actions amounted to saving her, but he would figure that out later.

The hot meal came first, and since the inn was located in the upper district of Norburg, it was not half bad—not nearly as good as Bilfred would have made it at Wardbrook, but pretty decent nonetheless. Theron hummed a tune as he ate and watched two servants fill his tub. He had been paying for the King's Suite, so his rooms had a monstrous bed, a tub, a hulking wardrobe, and a wonderful full-length mirror. The straw-stuffed mattress was fresh, the linens clean, and Theron counted himself lucky to have found such a miraculous place. Theron wasn't sure if he liked the mirror or the bath more.

When he was done with his meal and his bath, Caroline knocked at the door. *A perfect evening after a hard day's work.*

"Do come in," Theron called through the door.

"Missus Roche says you summoned me, my lord?" Caroline looked at Theron for a moment then blushed and looked at the floor. That was because he was standing in the center of the room in a wide stance and his hands on his hips, in the same garb he wore at birth.

She was a beautiful girl, and even more so when she was blushing. Red-haired, narrow waist, and curvaceous, she was what Theron called lower-class loveliness. Full and strong from a life of work, yet timid, unlike the women in court, who were stick-thin and arrogant from a lifetime of nothingness. He had to admit he liked the girls at court too—in fact, he had liked one just two nights past in the stables—but tonight he wanted Caroline.

"Please, my dear, call me Theron, and do close the door behind you. That cool draft will only diminish my splendor."

Caroline giggled and closed the door.

Some time later, Caroline helped Theron into a royal-blue doublet then a black vest over top. She tucked the shirt into his black trousers and her hand spent a little extra time up front. They stood in front of the mirror, and although Caroline was still naked from their romp in the sheets, Theron was all business now, and he was purely inspecting himself in the reflection.

"How do I look, my dear?" Theron asked.

"Like the most handsomest of princes, my lord."

He smiled, not at her but at himself, then unbuttoned the top of his shirt.

"Buttoned or unbuttoned?" he asked.

"Well, that depends—are you going to meet with another

lass?" She ran her hands over his abdomen; he tightened it out of vanity.

"I'm going to go see the count, actually."

Caroline laughed at this, and covered her mouth as she did. The way timid girls do when they are shy of their teeth.

"Then button it up, right up, or the count may think you are trying to seduce his daughter."

"Unbuttoned it is."

～

"Not here. I want it in the stables. I want the beasts watching me," said the lady with lustrous green eyes, the rest of her features concealed beneath her mask.

"What manner of nymph are you, woman?" asked the gentleman.

"I am no woman, I am a fiend. I am hungry and thirsty and I am a fiend. And I want to go now." She grabbed his wrist.

"Leave this lovely masquerade with food and drink? For the stables? I should stay and fortify myself. Tomorrow I must hunt."

"I will fortify you. We go now to the stables, so we can fuck like animals," she said.

The gentleman was a gentleman, but he did not say no.

～

CHAPTER FOUR

THE EMERALD WOMAN

*T**hey took her anyway, you damn fool.*
No.
They did, they took her. You counted them through the bars of your cage. Eighteen every time, not twenty, just eighteen. Two stayed behind and they took Alma. Probably raped her. You did that, Ken. She suffered. She is dead. Because of you.

Fuck you.

Think about it. Why else would they have stayed behind?

They were laughing. You heard them laughing. You know that laugh, the laugh of men who have become beasts.

Fuck you.

First you killed your wife. Now you killed Alma.

So much for burying Kendrick the Cold in the past.

Ken slammed his chained fists against the wall of the wagon.

He could have killed every last one.

He should have. He should have saved her instead of holding out his hands and letting himself be chained.

Should have wasn't the same as could have.

Kendrick the Cold could have killed them. But he was not

that man now. He was not cold. He was hot and sick, the rage a red film before his eyes. Impotent rage.

"I should have killed you all. I should have slaughtered you all, you fucking bastards, hung you in the woods by your own intestines, carved out your fucking eyes. Nailed you to the trees and let the ravens pick you apart. Should have done to you what I did for the count," Ken yelled into the darkness of the wagon. Should have done it to them so they couldn't do it to Alma.

No response came. Ken told himself it was because the bastards were afraid, but in truth, by now they realized that Kendrick the Cold was just another human being, another sniveling rat.

The wagon had been stopped for a while, and he knew he was there. He had returned home, his real home. Norburg. Fourteen years ago he had joined the count's men. Fourteen years old. The count's men joined the royal army and they set out to the east, the far southeast to bring the Luminescence—the God of Light—to the heathens. And in the far southeast the count's men became something inhuman.

The God of Light was a dark god.

The wagon had been still for an hour, maybe more. It didn't matter. Nothing mattered now. The doors opened.

"Kendrick Solomon Kelmoor. Welcome home, you bastard." Sebastian Calabaster, the man who'd recruited him all those years ago, was standing outside. He was thinner now, much thinner. His cheeks were sunken and his chain mail hung from his skeletal form like iron rags. His mutton chops had grown gray, his hair thinned, but Kendrick knew it was the same man. Calabaster had not gone to the far southeast. He had not fought there, but he fought at home. He fought the Rata Plaga, and that must have been just as bad, Kendrick reckoned.

"You are not little Kendrick anymore, the small, sickly

orphan that begged to join the regiment. You're a bloody bull now. By God you've grown," Calabaster said.

"It's been fourteen years, and it wasn't by God that I've grown. It was by force. You, too, look different, Calabaster, You look old, dreadfully thin."

"Thanks for noticing, lad. I do try, I certainly do try." The old man smiled, rotten yellow and black teeth nearly as gnarly as the bloody plague rats.

"Well, out you come, to the cells with you. You'll be hanged in a day or two," he said.

"Thanks for noticing," Kendrick said. "Don't sound so sad."

They both laughed, because Calabaster hadn't sounded sad. He hadn't sounded anything at all.

There was strange rumbling in the ground when Ken stepped down from the wagon.

"There it is again," mumbled one of the guards.

Calabaster turned to Ken. "Strange rumblings, in the ground around the city the past few weeks. First time I noticed it was when the Emerald Lady from the northeast arrived. Ground was rumbling so bad she nearly tripped and fell. The Honorable Count Salvenius caught her, luckily. Quick hands he has for a large man."

Ken scowled at the mention of the count, not much caring about the rumbling in the ground or this Emerald Lady.

Armed men closed tight next to Ken, and after a few steps a crossbow was at his back, steering him.

"I suppose there won't be a trial?" Calabaster asked.

"For the likes of him?" The surrounding guards laughed. "No, no, not for the likes of him."

∾

Atop a fine white gelding purebred, Theron trotted toward the count's keep. He was decked out in his lavish clothes, his long blond hair tied with a royal blue ribbon at the base of his skull. He rode with a short sword at his hip and his claymore on his back, the blades in black scabbards encrusted with gems.

He rolled up the sleeves of his shirt so the muscles of his forearms bulged as he gripped the reins. Every so often he would look down at them and twist his wrists to tighten the cords beneath his flesh. As he trotted past a fountain he pulled his horse to a momentary stop and admired the fine figure he made in the water's reflection with the quarter moon shining above his left shoulder before moving on.

It is a mad world, Theron thought as he stared at a thin girl of perhaps fourteen at most, being fondled by a man old enough to be her grandfather and large enough in the waist to fit four of the girl. He was laughing with some other so-called gentlemen as they stumbled drunk through an alley just off the main thoroughfare. Even in the dim light of the street lantern, Theron could see the purple bruising around the girl's eye. *These nobles call the lands outside of Brynth savage. They call the peasantry lowly, yet they see no issue in forcing young girls to marry old men. In leaving children to beg in the streets. This is the hypocrisy of man.*

"Are you looking at something, sirrah?" came the slurred words of the vermin with his hand around the girl's wrist.

"Nothing but a pack of rats in an alley," Theron said, his voice calm but tinged with venom.

There was a sad humor in the fact that he had just killed a monster in the defense of the people of Norburg, yet as he looked at the poor girl he wondered if killing just one monster ever did any good. *There will always be more.*

He spat on the ground, then carried on, and with each clop of his horse's hooves upon the stone cobbles and with each instigating yell from the drunkards, he imagined himself dismounting, killing the lot of them, and telling the girl she was free. *Free to do what? Have her father marry her off to another man of equal wickedness, or perhaps one even worse.*

He did not stop for a fight; there was no point, for if he fought over every injustice he would never get anything done.

Theron had no love for the count's city, but the city had had a monster, and Theron was a killer of monsters, so he came to the count's city and he killed his monster. It had not been an altogether terrible trip. Caroline had been a sweet thing, and the ball he'd attended two nights past had him loving a spry noble girl in a golden mask. A real demon, she was; dragged him to the stables, said she wanted it like an animal. Pretty, from what he could see that was not concealed by her mask. Green eyes, not of the forest. A different green.

Theron at last arrived at the keep, a perilously tall gray-stoned building, built with the design somewhere between a cathedral and a lordly estate. He dismounted and handed the reins of his horse to a well-dressed young lad in the court-yard, who bowed his head and walked away toward the stables with Theron's gelding.

"Careful with him, boy," Theron said, and when the boy turned around Theron tossed him a gold coin. The boy nodded and went on his way.

In the center of the courtyard was a great sundial, more a thing of richness than of any actual use, for the sun rarely shone down on the city of Norburg due to its almost constant cover of cloud. Past the dial, the wagon he had seen earlier on the road sat just outside the keep, with half the escort still milling about. The wagon was empty now, the prisoner gone. Theron felt a pang of sympathy, for the count's dungeons were notorious. He walked to the front doors, where a guard nodded and opened the gate.

"Lord Wardbrook," said the guard, and Theron was not at all surprised that though he did not remember the guard, the guard remembered him.

The interior of the keep was a thing to behold. It made Wardbrook seem mundane and poor in comparison, but Wardbrook at least had a sense of design. Black marble was the floor, black marble was each and every pillar, and black marble was each and every wall. Numerous paintings of the count that depicted him in his younger years, or in some fantasy realm where he was handsome and not grotesquely obese, adorned the walls. Trophy heads of exotic animals and beasts were jammed between and above the paintings. Their glass eyes seemed to follow Theron as he made his way down the long hall of nonsense things, past the heads and the paintings and the pieces of armor and ceremonial weapons. There was no order to it, and certainly not even a whisper of good taste. It looked altogether a bit mad.

He paused once and looked back. The eyes still stared.

Theron thought nothing one way or the other about the count. Salvenius was rich, even by royal standards, and his wealth neared that of the king himself. Much had been amassed through inheritance from his long and noble line, and enhanced by the brutal taxes he imposed. All that wealth went to the important things, such as big feasts, big parties, and big collections of nonsense.

Theron considered it common sense to make certain that those under his rule and care were well taken care of. It wasn't sentimentality. It was simple reason. Healthy peasants could work, yield more crops, enrich the estate. Starving peasants could not.

A crimson rug ran down the center of the black marble floor, right up to the lacquered oak doors that opened into the court. He put his hand on the door, and something in his chest seemed to harden and expand. He swallowed, feeling acid burn his gut. Anxiety. A sensation Theron was not usually accustomed to. A sensation he had not felt since Mother. Since Mother had done what she had done.

He looked at the jar he carried in his hand, at the black, rotting heart of the plagued she-rat. It had a dark shimmer to it, the same dark shimmer as the black marble. He took a deep breath; perhaps expanding his ribs would get that burdensome rock to fall from his chest. It did not fall; instead it grew. Theron had an urge to smash the jar and run, to sprint in the other direction, to leave Norburg and ride like all the devils in hell were nipping at his heels back to Wardbrook, where he would stay, stay for some time, his servants armed and his doors and windows boarded up.

Why he had this feeling he did not know. Theron despised feelings that he did not understand, and so he ignored the growing stone in his chest and opened the big oak doors.

The court had not a single sycophant at that late hour, and in truth, Theron thought he would be receiving his payment and handing the heart to one of the count's men. Instead he was greeted by the count himself, a strange woman standing just behind and to the side of the throne, and an absurd amount of guards lined against the right and left walls. The count was waiting, and he looked exponentially more grotesque than he had two nights before. He heaped over the sides of his lavish golden chair and his beady eyes looked as if they were about to burst from his head, more red in them than white. There was spittle on his greasy black beard, and his white tunic was drenched through at his armpits. Drenched and yellow.

The woman's elegant ringed hand rested on his shoulder, elegant but strong, fingernails painted emerald green. The woman was not his wife, for it was known to most that the count's wife had died many years ago. Mysterious causes. Most royal wives in Brynth were known to be taken by that plight, the plight of mysterious causes.

The emerald-nailed woman had black hair, so long it nearly dripped to the floor. If one black could be blacker than another, the woman's hair was the blackest, no shimmer to it, no luster. Just black. Full red lips, and eyes the same emerald as the polish on her nails. Her pale white breasts pressed against her black and green bodice, faint branches of blue veins running just beneath her milky skin.

Theron was not sure if he should be aroused or repulsed, for there was something baleful about this woman, and although he was not a man of God—far from it, in fact—he shivered at her unholy aura.

The woman engulfed his focus so entirely he had not registered the count yell, "Seize him." He heard him; he just somehow wasn't altogether receptive to the words, as if they were part of a scene that was of no importance to him.

It *was* of importance to him, though.

The armed guards surrounded him, weapons drawn and raised, snapping him out of his daze.

"Seize me?" Theron dropped the jar with the plague heart. It hit the ground with a clink but did not crack. He put his hand on the hilt of the short sword at his belt but did not draw. "What the bloody hell for?"

"For the defilement of my daughter, you debaucherous filth!" The count turned a deep shade of red then a bit purple. He stood from his chair, his fat legs shaking beneath his enormous weight.

"Debaucherous filth? Why I never. I am Theron Ward, Lord of Wardbrook, and I shall not have my name so besmirched, sir, Count of Norburg or no!"

The guards edged closer. They were wary, as they should

be. Theron could take a handful of the bastards right to hell, and they knew it, for the name Theron Ward was spoken far and wide and it was spoken with veneration... or at least so he told himself. He could kill a handful but there were too many, and Theron was not keen on dying in Norburg.

"Besides," he said, "I think I would have known if I had taken your daughter to bed, and I can assure you I did not. There is a mistake. Someone is spreading lies. Tell me who told you such a thing and I will make them spill the truth."

The count's face did not change color, but he did sit back down, prompted to do so by the dark-haired woman. She spoke then, her voice not at all like her features. It was too deep for her figure and had a hellish rasp to it, the rasp of old age, old age lived out in a smoke pit. Yet the woman was no more than twenty-five years in appearance.

Sorcery.

"It is true you did not bed the count's daughter," she said. "You ravaged her cunt in the royal stables. You fucked her from behind." The rock in Theron's chest had grown so large now it felt as if his spine was any moment to rip from his flesh. "You fucked her like a beast."

Theron stared into the woman's eyes. *Such a green, not like a forest, like a mist of poison, miasma, and rotten death.*

At this, the count's face turned from deep red to white then green, and he gave a malodorous belch, then made a choking sound, and then—Theron cringed as he steeled his mind for what was to come—the count hurled up thick chunks of his royal dinner onto his royal tunic and his royal trousers. Even at Theron's distance he could smell it, quail pie, bile, and stomach-churning rage.

The guards lowered their pikes, a veritable forest of sharp points leveled at his throat. Theron thought this a good time to raise his arms in surrender. The count had clearly just reached past the point of discussion, and so Theron would forfeit and find a way out of this conundrum in due time. The moment his hands went up, a guard came up behind him and pulled his hands down to bind his wrists. When he was bound and a man held him at each side, a third one sheathed his sword and stepped forward.

"Not the face, you bastard," Theron warned. "Don't you dare strike me in the face."

The man, a big, thick bastard equal parts muscle and fat, dared to do exactly that.

Shards and splinters of white in a puddle of red. Fragments of teeth and skull. The father was dead. The wife screamed. The children wailed. Kendrick had orders, and on the cross they would be nailed.

Cold as frost was his mind as their hot blood gave flow, yet as hammer struck spike, as they screamed, within his soul did the ember of self-hatred begin to glow.

Man to monster.

What man made this monster?

Count Salvenius must pay.

CHAPTER FIVE

THE SEEDS OF FRIENDSHIP

*A*ldous felt as if his head had been bludgeoned past the point of pain. It was just numb, a complete lack of sensation, as if he just existed in space. His muscles felt the same. He could move, but barely. *Stone floor. Not much light. Have I fallen asleep in the basement again? Why do I feel so weak? Father Riker will scold me terribly. I may even get lashes for falling asleep again.*

"At last, he wakes." The voice was deep and young, healthy and with good humor. It was not the voice of Father Riker.

With all his energy Aldous raised himself into a sitting position so he could see the man who was speaking. The figure was no more than an outline at first, but his eyes soon adjusted and Aldous saw him clearly.

He was a sight to behold; he was standing over Aldous like some golden giant. Perhaps two inches over six feet in height, and broad in shoulder. He had long blond hair and fierce gray-blue eyes. Every muscle was tight and rock solid. He wore nothing but tattered and filthy sack pants, and they looked strange on him, for he looked royal, and so Aldous thought he should be dressed so.

"Who are you? Where am I?" Aldous asked.

"I am the honorable Theron Ward, Lord of Wardbrook, at your service. And you are in a dungeon, my dear boy."

All of a sudden Aldous was very awake, and he used a nearby wall to assist him to his feet. He looked around, and although he had never been in a dungeon—unless he counted the basement of the church—this place looked enough like a dungeon that he could not question the man's words.

Empty, but for a rickety rotten bench on each wall, no windows, and made of stone, with a thick wooden door supported by iron. There was an unemptied slop bucket in the corner, the smell of piss and shit heavy in the air, and the walls moved with filth.

"What do you mean, I am in a dungeon?"

"I mean exactly what I said. You are in a dungeon." At Aldous' silence, he continued, "You are in the dungeon of Count Salvenius' keep, where he keeps prisoners under lock and key until they are brought to the torture chambers, and then hanged by the neck until they die." His tone was perfectly calm, and for some reason this upset Aldous far more than it would have if the man were hysterical.

"Prisoner? Torture? Hanged?" Aldous asked. He felt very ill, and he broke out in a cold sweat, trying to remember how and why he was there. He could taste bile in the back of his throat.

"Very good. You have just repeated the three key points of what I just said. It is clear that your mind is semi-functioning."

"Why am I a prisoner? I am a monk. I have done nothing wrong. Where is Father Riker?"

"Apparently you are not a monk. You are a sorcerer, and you burned this Father Riker alive. With your bare hands. Or so I have heard. I sincerely doubt that, though." The blond man snickered. "A fire mage, with no catalyst, at your young age. Not likely. But something happened and you killed a man, so you're here."

It all came back to Aldous in pieces, little fragments, like remembering a nightmare. Scattered screams and begging. Father Riker begging for his life and the flesh melting off his bones. Aldous could hear his own screams in the back of his mind, yet they were not his own, they were the furious cries of a demon. Not himself.

His skin began to tingle, to go hot as he remembered the fire... *the beautiful kindling fire.* He tried pinching himself, like a foolish child seeing if they are in a dream. It hurt; he was awake.

"No. That did not happen," Aldous whispered, more to himself than to Theron. He felt the heat of tears in his eyes, and he ran his hands through his hair, pulling at the ends.

"Oh, I think something happened."

"I did not mean to do it. I swear. I must tell them it was not my intent to do such a thing."

Theron gave a deep laugh.

"That is a good and brilliant plan. It will certainly get you out of your current debacle. Perhaps I shall do the same, right before they hang me. 'Uh, yes, Count Salvenius, your largleyness, I do swear I did not mean to fuck your daughter in the royal stables. It was an accident, so do release me.' No, no, young man, that strategy will not do."

The blond man slid down the wall he was leaning against with a long, dramatic sigh. Behind him, painted on the wall, was a strange symbol, the same blue as the eyes of the men that Aldous had seen right before his curtain was pulled. The paint seemed to glow, and looking at it made Aldous feel weak.

"What is that marking behind you?" Aldous asked, his voice quaking.

Theron looked up.

"A seeker's sigil. All prison cells in the country have them, as far as I know. At least the cells of any major city."

"What is a seeker's sigil?"

Theron scowled at him. "You don't bloody well know anything, do you? It prevents you from doing any of your wizardry so, in here, you are as weak as you look."

"I know no wizardry." Aldous tried to sound fearsome, then felt red as Theron just laughed.

"I believe you, but what I believe doesn't mean much right now."

~

They had been sitting alone in the cell mostly in silence for hours, except for Theron's occasional yelling outbursts to the guards, who may or may not have been outside. Theron was now kicking the door repeatedly and with all his might. He did this for perhaps five minutes straight, and his endurance amazed Aldous. Five straight minutes of furious kicking. Of course, the door did not budge, and so an exhausted Theron returned to his corner and sat.

"Damn me. Damn my irresistible features. I always knew that one day my pelvic propensities would result in my death, I just thought it would be in old age, my heart failing as a buxom beauty gave me one last ride." Theron looked down at his crotch and simply yelled. Aldous thought the man to be quite mad.

"Who are you?" he asked.

Theron looked up. His eyes went wide and he contorted his face into a scowling underbite. Aldous would have backed away if he weren't already against a wall.

"I told you who I am," Theron said calmly, his distorted facial features immediately returning to normal. He scurried across the floor, running his hand across the bottom edges of the wall, as if he were looking for something.

Aldous was not sure if he was more terrified of being in Norburg's dungeon or of who he was in it with.

"What are you doing?" He did not mean for his voice to come out as sniveling as it did. "You are really not making this situation any easier for me." Aldous began rocking back and forth, hugging his knees against his chest as he watched the handsome madman scurry across the floor muttering to himself.

Theron burst to his feet and stood in front of Aldous in a flash of speed that was hard to comprehend. The blond man aimed an imaginary sword at Aldous' throat.

"Who the hell are you, boy? What makes you think I care at all about the ease with which you are able to endure your current conundrum?" Theron slowly leaned his face down until it was inches from Aldous'.

"I am Aldous. Aldous Weaver," he whispered, and closed one eye, shying away from the imaginary sword.

Theron sheathed his phantom blade and sat back down, nodding to himself.

"Ah, Weaver. That's a good name. 'Twas the name of my favorite author. Darcy Weaver."

Aldous' heart thumped at the mention of his father's name, and he leaned in now, his fear momentarily replaced with interest.

"They burned his books, the bastards." Theron squinted. "Your order burned his books. But you redeemed yourself in my eyes. Good riddance to that priest you burned alive. They burned him, too, you know. They burned the great Darcy Weaver."

"I know," Aldous said, his voice hollow.

"You would have been a wee lad then. I was quite young

myself. About your age now." Theron paused and squinted at Aldous. "What do mean, 'I know'?"

"I know about Darcy Weaver. They said he was a sorcerer. They said that when he burned he went to the devil."

"Bastards," said Theron, "They burned him in a city not far from here."

"Yes. Aldwick. They burned my father in Aldwick," Aldous said, very quiet, almost a whisper.

"What did you just say?" Theron again sprang from his corner and grabbed Aldous by the shoulders, lifting him from the ground, as if he were a small child. "What the bloody hell did you just say?"

"Darcy Weaver was my father," he yelled.

"Say it again, and don't you dare be lying. I shall kill you here and now if you're lying. That man's words made me *me.* There is no one like him. He made me understand what a man must try to be. In my darkest moment when I thought my world was over, his words pushed me to become something better, something more, to become a monster hunter. He made me fight for what is good. Do you understand that? Do you have any damn idea of the importance in that?" Theron was nearly frothing as he yelled, his wide, crazy gray-blue eyes a maelstrom swirling down to the madness of his soul. "Don't you dare be lying!"

"Darcy Weaver was my father! I watched as they burned him alive. They took our lands. They burned his books and they sent my mother to a nunnery, where she slit her wrists. They sent me to the church. They sent me to the fucking church, where I burned Father Riker alive, where I cooked him as he screamed. I don't know how, but I did, I did, and so fuck him, fuck him right to hell!"

Theron stared down at Aldous and suddenly embraced him as the tangent reached its conclusion and the confusion that now entered the mixture of emotions he was feeling became almost too much to bear.

"This is destiny," Theron said. "You will not die here, not in Norburg. I will slaughter every single man in this city if I must, but I will get you, Aldous Weaver, safely from here. You will write. You shall write just as your father did, not copying out scripture in a fucking church, but truly write! My adventures will fuel your dormant talent. It is fate, most certainly fate."

~

Theron could not believe it. In his arms he held the living heir to Darcy Weaver.

The two of them sat in the cell, and for hours Theron spoke to Aldous about his father's writing. Things that the boy had no idea about, and in return Aldous told Theron about what Darcy Weaver was like as a man and a father, full of ideals, patient with his son, who had two questions for every answer. He sounded a lot like Theron's father in many ways, and this pleased him greatly. The hours went on and on until they were hungry, and then a few more hours passed until some slop was slid into their cell across the floor.

"I'd rather die then eat that filth," Theron said to Aldous, then screamed the same thing as loud as he could to notify the guards outside what he thought of their hospitality. Much to his regret, a good while later, he ate the slop with the wooden spoon provided. Aldous tried to eat his, but it only made him retch.

"Would you like my bowl of filth, Theron?" Aldous asked after trying to take a second spoonful and once again failing.

"You are sure you don't want it?" Theron asked, his hand already outstretched and on the bowl.

"I am sure."

"You are too kind."

"Please, it is nothing really. It will do me no good, and if you are going to be saving us, you will need your strength," Aldous said.

Theron chuckled.

The seeker sigils gave a quick glow, then faded. It was the seventh time they had done so since Aldous and Theron had arrived.

"What were you just thinking about?" Theron asked.

Aldous looked up from the finger drawing he was making in the dust on the ground between his legs. "Dogs."

"What?"

"I was thinking about dogs. I used to have three, and I was thinking about them. Great big wolfhounds," Aldous said.

Theron looked at the dust drawing on the ground. It was indeed a poor dust drawing of a dog.

"Why do you ask?"

"Not magic? You weren't thinking about magic?" Theron asked, as he glanced suspiciously at the sigils. They gave another glow. "There it is again. They just glowed again."

Aldous looked at the sigils now, but by the time he did they had already faded. "I did not see it," he said.

There came the slightest rumbling in the ground, or perhaps Theron just imagined it, but right after the sensation came again the sigils glowed, and this time for longer.

"Look."

"I see it. Why are they glowing?"

"Some sort of spell is being cast somewhere nearby, or something magical is active. Are you sure it's not you?" Theron leaned in and examined the boy. He put his hand on Aldous' head to see if he was taking on an absurd body temperature, but he felt normal.

The sound of a key turning rang through the cell and the reinforced oak door opened.

"I do hope I'm not interrupting, but the two of you are to come with us," said the jailor, a swarm of men behind him, all armed.

"Actually, you are interrupting," Theron said, and kept his hand on Aldous' forehead for an extra moment then slowly withdrew it. "I'd appreciate if you left us be."

"Sorry, Ward, can't be done. It's time to go down." The jailor's deep frown and sad eyes made Theron not much like the sound of the word *down*. "Really wish I didn't have to," the jailor continued. "I've always liked the ballads the bards sing of you. But an order is an order, you know how it is."

"No. I don't believe I do know how it is." Theron scowled at the man, but he was unarmed and knew there were several fighting men in the hall. He didn't have a chance, and he had to be certain of his actions, for he'd just vowed that he would protect Aldous Weaver. He looked at the boy then, his black hair all disheveled, his posture pitiful and hunched forward, in his tattered monk's robes. The world had broken him, and that broke Theron's heart. It broke his heart and it stirred a rage in him that he had not felt since he had been forced to eat the slop for lack of more appetizing alternative. *I will save your son, Darcy Weaver. I will save him from these bastards.*

"All the same, you have to come with us," the jailor said with a shrug.

Men flooded the room, two of them seekers, just in case Aldous actually was a wizard, Theron guessed. Nasty-looking fuckers, pale as snow, heads shaved, and lifeless in the eyes. Lifeless until they turned that burning blue.

Theron and Aldous were bound and shoved roughly forward.

They moved down a long, dim corridor toward stone steps that went ever deeper under the earth. The echo of anguished screams carried to them from the stairwell ahead.

"I think now would be a good time to start carving us a

way out of here, if you really meant what you said back in the cell," whispered a sniveling Aldous, as he took a hard shove from the back.

"Have no fear, my boy, the frenzy will start in due time. But as of now I am shackled and unarmed," Theron whispered back.

"Is due time soon?"

"It had better be, because I have no intent of joining that symphony of screams."

~

"How do I know when I have a friend, Papa?" asked the golden-haired boy.

His father smiled and tilted his head in thought.

"I am not entirely sure how to put that into words, my son, for I suppose every man and woman would give a different answer to that question."

Now the golden-haired boy tilted his head in thought.

"A friend is someone you trust, someone you trust with your life and their own life as well, until you do no longer. I suppose that is a friend," the father said and nodded now, more to himself than his son, feeling that he had just given both of them a valid explanation of friendship.

"But how do I know when I have a friend?" asked the golden-haired boy.

~

CHAPTER SIX

SOWN IN BLOOD

*K*endrick didn't scream. Thirteen lashes in and he still didn't scream. The pain was there, but he focused not on that, not on the whip. He focused on his stroke of good luck, for his captors had brought him to the keep of Count Salvenius. All that separated him from the man who had created the monster were the ropes that bound him, the door that blocked him, and the stairs he would ascend to his goal.

Another lash from the cat-o'-nine shredded across the flesh of his naked back. Still he did not scream. It wasn't about shame, it wasn't about whether or not he cared for the torturer's satisfaction, it was simply about calming his mind before he started a massacre, and the one that was coming was going to look like a royal slaughterhouse the night before Yule.

"You know what they told me to tell you?" the torturer asked.

Ken stared at the door, willing it to open.

It did, and a squad of the count's men shoved in two more prisoners. When Ken saw them, he felt a little burst of hope.

The more elements in the equation, the greater the chance for chaos, and two more men in the dungeon were elements that Ken liked.

The prisoners were roughly pushed forward, and their shackles were chained to the rusty rings attached to the floor right at the bottom of the wall. The group of guards and the two seekers left the chamber after placing the keys to the new prisoners' bonds on the torturer's table of tools.

The two men were perfect opposites. One of them was tall, blond, and built like a sculpture, handsome but he looked tough; he looked a killer, and Kendrick knew a killer when he saw one. The other was a short, scrawny lad, a bit younger than twenty years; he had a mop of greasy black hair, and he hunched like a kicked dog. Shoulders like a trout, and not a bit of muscle on him. He didn't much look like a killer; he didn't much look like anything.

It was the seventeenth lash that finally had Kendrick give a gasp.

"Ah, there it is," the torturer said, then he gave a giggle.

"You're the worst kind of scum, you know that," said the blond man. "How can you stomach that, you fucking coward? Striking a man suspended from the ceiling, unable to defend himself. You are everything disgusting about humanity."

"You know who I'm whipping here? This is a fuckin' kindness compared to the shite he's done. When I sledge all his limbs it will still be a kindness. This man here is Kendrick the fuckin' Cold. He is going to be whipped, beaten, and flayed until he admits to the last of his crimes, from killing a king's officer to butchering his own wife."

The blond man's eyes went wide, and he fell silent. The kid with black hair didn't seem to know or care who Kendrick was. He just looked at the torturer's table and the tools of his trade, fully horrified, certain of the suffering to come. Kendrick knew the face well.

"That's right, pretty boy," the torturer said. "Just keep your mouth shut until it's your turn. You can say whatever you like when it's your turn." Then, lifting the cat once more, he continued, "Back to our conversation, Ken, before we were rudely interrupted by our new guests."

$\sim$

There was a moment back in the cell when Aldous had believed Theron was actually going to get them out of this. That moment was gone. It took everything Aldous had in his being to stop from shitting himself then passing out as he watched the suspended man take the whip.

The tortured man was a few inches shorter than Theron, but what he didn't have in height he had in muscle. If Theron was a sculpture, this man, this Kendrick the Cold was a raw slab of stone. He must have had a good three stone on Theron, three stone of menacing meat. He had a jaw on him like an anvil and fists like two smithies' hammers. His matted, wild hair was thin, and a lifetime of fighting and pain was visible on the man's face. His nose was crooked and flattened, and a hundred small scars ripped in every which way across his features, one long one from ear to ear just under his eyes.

He took another hard lash to the back, his entire body tensing as it twisted a half circle.

"Silent again, eh?" asked the torturer. "As I was saying earlier. They told me to tell you she's dead."

"Yeah," said Kendrick, calm and low; his voice cooled the room. The sound of it caused gooseflesh to rise on Aldous' arms.

"Two went back after they got you. They said to tell old

Ken that. Yeah, two went back and they raped and killed your whore. Then they raped her again."

Aldous was afraid of the torturer, he was horribly, horribly afraid of the torturer, but as he saw the sick grin split the face of Kendrick the Cold, Aldous began to wonder whom he should truly fear.

"That is not a man to enrage," whispered Theron from beside Aldous.

"I'm going to pull out your tongue," Kendrick said, in a voice as calm as his expression. "Then I'm going to wrap it around your throat and choke you right to death." He did not yell the words, just said them low and calm, the way a man might state his daily affairs to a man that he was breaking his fast with.

Aldous could not see the torturer, for Kendrick's massive body was suspended before him. Yet Aldous was certain that the bastard with the whip was afraid. Afraid of a man who was bound and bloody. For who would not be afraid in the face of that grin.

The pause didn't last for long.

There came a screaming from the hall beyond the door of the torture chamber, the surreal sound of someone else's living nightmare adding to his own.

The blue symbols of the seekers on the walls began to glow.

There was another scream, not the scream of pain at the hand of a torturer, but the scream of death. Swords were drawn outside and there was a great deal of yelling, then more screaming, and at last came the sound of the squeals, the sound that nearly caused the blood in Aldous' veins to curdle and his spine to fully stiffen. Theron must have felt the same thing, for he stood and began to tug at the chain attached to the rusty ring at the bottom of the wall. The floor beneath began to shift.

Right beneath them. As if something were pushing up from below.

"Theron?" Aldous asked. Again bile rose in his throat, that hotness in the back of the throat with the singular chill in the belly that was the very physical sensation of fear. "This keeps getting worse and fucking worse." He was yelling by the end, his voice cracking like a schoolboy's.

"Not worse. We are in luck. There are things in the dungeon," Theron said.

"What things? What are you talking about?" yelled the torturer as he stepped out from behind Kendrick, eyes shifting side to side, fat jowls swaying.

"Chaos," muttered Kendrick, the way Father Riker used to mutter small prayers.

Again came a squealing from outside, and more screams, and Ken smiled at the sound.

The reinforced door to the chamber gave a loud thud. They all turned to look at it.

Again it gave a thud, followed by a sharp crack, a few splinters flying across the room.

"I suggest you unchain me," Theron said to the torturer. "For I am Theron Ward, the slayer of monsters, and those are monsters knocking at your door."

The door gave another heavy thud as a dark pool of blood seeped beneath, a slow-moving tide of deep crimson, shining back the reflection of the torches. Again, the ground beneath Theron quaked. A fact for which he was grateful, as it concealed the quaking of his knees.

"When they are done devouring the guards outside, the guards whose blood is now finding its way into your place of work," he said to the torturer, who now stood backed into a corner, trembling. "They are going to take down that door.

There is no way out for you. No one is coming to your aid. Undo my chains."

Aldous was not able to pull off the same façade. He sat on the ground hugging his knees to his chest as he rocked back and forth, eyes closed.

"Do something, Theron, do something," the boy repeated in a hushed voice over and over. Theron did not blame Aldous for his fear; a part of him would have liked to do the same—curl in a ball and beg a stranger for help—but a bigger part of him wanted to fight or die killing whatever came through that door. At least if he fought, he had a chance to win.

"I made a vow, Aldous. I'll get you out of this. Have faith, my boy." In truth, Theron was not as sure now, as he had been when he swore to protect Aldous earlier in the upper cell. By the sounds of it, there were a lot of rats out there.

The chamber walls covered in the blue sigils of the seekers were glowing madly. *Madly blue, but there is a haze of green. Not like a forest.*

The door splintered through in the center, leaving a jagged hole, and a gray-clawed arm, covered in black boils and dripping with blood, reached through. The boils pulsed and throbbed, and they seemed to drink up the blood and grow before Theron's eyes.

The torturer dropped his whip as he stared at the door. Kendrick the Cold began sawing the thick ropes that bound his hands side to side, then he swung up his dangling legs—blood dripping down his back—and planted his feet on the ceiling. With all his might and all his limbs, he pulled and pushed at the ropes.

"Rata Plaga," the torturer said, sinking to the ground in his corner, knees to his chest, a hum of terror surrounding him.

"Chaos," said Ken, his voice straining along with his

muscles as he pulled madly at his bonds, his hands turning purple as they tried to squeeze free from the tight ropes.

Aldous just kept rocking, back and forth, as if he were rocking to the sound of the hellish orchestra just outside the door.

"Kendrick, your bonds are too tight. Kick the table, man. The key ring to my chains… kick it to me." Theron's whole body shook, but his voice kept steady. *I won't die here, not here in Norburg. Not to the fucking rats.*

Kendrick swung his legs back down and looked at the table.

"Too far. Think of something else," he said.

Again the ground shook, and the arm breaching the door expanded the hole, and became an arm and a snout.

"Just try, try. Fucking try to kick it," Aldous wailed.

"Hurry now," Theron said as he looked from Ken to the door then back to Ken, then at the fanatical Aldous then finally back to Ken, all the while stepping up and down on the tips of his toes.

"Be still," Ken ordered. "You are like a child who has to take a piss."

"Just fucking kick it," Theron said, the iron shackles cutting into his wrists as he did his anxious dance.

Ken began to swing. He was now the pendulum that ticked and tocked away the precious seconds that would decide whether they lived or died. His toe almost reached the table. Almost.

Then he swung back.

The full head of the rat became visible now, its buckteeth gnashing and covered in gore.

"Anytime now, good sir," Theron said.

Again Ken swung to the table, his left toes getting well under it. The large man gave a grunt and flipped the table.

The keys could have fallen in any direction, but luck would have it that they flung toward Theron.

"There you go," said Kendrick with a glance at the door and the rat that was nearly fully through. "Now be quick. Be good and quick." Even Ken's voice had the sound of anxiety as he too gazed at the thing tunneling through the center of the door, the pool of blood from the hall outside running closer and closer to his dangling feet.

"Theron!" Aldous was all mad screams now.

Theron reached his toe to the ring of keys and slid it to himself. He crouched to grab it, but the most violent shake in the ground yet dropped him to his knees. He regained his composure and grabbed the ring.

Key into the hole.

The rat's head and both arms were now through the door, the hand of a second working its way in.

Wrong key.

The first one's torso came squeezing through, the creature so mad in its hunger that it gave no reaction as the splintered wood lacerated its befouled flesh. Black blood and pus squished from its open gut and ran down the door, slow and viscous, but the plague spawn kept wriggling through, its human eyes straining in the sockets of the grotesque skull.

Key in the hole. Right key.

"I don't want to die. I don't want to be dinner to that thing. Please, I don't want to die," whispered Aldous. He was corpse pale, and his words were slurred, as if he were soon to pass out from fear alone.

"You are not going to die, not here," Theron yelled, twisting the key in the lock. "Get a grip on your faculties, boy. You will not die here, but it is going to be some time yet before this is over. Find your guts."

Click.

Theron dropped the shackles and sprang back, away from

the wall, just as the shaking floor beneath him gave way and caved into the earth. There was a black hole for a single moment then a plague rat appeared in the space. This one was long and lanky, crusty, matted doglike hair covering its body. Theron turned around and sprang to a mallet that had fallen off the torturer's table, then turned back and went for the tall, shaggy rat fiend.

The thing went for Aldous. The boy was too rattled to even scream; he simply closed his eyes and waited for the gaping maw to rip apart his flesh.

I'm not going to let you die. I won't fail you.

Theron fed the creature stone; he swung the mallet in an upward arc right into the thing's open mouth, smashing through rotted teeth and unhinging the beast's jaw. The blow caused it to stumble forward into Theron, and he turned a shoulder to brace it as he delivered a mighty blow into the plague rat's knee. The bone shattered and the vile thing went down.

Still it dragged itself toward Aldous, hoping to get one bite before it died. Aldous slid back as far as he could, as far as his chains would allow. The rat reached out with a long, grotesque claw, and kept reaching. It raked the boy's lower leg, and a single nail sank into the flesh. The boy screamed and kicked the fiend in its shaggy face.

Theron brought the mallet down again, and again.

"I. Made. A. Vow." Each word brought another strike, blood spraying from the pounded meat up over Theron and the boy.

~

"I don't want to, Father, it is not fair. I have done nothing to deserve this punishment," the golden-haired boy protested as his father handed him the knife.

"This is no punishment, my son. And fair has not a bit to do with it. It is a lesson and a test wrapped into one."

"This is the job of a servant, not a job for me, a boy who will one day be lord."

His father laughed. *"A lord should never have a servant, or any other under his employ, do a thing that he himself would not be willing to do. That is what makes a man a tyrant."*

"I am no tyrant, Father!"

"Then understand the lesson, and finish the test. I am with you. We are in this together."

The boy gripped the knife until his knuckles turned white, and he steadied the blade as he put it to the throat of the goat that his father held in place. *"It is not like hunting,"* said the boy.

"A different thing entirely," agreed his father.

"He is not even afraid," said the boy, on the verge of tears, the blade against the goat's neck. *"I see no lesson here."*

"Your life comes at a price, son. So does the life of everyone else. That is the lesson. The test is finding out whether or not you will pay it."

The boy took a breath, and, with his eyes locked on his father's, he slit the goat's throat. It was the only thing he remembered about his ninth birthday.

~

CHAPTER SEVEN

A TEST

*A*ldous stared at the thing on the ground before him. It was grotesque, horror incarnate; it was the evil of the world manifested into a breathing, writhing, dying thing. Its matted fur was soaked with blood, and woeful human eyes peered out from a pulverized face. The thing was not yet dead, although it was clear it would never rise again. The hunter had made sure of that.

Theron stood above it; he no longer looked the gold prince. He looked the bloody savage. His muscles swelled in the combat, veins bulged in his arms and his neck, and his hair was wild and sprayed with the black blood of the thing most sinister writhing on the ground.

Theron threw Aldous a ring of keys, then turned and charged the rat that had gotten itself impaled as it wrenched its way through the shattered door. It retched, the wounds in its belly gaping and leaking as it did, then received a massive blow from a mallet-wielding Theron. The impact made an echoing thunderclap in the dungeon and blood shot out from its eyes. Two more blows had its skull was completely smashed, bits of bone and brain spraying across the room.

Aldous fumbled with the keys, the wound the rat had inflicted on him burning in his calf. He winced, and tensed his entire body to fight off his violent shaking so that he could get the key in the hole and free himself.

The shackles released, and Aldous struggled to his feet.

"Boy."

Aldous turned and looked at Kendrick.

"See that knife there?" Kendrick nodded at the knife on the floor with the other things sprawled out from the tipped-over table. "Take it, and cut me down."

Aldous was not sure what it was about the command Kendrick had just given him, but for the first time since this had all begun he felt his heart ease.

Theron was still at the door swinging at the limbs and snouts that were poking past the impaled rat.

Aldous reached down and grabbed the knife.

"Cut me down," said Ken calmly.

"Do it. We need him, Aldous." Theron grabbed a flailing rat arm by the wrist and bludgeoned it at the elbow. A squealing scream sounded from the other side of the block-ade, the remains of the door creaking under the assault. "And be quick. They're coming through."

"Don't do it, boy," came the quivering voice of the torturer who was, as Aldous had been moments ago, huddled in a corner, avoiding the fray. "Ward, tell him not to release that man. Assist me and get me to the count. I will tell him of your heroics and you will be pardoned. But do not release that demon. Do not release Kendrick the Cold. He is as likely to kill you as the rats."

The impaled, bludgeoned rat in the door that had thus far involuntarily helped in barricading the other creatures out of the chamber began shaking violently, and through the hole, Aldous could see the rats behind it feasting on its flesh.

"Cut down Kendrick," Theron said, his voice stern now. It

was an order and it was final. There was no more time to think over choices. Aldous took a step forward.

"Don't! Even if you escape, the count will hunt you. His men will chase you to the end of the earth. Release that man and you will hang. No matter what, you will hang." The torturer had no force in his words; he had crawled to Aldous and was begging. He did not even have the grapes to try and take the knife.

Aldous jerked his hand from the groping, whimpering man on the floor and righted the table, then climbed up so he was face to face with Kendrick.

"Good choice," Kendrick said. Cold and calm. As if the terrors of the world were not knocking at their door.

Aldous looked deep into the man's eyes. There was more emotion in the eyes of the rats than there was in his, and Aldous had a foreboding feeling that he may one day regret what he was about to do.

Theron yelled.

Aldous turned.

The rat corpse tore free, and the door was completely smashed through. The flood was coming, and, foreboding feeling or not, Aldous set to cutting.

The black-haired boy cut at Kendrick's bonds, using all his efforts. So fierce was he that Ken got a cut in the process. Nothing major, just a nick, really. The ropes sawed through, and he fell to the ground. He clenched and unclenched his fists, nice and tight, forcing the blood into his arms. The boy came down from the table and handed Ken the curved knife. It was a pretty thing, long and capable, looked like it could get right to the guts, no problem.

There were snarls from both man and beast as Theron

scrapped with a vermin behind him. More rats came through the door. Ken took a deep breath and leveled his gaze on the boy. The boy took a step back, indecision etching his features. Ken cracked his neck. He always took his time before the violence, for if there was one thing Ken had learned over the years it was that there was never any need to rush into the bloodshed. No matter what, there would always be something left to kill.

So he turned when he was good and ready and set to work. There were two dead at Theron's feet, and he was smashing the ribs of a third apart against the wall with the mallet he wielded. A fourth had gotten up behind him and was about to sink its filthy, festering claws into Theron. Kendrick didn't give it the chance. He burst across the room and plunged the long, curved knife into the rat's throat, pulled out and back in, ten times in five seconds, and the creature's head was more than halfway off, black blood spouting out like water from a hole in a broken dyke. It covered Kendrick and Theron both.

"You aren't going to turn into one of them on me when this is over, are you, hunter?" Ken asked, as he sank the knife into the throat of one of the monsters twisting on the floor.

"I have had much contact with these filth, and have not turned yet. Occupational necessity. What about you?"

"I've tussled with their kind before, but you never know for certain. What about the boy?" Ken turned back to look at Aldous where he leaned against a wall examining the wound on his leg.

Nothing serious, unless he was susceptible.

"The boy's a wizard," Theron said, his voice strained as he caught a rat and swung it into position for the kill.

"Wizards don't turn?" Ken asked, surprised. He stabbed Theron's rat in the head, sinking the knife to the hilt.

"I don't think they do," Theron said.

"I'm not a wizard," Aldous cried.

Theron and Ken both shot him a glance and said in unison, "You better hope you are."

There was a lull in the attack for just a moment after the first group had been slaughtered. Then came a brute, heaped with more muscle than Ken and Theron combined. Its arms were stout and it looked like it was having a great deal of trouble getting through the door.

Kendrick knifed it twice in the groin.

It fell to one knee then lunged forward, swiping its hulking claws. Ken sprang to the side and Theron came in with the mallet, striking it heavy on the head.

Ken went to the goliath's flank as it pressed at the hunter and pounced on its back; with one hand he grabbed hold of a tuft of hair, and with the other he set to stabbing. He plunged the knife into the creature's neck, but it was as thick as an oak and nearly as hard. He struck a boil and it burst. Hot, sticky puss ran warm on Ken's arm.

"You're quick for a large man," said Theron as he avoided the teeth and claws.

"And you're a talker? I should have guessed as much," Ken mumbled as he strained to keep his grip on the creature.

"Better a talker than a screamer," Theron said as he gave the thing a low crack in the ankle.

It roared and tried to reach backward to grab at Ken, but its stout arms would be its doom. It bucked and screamed as Ken held to the tuft of fur and kept digging his knife ever deeper through the dense muscle.

Theron brought the mallet down over and over on the brute's right knee as he dodged gnashing teeth. After six heavy blows there was an echoing crack and the pustulant titan went down.

"Aldous, lend us a hand in finishing this deed," Theron

called out as he wrestled to restrain one of the beast's powerful arms.

Ken was startled by the invitation. He couldn't see that they needed the boy's help. But he held his silence, because he'd often bolstered the confidence of his new recruits with similar tactics.

The black-haired boy looked around and set his eyes on a fire poker in the torturer's hands in a corner of the room. The boy grabbed the shaft and the two engaged in a most pitiful tug of war as the torturer sniveled. It was won when Aldous placed his foot firmly on the torturer's bald head for leverage and tugged.

Kendrick shifted his hand from the tuft of fur and lodged his fingers deep into the beast's eye; it screamed, its mouth opening wide. Ken ripped the knife from the rat's neck and wedged it into the open mouth.

"Shove it down the throat, boy. All the way down," he ordered.

~

The creature screamed and bawled; it frothed and snapped its tremendous maw of rotten, grinding teeth. Aldous wanted to lend aid. He wanted to help the two men be done with the thing, but every muscle in his body was stiff. With the poker held like a spear, he willed himself to move. His limbs began to shake, but still he could not charge.

"Do it, lad, do it," Ken ordered again, his voice loud enough to be heard over the gagging and thrashing of the beast, but it was steady.

"Kill it! Ram it down. Spear it like a fucking boar, boy!" Theron yelled, his voice not nearly as calm as Ken's, and Aldous could see every muscle in the blond man's body bulging and straining to hold the giant hell spawn's colossal meat hook of an arm in place.

"I've never speared a fucking boar!" Aldous yelled back with a moment of legitimate fury at his savior. "You don't need me. Please, you don't need me." He started to lower the poker. "Kill it yourself."

"We need you. We do. Be brave, Aldous. Show me what you are! Show me that we are in this together!"

He hesitated for a moment longer. "Ragh!" Aldous gave a meager roar and charged.

He drove the poker home.

The beast gagged from the depths of its fathomless belly, barfing blood. Aldous gagged, a symphony of gagging, his stomach convulsing from the stench of the fiend's breath. But he stayed the course. He was screaming and in a state of horror that nearly had him shitting liquid down his legs, but he stayed the course. His shoulders and forearms strained as he felt the poker drive through walls of organ tissue.

The creature lifted the arm it was using to balance, and swiped at Aldous, but he jumped back, releasing his makeshift spear as he did, and the rat fell face first, swallowing the poker all the way down. It convulsed for a few moments, then went still.

The three of them were huffing and covered in the devil's gore, but the fight was won. For now. The dead rats were strewn—mangled and mutilated—across the chamber floor. Kendrick looked to the corner. The torturer sat in a puddle of his own piss. Ken smiled at the pitiful man, the type of smile that said, *I told you so. You should have listened,* without saying anything, anything at all.

"Quickly, Kelmoor, before we are overrun. We must

hasten from this place!" Theron stood in the doorway, his boots mushing through the pieces of rat and chunks of the dead guards, gesturing for Ken to follow. The echo of squealing sounded from the tunnels below. Death beckoned from the black pit in the dungeon floor.

Ken turned from his prize and stared at Theron a good while; he knew there was no need to stay, not from a rational sense, at least, but Kendrick the Cold always saw the job done.

"I'll be just behind you," he replied.

Theron hesitated. It was strange that he did. For he owed Ken nothing; in fact, it was the other way around, for Theron and the boy Aldous had saved his life.

"Right on your heels, lad," Ken said.

Theron grimaced, and then looked past Ken at the torturer.

"All right, but be quick about it. It is not worth dallying over." Theron and Aldous made their way down the hall, the sound of their feet sloshing through the gore as they disappeared from sight.

Kendrick looked back at the torturer. He was glad he'd stayed.

Welcome back, Kendrick. Welcome back.

～

"Can we feed them?" the black-haired boy asked his father. Three stray wolfhound pups lapped at the water in the estate's garden fountain. They were dreadfully thin; their fur was matted and one was walking with a terrible limp.

"Yes, but be careful," said his father.

They fed the hounds, and the next day the hounds returned. Again the boy fed them, and again the next day they returned. After a week of this, the boy asked, "Can we keep them?"

"Why do you wish to keep them, my son?" his father asked.

"They need us. They need our help, can't you see?" the boy asked.

"I can. I most certainly can."

"And we can help them, so we must help them, just because we can," said the boy. His father smiled and stroked his black hair.

"You are right, my son, but you must understand. If you help these pups, if we take them into our house, if we save them from their own savage devices and the wild, then we are making them a promise."

"A promise?" asked the boy.

"Yes, for a good man must promise to never abandon that which he saves. In this moment you must be sure. We cannot simply save the pups' lives, only to leave them to their own devices when you have grown tired of their company."

"I promise," said the black-haired boy, a promise he was destined to break.

～

CHAPTER EIGHT

ESCAPE

hey passed, single file, through a narrow corridor with walls and floor painted in the mingled blood of man and plague rat alike. The upper dungeon was empty, with no sign of a struggle, but the guards were gone, the weapon racks were emptied, and the sigils were at a continual burning blue glow. Theron searched franticly through rooms and chests for his swords, hoping that this was where he would find items confiscated by the soldiers and added to their own coffers. He had a hunch that they had not seen the last of the rats, and even if they had, they were now escaped fugitives in a city filled with foes. He needed the instruments of his trade.

"Is this what you're looking for, hunter?" Kendrick asked from another room in the dungeon. Theron ran to the voice and found Ken standing with his claymore in hand.

"How did you know this was mine?" Theron asked. He cut a glance at Aldous, the boy he had promised to protect, and now that his claymore was found, the sturdy weapon that had never failed him, he truly began to believe he could keep his promise—he could keep the lad safe.

"Too heavy and fine for any common soldier," Ken said.

Kendrick threw Theron the blade then lifted a second sword—a short sword—of the same fine steel from the chest he was standing over.

"Borrow it," Theron said. "Better we each have one than I have two and you have none. Any of those swords from a common soldier have not the strength or flexibility of my blades, and might break when we need it most." He looked at the unarmed Aldous, deathly pale on the parts of flesh that weren't covered by gore.

"I'm more than happy with none," Aldous stuttered.

"You have your magic," said Ken, at the same time Theron said, "Very well, but stay close." Theron felt a fool after giving such an instruction, for the boy did not look as if there was anywhere else he would like to go.

"I have no magic," Aldous grumbled.

As the three climbed up the stairs to the kitchens, they did so in silence. Theron listened intently, but no sound came from above.

"Ready?" Theron asked, pausing at the door to the kitchens.

"Aye," said Kendrick, the same way a man says aye to being ready for a nap.

"Aldous?"

"Ready," said Aldous the same way a lad says he's ready for some surgery on his cock.

Theron threw the door open and charged forward into the kitchens, his claymore at the ready. The blade was hungry and Theron was angry. He was angry at his arrest, he was angry at the mistreatment of Darcy Weaver's heir, and he was bloody furious that the rats were back.

The floor of the kitchen was strewn with dead. The walls were spattered with blood and guts, and a few bodies had found their way into the roasting fire. This was no fight, just a massacre.

"You saw the sigils, hunter. You saw the way they burned with that strange green haze beyond the blue flame," said Ken as the three paused to study the savaged bodies.

"Yes," Theron whispered as anxiety built in his chest, an expanding stone.

"Yes what?" asked Aldous. "They were glowing. I saw it too. I thought you said they were glowing because of the rats."

"Aye, and if they were glowing from the rats, that means this plague is no thing of nature. They only glow in the face of magic," Kendrick said, and Theron shuddered. Magic was like a terrible storm, churning and gathering, uncontrollable.

"The plague is a spell?" Aldous asked incredulously.

Theron locked eyes with Ken and said, "There is some great and evil sorcery afoot. Black sorcery and a blacker betrayal."

"What do you mean betrayal?" Aldous asked, as he walked forward, looking up, away from the corpses on the ground.

Both men ignored him, and Theron said, "They appear to be acting with some sort of order, almost like an army."

"An army of rats needs a leader. A spell needs a weaver," said Ken.

"A weaver close by," Theron said, and shot a glance at Aldous. "And I don't mean our own."

"This sorcerer is within the city?" squeaked Aldous.

"Oh, she is. She most certainly is, and I think it is high time we absconded from this deplorable city and the presence of its capricious count." Theron motioned for the two to follow. Aldous did, but Kendrick stood still.

"I will not leave."

"What?"

"This is an opportunity for me to kill that bastard. Too

long did I serve under him. Too long did I carry out his evil on the weak and helpless. He sent me to do his evil deeds. He sent men almost as bad as me to rape and murder Alma. He will pay for that. I will be sure to see him off to hell for all that he has wrought."

Theron was unsure who this Alma was, but it was clear that Kendrick would not follow until he saw or created the count's corpse.

"We can just leave now," Aldous whispered to Theron. "Just us. We can leave him to his vengeance."

"We cannot," Theron said firmly.

Aldous looked around as if he were looking for the explanation to Theron's response. Theron felt a pang of disappointment in the young lad, but he could not begrudge him, for perhaps Theron would have thought in the same manner many years ago.

"We cannot simply save a man's life and then take his assistance in preserving our own, only to leave him to his own devices in completing what appears to be some sort of oath-bound quest. We must assist him in his endeavor." Theron clasped a hand firmly on the back of Aldous' neck and pulled him close. "It is the right thing to do, Aldous Weaver, son of Darcy Weaver."

The boy winced as Theron's words struck home. "It's as if you knew him better than me," he whispered.

"Stay or leave," Ken said. "I care not."

Theron felt for a pocket in his trousers. Not *his* trousers, the trousers they had made him wear in the dungeon. *No Brynthian ducat.* No coin to flip. This decision could not be made by chance, so Theron left the question to his morality instead.

"We stay," he said, and Theron Ward was his word—he was now committed to a killer.

"We are going to murder a count?" Aldous' voice grew higher in pitch.

"You say the word 'count' like it excuses him from punishment. Count or beggar, the man's deeds have woken the justice that now pursues him. This is an opportunity for heroics, an opportunity I will not abandon." Theron shook the boy then. "An opportunity you should grasp with equal vigor. You must be prepared to call upon your magic and reduce to ashes whatever foe we may next face, do you understand?"

Aldous looked with wide eyes and a drawn face at Theron, just at the mere mention of magic.

"I understand," he said, but Theron was not sure he did. Not that he doubted the boy could kill, because he had already proven he could, which had put him in this predicament in the first place. But Theron was unsure that Aldous could actually control his powers. "But," Aldous added after a moment, "to be honest, I really don't think I will be able to do it again." He winced and scratched the back of his head with the pitifully obvious symptoms of embarrassed guilt. Theron winced back.

~

Looking at the boy, it was hard for Kendrick to picture him committing a crime punishable by torture and death. "So it's fire, is it?" he asked.

"Indeed. Young Aldous here burned a priest to cinders with his bare hands. A nasty bastard, by all accounts," Theron said. "Well, only by Aldous' account, but I trust him. For he is the son of the great writer Darcy Weaver."

Kendrick gave Theron a blank look. "Never heard of him." Ken paused. "And that's a horrible reason to trust someone."

Theron's brows drew in. "Do you have a better one?"

Ken had not taken Theron Ward for a fool, but at those words he thought he might reconsider. "I don't trust anyone."

"That's just as foolish as trusting everyone," Theron said. "Let us find Count Salvenius and make certain of his death."

"Aye," agreed Ken, happy to leave this skirmish of words and head to battle.

"Do you wish to be the one to claim his life?" Theron asked.

"If the boy's a mage, I would prefer that he burn the bastard alive. The more brutal his death, the better. And like to like. The count has burned many," Ken said, as he stared into space, a cruel sneer curling his lip.

"I'm not sure I can kill a person," Aldous said, avoiding Kendrick's gaze.

Ken looked at the boy and thought of how many times he'd heard those words from boys who went on to kill dozens.

"If our wizard can't burn him, then he dies slow, by blades," Ken said.

"We haven't the time, nor do I have the stomach for torture," Theron said firmly, but without any anger.

Ken glowered at Theron, and had he been the man he was six years ago he would have come to blades with the hunter over that, but he was not the same man. Perhaps he was a better man now. Or perhaps he was simply a more patient monster.

"Fine," he eventually said, icy calm. In truth, it didn't matter how the count died, so long as he died. "Then to answer your question, hunter, no, I do not wish to be the one that kills him. It doesn't bloody matter now. Let's just go and fucking get it done." And he strode into the hall.

≈

They entered the throne room. The walls were adorned with the heads of dead beasts, glass eyes staring out, fur matted with the spattered blood of the slain who lay scattered across the floor, dead, filmed eyes staring at nothing.

"Same as the kitchens," Ken said.

"Not entirely," said Theron, kneeling over the half-naked corpse of a dead woman—more a girl than a woman, really. "She was raped, and her throat was slit. By knife, not by claw. Look around, Kendrick. A great deal of these wounds were made by sword, knife, and spear. Men, not rats."

"They're the same," Ken said as Theron lingered over the corpse too long for a man who knew death. "Who is the woman?"

"I don't know her name, but this is the count's daughter."

Ken thought there was perhaps the slightest bit of sentiment in Theron's voice, but he could not be sure.

Theron rolled the body over to inspect the girl's face. He stood abruptly. "Oh," he said, "no, that's not the count's daughter. I don't believe I know who this is after all." He shrugged, then gave one last glance. "Hard to tell, in truth, for she was wearing a mask when we fucked in the stables, so I can't say for sure, you see? But she was quite good, really."

Strange man, this Theron Ward.

Theron made his way to another set of stairs. These led to the second level at the back of the throne room. Aldous followed the hunter and, after a final look around, Ken did the same. The count's body was not among the dead, and he was too bloody fat to be missed even if he was half eaten.

There were more bodies still. Dead rats, dead nobles, and dead soldiers. Some of the soldiers appeared to have killed each other, and some of the nobles had taken up arms against some of the soldiers.

"I don't understand. I don't understand," Aldous repeated

to himself in a whisper as the trio slunk down the corridors of the royal chambers.

Ken almost told the boy there was nothing to be understood about chaos, but in the end, he held his tongue.

There was yelling up ahead and the sound of something heavy battering against a door. The noise was perhaps only fifty paces away and around a corner. And from the windows that lined the corridor came screams from the street below.

Kendrick went to a window that looked out into the city of Norburg. The city was in flames.

"Theron, come look at this. And you, boy, as well," he said, motioning his companions to the window. Hundreds, perhaps thousands, of the rats were swarming in the streets. They broke into the homes of the rich and poor alike and slaughtered and feasted with no prejudice.

"This is the delight of our world, is it not?" Ken asked. "One moment your back is being lashed just before you hang, legs twitching before the hateful screams of the people. The next moment, those would-be watchers of your death are being ripped asunder by a swarm of rats."

"You are a strange man, Kendrick the Cold," Theron said, and he too turned to look out the window. After a moment, he said, "It is her." He pointed. "Her hair has gone gray, but it is her, no doubt it is her."

"Who?" Aldous asked.

Ken followed the hunter's stare and saw amongst the swarm, walking through the center, a thing that caused even the voice in his head to fall silent in awe: a woman, wearing emerald green, her black hair streaked with gray. Around her marched fifty of the count's guards and several seekers, but not as her captors. They were her escort.

"She is a dried husk, drained by her spells, but the same witch," Theron said.

A witch. Suddenly, Calabaster's words—at the time of

their utterance, meaningless words—echoed in Ken's mind: *The rumbling in the earth started the same day as that Emerald Lady arrived from the northeast.* There had long been rumors about the black sorcery and dark deeds of those who lived among the mountains of Romaria, whose towns edged up against the darkest woods, whose people were said to have ties to demons and darkness and all manner of legends. Ken could believe that such a woman might be a witch.

Behind the Emerald Woman and her entourage was a procession of women held in chains, some screaming and begging, others wailing in lament as they were dragged forward. Dragged forward into the angry sea of rats, the writhing, furious tempest of black boils and smoldering pus, gnashing teeth, and imprisoned eyes.

Ken glanced at Aldous and saw the true horror in the boy's eyes, and when he shifted his gaze to Theron, he saw the mixture of dread and impotent rage etched into his visage.

"Go," Ken said. "You are probably already regretting your decision to stay."

"I am," Aldous said, and plucked at Theron's sleeve.

Theron pulled his arm away, and said, "Do not question my honor."

Ken shrugged. "See how the creatures of the plague part, how they split and make way for this Emerald Woman and her parade." They squealed and shrieked as she passed with her convoy, and they hissed and snapped at the enslaved women behind.

But they let them pass through, untouched.

＊

One cannot both be a ruler and righteous. To be righteous, truly righteous, a ruler must be able to justify each and every one of his actions, from the way he eats his dinner to the way he wages his wars not only to himself, not only to those close to him, but he must justify all to each and everyone of his subjects. Only then can a ruler be righteous, and that is simply a thing that cannot be done. Therefore a ruler must be powerful enough to make his subjects forget entirely about the concept of righteousness.

—The Honorable Count Salvenius of Norburg, excerpt from the text Sovereignty.

＊

CHAPTER NINE

WHAT IS RIGHTEOUS

*T*he three of them slunk down the hall, quiet as cats —Theron up front—as they approached the sound of hard wood and bodies bashing against a door. There came a monstrous crack, a momentary pause, then screams of fury and steel against steel.

"Slay these traitors, men! They abandoned me for that bitch!" The bold cry was that of the count.

"That's him. The bastard's still alive," whispered Theron as they hid around the corner, mere feet now from the chaotic bedchamber. He peeked his head out to get a look. The attackers were pushing their way through a smashed-in double door. On the ground lies a sturdy, solid oak wardrobe, a real monstrosity of a furnishing that had been used by the betrayers as a battering ram.

Theron moved to step out from cover and enter the fray, but Ken grabbed him by the wrist.

"Give them a moment," Ken said in a hush. "Let them settle in to each other. When they are good and tired, nearly dead, we go in for the kill."

"Like vultures?" Theron asked.

"Aye. Like vultures." Ken smiled.

"I don't know about this," said Aldous, reaching out to grab Theron and tug him back behind the wall. "I mean, that sounds like a lot of swords. And a lot of screaming. If we were vultures I don't think we would go in for the kill. I don't think vultures do any killing, in fact. They just eat the dead. So can't we just wait until they are all dead?"

Ken shot him what might pass for a smile. "That won't do," he said. "I need to see him die."

"What difference does it make? How could you possibly *need* to see that? All that matters is that he does indeed die, right? That's what you said, right?"

"Wrong," said Ken.

"No, no, my good man. The boy is right. I believe that is exactly what you said," said Theron, suspecting that Ken's earlier easy acquiescence had been a ruse.

Ken shot him a dark glare and stood, clearly having decided it was now time to enter the fight.

"Stay close, Aldous," Theron said. "I'll be outraged if you get yourself killed after we've made it this far."

"I don't even have a weapon."

"They will be dying fast, and the dead won't protest at your taking one of their blades," said Ken, his back against the wall just outside the door. He looked at Theron.

Theron gave a nod. *Courteous of him to wait for that.* They charged into the chamber.

A crowd of armed men were in the room, and at the back of it, Count Salvenius himself stood on his royal bed in his silk nightclothes. Hanging from the wall behind him was a painting of a great sea monster, a Leviathan, bursting from the depths.

It was a large room, but not large enough for so many men to slaughter each other. It made Theron's job easy enough from a physical standpoint, for none of the men in the clash had expected to be flanked by Theron Ward and the infamous Kendrick the Cold.

The easier it was to kill a man physically always made it harder for Theron mentally, for the deed of driving a sword through a man's back did battle with Theron's scruples.

Kendrick had no such scruples.

He slit his second target's throat before his first corpse hit the ground, the severed artery spraying blood like a fountain.

"Stay right behind me, Aldous. I won't let them get to you." Theron went into the thick heap of men with a wide stroke of his claymore, neck level. His blade was hand-forged and strong, brought home to him as a gift from his father. It was the greatest gift Lord Wardbrook ever gave his son, for it never failed in cutting, not once since Theron took up the hunt. The claymore took the heads of two men in a single stroke and cut deep into a third. Three men dead in a moment, three human lives taken in one tick of the clock's quickest hand.

One of the count's betrayers slit open the belly of a guard and tossed the corpse to the floor, only to take a spear point to the chest from the guard just behind. The spearman drove the betrayer back, impaled him straight through, and barreled toward Theron, who twirled away from the threat and came shoulder to shoulder with another foe. His enemy turned fast enough to see how he would die, but that was all. In the tight press, it was hard for Theron to swing, so he stabbed his claymore from up high, down through the man's clavicle and into his heart.

As the man gurgled his last bloody breath, still standing when he died, Theron was taken aback by the vibrant emerald glow of the man's irises.

"Theron!" Aldous yelled.

Theron whirled round to see he and Aldous were now separated by the spearman.

"Pick up a sword," Theron cried as he lunged at the boy's attacker.

Aldous obeyed, and just in time, for as he ducked to grab a blade of one of the fallen, the spearman stabbed out, barely missing the boy's throat. The spearman retracted and readied for another thrust. Theron chopped him hard in the knee, nearly taking the leg off completely, and the man went down.

With his eyes closed, Aldous flailed, his sword coming down on the screaming man. Theron was not surprised when the blade bounced off the guard's plate mail half-helm.

He ended the man's pain with a quick and accurate heel to the throat.

Aldous opened his eyes, his gaze darting around, half crazed.

"Stay close now, one hand on my back, the other on your sword," Theron said in the most soothing tone he could muster, for he feared if he did not in some way diminish the lad's anxiety he would lose his faculties completely and end up wandering off and getting stabbed, or worse, eaten by some rat still lurking in the corridors.

Theron surveyed the room for Ken and quickly found him; he had a sword in each hand and was parrying the blows of two men, one with a mace, the other with a short-bearded axe.

The one with the axe came down with a hard swing. The man's head tilted up, and for a split moment Theron locked eyes with him.

A vacant green glow.

He knew that glow.

Here was a spell incarnate.

Theron stepped in to aid Kendrick, his claymore coming up to block an incoming mace. The defense freed Ken to turn both swords on the man attacking from the right. One blade went low, sticking the man in the groin; the other opened his throat, spraying blood onto a painting of the count hanging from the wall, leaving splatters of blood across his throat.

The attacker with the mace swung again, too slow, and he lost his hand at the wrist for it. For a moment he stared in shock at the hot red spurting from his mutilated stump, then Ken stuck him through the ribs, a blade on each side.

Thirty had turned to fifteen, but still no one threw down their arms. It was fight to survive or fight to the end. As the men died, the tides of blood drifted to the dangling dust-sheets of the count's bed, white silk hem turning red.

Theron parried, countered, and beheaded one of the count's men. The tide licked up and touched the feathered mattress.

Kendrick gave riposte, dodged, and impaled another, lifting the man from the ground with a tremendous roar by the blades skewered through his foe's chest. The tide sprayed onto Salvenius' toes. The count shrieked and danced like a woman who'd spotted a rat scurrying across her chamber floor.

"Theron Ward! Hunter, you've come to save me!" yelled the count over the cries of the living and the gurgled moans and sobs of the dying, as the bloody tide stained his night-dress to the shins.

Theron answered this by plunging his claymore through the shabby hauberk and meager guts of the next man to die. He twisted the blade and wrenched it upward, the man and his splitting mail screamed in the same pitch. The count was drenched in red to the chest.

"Enough! Please enough," cried the count. "The betrayers are dead. You've done them in. Men, lay down your arms. Let us talk. Let us be civilized."

Civility was a façade, lost when the sword comes out.

The remaining guards did not lower their weapons, but they edged back, and had no menace left in their posture.

"Civilized?" asked Kendrick, voice calm as always. "Let us talk? Like the way you had me talk to the easterners?"

The count's eyes went wide, as if he'd just then realized who the second gore-splattered stranger was.

"Kendrick Solomon Kelmoor? Kendrick the Cold?"

"Aye. You were waiting for my execution before you came to say hello? Too busy being civilized?"

"Kendrick, please, I wasn't going to have you executed, I... I..."

"Shut up." Even now Ken did not yell, and he lowered his swords to his sides.

One of the guards thought that this was perhaps a good moment to strike. He sprang; Theron saw it coming and took off the man's head. The others finally dropped their swords before the head hit the ground.

"What about me? Were you going to have me executed?" Theron asked. "I didn't even know it was your daughter, and even if I did, torture and execution? Over that? She was willing. More than willing."

Aldous made a choking sound.

Theron turned to Aldous and smiled. "I suppose there isn't much in *your* defense, though, my boy. You did burn a priest alive." Aldous shook his head. "And you did so with sorcery, no less."

Aldous' brow caved in and his jaw clenched; his lips curled down in a furious frown.

Theron felt regret at the boy's expression. Perhaps he had taken the joke too far.

"Pardons, for all three of you. Full pardons," said the count.

Theron did not speak. Ken did not speak. Aldous did not speak.

"And... and gold. Ken's weight in gold," the count said. "That's a lot, that is a fair deal."

"No deal," said Ken.

The count was about to protest, but an unexpected voice spoke first.

"What happened here?" asked Aldous, his voice cracking. Theron turned to look at him, uncertain what it was he was asking. "Why did your own men try to kill you?"

"Why does it matter?" Theron asked.

"Because he is a bastard," said Ken.

"Who was that woman? Where did the rats come from?" Aldous stepped out from behind Theron now. "Don't you want to know?" he demanded, and then turned to Ken. "Don't *you* want to know?" He walked forward, toward the count. "Start talking, you fat, cowardly bastard, or I'll burn you alive like I did to your fucking priest! I want to know what happened here."

Theron shrugged, startled by the lad's vehemence. "If the boy wants to know then the boy should know."

Ken glared at the count, and Theron was certain that Ken couldn't have been less interested in the answers.

The count looked more afraid now than he had been during the fray. He sank to his knees on his bed.

Aldous took another step forward, his shoulder brushing Theron's as he passed, and Theron could feel the heat of his skin even through his clothes.

"I shouldn't even be here! Do you understand me? I should have never been in that church. I should be at home. My mother should be alive, and my father should be alive." Theron exchanged a glance with Ken. Aldous moved to the foot of the bed, and yelled, "My dogs should be alive! And you took them from me, you took my life from me." The count scuttled backward on the bed. "I had done nothing wrong. My family did nothing wrong!" Aldous climbed onto the bed, his bloody hands leaving prints on the sheets as he crawled up and screamed right in the count's face, spittle hitting the count's cheek. The count's hands flew to his cheek as if it burned.

"Help me," the count said to his closest man, who in turn looked at Theron and Ken. They shook their heads. The guard backed away. Count Salvenius pulled up his sheets, like a child hiding from the monster under his bed, and his beady little eyes turned to Aldous. "I don't even know who you are, boy. I've never wronged you."

And Theron believed him. But he did not stop the boy.

Aldous punched the count hard in the face, pulled his blanket away, and punched him again, piteous punches lacking both aim and force.

"Tell me who she is!" Aldous screamed.

"I don't know," cried the count. "That is the truth! She was here for a few weeks. She said she hailed from Romaria, that she was a rich duchess, that she believed we would make powerful allies through marriage. I was bewitched by her beauty. Do you understand? Bewitched!" The count blubbered. "I don't know what this is all about, I swear! An infiltration? The beginnings of a Romarian invasion?"

Aldous hit Count Salvenius again.

"I'm surprised you're letting this happen," Ken said to Theron.

"Why?"

"I thought you don't stand for torture. Yet here you stand watching death by a thousand tiny fists." Ken's tone did not have the slightest bit of humor in it.

Theron chuckled. "A joke?"

"A joke," Ken confirmed, straight-faced.

"Hard to tell," Theron said as Aldous yelled and the count yelled.

"He knows nothing," Theron said to Aldous.

"Agreed. The man is a fool," Ken said.

Aldous landed another punch.

"Aldous, that's enough."

The boy didn't hear. He just kept hammering his tiny fists into the sobbing Count Salvenius, who swiped his hands before him and batted ineffectively at the boy.

"Aldous!"

He finally stopped and looked at Theron, his knuckles bloody, and the count's face a swollen pulp.

"You should be the one to finish this, Ken," Theron said.

"This isn't how I imagined it," Ken replied.

Theron took a good look at Ken. He was wounded, from the open lashes on his back, to a hundred small and substantial cuts and bruises from the battles they had just fought. Theron too was wounded. He was beginning to calm from the adrenaline of the fighting, and the pain in his body was beginning to set in. A warrior never knew he was injured until a good while after the fight. Many died and never even realized they were injured. They fought out the whole battle and only after it was done did they fall dead. That was the type of exhaustion that was dawning on him now.

The count slid out of his bed and landed with a thud on the floor. Aldous remained lying in the blood-soaked blankets, taking deep breaths. It was dreadful, and, in some dark and depraved way, a most humorous scene. The fat count, bruised and bloodied, evicted from his bed by a fragile, black-haired boy.

~

The count slid like a slug across the blood-soaked ground, past the bodies of the men who had given their lives for his miserable existence. Ken followed, the point of his sword hovering over the back of Salvenius' neck.

"Kendrick," sniveled the count.

Ken pressed the sword into the back of the count's skull,

slowly lowering his weight down on the hilt. There was a crunch as the bones split apart, then came the squish of sharp iron eviscerating brain. He rolled the corpse over and stared at Salvenius' face. It was not only bruised from Aldous' strikes, but there was something else. Something...

Burns. There were burns in the shape of the boy's knuckles.

Or perhaps Ken was just mad. He took a deep breath and sighed. *It's over.* Until it began again.

"How did it feel?" Aldous asked from the bed, lying flat on his back, looking up at the ceiling.

"Not like much, lad, not like much," Ken replied, as he stared at the boy on the bed and wondered if he truly was a wizard.

~

Theron looked at the painting hanging on the wall above the count's bed. The great green Leviathan, tearing through the surface, causing tidal waves, the sky black behind it and lightning ripping across the canvass. Specks of blood had reached the piece of art. The red droplets gave the monster dreadful life, and a shudder of dark premonition reached up from the depths of Theron's soul.

"I think it is high time we left Norburg."

~

"I'm cold, sergeant. I'm really, really cold," said the lad in the sergeant's arms under the hot southern sun, one arrow in his belly and the other in his sternum. The arrowheads were barbed and there'd be no getting them out.

"That's all right, Peter, it's all right. Your fight is done. Your war is done." Tears welled in the sergeant's eyes, for Peter was a new recruit, and now he was going to die. The last bit of innocence lost.

"Was it right?" Peter asked as he coughed up blood.

"Was what right, lad?"

"What we did here, sergeant."

"Ken. My name's Ken. Don't call me sergeant, not now." Kendrick clenched his teeth hard, fighting with everything he had not to weep in front of rest of the men. Behind him, the easterners screamed on the crosses as their village burned.

Peter died.

Ken's men were about to hammer the first nail into the brown-skinned child that had struck Peter from the bushes with the arrows.

"Don't!" Ken roared. He stood and drew his sword, putting it to the throat of the man with hammer and nail. "Let him go."

"Sergeant?"

"Let him go, Sebastian, or I will put you on a cross right next to him."

Sebastian stood down and let the child go. The brown-skinned boy looked at a woman nailed to the cross. He looked at the little girl dying beside her. Then he looked at Ken with a hatred beyond any word of any tongue, and that was the first time Kendrick the Cold understood that he deserved to die.

~

CHAPTER TEN

GETTING OUT ALIVE

*T*hey waited by a window in the keep that looked upon Norburg until the sun rose and the fires died, until there was only ash and death.

The trio made their way down to the ground floor and exited the keep into the smoldering ruins. What a sight they must make for some great bird high above, Aldous thought. Three battered and broken forms, wounded and drenched with blood—their own and that of their butchered foes— casually strolling down the corpse-covered cobbles of Upper Norburg's main thoroughfare.

Theron led the way, his shoulder bleeding badly, his forearms cut and scraped raw.

Aldous was the lucky one; the deep gash in his calf from the rat's claw was all he had sustained through the ordeal, and although it hurt terribly, he kept his mouth shut as he followed behind Ken. The man was hunched forward, the crisscrossed wounds on his back oozing, and he was too careful with each step he took. He had lost a good amount of blood, not only from where his back had been carved up by the whip, but from a series of cuts on his arms, and, worse still, he bled heavily from a puncture just under his ribs on the right side.

"Kendrick?" Aldous reached a hand toward Ken's shoulder, then yanked it back and said, "You are bleeding pretty bad."

"Aye, I'm aware of that, lad." Ken's voice was heavy with fatigue, but there was no rasp or coughing up of blood. Even with the limited knowledge of medicines and herbs that Aldous had learned from the brothers, he knew that was a good sign, at the very least.

All around them were corpses and ruin. The only life to be seen was the gathering of the crows, and their small group of three, picking their way along abandoned alleys. Aldous greatly feared they would soon be a group of two if they did not treat Ken's wounds.

"What do we do, Theron?"

"We must go to my estate. I have a full staff, and adequate medicaments to heal Kendrick."

"How far?" asked Ken.

Aldous thought the distance was of little importance, since he doubted Ken could make it another twenty feet.

"Just under half a day on horse, if we ride at a good pace," Theron said.

The word *horse* did not sit well with Aldous. He had been riding twice in his lifetime, the second attempt worse than the first.

Kendrick snickered, but it was a halfhearted attempt. "I hope the rats were only interested in eating humans today."

Theron sighed as he trudged on. "The stable is next to the inn where I stayed for a couple of nights. We must go there anyway to clean our wounds and gather provisions to prepare for our journey."

As they walked through the thoroughfares of the city, Aldous realized he had completely run out of fear and disgust. They passed scores of corpses ripped asunder, limbs and guts strewn across the gray cobbles, and Aldous felt nothing. One week ago, he had been doing a poor job of copying out scripture in Father Riker's church basement. One week ago he had been trying to write a book dedicated to his father. One week ago he had not even imagined horror such as this.

"It is impossible to prepare," Aldous began. "It is impossible to expect what the next hour may bring. I had not the slightest clue the day they took my father, not the slightest hint that my family would soon be decimated. After that I swore to always be prepared for the worst, to always expect the worst of man and the world." He moved his hand to gesture at his surroundings, though neither of the two men was looking at him. "Yet how could I have even fathomed this as a possibility?"

"We do not decide what destiny puts before us, all we can do is choose how to confront it," Theron said. His voice was even, calm, and despite what Aldous had just said, he thought that Theron Ward *was* prepared. Prepared for anything.

"Destiny." Ken scoffed at the word, then cringed and held his side.

"You deny destiny, Ken? You deny any governing force that exists beyond the realm of human understanding?" Theron asked, his voice quiet with fatigue.

"Is this the time to best discuss philosophy?" Aldous asked.

"We nearly died, and we're not out of it yet, so I see no better time," Theron said, as if his answer made sense. Which it sort of did. Which, in turn, made Aldous very nervous.

"I do not believe in God, Hunter," Ken said.

"I am with Kendrick on that." Aldous nodded, heavy with furious thoughts toward the church and the Lumines-cent, so consumed by his anger that he nearly fell face first

117

into the gleaming entrails of a corpse with its gut ripped open.

Theron gave a bitter laugh. "I did not say God. I made no mention of the Luminescent. You let your scathing hatred for the Brynthian church and royalty ruin your connection with any greater force. It is childish." Over his shoulder, Theron scowled at Aldous and Kendrick both. "There is something you despise, so you narrow your minds into only accepting the direct opposite. Instead of making an attempt to walk down any of the other near limitless paths of spirit, you choose to abandon them all because of a hatred for one."

"Watch yourself," Ken said, and Theron turned and side-stepped just in time to avoid a falling timber from a smoldering building. "Chaos," Ken continued. "I believe it is all just chaos."

"Then that is your God. That is your greater force. I call it destiny, you call it chaos. They are the same."

"If you say so," said Ken. "You have clearly thought about this a great deal more than I."

"Then what do you think about?" Aldous asked, but Ken just walked on without offering an answer.

When they arrived at the stables, it was as they had feared. The horses had been slaughtered and half eaten. Theron knelt over a red-stained white gelding, its ribs exposed and guts hollowed. Aldous saw him brush at his eye, and had he not witnessed the brutality he had last night, he would have thought that the man was brushing away a tear.

"I did love that horse," Theron said. He ran his hand across a scar on the horse's shoulder. "He acquired this when he took a spear blow in my place, against a hill-man far to the north, in the land of Ygdrasst. I thought I was going to lose him there, but he pulled through. Many great fights and many great hunts we rode together." Theron stood. "It is a foolish thing to grow so attached to an animal, but it is hard to avoid whether you know it to be foolish or not."

"Did he have a name?" asked Aldous.

"No, I stopped naming my horses some time ago. It wrenches too hard upon the heart when they die." Theron looked at the gelding all the while that he spoke, and it hurt Aldous to see such a strong man fighting off the pangs of melancholy over the loss of a beast.

"I lost a good horse," Ken said. Aldous turned to him, surprised at the emotion in his tone. "I named her Steadfast. It was near the most painful loss of my military life. I'm sorry, Theron." Ken momentarily clutched Theron's shoulder with one hand as he held on to his bleeding side with the other.

"It is an absurd unfairness for the horse, and it plagues me with an equally absurd guilt, for who was I to force the creature here to his death?" Theron asked, and moved from the stables toward the Inn.

The building had not burned to the ground during the assault, and in the kitchen was a good amount of food—the appetite of the rats was not for bread, fruits, and cooked meats.

They gathered what they could and took four canteens of water, and a skin of wine. Theron spent a bit of extra time going room to room, looking at the faces of the dead as if he was searching for someone, but he said nothing, and when he had made a complete inspection of the premises, Theron mumbled, "Not here."

"What's not here?" Aldous asked, but Theron made no reply.

Upstairs Theron took to the chamber he had rented. Aldous reached for Ken to help him to the bed, but Ken only cast him a glower and made his way on his own.

Theron went to the fireplace and grabbed the tinderbox from off the mantel. Quickly he got a fire going.

"Aldous, at the foot of the wardrobe lie some of my daggers. Be so kind as to bring me one," Theron said from his place by the fire, his eyes on Ken.

"Do we have to?" asked Ken with a dark laugh, as though he and Theron were party to a jest that Aldous was not.

"Let me see it," Theron said.

Ken removed his hand from his side, and immediately blood began cascading down.

"Indeed we have to," said Theron, grimacing so hard at the wound it was as if he were the one that suffered it.

Aldous opened the wardrobe and grabbed the longest of the three daggers. "Here," he said as he unsheathed the blade and ran it to Theron.

"Kendrick, bite a pillow," Theron instructed.

Aldous looked at the knife, then at the fire, then at the man.

"Sorry, hunter," Ken said, "I've never been much of a pillow biter. I'd prefer to take it standing up." Ken winked at Aldous. "You're looking pale, boy."

The blade started to glow in the fire. "Aldous, hold him still."

Aldous and Ken exchanged a glance.

"Just do it, hunter," Ken said, and then he took a deep breath, readying himself.

"Fine, but don't you strike out at me."

"I won't, just do it. I've had worse."

Theron pulled the red-hot dagger from the fire and crossed the room. His hand began to shake. Aldous figured surgery and killing took two different kinds of toughness, and he wasn't entirely sure Theron was equal in both.

Aldous took a large swig from the skin of wine he had grabbed in the kitchen, and grimaced as if he were the one about to feel the hot metal. Theron took a moment to position the knife over the wound. Ken started a low growl before the fire-hot steel touched his flesh, and when Theron brought the knife down, close, so close, he tensed.

Aldous backed up until he hit the wall.

Theron stood poised above Ken.

"The knife cools," Ken said, and when Theron still did not bring it to his flesh, Ken grabbed the other man's wrist and pulled the steel to the open wound. The veins in his neck looked as if they were about to burst, and he let out a scream that could shatter stone.

The smell of burning flesh hit Aldous. *Father screams at the stake as the fire eats his legs. Father Riker screams in my hands as I melt his flesh like smoldering wax off his wretched bones.*

He blinked.

Kendrick was done screaming. His teeth were clenched tight and his eyes were wide with pain-induced madness.

"It's done. It's done now," Theron said. He sat at the foot of the bed. "I had to seal a wound like that once before. The fellow writhed around and jerked up when the heat touched him. I damn well slipped and the heated blade slid into his heart."

"Thanks for not telling me that until now," Ken said, then looked at Aldous and held out his hand.

Aldous looked back, not entirely sure what the man wanted.

"The wine, lad. Give me the wine."

"Ah, yes, of course." Aldous reached out and gave Kendrick the wineskin. He chugged it dry in a single go.

"Now what?" Aldous asked.

"Now we bandage our wounds with linens from the beds and then we rest," Theron replied.

Some time later, the trio donned fresh clothes from Theron's wardrobe.

Aldous had enough spare fabric in his outfit to fit another Aldous, and he couldn't help but feel bad that, even with a belt, the pants he wore dragged across the ground and caught under his filthy shoes. Of course, at this point Theron likely did not care, but Aldous felt the tinge of guilt nonetheless.

"My father told me that there was still goodness hidden in the world," Aldous said. "That it was lost and hard to find, but it was there, like the reflection of one golden star on the sea during a clouded night. There will always be one golden star in that black infinity."

"Which of us is the golden star and which the black infinity?" Ken asked, unsmiling.

"A joke?" Theron asked.

Ken did not reply.

~

"Why are you doing this?" Aldous asked many hours later when they had left the inn and Norburg far behind.

"You have such difficulty accepting a good deed?" Theron asked.

"When I first arrived at the church," Aldous said, "I was told that it was only out of kindness that Father Riker and the other monks had taken me in. That it was the kindness of the Luminescent." He paused, remembering. "There is nothing luminous in Brynth."

From then they walked in silence. The band made their way through a dead ravine, under the fathomless gray sky. It was late summer; a cool summer, but still the season of life, yet there was not a leaf on a tree. *Sorcery.* The trees towered like buildings and their branches mingled and broke against each other, so that they formed a series of archways above the hardened dry mud floor.

Every so often Aldous looked back to check upon

Kendrick, who now trailed them by a dozen feet. The large man's lips were purple and he was shaking. He looked not the fearsome killer that had delivered such slaughter the night before. He was vulnerable; they all were vulnerable and very human.

Night fell, only a few shades darker than the cloudy day. They were far from the ravine and the land was flat and straight now.

"How much farther, Theron?" asked Aldous.

"We made it further than I thought, much further. I say only four more hours, five at most. Sanctuary is close," Theron said as he stopped, then bit into a loaf of bread and sipped at a canteen.

"I'm done, lad. I can't carry on," Kendrick said, then dry-heaved twice before hurling up the water he had been drinking during the day.

"Then we shall camp and make an easy trip in the morn," Theron said.

"Won't make it. I feel the fever. You did what you could. Both of you did, and I thank you for that, but I don't have the fire to keep on. Leave me. That's the way of this country, the way we've been made. Carry on. No point in waiting for me to die," Kendrick said calmly before he buckled at the ankles and knees and fell to his side like a tree broken by a storm.

Aldous reached him first and leaned close. "He's still breathing. Barely. But still breathing and out cold." He looked up as Theron reached his side. "He's right. We need to leave him..." He regretted the words as they left his mouth, for Theron's stare made him feel more a villain than Kendrick the Cold.

"We camp here," Theron said. "No fire, for I am in no condition to entertain guests. Kendrick will wake in the morning and we will reach my estate early afternoon."

Theron's words were a command; Aldous had no say in the matter, that much was clear.

He wanted to laugh and cry at the same time as he thought of his predicament. *Of course I have no say in the matter. What am I to do? Disagree? Decide to go my separate way?*

"How were you not afraid?" Aldous asked as they lay on the grass in the blackness of night, Kendrick shivering close by.

"Last night, you mean?"

"Yes. Not once did you freeze, not once did you slow. Even now I see you are in horrible pain. But you are not afraid of death."

Theron gave a laugh. It was a weak laugh, but it was defiant, too.

"I was afraid. I am afraid. Death is my greatest fear. Life is my greatest love. So I do what I must to carry on, but not only for myself. I was given the chance to save your life, Aldous Weaver, the son of the greatest writer, the man who inspired me." Theron gave another little laugh. "In many ways, your father saved you."

Aldous clutched his belly in the dark, Theron's words worming through him.

Theron stood up and removed his cloak, and put it over Ken.

"How did my father save me?" Aldous asked as Theron lay back down, hoping his tone did not betray his emotion.

"Because he was instrumental in the shaping of my mind. Much of my outlook on this world is your father's. I never even met the man, not in this physical plane, but I met his mind."

Aldous was not sure if Theron was fevered from his wounds, or if his words were some sort of brilliance.

"I was given the opportunity to save your life. I thought that if you live you might one day write like your father. You might one day affect even one man or woman as your father affected me. So, yes, I was afraid. Every moment of last night's events nearly brought me to my knees, but my love of life, and the love of the potential of yours, and even Kendrick's, overcame that horror of death."

Aldous marveled at the man's positivity. It reminded him of his father in many ways, and that was why he felt all the guiltier about his own negativity. Father always spoke with certainty, like he understood some future factor of his life's plot that no one else could see. Even when they'd burned him, right there, moments before his death, he spoke with positive inspirational words to his son. Aldous thought that his message must have been: *Carry on in goodness, my son; be that lone golden star and do what you can to cast a reflection.*

Theron Ward cast that golden reflection.

"It's just hard for me. It is hard for me to trust," Aldous said, bowing his head as he spoke, not wanting to look Theron in the eyes.

"Of course it is, but just because something is hard doesn't mean you shouldn't do it."

"Do you not think that misplaced trust can be disastrous?"

"It does not become misplaced until you lose it." Theron sighed.

"What does that even mean?"

"I'm not sure. I thought it sounded good, and I wanted to finish our conversation. Go to sleep and wake up with trust in your heart. You'll need it."

Aldous shook his head in astonishment of the strange man, and he too lay back. The night was cool but not cold, and he was tired enough that he would find sleep, out there with a murderous, dying army deserter and a madly eccentric hunter. Maybe that was the beginning of trust.

As Aldous looked up at the dark clouds in the sky, he

thought of the time when it was always filled with stars. He would sit outside with Mother and Father and they would look up at the stars until Aldous had fallen asleep, then his parents would bring him into his bed and tuck him in. Sometimes he would pretend to have fallen asleep just so he could feel the weightlessness of Father carrying him down the halls of their country estate, placing him into bed, and tucking him in tight. *I love you, my son,* he would say, and Mother would kiss him on the forehead. Aldous felt a warmness roll down his temples; he was crying. As he wept in silence he saw it: a single golden star fighting its way through the clouds, fighting alone but fighting brilliantly, because it shone, it shone and it lulled Aldous into an easy sleep, and despite the horror of the previous night, he dreamed of his childhood and he dreamed well.

In the morning when he woke, he saw Kendrick first. He was still unconscious and sweating profusely. His chest rose and fell in a rapid, shallow rhythm. Aldous barely knew the man, but he had helped save his life, and it saddened him to know that this man would not rise. He would not make it a five-hour journey to Wardbrook.

Aldous turned to his other side to see what Theron had to say on the matter, but he was not there.

Aldous looked all around, and he felt like a fool, not only for the part of him that hoped to spot Theron Ward, but because the ground was mostly flat in all directions, but for a hill to the east. He began to panic, for he had not the slightest clue where he was. He was alone with a dying man, and with limited rations and no weapon to defend himself.

Panic soon turned to rage.

After all he said, he left us. The bastard left us. He thought we would slow him down.

"Theron!" Aldous screamed at the top of his lungs. His eyes strained and his throat grated.

He screamed for a minute or so then, exhausted and coughing, sat back down and began to weep. He looked up once more to the eastern hill, and in his tear-blurred vision he saw him. Theron was there, dragging something behind him. As he got closer, Aldous could see it was some sort of makeshift sled.

~

Dreams, they are the most mystifying of all things in the magical realm, the most unfathomable. The most sinister. For in my dreams I feel a thousand pains, I sob at a thousand woes, I indulge in a thousand pleasures. They often feel more real than life, yet they are nothing. When I wake they are nothing. Dreams encompass all that I have experienced in my life, both sensory and through thought, whilst at the same time a dream is capable of forming new experience. Who has not remembered a dream they once had in the waking world, then thought of it so much they dreamed of that dream once again? But they dreamed of it as they thought of it as a dream!

Oh, such strange madness it is.

Why may I not just sleep? Close my eyes then wake with the night past; why must I leave this strange world to another, ever stranger? A world that I have made and diluted and disrupted, mangled and perverted, a world, or perhaps many worlds, infinite worlds, entirely my own, yet of which I have no control. A wise man once said, "Every man is king of his own mind." I disagree. Oh how I disagree, for dreaming only involves the mind, and dreaming is madness. Of madness there can be no control. Death beckons me forth, a promise to end the dreams, but what if it lies? What if to die is to dream? To dream forever?

—The scribblings of a madman, unnamed, found dead in his cell, deep in the dungeons of the Imperial City.

~

CHAPTER ELEVEN

FEVER DREAM

*S*ix days had passed since they had arrived at Wardbrook, and for six days Kendrick had remained in a delusional state, half dreaming and half awake, the fever fighting to take him. He fought back. He screamed in his dreams, wailed and sobbed, and when he did wake it was in a mixed state of terror, rage, and unbearable sadness.

He had already torn two rooms apart in these states of madness, tearing apart the mattresses with his bare hands, tipping over the furniture and pummeling it with bloody knuckles. Theron had been hard-pressed to subdue him.

When Ken became exhausted, Theron would call for his servants, and together they would spoon water or broth between Ken's parched lips. In his delusional fury he would demand that Theron and his staff tell him where he was and who they were. He would demand they tell him where his wife was, then after a while he would begin to weep and soon fall back into his dark sleep.

Of Aldous, Theron had seen little, for the sick room was more than the boy could bear. So Theron sat by Kendrick the

Cold's bedside on the seventh day, just as he had through the first six.

The fever had broken in the night, and Theron was certain the man would live. But his fight was not over, for the attack of nightmares was yet to cease. And fight Ken did. Whether he knew it or not, he had a formidable will to live.

Ken sat up fully in the bed and screamed. He roared, a bestial sound that would quake the resolve of a hungry bear. His eyes were wide and mad tears poured down his face, veins bulging in his neck. Yet he was not awake.

Still he fought the madness, and after a time he lay back down, calm again until the next attack.

"Keep on, my friend. Do not kneel to the devils that haunt you," Theron whispered.

There was a faint knocking at the door.

"Come in."

"How fares he?" asked Aldous. Each and every time Ken engaged his enemy and entered a fit, Aldous would knock at the door, but he never walked through the threshold. Theron knew the boy was sitting outside the room most of the time. He was too afraid to sit as close as Theron, especially after seeing the aftermath of the first destroyed room, but he cared enough to spend many of his hours outside in the hall.

"He is going to live, of that I am certain. The fever is losing, but some darkness inside him lingers."

"He is a frightening man, even in this state," said Aldous as he looked toward where Ken lay in the bed, as if he were a wounded lion that, with a sudden burst of strength, would lunge and tear out his throat.

"Perhaps most of all in this state," Theron said, without taking his eyes from Kendrick. "Tell me, have you been doing what I asked of you?"

"Yes. It's fascinating to read something other than scripture. Last night I started a book on the alchemical properties of void dust. Very interesting stuff," said Aldous.

Theron smiled. It was certainly not interesting stuff, and he knew for a fact that the boy could not understand a bloody thing in any book on alchemy, unless he was secretly man of science as well as magic. Yet it pleased Theron all the same that he was putting in an effort.

"There is something I want to give you." He closed the book in his lap, stood, and handed it to Aldous.

The boy took it. *"The Indisputable Science of Goodness,"* Aldous read aloud, then paused. "By Darcy Weaver," he continued, his voice growing faint as he reached his father's name. "My father..."

"Yes," said Theron, smiling.

Aldous ran his fingertips along the title on the spine. "Thank... thank you, Theron. I... I don't know what to say. I've never read any of his books. I was too young." Aldous' face was red, and his eyes shimmered with the formation of tears.

"Say nothing. Not until you have read it. Return it to your chambers, then come back here and sit with me and our friend." It was not an invitation, it was an instruction, and Aldous obeyed.

At the door he paused, and asked without looking back, "How do you even have this? I thought they burned them all."

"Do I look like a man who would burn my books?"

∼

The old woman did not protest as he tied her to the cross. She cackled instead.

"You are cursed. Cursed by my god and your own, cursed to walk with that demon of chaos that is your wretched soul. You are

cursed and you are weak," said the old woman as he strained to tighten the final knot round her bony wrist.

The sky was red, and the moon was black. Mountains of corpses surrounded them, surrounded Ken and that old crone on the cross. Thousands of dead children, their innocence only understood after their slaughter, after their screams and sobs carved eternal scars into the soul of a man turned monster. A man who once, like them, had been an innocent child.

"I will not do this," said Ken to the old woman as he held the first nail against her palm.

She laughed, a high-pitched cackle. "You already have, you broken fool. A thousand times, you already have."

"No, I will not do it again," he said as he brought the hammer down, and the clink of the mallet striking the nail mingled with the shattering bone. The old woman became a screaming child, then a mother, then a husband who loved his family. They wept and begged, and so did Ken.

"Enough!" Ken cried. "Enough, damn you, enough. I know what I have done. When can I forget?"

Again the form on the cross was the crone. "Never, never will you forget. You may die and be reborn for time eternal, but never will you forget what you have done. You turned your back on humanity, you blackened your soul." Again she cackled. "Man is fire and the devils are cold."

The mountains of corpses shrank and turned to trees and homes, the red sky turned gray, and the black moon turned yellow.

He was back home, the west, Brynth. The houses were boarded shut and in the streets they walked, men and women covered in black and yellow-green boils. They puked and bled as they screamed and crawled through the mud. When they saw Kendrick, they turned and began to squeal.

Somewhere in his thoughts, he was repulsed, he was afraid. That place was buried deep. The foul things, once human, turned and faced him; they stared in silence. That silence called Ken forward; it told him to set to work. He pulled his hatchets from his belt and he got to that terrible work on the whole town.

Alone in that dark village stood a chapel. Cloud white, a hopeful beacon in that endless gray infinity. Ken walked to the chapel. He opened the doors.

They hung from the rafters. The survivors, those who had not turned into the rats, hung themselves from the rafters, and at the altar lay the priest, knife in his hand, his wrists slit to the bone. Mothers and fathers hung next to sons and daughters. The silence of the dead town screamed in Ken's ears. The wickedness of the Luminescent and the wickedness of man were one and the same.

Wake up. You're dreaming. This is done. It is over. Just wake up. You don't need to see the rest.

"I cannot!"

You must. I can't look at the rest. Please wake up, please, please don't go home.

The chapel warped before Kendrick. The corpses on the rafters disappeared. The priest rose and turned his back; his hair grew long and he was Eleanor. She knelt by the fire. She was waiting at home.

"Eleanor, my love, my sweet love, I came home, I came home for you. To protect you."

Wake up. Damn you, wake up, don't do this to me, don't you go any closer to her.

In his house, Kendrick fell to his knees. The baby was soon to arrive, and his wife...

He was right behind her now. She was so grand, so magnificent, her golden hair shining brighter than the fire she sat by. Kendrick reached to touch her.

You fucking bastard. You know what happens next. You already know! Just wake up! Wake up—

He touched her.

She turned.

Kendrick opened his mouth to scream, but no sound came.

She wore white, stained black and red. The boils covering her neck swelled as the hot blood ran from them, like a sack of spider eggs begging to burst. The blood... Their unborn child, torn from her own guts.

She too was on her knees, Eleanor's monstrous buckteeth gnashing through the little bones and the squishy fat as she hungrily devoured their daughter.

He tore her apart. With his bare hands he tore Eleanor apart.

~

Kendrick twitched and twisted in the bed. He cried out and sat bolt upright, eyes wide and crazed, breathing heavily and drenched in sweat.

Aldous had half a mind to run. For even weakened by the fever, Ken was still a terrifying sight. The black bags and scruffy beard he had acquired made him all the more alarming. It was when, with eyes wide and bloodshot, Kendrick screamed the name "Eleanor," foam spewing from his mouth, that Aldous' mind went from having half the desire to run to a full desire to run.

Theron caught him by the arm.

"He will not harm us," Theron said calmly.

"I'm sorry, but I don't trust you on that," Aldous said as he tried to tug his arm free of Theron's grip, but there was no use. So Aldous decided to simply close his eyes as the wrathful Kendrick walked toward them on trembling legs, roaring the name "Eleanor."

Aldous could feel the heat from a very close Kendrick, and so he opened his left eye just a bit. Kendrick stood face to face with Theron. He snorted like a bull. His eyes went soft and tears dripped off the bottom of his chin. He collapsed to his knees and sobbed.

"Help me drag him back to his bed," Theron said. "I

believe he has survived the worst, and when he next wakes our friend will be back." He grabbed Kendrick by one arm and nodded for Aldous to grab the other.

"Our friend?" Aldous asked incredulously, as he followed Theron's silent order. Theron he could call a friend, for Theron had saved him and they had spent the last week together in his estate. They'd talked about a great many things, and as many differences as they had, there were equal similarities. Indeed, he could call Theron friend, his only friend since he was a boy.

Kendrick was something else. They had only known each other for a day, and whatever else Aldous knew of the man was through stories. None of which depicted friendship material.

"Indeed," Theron said.

"I don't know if I consider this man my—" Aldous began, but Theron abruptly dropped Kendrick's arm, and alone Aldous could tug the beast no further. He looked up, and Theron had a look of utter contempt on his face.

"Then leave him," Theron said. "I will tend to him myself and you can go back to your quarters and read the book of your father's that *I* just *gave* you."

"What? No... I—"

"You heard me. Go. I won't stop you. Despite the hell I went through to keep him alive this long, if you don't call him friend then walk away right now."

"I don't understand." Aldous was overwhelmed by guilt, confusion, and fear all at once. Theron was a frightening man when he was angry, and the fact that Aldous could not comprehend where the sudden burst of rage had come from made him all the more intimidating.

"We saved his life. You and I together saved this man's life. We are now responsible for him, and so he is our friend." Theron's voice had again calmed and become completely flat.

His quick burst of rage—Aldous was now understanding—was a quick burst of impatience.

"You say that as if it makes sense."

"Say he is your friend." Theron's eyes were animal intense in that moment; they were loving and violent, hypnotizing. They were the eyes of a leader, the alpha of the pack.

"He's my friend?" Aldous offered, knowing then that there was nothing else to say.

"Good." Theron grabbed the arm he had dropped, and together they heaved the wallowing Kendrick back into bed.

～

Aldous rocked back and forth in the chair for some time, simply starring at the book, *The Indisputable Science of Goodness* by Darcy Weaver. He read the title aloud every ten minutes or so. But Aldous could not bring himself to start the book.

Why this particular book? Why his philosophy and not his fiction? Why this volume of philosophy? What if I disagree? The last was the core question and the main force that stopped Aldous from opening the book. Not once in his youth had he disagreed with his father. Essentially, it was a fear of having his very first argument with his father that would not let him even open to the first page.

A knocking came at the door.

"Yes?"

"It's me," came Theron's voice.

Theron entered the room, about to speak, but before he could Aldous did. "Why are you doing this? Why have you done all that you have, not just for me but also for Kendrick?"

"I'm getting sick of you asking me that question. There is

no other rational way to be," said Theron as he stepped into the room.

The matter-of-fact answer irritated Aldous. He was not sure why, but it did. He was suspicious; he could not help it, for what man behaved as this Theron Ward? Born into wealth, sickeningly abundant wealth, with no need to ever do a bloody thing, yet he did so much. He made himself into so much more than his birthright. Aldous felt a spiteful, cynical monster in that moment, but he could not help it. The man's positivity and compassion had all of a sudden become irksome.

"Of course there is, are you mad? You have everything, yet you risk it all to be a hunter to defend the weak, to try and save and change the villainous. You could sit about and—"

"And do nothing?" Theron snickered in a way that made Aldous feel like the greatest fool who'd ever lived for speaking the way he just had. "That is rational, you think? To sit about and do nothing?"

"You can't win," Aldous said in a weak voice. He was blushing now, and he looked down at the book, the book that belonged to Theron, and stopped rocking in the chair that belonged to Theron. He felt very much like an arrogant child, arguing just to argue. Disagreeing just because it took trust to agree, but despite this he whispered, "You can't win, you can't change the world; the evil in it will never leave." He thought of his father, his brilliant, hopeful father, burning alive.

"Neither will the good." Theron stood over Aldous, a great and powerful form.

"They killed my father because they believed him to be evil, because they thought they were right. In the end it is a matter of perspective," Aldous said.

"If you truly believe that, you have lost. You have lost and you are not your father's son. Such a belief is an escape. Saying that all is relative, or a matter of perspective, is to say you accept evil. Torture is not a matter of perspective; rape is not a matter of perspective; burning a man alive for questioning a church that flays and burns and crucifies any who do not kneel to the Luminescent is no matter of perspective. It is evil." Theron tilted Aldous' head up so he was looking into his eyes. "There is no arguing this. There is good and there is evil, and every man and woman must face this reality."

"It's not that simple," Aldous said, with a bit more venom in his voice than he intended.

"Read your father's book, Aldous." Theron sighed. "I will be leaving Wardbrook for a short time. I have business in Baytown and I mustn't be late."

He turned his back and walked from the room without waiting for a response from Aldous, then over his shoulder said, "Sir Hakesworth will be in charge of the estate while I am gone, and will continue to make sure our friend Kendrick is in the process of good recovery."

Aldous said nothing, just watched Theron walk down the hall until he had turned a corner and was out of sight, and then he closed the door and walked to his bed to again look at the book.

～

"They're home! They're home!" The blonde little girl ran down the path, lush green grass to either side. She spun once, and twice, her little dress rising and twirling in the soft summer wind. Her smile beamed. She closed her eyes tight, her head tilted to the warm sun, as she twirled toward the two figures of her affection that rode down the path back home.

"They have only been gone three days, child, just three days." Her mother laughed.

"It felt longer! It felt like forever and ever. I'm so happy they are home!" The little girl's voice trailed like her long golden hair as she ran ahead down the path.

"It will be a most cherished reunion," whispered her mother.

～

CHAPTER TWELVE

REUNIONS

*K*en stood from the bed and walked to the window. *Glass.* He ran his hand over the smooth surface. Keeps and churches were the only places he had ever seen with glass windows, which made him wonder where he was.

What was the last thing he remembered? It wasn't a good thing. There was an aching in his back, and the image of the torture chamber in the depths of Norburg Keep flashed across his mind, along with the memory of ten armed men dragging him from slumber.

"Alma," Ken said. "I am sorry. I truly am. I hoped they would never find me, and for that I am a monster. For gambling your life on what I hoped."

He turned and looked at the bed. All his life he had slept like a cave bear; as a boy and as a murderous man, not a thought stirred while he slept. Yet he knew that, in that bed, he had dreamed.

He remembered the blond man with the features of a northern warrior prince. Theron Ward, the monster hunter.

He saved my life. There was another too, a young man. Black hair. Aldous Weaver.

He looked around the room. The walls were a deep maroon. A great fireplace was lit on the wall furthest from Ken, ten pointed antlers on a plaque above it. The floor was a dark wood, and in front of the fire was the pelt of a snow-white wolf. He turned his head back around and looked at the bed. It was royal. There was no other word for it; the bed alone was the size of Ken and Alma's modest hovel.

He walked across the room toward the immense dresser, on which a large—and, to Ken's taste, offensively decorated —mirror was fastened. The frame was rich wood, with a delicate relief of angelic creatures carved into it.

It had been a long time since he'd stared into a mirror.

Ken took a moment to comprehend the man in the reflection. His chin was clean shaved, and his once long, matted hair was trimmed down to the skull. Ken did not remember much, but he was sure that he was not responsible for the clean shave. The black bags beneath his eyes, the bandages around his torso and arms, and the overall look of depletion was likely the doing of fever, for that would also explain the dreams.

Looking in the mirror confirmed how he felt. Weak. Horribly weak. A sensation he had not felt since he was a boy, a sensation he despised. He wanted to strike the mirror, smash it to shards and obliterate every part of the strange, lavish room he had woken into. He expected the voices of self-loathing that haunted his mind to speak, to chide him, to ridicule him, but for the first time in a long time, the voices were silent. He took a deep breath and accepted that something had happened, something terrible, and for whatever reason he was still alive.

Chaos.

The door creaked open behind Kendrick and he turned

from the window and saw the boy, Aldous. He looked both afraid and surprised to find Kendrick by the window.

"Where am I? I don't think I'm supposed to be here," Ken said, confused and embarrassed.

"You are supposed to be here. I just didn't expect you to be out of bed." The boy came no closer.

"Why? What has happened? Am I dreaming?" Kendrick was beginning to feel more than a bit uneasy, then he noticed the tray in Aldous' hands. There was a cup of tea, or water maybe, and what looked like oats. *Hot oats with milk and water.* He sniffed the air. There was a spice... *Cinnamon?* Another symptom of wealth—or he was back in the east, for that was the only place he'd ever encountered such a spice. He hoped for the former.

"I hope not. I hope you're awake and sane. For seven days you were ebbing in and out of this life and screaming madly in your dreams. In your most recent outburst, I feared for my life," said Aldous, nervously extending the tray.

"I think I'm awake. Where are we, and why are you here? I remember the fight, the slaughter." Ken paused. "We killed Count Salvenius. Or was that a dream?" He took the tray, and again smelled the cinnamon.

"No, that was real. That night was real. The count is dead and all of Norburg is in ruin. The rats were real, too." Aldous shuddered.

"I remember a woman," Ken said, setting the tray on a low table. "And the rats parting to let her through."

"Yes." Aldous shuddered again and sidled a little closer. "You were wounded and exhausted. We set out for Wardbrook, two days' march from Norburg. You were fading the first day, but somehow managed to keep up. Do you remember any of this?"

Ken shook his head. He didn't remember any of it, except

what mattered. The dead count. And the witch, though why the witch mattered, he couldn't say.

"By nightfall you collapsed and looked like you weren't going to make it. It guilts me to say, but I simply thought we were going to leave you." Aldous bowed his head and looked to be in genuine shame, a disposition Kendrick knew much of.

"Why didn't you?" Kendrick asked. "Leave me, I mean. You should have. I deserved to be left there." He was angry now, and he stepped forward, but then felt woozy and sat back down on the bed. "I deserve to die," he said softly, as he thought of Alma.

Aldous handed him the cup, and Ken took a sip. It was tea, with milk, warm and pleasant and sweetened with honey.

"Theron didn't think so." Aldous said, still standing. Ken stared at the boy, who was clearly uneasy, not sure if Ken would bite.

"Why? He knows who I am, as I have no doubt you do as well. If not when we first met, our host has informed you."

"He has," Aldous said in a hush.

Ken gave a snort of laughter. He forced it out. Nothing was funny.

"Whatever he told you, the truth is far worse." He finished the tea and handed the empty cup back to Aldous then wiggled his fingers at the porridge. The boy handed him the bowl.

"Are you an evil man?"

"Don't be childish," Kendrick said, but when he looked at Aldous it was clear the question was serious. "Yes."

"Theron thinks that can change."

"He does, does he? What do you think?"

"I'm not sure. Maybe you're a good man who's done evil things. Your punishment is living with that."

"That's a pretty easy punishment," Ken said. He tried to sound cold, tough, and emotionless, but the boy's fear was gone and he stood up to leave the room.

"I disagree. I doubt there is anything worse." Aldous walked to the door.

"The fuck do you know about guilt, boy?"

"I watched the church burn my father alive. I watched and I did nothing, his screams ringing in my ears. Then I spent the rest of my life copying the Church's scripture. If I didn't, I'd be branded a heretic, so I bent my knee to evil. I want to make up for that guilt. I don't know how, but I want to do it." Aldous spoke quietly, and looked past Ken as he did; he looked down the path of hatred. It was cloudy for the boy now; the fog on the road was thick, but Ken knew that all one had to do to clear the path was keep on walking.

Theron had arrived at Baytown in good time. He smiled as he took in the salty air gusting in from the sea, through the wide, muddy thoroughfares of the town. Baytown was one of the rare places in Brynth that always looked and felt the same. A heavy fog drifting about the wooden shanties; bearded, grim-looking men weathered by the sea, always talking about their most recent catch. The issues of the world were lost on these people, unless those issues had to do with fish. The sound of the gulls cawing above as they circled in the sky, waiting for a morsel of any kind to make itself known through the fog below, whether it was a fish in or out of water, or perhaps to sneak into a bucket of bait whilst a fisherman was not looking. Baytown was a place where hunger ruled all in some ancient way, and a full belly was the only blessing asked for from the gods of the sea.

The last time Theron had been here, he himself was

returning from the far northern isle of Ygdrasst. On a ship given to him by a great Jarl—the *Storm Lurker*. It was a lean vessel, half schooner and half dragon ship of some past era. It was a long ship, but it glided low on the water and moved with tremendous speed when the sails were full, and even when all that pushed her were the oars.

It was the ship Theron looked for now as he dismounted his horse and walked down the long dock that stretched out into the calm, lapping waves of the sea. He saw the bulkhead first, emerging from the heavy fog, the carved visage of a furious serpent, tongue like a snake and teeth like a wolf. Gulls floating on the water took flight and fled from the cruel face of that formidable beast of the blue. The sails were down, and the oars were out rowing hard toward Baytown.

He could see the girl at the head of the bow as the *Storm Lurker* glided from the mist. She was not the girl he remembered, and the way she stood at the head, it was as if she were captain—a position she had not held when she left Brynth. Even at the distance, Theron could see her shoulders had widened. She wore light chain mail, and the sides of her blonde hair were in tight braids with the center loose and wild.

She returns a hunter.

Theron smiled so wide it hurt.

"Chayse!" he called.

"Theron, you fool! You came to escort me home?" she called back as the *Lurker* neared the dock.

"But of course. I planned the trip the moment I received your letter."

When the ship was aligned and the oars were taken in, the crew set to the task of pulling the schooner to dock. Chayse, apparently unable to wait for the ship to be fully settled, leapt from the deck to the dock. Theron caught her in his arms and squeezed her as he had when she was a child.

When *they* were children.

"You've grown," he said when he placed her down.

"Excuse me?" she asked, flushing red in an instant and punching Theron in the arm. "That is not a thing you say to a lady."

"In a good way." Theron laughed. "You were meager when you left, could barely draw back your bow."

Chayse drew the longbow that she wore on her back and flexed the sixty-pound draw all the way so that the yew of the shaft gave a bit of a bend. Chayse had been better than anyone Theron had ever met with a bow before she left; he figured her trials far away had honed her talent to the point of being frightening.

Theron squeezed her drawing shoulder. "Carved in stone!" he said, much impressed.

"Just like you," Chayse said as she released the string, then gave Theron a hit to the gut.

They looked at each other for a long time. They laughed and embraced, then looked at each other once again. She was a stranger; she was a changed woman, physically and mentally. She was certainly altered from her time away, but she was still the same Chayse.

"How did the *Storm Lurker* serve you?" Theron asked.

"Well. She is small, but her craftsmanship is superb, for she rips through the tide quicker than any ship her larger."

"Just as I said she would."

"Yes, Theron, just as you said. You know all there is to know about ships." Chayse gave him a playful shove.

"What can I say? I am an expert on a great many things." He smiled wide at her again. Not the smile he gave to strangers, or even the one he gave to himself in the mirror. This was a special smile just for Chayse. They embraced once again.

By now the rest of the crew had come off the ship. Some

men Theron knew, for they had adventured with him before. They embraced and offered one another a reminiscent joke. The men Theron did not know shook and embraced anyway, for they all knew *of* him, whether or not he knew of them. They exchanged jokes about what it was like to spend two years serving under the likes of Chayse.

It was clear that the fact that she was only twenty years and a woman meant little to most of these men, for their respect was obvious. And those who were too primitive in their beliefs to admit respect for a woman looked as if they feared her enough to keep their opinions to themselves.

"What say you we stay one night in Baytown before we head back?" Chayse said. "I'm sure the lads would love to tell you stories and hear some of your own. Two years is a long time for racking up a good adventure or ten."

"I would love to, but—" Theron began.

"But nothing, ye handsome bastard! Two years is a while to be free of having a drink with Franklin the Fierce," said Franklin the Fierce.

"All right, all right. One night I shall stay, but then Chayse and I must depart, for there are guests waiting at the estate." The group cheered, all of them madly excited about getting drunk, for every man knew that the only thing better than a voyage at sea was getting drunk when that voyage was done.

"Guests?" asked Chayse, eyes narrowed. "You didn't go and get married, did you? Have some girl and her kin back at home?"

The group all had a good laugh at this, for if Theron Ward was known for one thing as much as his monster slaying, it was his womanizing.

～

The Scathing Skeemer was Theron's type of tavern, although

the misspelling of the word *schemer* on the sign outside did drive him a little mad. The place was filled with as much joy as it was with drunken sailors and fat, jovial concubines. It took Franklin the Fierce a matter of seconds before he had coin out and was smothering his mangled face in a plump, pale pair of teats. Chayse laughed at the sight and slapped Franklin hard on the ass. He raised his head and yelped, but his lady pulled him back down into the warm abyss of her mighty mams.

When they had slowed down a bit after the initial excitement of their reunion, they took to serious talking—well, Chayse, Theron and a few of the older, more weathered hunters. The younger ones and the crewmen who manned the ship stuck to drinking and whoring.

"So what was it like? The south Chayse, the south!" Theron grabbed her by the face and mushed her cheeks in his palms.

"It was hot," she said when Theron released her. "Hellishly hot, but beautiful. The landscapes and vistas put the hillsides and valleys by Wardbrook to shame. The colors were powerful, I mean really powerful. We have no green in our fields of Brynth like the green in the forests of Azria. We have no flowers like their flowers, or even the water in their streams." Chayse tilted her head back and sighed as she reminisced. "Azria is a truly wonderful place. You would like it there. Although you would have a bit of trouble with the women."

"Hideous?" Theron asked with a wince.

"Not in the least. They are some of the most beautiful I have ever seen."

"Then what's the problem?" Theron asked.

"They're as tall and mighty as you, lad. One might decide you belong to her and put your stones in a vise, and a collar round your neck," said old One-Eyed Welfric with a laugh.

"Then I suppose there are no real men there to keep

151

things in order," Theron said, slapping his hand hard on the table and staring at Welfric in anticipation, waiting for the old man to laugh. Welfric howled at the jest, and only then did Theron begin to safely laugh at his own joke. Chayse shot both of them a glare that could kill, and they abruptly stopped their fit of laughter at the not-so-funny joke mid-wheeze.

"How were the contracts? Anything ferocious?" asked Theron, after he had fully regained his composure.

"Nothing quite as horrific as the rats, but there was a particular contract that nearly got the best of us."

"Aye, we lost two local hunters, and that boy Chaff from Dagund got done in," said Welfric. "Franklin said he'd be the one to bring the news to the boy's folks." He took a big swig of ale.

"It is the risk of the profession, but it is never easy to loose a comrade," said Theron. He thought of Kendrick back at Wardbrook, and wondered how Aldous was managing. If Ken was awake and functioning, were they getting along? *What if I return and Ken has killed my entire staff?*

"The locals called the creatures *Eloko,*" said Chayse.

"Nasty little brutes," Welfric added. "Mangy dwarves with fangs and beastly strength. A tribe of them was preying on local hunters and caravans that were essential to the profits of Azria's capital city. We got contracted to track them wee butchers to their grotto and take them out." He shook his head. "We had no bloody idea that there would be so many." He lifted his tankard and took a long swallow.

"Must have been a hundred," Chayse said. She, too, took a swig then looked up at Theron. "What about here? How have things been at home?"

Theron took a deep breath and let out a sigh.

"Uh-oh," said Welfric.

"Norburg is in ruin, its citizens butchered, and the rats

have emerged once again, larger and more grotesque than I have ever seen. They attacked as a swarm and I believe dark sorcery to be what directed the destruction."

Welfric, Chayse, and the others stared at Theron wide eyed, with disbelieving looks carved into hard faces.

Theron went on to retell in depth what happened that night. He altered the story slightly when it came to his arrest and how he had met his companions in the torture chambers. He also omitted whom exactly his companions were, and that they together slaughtered the Count Salvenius.

Other than those meager alterations, he kept the story the same. For Theron trusted Chayse, and he trusted Welfric as well, but to divulge that he was responsible for the death of Count Salvenius—and that Kendrick the Cold and a wizard were holed up at Wardbrook—in a tavern with the name The Scathing Skeemer was likely not a wise plan. For if the wrong ears became privy to such information, Theron would become a fugitive along with the company he kept.

"That Emerald Witch, you believe her to be the dark designer of Norburg's ruin?" asked Welfric, in a voice too loud for Theron's comfort.

"Yes." Theron looked around with unease. "Lower your voice, Welfric. I know not her ultimate plot or the extent of her power. She could have agents lurking in the shadows here and now." He leaned in and motioned for the others to do the same, and continued his tale in a whisper. "Her and an entourage of the count's former men-at-arms and several seekers, with a procession of chained women, marched through the center of the swarm like the king's men parade through the Imperial City crowds." Theron took a sip of ale. "The beasts were frantic and mad, but they were obedient. They feared her, and they understood her agenda for her company remained unharmed." Theron finished his seventh pint of ale, but the dark thoughts kept him sober.

The group talked and brooded late into the night. They passed out there in The Scathing Skeemer, and when they woke they said their farewells. Tears welled in Chayse's eyes as she gave her goodbyes to her closest companions of the past two years.

"She cannot help but cry," Theron said. "She's tougher than any woman I know, but a woman still."

One-Eyed Welfric turned to him, tears pouring down half his face, and nodded. "Aye," he said. "Aye."

~

"So what did you not tell the others that you are now going to tell me?" Chayse asked when they were a good twenty miles from Baytown.

"I was arrested. Sentenced to be hanged, or beheaded maybe. Sentenced to die," Theron said, grinning.

"What have you done, Theron?" Chayse was not grinning.

"I had a drunken tumble in the hay with the count's daughter. She was a fiend."

"I do not care about the girl's sexual appetite," Chayse chided.

"No, truly, when I think back on it, she was as mad as a fiend. She howled like a beast. She was possessed. It was part of the Emerald Witch's plot. I don't know why, but that she is out to get me. Yes, indeed, it was a conspiracy most... coital." He smiled, impressed with his word choice.

"Or you were drunk, the girl was drunk, and you fucked her like you always do and it finally got you into a proper bit of trouble," said Chayse, finally grinning.

"No, she wanted me in the dungeon when her rats attacked. She did not want me to interfere. I escaped, but I still failed in saving the city." Theron lost his zest, and stared at the ground, downcast as he thought of all the people that had died in that brutal slaughter.

"Don't be ridiculous, Theron. There was nothing you could do against such odds. At least you saved the two guests that are now safe and recovering at Wardbrook. That is who the guests are, isn't it? People you saved?"

"In a manner of speaking."

"Theron?" Chayse scowled.

Theron gave a smile. "Aldous Weaver, the son of the great Darcy Weaver, is now in our very home."

She stared blankly at him for a moment then rolled her eyes.

"In the flesh," Theron said.

"You lie!" Chayse was now grinning too, like a little child.

"I do not. I swear I do not."

"And the other?"

"A man by the name of Kendrick Kelmoor, known locally as Kendrick the Cold."

Chayse went pale, and so ferocious was her stare that Theron was forced to look away, for if there was a wrath he feared it was the wrath of Chayse.

As they trotted down the path back home, Theron could feel that the eyes of his sister were not the only ones burning a hole in his back. He stopped, turned around, and stared out into the tree line—a dark shadow beneath the early morning glow.

At first he saw nothing amiss, and then there, on an eastern hill, a hunched form. He narrowed his eyes. The form did not move, not forward, and not back. It stood perfectly still, like a cat confronted by a stray dog.

But this was no cat, and no dog.

"It's a... rat," Chayse said from behind him. "Rata Plaga. Out in the open."

"Impossible. They don't watch. They attack." But it wasn't

impossible. Because this was most certainly a rat, and it was most certainly watching him.

An image jumped into his mind of the Emerald Witch walking through the mass of rats, and the rats parting to let her through. As if she was their royalty.

No, more than that. As if she pulled their strings.

He stared at the rat on the hill once more and wondered what exactly the Emerald Witch wanted from him.

~

The jungle canopy towered as high as a mountain, trees as old as time. Their massive deep green leaves funneled the torrential downpour from the high heavens into thick cascades of water that came crashing to the jungle floor so far below. Even in the downpour, the heat was nearly unbearable, and the air was so humid that to breathe was to inhale some of the visible blanket of moisture that hovered before the eyes, even in the dim evening light, and the shade of those monolithic trees. Most of the creatures that dwelled in that dense bush took to hiding in their little holes, waiting for the weather to pass. All hid but the big game—the big game and the huntress from across the sea far to the northwest. They prowled the jungle, taking solace in the blanket of mist and the noise of the cascading rainfall.

A fine predator was the great shadow cat of the Azrian rainforest; a better predator was the huntress from Wardbrook.

She notched her arrow.

Took a breath.

The shadow cat's golden eyes glowed.

She drew back.

The shadow cat's golden eyes glowed.

The arrow released.

~

CHAPTER THIRTEEN

ADJUSTING

endrick was already in the library when Aldous walked in. He was sitting by the fire, staring at the flames. Theron had been gone ten days. In that time, Kendrick had improved immensely, but the man was still not in top form. He had lost a considerable amount of weight and he said less than little, always staring into the flames or out the window, or anywhere else that did not force him to interact with other people.

"Kendrick," Aldous said as he opened up his father's book and sat down in a chair close by Ken and the fire to—for the third time—attempt to read his father's writing.

"Aldous," Ken said, nodding, still staring at the fire. "Theron's kitchen staff made quail eggs and fresh-baked bread. You should eat it whilst it is still warm."

That surprised Aldous, for it sounded like the man cared.

"I'm not hungry, but thank you." Aldous offered Ken a courteous smile, which was lost on him, for he had not looked away from the flames, as though he searched for some sort of answer there. Aldous knew that feeling.

He opened his book and began to read. Each day it took

him less and less time to become irritated with the words on the page. It was an endless slew of subjective ideas, like justice, honor, loyalty, and, of course, goodness, described in an objective way. There was no art in the writing—it was painfully bland—and that had been the first thing to take Aldous by surprise.

Ken began laughing, a quiet chuckle.

Aldous looked up from the pages and saw that Ken was looking at him.

"What's funny?" Aldous asked.

"You're looking at those pages like you want to throw them into the fire," said Ken. His tone was sinister, and he looked the part, sitting in that lavish armchair with burgundy cushions and lacquered dark wooden limbs. The fire cast a shadow on his hollowed features; his pale shaved head and face looked almost like a skull in the dim light of the library.

"Don't say that. I want to do no such thing!" Aldous said. "This is my father's book, you know."

"It's Theron's book," said Ken, turning away from Aldous and looking back into the fire, the flames glowing in his dark, heavy eyes.

"My father wrote it."

"I know, but every day while I am in here sitting by the fire, you read it, and you have the same look on your face." Ken brought a handkerchief to his runny nose, the last symptoms of his near death still running their course. "I haven't read too many books in my life, boy. In fact, I've read none. Read a lot of faces, though, and yours is easy."

"What does it say?" Aldous asked, with as much genuine interest as irritation.

"Contempt."

"I do not hold contempt toward my father, Kendrick." Aldous felt a heat rise in him; he felt the pages underneath his thumbs growing terribly hot, hot enough to burn. He slammed the book shut and tossed it down, to preserve it. The book landed dangerously close to the fire.

Aldous' heart leapt in fear, and he could swear the flame did the same, leaping and twisting and reaching for the book. Aldous snatched it and shoved it to the side.

Ken didn't take the hint to leave things alone, or he just didn't care; Aldous assumed the latter, as Ken said, "I never said that you hold contempt for your father, but your father is not his book. The book is just a book, just words. If you don't like the words, don't read them, and don't feel bad for it."

Aldous sighed and felt the furnace in his belly cool slightly.

"Just words? Theron swears that these words inspire him to act in the manner he does. He told me they were his call to action, and my frustration comes from the fact that I am having great difficulty finding what he found in them." Aldous turned the book over in his hand and examined the spine, as if that would give him the insight he needed. Instead, that insight came from a cold-blooded killer who did not choose to read.

"You'll never find it," Ken said, finally looking at Aldous and holding his gaze. "You aren't Theron, you're Aldous. I don't give a damn what our gracious host says... he is the way he is because he is a good man first. He saw whatever he saw in that book second. You find what you are in the things you do, not in what you read in some book." Kendrick stood and placed his hand on Aldous' shoulder. "You're a good lad, and don't you worry on that." He turned away. "I'm going to go help myself to some more of those boiled quail eggs and fresh bread."

Aldous felt a chill. The way Ken had stood and patted him on the shoulder brought back memories of his father, and the association was not entirely pleasant. He did not want to think of Ken like his father, or of his father like Ken. Yet what Kendrick had said put Aldous at ease and released some of the pressure and guilt surrounding his father's writings.

"Come and eat, Aldous," Ken said. "Then we will go outside and I will teach you how to use a sword. It will do you better than books when we face her again."

"Her?" Aldous asked, then before Ken could respond, he realized… "What makes you think we are going to face her again? What makes you think I am going to take any part in a witch hunt?"

"Because you hate magic—you hate it and you fear it. She's what you hate; she's what you fear you will become. And given what you are, do you really think that at some point she won't come looking for you?"

Aldous jumped from his chair and paced back and forth. "What do you mean, come looking for me? Why would she do that?"

"Because you hate magic—you hate it and you fear it. But you *are* magic. It's what you are."

"I am beginning to get sick of other people telling me how I feel, Kendrick, very sick of it." The rage was coming back, and it grew all the worse, feeding off itself. A flash sweat came over him, hot, then cold, then hot.

"Am I wrong?" Kendrick asked, his back to Aldous as he stood in the doorway.

Aldous wanted to yell that Kendrick was wrong, that he didn't know Aldous' mind, know his heart. He wanted to yell that he was a man, not a boy to be told how to think. And then he no longer wanted to yell, for only a boy would rant. A man would think. "You're not wrong," he said at last. "What about you, Ken? Why do you care about the witch? You're alive, she is gone, and Theron is gone. You could just leave."

"We saw evil, lad." Something in Ken's voice sounded like

fear. "We saw real evil. We saw the thing that wants nothing but death for the whole human race. I've done terrible things, Aldous. I deserve a thousand deaths in the worst kind of ways." He paused. "I don't want what I deserve. I want redemption."

Kendrick turned, and Aldous looked in his eyes, his dark, cruel, beady eyes.

"Killing her, will that wash away all the blood on your hands?"

Ken gave a short laugh, a sad laugh. A terrible, lonely sound.

"I took part in an attempted genocide, lad. Nothing will ever, in this life or any other, wash the blood off me. It runs deeper than flesh and it drowns my soul."

"Then why try?"

"Because I don't want to die, and the only thing that stops me from dying at my own hand is a purpose that makes me better than I was," Ken said in his perfectly calm tone. He turned and walked down the hall. "Now come and eat before I show you how to pick up the sword."

Chayse had been questioning Theron about Kendrick since the moment he'd told her that the man was a guest at the estate. She had been hard to calm as a child when she latched on to an idea, and it appeared that she was even more diffi- cult to appeal to as a woman.

"I don't like this. I don't trust him. He could have robbed us blind and murdered everyone under your employ while you were gone!" Chayse said for the hundredth time. They were nearly home now, and her agitation only escalated the closer they got.

"I already thought of that," Theron said casually, and bit

into an apple he had picked from a tree in an orchard. It was sour, and he frowned at the fruit before he tossed it.

"You already thought of that?" Chayse laughed and shook her head. "And you left him there anyway?"

"He has honor. He is not some mad rogue who kills indiscriminately."

"That's exactly what he is! He is a cold-blooded murderer. He killed his own wife, murdered her after deserting the army."

It was Theron who laughed now. "How do you know? Were you there? Don't be so ignorant, little sister. I expect more from you than to believe every rumor you hear."

"He took part in the king's genocide in the east. That is not rumor. At least admit that. He slaughtered Brynthian citizens who stood against the king's campaign. How can you not feel ill at the mere sight of the man?"

"You speak in the past tense, Chayse. He did those things. Or so it is said. But even if he did, even if he was that man, he is that man no longer. He was a man who did as he was ordered. When you were in Azria you did the same."

"How dare you! How dare you compare me to that monster."

Theron turned to his sister. She was on the verge of tears, and this was not what he wanted, especially since they had just so recently reunited. "Do you really believe that? Do you really believe that orders justify genocide?"

"I saved his life," Theron yelled. "In the dungeon, I saved his life. I'm responsible for him now." He paused, and when his sister didn't answer, he said, "Chayse, please. Just give the man a chance to prove his worth."

"I will be civil, that is all. You are Lord of Wardbrook, and so I will be civil to your guest. Do not ask anything else of me."

"Thank you." Theron offered his sister a smile; she did

not return it. "And do dry your tears, sister; we are home, and I would not have you puffy-eyed and red-cheeked when you meet our guests."

Chayse gave him a look of such venom he thought she might draw her bow and shoot him dead where he was.

~

Aldous was in the courtyard, armed, standing side by side with Ken. He watched intently as Ken demonstrated sword strokes, then nearly tripped over his own feet when a shrill whistle sounded from behind.

Ken turned. "Lord Wardbrook!" he called out, and waved his hand.

"Theron! You've returned," Aldous cried, and made an attempt to casually stick the sword he had been practicing with into the grass; it penetrated topsoil then fell over. Aldous looked at it, aghast, and said, "Heavy hilt."

"Don't start calling me lord just because you've seen the estate," Theron said after he closed the distance and hopped down from his horse.

Ken looked at him for a long moment, and then said, "Thank you."

"What for?" Theron asked.

"You know what for, you bastard." Ken's mouth twitched on one side in what Aldous thought might be a smile.

Theron smiled back and reached over to clap Aldous on the back.

"My friends, there is someone I would like you to meet. This"—he made a grand sweep with his hand—"is Chayse."

Aldous felt woozy just looking at her. She was magnificent. Completely and utterly magnificent. She sat high atop her black mare like some ancient goddess. She wore a sleeveless chain mail shirt; her arms were muscled, and tattooed

165

from the shoulder to the elbow with black-inked symbols from a faraway world. One of the brothers in the church had such markings, for he had been a hardened sailor before he joined the priesthood. Brown leather covered powerful thighs that clung to the black mare with potency. Despite her formidable physique, her face remained feminine and elegant. She had high cheekbones beneath wide yellow-brown eyes, a small nose, and full lips with a sharp jaw. She was... She was... She—

"Aldous, land ho, wake up, sailor!" Theron waved his hand in front of Aldous' face.

"Theron?" he asked as if being woken from a dream.

"Indeed."

Kendrick was snickering to the side—at what, Aldous was not sure.

"Thisssss," Theron began very slowly as he palmed Aldous' head with one hand and pointed to the goddess with the other. "Is. My. Sister. Chayse. Say. Hello."

"Chayse." Aldous repeated the name like a man possessed. She hopped down from her black mare and extended her hand.

Aldous felt his face burn, and his palms got sweaty in a flash. He extended his hand and although everything in him screamed *don't you say it,* he said it: "You are a goddess."

"A goddess, am I?" the goddess asked.

"She most certainly is not," Theron said with a laugh.

Aldous took her hand and he blushed.

There was a terrible noise that tore Aldous from the moment, and he turned to see Theron holding his sides and laughing like a madman.

"A goddess, he says!" Theron howled and shoved his sister, who turned to her brother, fury in her eyes. "Yes, indeed, young Aldous Weaver. My sister is a belching, fart-ing, feasting, beast-slaying goddess. Wait till you see her at dinner! Or even worse, in the morning!" Theron howled until there was the crack of the back of Chayse's hand up the side of Theron's head.

"Ow!" Theron yelled, then he turned to Ken and Aldous. "It has claws." He snickered for a moment then received another hard slap.

He stared at his sister in complete befuddlement.

"I am a little girl no longer, brother, and if you aim to bully me as you did when we were children, you will be in for a thrashing."

Her fury only made her more wonderful in Aldous' eyes. Watching a woman strike a man such as Theron was a most exciting thing to see. He readjusted his trousers so that it was not visible exactly how exciting he thought it to be.

"Oh, no. You're a strong woman now. There will be no more teasing." Theron bowed then turned back to Aldous. "You are right, she is a most magnificent specimen."

Chayse then turned to Kendrick, who tilted his head down and looked at her.

"This, dear sister, is my friend Kendrick. He helped save the lives of me and Aldous from a most certain and horrific fate," Theron said in an attempt to break the obvious tension. Aldous assumed Chayse had heard about Ken what most people had heard of him. And she was clearly not entirely pleased with the reputation that preceded the man before her.

"My lady," Ken said, bowing his head a bit more.

"If my brother has you calling him Theron, then do call me Lady Chayse."

"Good," Theron said. "Introductions have been made. I was going to say be ready to start training tomorrow, but it appears you two have already begun."

"Training for what?" Chayse asked.

"Preparing for our great foe." Theron's smile faded, and

Aldous wondered what had stolen his good humor. "You three will be joining me in my hunting from hence forth, and ultimately together we will take the head of the Emerald Witch."

"Why hunt her?" Aldous asked. "Why not just let her be? She's gone. She left. Why not leave it at that?"

"I saw a rat on the road. If they are not gone, then neither is she. So we hunt monsters."

"That's strange," said Ken.

"What is?"

"I do not remember agreeing to taking up the profession of monster hunting with you."

"Ah, I apologize. I must have forgotten to ask. Do you have more pressing things to attend? Or perhaps a dream to start a farm?" Theron asked. "And you, Aldous, you too look dubious. Perhaps you would like to go back to copying scripture?" Theron paused and scratched his chin. "I doubt they will have you back, though. You would have to ask nicely."

Aldous tried to form a rebuttal, but before he could utter a sound, Theron continued, "No. Won't happen. You're not going back to scripture, and Ken's not going to start a farm. We are bound by friendship, we are bound by battle, and now we shall be bound by the hunt. Objections?"

"Well, you did say we were friends."

"Indeed, and friendship goes both ways. We shall survive on my wealth, my land, and the influence of my name, and you will share my fights. All of them. Do we have a deal?"

"I've fought on shitty terms for men far worse than the likes of you, you scoundrel, so yeah. We have a deal," Ken said.

"You have always hunted alone, Theron. You told me so back in the Norburg dungeon," Aldous said. "So why do you need us now? Ken I can understand, but what use could I be?" He thought of his father, who had not fought the monsters who came for him, who burned him alive.

"Your use is twofold, good Aldous, and therefore you are the most important to our band," Theron said.

"I really don't want to be the most important," Aldous mumbled.

"You are the most important because not only—" Theron said, at the same time Aldous said, "Ken, tell him I am not the most important." Aldous shook Ken's thick arm, but Ken pulled away, and with one large hand palmed Aldous' head and turned it back to Theron.

"—not only because you are a wizard, Aldous, but because you are a writer. You will one day document all of our great journeys, the adventures of the legendary Theron Ward and his hunters."

Chayse coughed. "Your hunters? I'm going inside. It's been a long time since I've had a bath. It was a pleasure to meet you, Aldous Weaver."

Butterflies of excitement and nausea mixed in his stomach at her words.

Chayse nodded to Aldous and trotted off toward the estate.

"The... the pleasure was mine," Aldous said to her back before returning his gaze to Theron. "Theron, listen. Listen. I thought that maybe I would take up this quest, to save Brynth and all that. I thought that this very morning, but, well, me and Ken have been out here for hours and I can't even stab the ground properly. I don't think I will be much help in a fight."

Ken ruffled Aldous' hair. "It takes time, lad."

Aldous continued to protest, but Theron stopped listening. He simply stood there and smiled.

~

"Where did they go?" she asked, tears filling her eyes, her golden hair untamed from sleep.

"Away. They went away," he replied, his tone hollow, his eyes vacant.

"Where is away? For how long?" she asked. She grabbed her older brother and tried to shake him, for he was taking his time to respond.

"Father said he wouldn't leave when Mother left," he said to the air, to the empty house, more than to her. "He lied," he whispered to the vacant home. "He lied! He lied and they abandoned us!" His screams echoed in the lonely palace.

She began to weep and weep. "For how long have they abandoned us?"

Again she shook her brother. She wanted him to come back to her, for he was not there. He was hollow like his tone, hollow like their home. "For how long?"

He sneered, drying tracks of tears rolling down each of his cheeks. "Abandonment is forever."

~

CHAPTER FOURTEEN

BATTLE WITHIN

*H*is arms were heavy, the shield was heavy, the wooden sword was heavy. After a thousand strokes, and a thousand blocks, anything became heavy. *Tomorrow they will be lighter,* Aldous told himself. He took a deep breath; the cold early winter air cooled his burning lungs. A single snowflake fell before Aldous and was white on the dark mud for an instant before it faded.

He slowly circled his foe, a monster of a man, a mountain of muscle who stood sneering in the center of the hard mud circle. He looked for some weakness in his foe's defense, as he had each and every day, before he charged, and each and every day he ended up on his back, unable to breathe.

Every man can be defeated, even him.

As the days had turned to weeks and the weeks to a month, Aldous had begun to enjoy the pain of combat. He enjoyed how physical suffering was the currency spent to purchase physical strength. He could see in the mirror as his soft cheeks turned sharp and hollow, as his bony arms thickened with wiry muscle, and how the reflection of the eyes of the frightened deer turned to those of the hungry wolf.

Commit to the finish before you attack. Theron had told him that. One last breath and Aldous charged, as he had charged the rat a month ago. But he did not waver now; he was committed, so he charged in silence and with great focus.

Shield up. The wooden staff of his foe crashed hard into the buckler. Aldous did not take the blow in full force; instead he spun off it to the brute's right flank. *Sword raised. Strike!*

He felt impact on the back of his knee... he was off his feet... he was in the air. He was on his back. Unable to breathe.

"Up you get, wizard! Until you learn a spell you're going to have to get used to weapons and taking a beating up close," said Ken.

Every man can be defeated, even Ken.

Aldous rolled over and onto his knees then dug his sparring sword into the mud and flung it into Ken's face. It hit the mark more out of luck than pinpoint accuracy, but that didn't matter. All that mattered was taking Ken down, even once.

Aldous sprang to his feet, sword at the ready.

"Bravo!" shouted Theron from outside the sparring circle. "You're learning, boy."

Ken did not so much as attempt to brush the mud from his eyes. He charged at Aldous, swinging his wooden staff with cold intent. Aldous raised his shield and took a hard blow. Only when the blow connected did Aldous realize his mistake, for the block gave away his position. *If I had dodged, Ken would not be certain of...*

The staff drove into his sternum with such force that Aldous was sure he was impaled and soon to die. Only when he hit the ground, foaming at the mouth, did Ken brush the mud from his eyes.

"Good attempt, lad, good attempt," Ken said before

walking out of the circle to sip from his canteen.

Aldous tried to sip at the air, desperately attempting to get some life back into his lungs. Ken had never hit him that hard before. *I shouldn't have flung mud.*

But this *was* the first time Ken had hit him that hard. That had to mean something.

The price of progress was the bruise he'd have by tomorrow.

After what felt like eternity, Aldous could again breathe at his own will.

"You still alive?" Ken asked, snickering. He was sitting on a stool outside of the circle, completely relaxed. The man could have taken down ten Aldouses and still not have broken a sweat.

"I think so," Aldous said, coughing. "I'm just glad we are on the same team, when the real fighting starts."

"Yes, we are quite lucky to have Ken," said Theron, "and I don't doubt that you will prove to be just as useful when the time comes. But until then, Ken is your enemy. Take a breather, and some water, maybe some wine, and then ready yourself for another round."

This was how it went most days. The first time Aldous tried talking his way out of further sparring, he had told them he was too tired. Chayse had been most irritated by that, and gave him a few hard slaps upside the head, along with a splash of cold water to wake him up.

So now Aldous only sighed and prepared himself for another round.

"You can take a break, Weaver." It was Chayse who spoke now. She was walking up the hill toward the sparring circle from where she had just been further honing her skills with the bow in the field below—not that they needed any more honing. She took off her quiver and put down her bow. "I'll take this round. Ken, what do you say?"

Aldous shot a glance at Theron and noticed his frown. Chayse was normally not so jovial in her interactions with Ken. She was polite, but distant, and always, her dislike was just below the surface. So her easy manner now made Aldous wonder—and from Theron's expression, made him wonder, too—what she was about.

"Sure." Ken stood.

Aldous hurried from the circle. He had watched the two of them spar before, and Theron had to break it up more often than not. Chayse usually went at Ken with all of hell's fury.

Theron tossed his sister a sparring staff from the weapons rack; she caught it in one hand.

"Don't go easy on me, Ken. I'm sick of it," Chayse said, ignoring her brother's scowl.

Uh-oh. Aldous backed up another step.

"It's a spar. The whole point is going easy," Ken said as he walked into the circle with his staff over his shoulders, as if he were going for a stroll.

Aldous knew he was taunting her. It was subtle, but that was how the large man operated: with a calm subtlety. Chayse knew it, too.

"You're just afraid," she said. "You're afraid that if we both go at it, that if you actually try and end up losing to me, you'll have lost to a woman."

Ken huffed. "That has nothing to do with it, kid."

"Kid?" Chayse said, her grip tightening on the staff, her knuckles going white. "Kid!" Chayse yelled as she charged.

Uh-oh, Aldous thought again.

"Uh-oh," Theron said.

Ken raised his staff, blocking the first two-handed strike. Chayse delivered a roundhouse kick hard to Ken's ribs. Aldous winced, but Ken did not. It was enough to back him off, but clearly not enough to hurt him. He stepped back, then circled right, twirled his staff, and swung at Chayse's left side. She was quick and blocked the blow, but it was too heavy for her to deflect, and it sent her off her feet. She rolled and sprang back up, right on the edge of the circle and nearly into Aldous, who was standing just outside the ring.

Aldous shot a glance at Theron, but the other man's face gave no indication of his thoughts.

Kendrick rushed forward now, holding the staff like a spear. Chayse met him head-on, using the grip of a two-handed sword. Ken thrust, the same movement he had used to drop Aldous, but it did not have the same effect on Chayse. She deflected the thrust and stepped forward into his guard, too close for Ken to use his weapon.

She forgets that Ken is the weapon.

Chayse tried to bash Ken in the face with the pommel of her staff, but the large man snapped his head forward and cracked the hard part of his brow against her fingers where they held her weapon. Chayse gasped and dropped her weapon, pain and rage mingling on her beautiful face.

Ken bumped her with his shoulder and forced her back far enough to use his thrust. Teeth bared in a snarl, she twisted out of the way, making a quick recovery, and grabbed the shaft. She pulled. Ken did not budge, but the momentum threw her forward and, using it, she drove her knee hard into Ken's groin.

Ken groaned.

Chayse pulled back on the shaft with her full weight, and aimed a second blow at Ken's groin, this time with her foot. Ken twisted to the side, taking the blow on his thigh instead of his stones, but the move gave Chayse the momentum to pull the shaft from his grip.

Now he was the one disarmed.

Aldous dropped both hands to cover his stones even as he silently cheered for Chayse.

"I told you not to go easy on me this time," Chayse said, grinning as she twirled Ken's staff and circled just outside his reach.

"Unfair, Chayse. Very unfair," Theron said from the sideline, but there was too much mirth in his voice for it to be a scolding.

"All is fair in a fight," said Chayse. Again she twirled Ken's staff and kicked her own that she had dropped out of the circle. "You're unarmed, Ken. You're done."

"Not likely. I've gotten through a lot worse than sore stones and no weapon." Ken adjusted his posture, hands ready, legs sturdy, torso bent a bit forward at the hips.

Directly behind Ken's left foot was the crevice Aldous had created in the mud with his practice sword. He wanted to warn Ken as he watched Chayse rush forward. But if he warned Ken and because of it Chayse lost... well, he feared her wrath—and worse, her dislike—perhaps more than he feared Kendrick, and so Aldous remained silent.

Besides, hadn't Ken taught him that a warrior should always be aware of his surroundings?

The staff came down, perfectly straight. Ken leaned to his left at the same moment as he slid his left foot back in an attempt to wheel out of the way. His heel caught, and he went off balance.

Chayse's eyes went wide. Her foe was not down, but his arms were outstretched as he tried to recover his poise. She did not fully follow through with her downward strike; instead she back-swung halfway through the motion and caught the Ken hard in the temple with the shaft.

If the blow had hit Aldous in the temple, he was certain that he would never wake. Ken was a different man, with a different kind of head. He went down, but was quickly stumbling back to his feet. His eyes were dazed and wild, but he was conscious.

It was an impressive show of constitution, but it did not matter. He was too rattled to defend or dodge the next blow, which swept his legs out from under him. Aldous gasped. How could anyone take down Kendrick the Cold? But he couldn't help but grin, for Ken had done the same move on him over a hundred times, and he reveled at the sound of the air leaving Ken's lungs as he hit the ground.

Chayse stood over Ken and put the edge of the staff at his throat, her face lit with triumph.

Aldous could not tear his gaze away. Her hair was down that day, strands of golden light flowing beneath the winter sun as the snow falls from the heavens. She was a painting, not yet captured, for what painter could capture such perfection? She was a northern goddess of battle.

Theron clapped him on the shoulder. "Put your tongue back in your mouth, boy."

"I told you not to go easy," Chayse said to Ken, her tone annoyed.

"I didn't," Ken wheezed from the ground, and brought a hand to his temple.

"Did I just witness that?" said Theron.

"You did, brother," Chayse said, her eyes only on Ken, the staff still at his throat. Aldous thought she would be more jubilant at the win, but she sounded wary… questioning.

Theron grabbed the staff and yanked it from her hands, then heaved Ken to his feet.

"I'm sorry, sister, but that was luck," Theron said, shaking his head. "Ken tripped, and he tripped in that little hole Aldous shoveled out with his sword." Theron then turned to Aldous and raised an accusing finger. "Were you in on this? Did the two of you plot this? I find it all to be very convenient."

"Chayse won and that is that," Aldous said. "We had no previous discourse."

It was Ken who now turned his gaze to Aldous, and at the cold stare, Aldous shrank away a step or two.

"What do you say, Kendrick the Cold? Did I win?"

Aldous couldn't believe she was asking the question as if there could be any answer but *yes*. She had won. That was all.

Ken turned back to Chayse. "Yes." There was no emotion in his tone, no spite, no embarrassment.

"But it was unfair. She struck you in the stones, and you tripped," Theron protested.

"Why can't you just accept that I beat him? Why must you always belittle me?" Chayse took a step toward her brother, as if she was ready for another round, but with Theron this time.

"Because *I* can't even beat Ken, so—"

"So how could I?" Chayse laughed. "Your ego truly is boundless, brother." Chayse turned and sauntered away, back toward Wardbrook.

"What a woman," Aldous said. No one was listening.

"I don't know if I want you teaching me anymore, Ken. Losing to my sister, and clumsily falling about like that..." Theron said with what looked and sounded like complete sincerity.

Ken laughed with the same sincerity.

"Well, Ken?" Aldous said, stepping in between the two.

"Well what, boy?"

"Do you think it was a fair win?"

"No." He shook his head, and in that moment Aldous wished he had the balls to give Ken another kick in his, but then Ken surprised him: "It wasn't a fair win because it was never a fair fight. The odds were in my favor. I've fought as many battles in one week as Chayse has in her life. Killing is killing; combat is combat. She won despite my vast advantage."

"Why don't you tell her that? It would please her," Aldous said.

"*You* can tell her that, wizard. I think you're the only one interested in pleasing her." Ken winked at Aldous, and his cheeks set to burning in an instant.

"Unbelievable," Theron muttered. "I'm really not sure that I'm willing to accept this, Ken."

"What? That the boy pants after your sister?"

"Not that." Theron made a dismissive gesture. "The win!"

Ken shrugged. "Choosing to accept or deny reality doesn't change it."

"You should be proud of her, Theron. Not jealous," Aldous said, and at Theron's thunderous look, he thought for a moment he was going to receive a thrashing. But Theron Ward, as usual, was a surprise.

"Yes, you're right, young Weaver," he began, in that pleasantly positive tone he often took on. "You are most certainly right. As you know, I am a man with many strengths and upstanding morals, but modesty is a policy I still struggle with, and a most difficult struggle it is."

Aldous could not help but wonder if Theron was a very foolish or very intelligent man.

Ken's stomach growled.

"I suppose that is just as good as the dinner bell," said Theron.

As they walked back to the estate, the light snow falling, Aldous felt he was among friends, strange and extraordinary friends. He wondered if maybe he was happy. He wondered if he felt safe. He thought he did.

But that was just for a moment, because he knew that after they ate and he went to his chamber, sleep would come, and with it dreams of his father burning, the ravens watching, the wolves howling.

Every man and woman is subject to seasons within the self. Most do all they can to make an endless inner summer, do all they can to pursue and hold the warm season, the season of joy. That is the pursuit of the many, and a foolish pursuit it is. Humankind does not pick the seasons of the outside world. It is beyond their power; so too is controlling the seasons within. The fall must come when joy runs its course, and at the bottom of the fall comes the long season, the true season, the human season: winter. For woe is man, woe is his soul, and woe is his flesh. If it were not this way we would never cherish the warm rays of the sun when the summer finally comes. An endless summer would be nothingness. Endless happiness is nothingness. We can love the warmth only when we have suffered the cold.

Excerpt from Seasons of the Soul, by Darcy Weaver, written and published two years before he was burned at the stake.

CHAPTER FIFTEEN

WINTER

*I*t had been a week since Ken lost against Chayse. They had sparred twice more since, and Ken had won both bouts.

"I won't lie, Theron. I'm worried to fight alongside your sister," Ken said, as he stretched side to side, getting ready for another round of grappling with Theron on the cold-hardened grass.

"She can handle herself. You should know that by now. She did drop you on your ass." Theron widened his footing and raised his hands, flexed like claws ready to grasp, a classic southern wrestling stance that Ken had just recently taught him.

"I don't doubt that," said Ken, as he circled the hunter. Ken had been winning on every takedown since they started their grappling, for he had the advantage of weight and Theron was relatively new to wrestling. But each day Theron became a more difficult adversary.

"Then what's the problem?" Theron asked just before he lunged.

Ken back-stepped and swatted away the incoming hands.

185

"I fear she may mistake me for the wrong kind of monster and put an arrow through my throat."

Theron snorted.

Ken continued to back-step and shift side to side, swatting away grasps. "Stop clawing like that, you'll—"

Theron performed a pirouette and hooked his heel behind Ken's knee, then the hunter brought his forearm hard across Ken's chest, trying to knock him down. It was so quick another man might have been lying on his back on the ground. But Kendrick wasn't another man, and so it was Theron who stared up at him, flat on his back.

He held out his hand to Theron and hauled him to his feet.

"She doesn't hate you that much," Theron said.

"But she *does* hate me."

"Certainly."

"I am a changed man," Ken said.

"I know you are, and I don't hold your past against you."

"We aren't talking about you, we are talking about your sister."

"Is that why you let her win? Because you care what she thinks about you?"

Ken was tempted to knock the man down again, because he was tired of this question. "I didn't let her win," he said. "Get back in position."

But Theron wasn't inclined to let the matter drop. "Short of rescuing a litter of puppies from drowning in a river just before you leap into a burning orphanage and save all the children, I don't think there's anything you can do to change her mind."

"I would do those things now. I would save those puppies." Ken growled. *I would, now.*

"So you *did* let her win."

≈

Dinner was meat pies, everyone's favorite, except for Aldous. Back at the church Aldous would stare miserably at his plate of stale bread, pissy soup, and sometimes mutton with a longing for something substantial. After two months at Wardbrook, Aldous was nearly certain he never wanted to eat a substantial meal again.

"Eat, boy!" Ken ordered with his mouth full, halfway through his third pie, while Aldous worked on his first.

"I'm not entirely hungry, Ken."

"You're never hungry. No more of that excuse. Eating is part of your training. You must become like Ken and myself." Theron flexed his arms at the head of the table, reached across to Ken and punched him in the shoulder, then shook out his hand, making a face of mock pain.

For an intelligent man, Theron played a great fool.

"Leave him alone, you ape," said Chayse. "Aldous has a different kind of masculinity than you two meat piles. If he is not hungry, he need not stuff his face until he becomes ill."

Aldous had a warm sensation in his body when Chayse came to his aid, mostly the lower half.

Across the table, Ken said nothing, only continued shoveling meat pie into his mouth.

Theron rolled his eyes. "Chayse, there is only one kind of masculinity, and it's called being a man." He turned back to Aldous. "Eat."

Aldous looked back at the pie, then after a moment returned his fork to it.

"Don't you eat that, Aldous. You're not hungry," said Chayse without taking her eyes from her brother.

The warm feeling disappeared, for now he was aware that the sole reason Chayse came to his aid was because she wanted to fight with Theron. Besides, he *was* starting to feel hungry.

Aldous looked at Ken, who shrugged and went back to his food as the Ward siblings' bickering about what Aldous should or should not eat turned into an argument about something else entirely. It was a frequent occurrence, and things were brought up that were of no interest to Aldous, so when the dinner table turned into their battlefield, he and Ken ate—or did not eat—in silence.

Aldous thought he heard a bell chime.

"You don't even know what that word means, you dolt!" Chayse yelled.

The bell may have sounded again.

"Excuse me," Aldous said, lifting one finger.

"Of course I bloody well know what it means," Theron yelled back.

"Tell me then, brother, what is a philistine? Because if you knew the word you would know it is you, not I—"

Aldous was certain now that he heard the bell. "Excuse me," he said again.

"Don't bother," Ken said, frowning, and Aldous wondered if he, too, had heard the distant sound.

"—are a philistine," Chayse yelled.

The bell certainly was sounding, and it was frantic, clanging again and again.

Ken pushed back from the table and got to his feet.

"Quiet," Aldous said as he perked his ears to the bell. He rose from his chair and slammed his hand on the table. The candles lighting the meal gave a momentary flare, and all eyes turned to him. "Silence!"

The others tuned in to the sound of the bell.

"They are here," Ken said, already striding from the room.

"The village," Theron said, rising from his chair with such

force it flew back and clattered to the ground. "Arm your-selves—we are under attack."

Aldous tried to rise, but there was a weight in his head that burst into excruciating pain, dropping him back into his seat. The flame of the candle before him on the table snuffed. He blinked, trying to clear his vision, to see the room before him. But he saw only burning blue eyes, close but far away. He heard the squealing of rats in his mind, not his ears, and he could smell burning flesh.

It felt like hours, but it must have been seconds, because when he finally bolted to his feet and ran after the others, they weren't far ahead.

They moved through the estate quickly. The butler and once knight Sir Hakesworth came to them with Theron's claymore and Chayse's bow and quiver. A servant was right behind carrying a two-handed bearded axe for Ken.

"What about me?" Aldous asked, as he ran with the other three from the front doors and into the courtyard. The manor house sat atop a hill, with the village below. Smoke rose from fires nipping at the town, and they could hear screams.

"You need no other weapon, but take this if you must." Ken tossed him a sword. Aldous grabbed for it, fumbled, and at the last second got a grip. "Burn the bastards. I know you can do it, lad," Ken said.

They were in a full sprint now across the field, and Aldous saw the first of the rats. Covered in boils and grotesque, heaping muscle, just like the ones at Norburg. Fear was something that he hadn't quite remembered in all its detail until he set eyes on the rats again. Fear and anger. The hilt of the sword heated in his hand, followed by a pang of pain that shot up his arm.

His vision hazed and again he saw the blue, blue eyes.

The rat squealed before it came charging to meet them,

and Aldous forgot about the heat and the eyes, and thought only about staying alive.

Chayse stopped, notched an arrow, and loosed it at the charging rat that was now under twenty paces away. The shaft went feather deep into the thing's skull, and it was dead before it fell.

They reached the village, Ken cutting down two more rats and Theron taking down one.

Men and women alike were fighting the rats with whatever they had—a pitchfork, a broom, an iron skillet. A stocky, mustached man that Aldous recognized was clobbering a rat with a rolling pin in one hand and hacking it with a meat cleaver in the other.

Theron swung his claymore and assisted the man by plunging the blade into the vermin's spine. It screamed, and the man—Bilfred, the cook, Aldous remembered now—chopped off the upper portion of its snout with his cleaver, the lower jaw and tongue dangling.

"I don't want you using that for any more cooking," Theron said with a laugh. Aldous swallowed back the vomit that rose in his mouth. Bilfred's eyes were wide and filled with terror, but he managed to chuckle.

"Thank the Luminescent you've come," said the cook. "They came with no warning."

Clutching the sword with both hands, Aldous spun, and spun again. He heard a scream from his left. A woman was on the ground, two rats atop her, ripping open her belly and feasting on her guts. Chayse shot one of them dead, an arrow through the eye. Ken and Theron rushed the second. Ken hacked off an arm and Theron took off its head as the vile creature bawled.

Bilfred began to run, and Theron caught his arm and yanked him back. "Stay behind us, man!"

Bilfred looked at him, wild-eyed. "Theron—my wife, she is at her sister's."

Another two rats came running down the thoroughfare from behind them. Aldous was closest. He turned around to face them, his arms shaking, every part of him wanting to turn back and stand behind Theron and the others. Instead, with hot bowels and hazy eyes, he charged.

"Aldous!" Theron yelled from behind; Aldous could hear the hunter taking off behind him, and Ken's heavy footsteps as well.

He could have slowed down, he could have let them make first contact, but something in him pushed forward, something made him want to prove to the others that they were in this together.

Under ten paces.

Aldous yelled.

Something sharp cut his ear and the first rat had an arrow down its squealing throat.

Five paces.

Aldous readied his sword. The claws came at him. He slashed out. Hot blood sprayed across his face and then Theron and Ken were upon the beast, hacking down on it, carving the thing like a ham. Its arms and head were off so quickly it was hard to tell who'd cut what.

Both men clapped him on the back, so hard he almost fell over face first in the dirt and blood.

Aldous looked at Theron, waiting for the hunter's command. In the center of the village a few militiamen stood outside the town hall, fighting back a score of the rats.

"Chayse, Ken, go with Bilfred. Quickly. Aldous, with me. We will aid the militia." Theron gave the order, and they acted on it.

Ken and Chayse sprinted to keep up with the cook. He was a man of nearly middle age and he was on the hefty side, but his rage and fear for his beloved wife stirred him into frenzy, and he ran with all he had to a farmhouse on the outskirts of the town. They ran at it from the west, and a pack of rats converged on it from the north.

"Hurry." Bilfred coughed. "They will beat us there."

That was true, and worse yet, Ken could see the door had already been ripped asunder. He feared the worst, but he said nothing. He felt so much empathy for the man it hurt. He had lived the anguishing fear of knowing an evil as foul as the Rata Plaga was descending upon the one you loved.

"You fucks! Turn here, devils!" Ken roared as the rats reached the farmhouse. They squealed and charged down on all fours, vile claws slipping in the snow as they hungrily came forth.

"Chayse, Bilfred, go around; get to your wife and her sister. I will send these vermin to the devil myself. I fear there are already more inside."

Chayse nodded. If she wanted to protest Ken giving her an order, she held her tongue, and she and Bilfred cut right as Ken ran straight ahead.

$\sim$

"Ready, Aldous?" Theron whispered as they hid behind the wall of the blacksmith's shop and peeked out at the skirmish between the militia and the score of rats. "We are going to flank them."

Aldous felt woozy. A searing pain shot through his skull and he saw the image of glowing blue eyes once more. He had an ugly feeling he knew what these visions heralded.

"Are you ready, boy? Ready to use your magic? I need you." Theron grabbed him by the shoulders and shook him.

The pain exploded in Aldous' head. All he could see was the glowing blue now, glowing blue in a river of green.

"Theron! My head... I can't see." He fell to his knees. The pressure was building. "A seeker... there is a seeker! He is close!"

～

Theron stared at the boy crumbled on his knees as he screamed in horrific pain. He was about to kneel when he heard the snow crunch behind him. In an instant he ducked down and stabbed out at the thing that came at him from behind.

His blade was met by the seeker's and deflected. He was not surprised. They were rumored to be the best swordsmen in the kingdom, but this was the first he had ever had cause to face one. The seeker's face was as white in the night sky as the snow on the ground; his eyes burned with blue flame from beneath the brim of his hat.

"The Emerald Queen sends her regards," the seeker said in a courtly tone, and then began the dance. He wielded a thin saber and was perilously fast.

"Her regards sent from a seeker? Strange. Are seekers not tasked with removing the threat of sorcery?" Theron said as he met his advance and blocked the oncoming assault.

This wasn't Norburg. This was Wardbrook. His home. His village. His responsibility. And he had brought her here, because since the night that she had lured him in the guise of the count's daughter, she had been hunting him.

His foe's blade was lighter by far than Theron's claymore, and if he kept up the game this way, Theron would eventually fatigue and the seeker would get the better of him. Between the clanging of their blades, Theron could hear the militiamen screaming as the rats overwhelmed them. Aldous was still on his knees wailing, and Theron now understood it was the seeker's effect on him, a dampening of his magic.

Theron lowered his guard and ducked the next sweep aimed at his neck. Instead of stepping away, he went forward, his head low, too close to swing his claymore. He dropped it, wrapped his arms round the seeker's waist, and thrust his shoulder into the other man's abdomen, taking him to the ground. They rolled. The seeker was stronger than he looked and ended up on top, where he twirled his saber in his hands and plunged it down at Theron's head. Theron bucked his hips and drove a knee into the seeker's low back, knocking him off balance and causing the descending saber to sink into the dirt beside Theron's ear. They rolled again, Theron back on top. He caught the seeker by the wrists as the man was reaching for his daggers at his sides.

There was another scream from the militiamen by the town center, then the wail of a woman and the unified squealing of pustulant rodents.

Theron removed his hands from the seeker's wrists and went for his burning blue eyes. He plunged his thumbs into the glow, giving the seeker the choice between his daggers or his eyes. The seeker tried to preserve his eyes. He grabbed Theron's wrists and fought with everything he had.

In the end the seeker acted like any man as Theron's thumbs poked at his eyes: he screamed as they warped from the pressure, and he screamed all the more when they burst.

"Why is your order aligned with the witch?" Theron demanded as he rolled the anti-mage over, and pressed one of the seeker's own daggers against a gouged socket.

The seeker screamed out.

"Bastard," he said, his whole body convulsing. "Kill me, end it."

"Tell me," Theron shouted.

"Brynth is weak, the king is weak... and they... they have power." The blue-cloaked man was convulsing from the pain now.

"They? Who is *they*?" Theron delivered a pommel strike with the dagger.

"Leviathan," the seeker spat through his agony. "Leviathan! The beast of many heads has risen, and all will choose to bend knee or die."

The words meant little to Theron, and he had no more time for further conversation, so he buried the knife hilt deep in his enemy's skull.

He stood above the dead man, chest heaving.

He stalked around the corner to the score of rats that infested his village, vaguely aware of Aldous scrambling to keep up with him, the seeker's effect on the boy now nullified. The rats were attacking his people, killing the people whom *he* was sworn to protect.

It was the first time Theron Ward had felt like he failed.

"I'll find you," he whispered as he cut into the first slab of rat meat. It died without a noise.

He dodged right, cut left. Ducked, pirouetted. Hack. Slash. Angry. Focused. Two more dead. Another. And another.

"No matter how long it takes, or how far I need to go, I'll find you. And I will know why you hunt me," he whispered into the face of a dying rat as he carved out its guts, seeing only the face of the Emerald Witch.

Ken made quick work of the four rats outside. They lay in pieces at his feet, some still, some still twitching. All dead. One of them had landed a glancing blow with its claw to his right shoulder, but Ken could still swing his axe, and that was all that mattered.

Ken heard a woman scream, and stormed the farmhouse.

It was a large abode, three rooms and walls of stone. There were three little, mutilated corpses in the front room. *Children.* Ken cringed.

A dead rat lay in the center of the floor, its brains cudgeled out. Ken turned the corner. Bilfred was leaning against the wall, staring wide-eyed at his own intestines hanging from his split belly, and the creature that lay at his feet had a cleaver in its brain. Another two rats were dead on the ground, felled by arrows.

Chayse.

The huntress was on the ground in one corner of the room, grappling with one of the larger fiends. It had her pinned, and she kicked and pushed at the thing's face as it snapped at her.

In the other corner was a human corpse, gender unknown from the mauling it had received, and next to that, a woman screaming as the buckteeth of long, lean vermin bit into her arm and shook it violently.

"Ken, save her, I'll manage!" Chayse shouted.

Both the rats were formidable, and they would not go down from a single blow.

Fuck. Make the choice. Make it now.

The woman screamed. Chayse groaned as she held the mouth of her monster open, so the teeth would not sink into her neck.

There is no choice; you know what must be done.

In two strides, he was upon Chayse's rat.

"The woman! Save the woman!" Chayse screamed as she struggled with the rat.

He swung hard. The long axe clipped the wall, and so the

strike was slowed. It bit into the wretched thing's flank and caused it to spin away from the huntress.

Furious, it set eyes upon Ken and came forward. He raised the axe for a downward strike. *Too tight.* It caught on the ceiling and he just barely dodged the incoming claw.

The screams of the woman behind him turned into a suffocated gurgle.

Chayse snatched her bow from the ground and let fly an arrow past Ken and the rat that faced him. The one attacking the woman squealed. Chayse let fly another shaft and the rat went silent.

Ken used the axe like a spear and stabbed the vermin with the spike on the weapon's top. That blow forced it back. Chayse stepped out to its right side, and at less than two feet away she crouched and shot it in the ribcage. It twisted from the pain. Ken hooked the beard of the axe around the back of the abomination's neck and planted a foot on its chest. He pulled the axe as he pushed with his foot; the blade of the axe's beard slowly severed the creature's spine, as Chayse pulled the arrow from its ribs and set to stabbing it again and again, her face a rigid mask of fury.

When it was done, Chayse looked up at Ken, her eyes immense and white, staring out from her black gore splattered face.

"I had it under control," she said. She nodded to the two bodies behind Ken. "That is on you."

Chayse was out of the farmhouse and running back toward the center of the town to aid Aldous and her brother before Ken had a chance to defend himself.

Always the villain.

～

We have been wrong, we have been unjust, and we have been wicked. Treat a thing as a beast and a beast it shall become. We have made magic evil—not those who wield it but us, the ones who fear it. They gave us medicine; we burned them at the stake. They kept the wolves from our door and we put them on the cross. They protected us against nature's wrath many a time, and still we bound their hands and cheered as the plank was dropped out from under them. We laughed as they did the gallows dance.

We are the monsters, we know our own wickedness, we fear our own wickedness, and in our paranoia and self-loathing we projected our nature onto them. The Arch Servitor says they are heretics playing at God; it is not they but us who is playing at God. For we are the ones who have bestowed ourselves with the power to judge them by their very existence by their very God-given nature. We are the sinners and we must repent; we must ask for their forgiveness before it is too late.

Darcy Weaver's appeal to the King of Brynth before the night of mage bane, when twenty men and women were burned alive. A week later Darcy Weaver was arrested and burned alive on the stake. There was no trial.

～

CHAPTER SIXTEEN

SOMETHING USEFUL

*I*t was when the snow had melted and the earth had softened that Theron finally stopped searching for tracks, or clues, or anything that could lead him to the rats' point of origin. He was a patient man, and an even more patient hunter, but it was spring, and he had no idea where his enemy hid. He sent messengers and riders to nearby cities and towns to make inquiries, in an attempt to discover if anyone had seen anything, if anyone could give him anything at all.

There was no success. At the funerals of his townsfolk all he could say to the weeping families and friends was: "I will avenge them." How he would do so, he did not say. The families of the slain believed him. Aldous believed him. So did Ken and Chayse, but as the snow melted and the days grew longer, he no longer believed himself. The loss of confidence was a foreign emotion, one not pleasant in the least. An ill feeling crept over him. It was a sense of dread, the dread of a nemesis.

Theron sat in a brass tub, freshly filled with hot water by the servants. He lifted a petal of lavender from the water; it was not yet waterlogged and the beaded droplets rolled off the petal, unable to penetrate.

"You will lose, eventually," Theron whispered to the petal.

Ken was also in a brass tub and had been talking for some time, but Theron had not been listening. He was not himself, and he knew it. The attack had changed him. And in a strange reversal of roles, Kendrick was the one who had more to say than Theron.

"What say you to that?" Ken asked.

"To what?" Theron dropped the petal and turned to Ken.

"To being a hunter and bloody well leaving this estate in search of monsters. We have been here for too long."

"I looked for them. I have done everything I can to hunt for clues. So did you and Aldous and Chayse, and everyone under my employ. The tracks lead nowhere—not one bastard in Brynth seems to know a bloody thing."

"I'm not talking about the rats and their witch. Maybe it is time to move on. You are a sworn hunter. So hunt."

Theron had realized early on with Ken and Aldous that having friends was a great deal more difficult than having subordinates. Friends always had something to say—even Ken, who spoke little, and Aldous, who was often too afraid to speak—and with Ken and Aldous, things were said with enough value to be considered.

"Hunt other monsters? While the Emerald Witch is still out there? She has spies, Ken. What if we leave, only to return to ash? What if she strikes again?"

"Why here a second time?" Ken asked. "Why would she come again? She attacked only to lure you from your den. Leave here to hunt monsters, use yourself as bait, and she will come to you." And when Theron made no reply, because he could think of no reply that at this moment he could offer, Ken pressed, "Who is she, Theron?"

"What do you mean, who is she?"

Ken's stare was unsettling, even if he was in a warm bath filled with lavender petals while he was giving it. Perhaps that made it even more unsettling. Ken was always calm, always relaxed, but his guard was never down; his sword was always drawn. If there was a time right at the start when Theron thought Ken to be no more than a brute, that time was long gone.

"I would tell you if I could, Ken. I swear. No doubt you find it as suspicious as I that she has appeared to take an interest in me, but I cannot say why. I have many enemies from all around the world, but I had never imagined an enemy as great as her."

"Who are your parents, Theron?" There was no implication in Ken's tone, for there was rarely anything in Ken's tone, but his eyes said enough. He was a smart man, far smarter than he appeared. He had an apish brilliance, a kind of instinct that bypassed philosophical explanation and homed in right on the questions of things, the ones that begged answers.

Theron's stomach turned at the mention of his parents. He felt that newly familiar anxiety growing in his chest, the ever-expanding stone of dread.

"Within the week, Ken, we shall go out in search of contracts," Theron said firmly, his eyes locked with Kendrick's. "You are right," he continued. "I cannot be ruled by fear, even if it is a fear for my people. There is more evil in Brynth than just the rats, and as a hunter I am obligated to find it." Theron motioned a female servant standing in the corner to come forth with a towel. He rose from the bath and raised his arms as she dried him. He did not look at Ken, but he knew the man's eyes were looking for his. The evasion of the question regarding his parents would not be ignored, but luckily Ken left it alone for now.

~

"I'm still having trouble with it," Aldous said to Chayse as he closed up his father's book and looked over at her sitting in a reading chair to his left in the study. She was perhaps most beautiful when she was focused on a book. She held a great majesty of both physical and intellectual prowess as she sat with her powerful legs crossed and her hair tied back as she read *Hagalaz: Bestiary of the North.*

"Having trouble with what?" she asked without looking up from the words.

"Accepting what my father wrote as completely viable," Aldous said. Saying it aloud to Chayse made his stomach turn a bit, for who was he to say that his father's work was outlandish? He was only seventeen. Yet he had experienced much. He'd experienced his father's only great conflict; he'd experienced his father losing that conflict; he'd experienced a count's dungeon; and the rats. He'd experienced the seekers, and, worse yet, the Emerald Witch. As he thought this, the guilt in his gut faded and turned into resolve. He was young, but in his young age he had experienced enough to develop his own opinions on the world. Hadn't he?

"I mean, it still feels to me almost pompous," Aldous continued. "I know my father was an adventurer. He told me his father was, too, but I know Father never engaged in anything like you or Theron, or certainly not Ken. I don't think he ever had to make one of the choices that he talks so certainly of in his books. It seems… high and mighty." He let the last words out with a sigh, on a single breath, as if they were forced from him.

"Of course it is high and mighty," Chayse began with a comforting smile. "I believe your father was writing down standards that every man and woman should strive to uphold. Impossibly high standards, so even if they were to fall short they could still be good people. The desire for vengeance and justice to be trumped by a hope for restoration is not a ridiculous notion. It is a perfectly rational one. Yet, despite its rationality, it is hard to imagine carrying it out." Chayse paused and shook her head, as if she just in that moment came to some realization. "Yet I suppose we are overcoming that desire for justice right now in this house. At least, I am. Theron overcame it right away."

"Kendrick?" Aldous whispered.

"Yes. If Theron ends up truly driving Ken to do good with the rest of his life, then your father's theory will be true. But it was easy for Theron to have the power to choose Ken's *recovery*, as your father would call it, over justice, or vengeance, because Ken had never harmed him. Had I been one of Ken's victims or even the victim of any man who was *just following orders*, I wonder if Theron would have had such an easy time deciding on giving Ken a chance."

"Exactly. That is why I say it is relative," Aldous said, excited that he and Chayse were on the same page, for if he had taken up this conversation with Theron, he would not hear the end of the hunter's well-constructed but still circular reasoning. "Goodness," he continued, "righteousness, and bloody everything else, for that matter, is relative." That was very plain to Aldous; relativity seemed inarguable because it encompassed every argument already.

"That is why philosophy is a most tedious thing." Chayse closed up her book and leaned over to Aldous. "I often find it nauseating and a fruitless effort to delve into these things, endless circles of reasoning that just become more unreasonable each and every time the circle makes a full rotation. In truth, I read what Theron read so he had someone to talk to about all of that noise. Perhaps there is truth in it." Chayse paused, and then said, "Or perhaps it is the way smart men intellectually indulge in nonsense." She smiled. "Don't tell

Theron I said that. You're a different man than your father, Aldous. You don't need to force yourself to believe what he did. It doesn't change the fact that you love him. I promise you, I don't see eye to eye with my parents. I don't think I ever did, but I can't help but have some memories of fondness, and I can't help but love them. Your father was a good man, and he did what he could with what he had."

Aldous stared at her, hearing some of her words, but not the others. "You said you don't see eye to eye with your parents," he said, confused. "You're talking about them as if they're alive…"

Chayse looked away. "It's likely," she said after a moment.

"Likely?" Aldous asked, even more confused.

And in the silence that followed, he sensed that she wanted to be alone.

"Thanks, Chayse." Aldous closed the book and stood from his reading chair. He walked away from the fire, down the hall to his chambers, and stuck Darcy Weaver's *Indisputable Science of Goodness* on a random shelf where it could fit.

"Sorry, Father. The only thing that is indisputable is conflict, and that is solved with action, not words." He ran a finger down the spine of the book and walked away, back into the library, where Chayse was still reading, and he scanned the shelves, looking for something else, something clearer, something he could use. The titles all ran together. There were books about plants and philosophy and farming. There was one titled *The Botany of Moonswidow,* another titled *Utopia,* and a third titled *Leviathan.* Aldous stepped closer and tapped his finger on the title. Almost did he pull it free and open the pages.

"Done with it?" Chayse asked.

He looked at her for a moment and then understood that she spoke of his father's tome. "Done with it," Aldous said. "Do you have anything on magic? Not alchemy, but real magic." He was looking at Chayse when he asked, and she looked up right away.

"That would be condemnable by death," said Chayse, a sinister sneer curving her full lips.

"I'm already condemned to death."

"So you are," Chayse said. She was quiet for a moment, her expression contemplative. And then she gave a small nod, as if she had reached a decision. She closed her book and rose. "Come with me."

Chayse led Aldous down the hall of the lower level in the east wing, past the baths.

"Where are you two going?"

Aldous and Chayse turned to see the towel-clad Theron and Kendrick emerging from the room, steam gliding into the hall behind them. Theron looked stern, and all of a sudden Aldous felt like he was doing something very wrong.

"It's dinnertime. Come along. Whatever mischief you think you're up to, leave it be." Theron's tone was easy, but something about him in that instant left Aldous feeling uneasy. And when he glanced at Chayse, she looked as uncomfortable as he felt. She narrowed her eyes at Theron and Aldous thought he was about to witness yet another sibling argument. Tension passed between them before Chayse turned and walked silently back the way they had come.

There were no words at the beginning of their meals, and sometimes no words all the way through—unless Theron and Chayse were having one of their brother-sister spats. That evening was no exception. The meal was one of Ken's favorites, beef and venison with pudding. Had they not trained the way they did every day, each and every one of them would no doubt look much like Count Salvenius by now. In the midst of the devouring of meat pudding and the guzzling of dark ale, there was a trumpet sound from outside the estate, followed soon after by a hard thumping on the heavy brass knockers of Wardbrook's mighty doors.

Theron lifted his head from his plate and, mouth stuffed with food, called, "Hakesworth! Door! Messenger... trumpet! Door!" He swallowed. "Everyone get yourselves together. Act respectable. Especially you, Ken. Stop stuffing your face like that. It's barbaric," Theron said with contempt as he wiped more than a bit of everything from his own face.

Ken looked at the others at the table, who were all stuffing their faces in the same manner as he, cheeks puffed up like chipmunks, sweat on their foreheads.

"Who's here?" Ken asked, feeling a bit nervous about a guest. They had been in solitude with only each other and the staff of Wardbrook for months now; the only guests had been the rats.

"A contract. I can feel it in my guts," Theron said as he rubbed his food-distended stomach.

They waited a pregnant moment. Theron shot Aldous a glare. "Wipe your shirt. You have crumbs."

Sir Hakesworth appeared in the doorway of the dining room. With him was a royally dressed man in garb just as fancy as Theron's, escorted by two silver-clad guards. They all wore red cloaks.

The man in front was skinny, with a long face and a thin black mustache that looked painted on his upper lip. He had one of those faces that Ken just wanted to punch. It was the face of the type of man who talked a lot of fire, stared a lot of lightning, and did a lot of nothing when things got gritty.

"Lord Wardbrook, I present to you the royal messenger of His Grace, the Duke of Dentin," said Hakesworth.

The messenger stepped forward.

"I am sorry to interrupt your... dinner," the skinny, spick-and-span man said. He made no effort to hide his displeasure at the sight of the hearty meat pudding and thick potato and onion soup, as if he were somehow above a strongman's meal.

"Not at all, not at all. Please, sir, sit down. You and your escort are welcome at my table. There is plenty to go around." Theron stretched his hands to the many free chairs around the massive dining table.

Ken fought back a scowl and hoped the man did not sit, for those were his third and fourth helpings Theron was offering this stranger.

"Thank you," said the thin-mustached man. He snapped his fingers and his two men removed their helms and took a seat with the messenger. Hakesworth left the room and promptly returned with plates and utensils for the guests.

A servant poured the messenger and his two men ale. The messenger waited until his goblet was full before asking, "Do you have any wine? An estate of this caliber surely has wine." The air of superiority in the man's tone reminded Ken of the Brynthian officers in the army, men—if they could be called that—who paid for their station in the military. They went to school to learn about war, when men like Ken had to learn about it in the fire of combat and struggle to stay afloat in the sea of blood left by the dead.

"You don't like ale?" Ken asked, no doubt to Theron's displeasure, but Ken wasn't looking at Theron; he was glaring hard at the messenger, angry at the insult to his friend's hospitality.

"No. I have developed a finer taste in the Dukedom of Dentin."

Theron lifted a brow at Ken, but Ken ignored the warning.

"Ah, well, have some of this. I take it you are hungry." Ken slid the massive serving bowl, filled with meat and shire pudding and drippings, toward the messenger and his guards.

The man offered Ken a tainted smile and scooped up a scant spoonful onto his plate, and then slid it down to his men. They took proper servings. They were, of course, doers, and doers knew what was what. That included knowing that when you have a hefty meal before you, always, always eat it, for it may be your last. The talkers never seemed to get that; instead, they developed *finer tastes*.

"So, honorable messenger of His Grace, the Duke of Dentin," Theron said, "what message do you bring all the way here to Wardbrook? At this late hour."

"I bring not a message but a contract, for you: *the great hunter* Theron Ward," said the messenger, that smug smile still on his face. It was as if he were making an effort to act like a right bastard.

The messenger pulled a piece of parchment from a satchel; it was rolled, tied, and sealed with red wax and the sigil stamp of a fox. He handed the parchment to one of his guards, who then stood and walked it over to Theron. Ken wondered if the man's legs were broken, that he couldn't walk it himself. Theron took the scroll, all the while staring hard at the messenger.

Ken could see that he was assessing the man, perhaps assessing his legitimacy. Just because a man said he was a thing did not mean he was indeed what he said himself to be.

Theron opened the parchment and read, his face unchanging. After a minute or two he said, "Yes, we accept."

"We?" asked the messenger.

"We," said Theron.

The messenger looked down his nose. "I was under the impression you hunted alone. That is what the bards sing about, at least." He squeaked a short laugh, and still he had that smile on his face, his thin, stupid mustache drawn on top. Worse still, he slid his untouched pudding into the center of the table.

Don't kill the messenger, Ken. But oh, he really wanted to do just that.

"I did," Theron said. "Now I don't."

"I carry his things," Ken said.

"You're a bit old to be a squire," said the messenger. He had another quick laugh as he looked Ken up and down the way one might appraise livestock. Ken wanted to tell the man who he was, tell him what he had done, and what he would do if the weasel didn't smarten up, show some respect, and eat his damn pudding. Ken had spent years trying to put his past behind him, but in this moment, he would have garnered pleasure in having it known. Of course, Ken said nothing. He just stared back at the bastard.

"Theron is not a knight," said Chayse. "He does not have a squire."

"He has a man to carry his things," Ken finished.

Theron remained silent. It was hard to say what was causing the tension in the room, and Ken wondered if this was always the atmosphere when Theron received a contract. He doubted it. There was something else. Whatever Theron had read on that parchment, he did not like, yet he still accepted the contract.

"And who are you?" the messenger asked Chayse.

"His apprentice," she said.

The messenger looked back at Theron, snickering. "You have taken a woman as your apprentice? You really are singular in your methods."

"You should ask the beasts and men she's slain if what is between her legs had any effect on their heads leaving their bodies." To everyone's amazement, it was Aldous who

211

released that fiery response. Ken had forgotten the boy was even at the table.

The messenger scowled.

"And you are?"

"I am a writer. I am the man who documents Theron the Great and Mighty's hunts and adventures," Aldous said without a moment's hesitation.

"As I said, we accept the contract. We will leave tomorrow at first light," said Theron.

"Very good," said the messenger. "The duke will be very pleased."

"You should stay here at Wardbrook until morning. We can voyage together, perhaps develop lasting friendships." It was the least inviting invitation Ken had ever heard. Theron said what he said, but it sounded to Ken like: "Leave my house, leave me to my pudding and ale, and I will see you in a week when I arrive in the Dukedom of Dentin."

"No, no. We will begin our trip back now. Perhaps camp at midnight. The duke does not like to be kept waiting," said the messenger, no doubt implying that Theron and the others should be heading out with them.

"Very well," Theron said, his tone hard. "You go on ahead. You can forewarn the duke of our acceptance of his contract. We will be hot on your heels, and we will kill his monster."

The messenger protested no further. He stood and bowed. His men had not finished their meal and looked to be displeased to be taken from it, but they left all the same. And so the contract was accepted, the duke's messenger left, and Ken went back to stuffing his face with a hearty meal, for he did not know if it would be his last.

~

Curse your broken world, world of men, world of filth. A thousand kings, kings of dirt, kings of gold. Great masters of the old, masters of the mold, your day reaches its zenith and the twilight is nigh. The long night is here, and under the endless moon man shall learn he cannot eat his gold when all his dirt and soil turns to ash, when he runs to the edge of the world and the edge is not far enough, when he jumps from the cliff and the fall is not long enough, when with trembling hands he ties the noose around his neck. Man and his thousand kings will know that not even in death will they have found solace from the wrath. The wrath of the flame, the wrath of the wizard, as they burn, they will finally see.

A letter to the King of Brynth, written by Arch Mage Phelix Calliban from his cell one day before he was burned at the stake.

~

CHAPTER SEVENTEEN

MAGIC

*T*hey were up an hour before sunrise and met outside the armory, as Theron had told them to do the night before. Aldous was anxious; he was afraid, yes, that was certain, but for the first time he also felt a faint flare of anticipation.

"The contract is for an Obour," Theron began. "A walking corpse, a spirit that exists in our world in a state of... undeath, so to speak. For forty days and forty nights it walks in this state and does mischief most foul. They spread their dung on the walls of villagers' homes, and tear the udders from cattle to drink their blood and milk. On rare occasions, they attack and kill humans."

"Sounds like a nasty pest, but not a monster," said Ken, but Aldous thought it sounded quite monstrous. "Why would the Duke of Dentin send a man all the way here to get a pest taken care of? Hell, they could have just rounded up a few lads with scythes to kill a single fiend."

Theron shook his head.

"The situation is not so simple," he said. "The Obour was first spotted twenty-eight days before the letter was signed.

The messenger took at least five days to arrive here. We will take six to get there, for I am not well versed with the route to Dentin, although I do know of it. I assume the Obour was not spotted the very first day it rose, and even if it had been, that only gives us a day or two to find it in the form of an Obour." His lips almost curled into a smile.

"What other form would it be in?" asked Aldous. The fear went up a notch and the anticipation went down.

"On the forty-first night, the Obour turns into an Upir," said Chayse.

"And mischief most foul becomes something altogether more sinister," said Theron. "So there is a small chance it might be an Obour we come across, in which case we take off its head and call it a day." Theron grinned, a grin that made Aldous a bit more nervous. "But more likely it will be a full-fledged Upir."

"So in the case of a full-fledged Upir, what do we do?" Aldous asked, and swallowed the bit of bile that he told himself was from morning hunger and not fear.

"We take off its head, then we burn it and call it a day," said Ken, and he too was smiling. He was excited; there was no doubting that.

Aldous turned to Chayse. She was beaming; the other two were smiling, but Chayse was beaming. "So exciting!" she said, and shook Aldous by the shoulders to get him to be excited, too.

Her tactic failed, and the shaking simply further stirred Aldous' guts.

"Ken, what will you be taking?" Theron asked as he opened the door to the armory like a gateway into some majestic oasis.

Ken pulled a one-handed bearded axe from a rack. He swung it and twirled it in his hand. "This," he said, then moved down the rack, and lifted a mace in his other hand.

Had Aldous been using the thing, he would need two hands, but for Ken it was a toy. "And this."

"Armor light, Ken. You will need to attempt to match the thing in speed, for an Upir is a creature egregiously swift," said Theron.

Ken donned a cuirass of black boiled leather. It thickened his already immense frame. In that moment, Aldous greatly envied Ken's size, for he thought it might take only a single swipe for even the less threatening Obour to knock him down.

Chayse wore a light chain mail vest, no sleeves, and leather breeches, like she had when Aldous first saw her. She threw a black cloak over her shoulders, and took her bow and belted two short swords.

Theron pulled a light chain full shirt over his head, then a black coat atop it. He sheathed his claymore on his back, along with a small hand crossbow the likes of which Aldous had never seen. It looked quick, versatile, and deadly, without the cumbersome size and weight of the traditional weapon.

The last thing Theron put on was his helm. It was forged from black iron, and engraved with ancient northern symbols that Aldous could not decipher. There was a spiked horn on each side, with smaller spikes on the crown and scalp of the helm. It was an old, brutal, sinister thing that looked as if it had once been alive. When Theron pulled it onto his head and his eyes peered out from the circular holes, the armor seemed to become part of him, as if the iron were scales and the horns and spikes grew from the hunter's skull.

"Where did you get that fine piece?" Ken asked.

"It was gift," said Theron. "My travels took me to Ygdr-rast, far to the north and across the sea. I met a great Jarl there, by the name of Vulknoot Therickson. His brother was slain in a hunt for a frost boar. To this day I have still not seen such a beast." Theron stared before him, his muscles tensing, as if the boar were down there in the armory with them. "Twice the size of the biggest bull was that gargantuan swine. He had tusks as long as spears and thick as oaks. His eyes were as wild as a thousand reeling maelstroms." Aldous thought for a moment how such eyes would look, then decided it was a thing better left un-thought. "Jarl Therickson and I, just us two. Together we achieved conquest over the most quarrelsome quadruped. It took eight spears to slow him enough to get in close, but even then the white behemoth fought to the teeth. Blood stained the snow, and its squeals echoed through the mountain pass. The Jarl got his axe in its belly and my claymore found its throat. We feasted like Therickson's gods that night as we took shelter from the elements in the boar's carved-out rib chasm."

"I am certain that story told of some great adventure," Ken said. "But I was unable to understand it for all the words. Quadru-what?"

Ignoring him, Theron took off the helmet and stared at it in admiration. "When we returned to his great hall, as a gift he gave to me this helm, the helm of his fallen brother... Fine men, the Thericksons... fine men. "

Aldous looked at the size of the helmet, wondering if he would even be able to lift it. Already did he feel small and weak next to just Theron and Ken. He could not imagine an entire hall of Therickson behemoths.

After a moment, Theron placed the helmet back on his head and turned to Aldous.

"And you, Aldous? What here in this great armory lights the kindling of dormant violence in your chest?"

"I can read your fine mood, brother, in your flowery language," Chayse said.

Theron ignored her as well, and said, "Aldous?"

Aldous winced. "Perhaps a quill and parchment? Is that

not the task you assigned me when we were in the dungeon? That seems best suited to my skills."

"That would be magnificent, good Aldous," said Theron. "This is a desire I have held since our first meeting, but you cannot write in the thick of the action. In the thick of the action, you will need a weapon, so it would seem you have two mighty tasks, whereas the rest of us just have one." Theron turned his back to Aldous and went through the racks.

"He has been practicing well with short sword and shield," said Ken. "Let him try with that in the field. In sparring, he fares better than most would."

"What say you to that, Aldous?" Theron asked.

Before he could respond, Chayse spoke. "Give him the sword and shield, but why isn't he using his gift?"

They all fell silent at this. And in the silence, Aldous' anxiety heightened.

"Why shouldn't he be using his magic?" Chayse continued.

"Aldous is yet to repeat whatever spell he called upon in the chapel. When the rats attacked the village..." Theron let his silence speak for itself.

"Magic cannot be summoned at the snap of a finger," Chayse said. "Even our mother, skilled as she is, needed a catalyst, brother."

Ken's axe clattered to the ground.

Aldous felt like all the breath had left his body. He thought he must have misheard Chayse, but there was no other way to interpret her words. She spoke of magic. And she spoke of her mother—Theron's mother—in the same breath.

Theron and Chayse, the two people he thought most of in this world, had magic in their blood. The revelation made him feel terror and wonder and despair and hope all at once.

Theron stalked toward Chayse, his good humor evaporated.

"Tread carefully, sister." Each word sounded like it was bitten out between clenched teeth.

"We must help Aldous tread carefully, must help him hone the skills to control his magic," Chayse said, not backing away. "We are going into the hunt with Aldous, so trust him. You spent too much time alone, Theron. Surviving alone is about trusting yourself. Surviving as a pack is about trusting the individuals that make up that pack. You asked me to trust Kendrick the Cold, to live under the same roof, to eat at the same table, to fight by his side… a killer, a monster in human form." She shot Ken an apologetic look.

He shrugged.

"If Aldous truly has a dormant power," she continued, "then let us trust him. Let us use the keys we have in this very house to unlock that power."

Though a part of Aldous didn't want to know his power, the bigger part of him wanted to unlock it just as Chayse said.

"It will take time, Chayse," Theron said. Aldous wasn't sure if that meant Theron had agreed to share the secrets or not. "He will not be able to simply loose bolts of lightning and flame just because he has scrolls and a catalyst."

"Scrolls?" Aldous whispered.

They both ignored him.

"So let him learn as he goes," Chayse said. "He has already proven to be a quick study with a sword." Ken snickered. "He will be equally quick with magic," Chayse finished.

Aldous turned to Ken with a scowl, and the large man rolled his lips inward in mock fear.

Theron reached into his pocket, and from it he retrieved a Brynthian ducat.

"Theron, really? Now?" Chayse shook her head in dismay.

Theron ignored her and flipped the coin. It spun in the air end over end. Aldous' stomach was in his chest with anxiety as he struggled with the reality that this coin would have a pivotal role in his life.

Theron caught it. He slammed it on his hand. The face of the king.

The hunter scowled at the coin for a long moment then flipped it over.

The face of the dragon.

"Very well," said Theron. "Very well, but he is taking a sword and shield nonetheless." He turned to Aldous. "Do we have a deal, wizard? You fight no matter what, whether your magic can be tamed or not."

"Yes," Aldous said, the excitement rising again, rising to the thought of a dormant power and the new and unexpected opportunity to learn about that power. He lifted a light wooden shield from the rack and belted a sheathed short sword.

"Follow me," said Theron, his voice stern, his presence more formidable than ever in his armor. They were about to pass some sort of threshold; an irreversible step was about to be taken, and although afraid, very afraid, Aldous Weaver followed, ready to study and learn and grow his power.

Lady Wardbrook's hidden study was past the baths at the very end of the hall. A loose brick, when pushed in, activated some mechanism incomprehensible to Aldous, and as if by magic, but more likely by magnificent engineering, the wall simply opened.

"Sneaky," said Ken as he watched the secret gate part.

There were steep stone stairs that led down into black. The torches on the wall burst into flame, illuminating the stairwell. This was certainly by magic. It was just like in the chapel when Aldous lit the candles with tinder or flint. Aldous looked at his hands.

"It wasn't you," said Theron. "My mother put a spell on the torches to illuminate whenever the gate was opened."

"Why didn't you tell me your mother is a sorceress?" Aldous asked.

"I'm more than telling you now," Theron replied.

"Where is your mother?" Aldous asked, following Theron as they descended deeper under the earth, Chayse and Ken following behind. Cobwebs ran across the ceiling and walls, causing all of them to swipe in front of their faces to remove the things from their path. It had unquestionably been a very long time since anyone had been in this deep, reclusive part of Wardbrook.

"My mother's whereabouts are more unknown to me than those of our mortal enemy the Emerald Witch, so please let us deal with one demon at a time," said Theron. His tone —and the cracking of his knuckles as he clenched his fist— made Aldous think it wise to immediately stop that line of questioning.

The further they went down the stairs, the stranger Aldous felt. His palms grew hot and moist, and an icy, damp sensation slithered down his spine. He thought he heard Chayse whisper something, but when he turned around to look at her, it was clear she had not spoken.

They reached the bottom of the stairs. The ceiling was perhaps only nine feet high, but the room extended for at least a hundred. Like many other rooms in the estate, the walls were all lined with books.

"Are these all...?" Aldous approached a shelf and read a single title at random: *Lightning Possession.*

"Yes," said Chayse, "they are all tomes of spells."

"Does your mother—"

"Yes," said Theron, "she knows them all."

A shudder shook Aldous' frame. He again took in the vast

room: thousands of books, tens of thousands of spells. *What power would such a person possess?*

You will one day know, Aldous Weaver. The voice was a hushed whisper, nearly a hiss, it was the voice of a woman.

Something tugged on his chest. Something was pulling him.

"What is a catalyst?" Aldous asked, as he looked around the room for the voice, or the thing that pulled him, wondering if that, in fact, was this catalyst they described.

"It is a magically imbued anything," Theron said. "Well, inanimate as far as I know. It is magically imbued by an arch mage and passed down to disciples, so they may, with greater ease, access their powers."

"The first time you called fire, what was in your hand, Aldous?" Chayse asked.

Aldous thought back and replied, "Father Riker."

Chayse and Theron exchanged a glance. "Nothing else?" asked Chayse.

"Nothing else."

"What is so fascinating about you, Aldous, is that the very first time you used your powers you had no catalyst," Theron said. "Arch mages spend most of their lives trying to reach that point."

"Could a sword be a catalyst?" asked Aldous, as he gripped the hilt of the blade at his hip, and in his mind's eye he saw the weapon ablaze, hordes of rats closing around him, and he was not afraid.

"Yes, as I said, any inanimate object," Theron said. "An arch mage could imbue a spoon if he desired, or a chair if they had an urge to watch their disciples run round shooting bolts and blasts from a chair." He snickered.

"In the far east I saw a battle mage," said Ken. "He wielded an axe that blazed with hellfire. It set men ablaze by the score and cut through the heaviest plate like a hot knife through butter. He and twelve of his men held a mountain pass against three hundred of us."

"How did you defeat him?" asked Aldous.

"They say that the practitioners of magic use their own life force to generate their spells. After killing over two-thirds of our force, his twelve followers long ago butchered, the battle mage simply wore out. He was exhausted, and his axe fizzled. He became a normal man. I shot him in the eye with a crossbow."

"Ah," said Aldous. He thought of what Ken had just said about the use of life force as a currency for spells. He remembered the feeling after he'd set the chapel ablaze; it was the feeling of slipping into death's black fade. It was painless, but it was the temptation of an embrace much unlike sleep, for sleep promises of awakening. This had been different, a sweet song that sang only of eternity.

"Here," Chayse said as she opened a chest next to a massive oak desk and from it pulled out a four-foot wooden short staff. "This was one of my mother's earlier staffs, given to her by a great druid who dwelled in the Nevidian forest." She walked back to the others and extended the staff to Aldous with both hands.

He took it with the utmost care. It was fashioned from ash and perfectly smooth in the center. The rest was carved with the most intricate details, a relief of an unkindness of ravens on one half, and a pack of fang-baring wolves on the other.

The dreams. Dreams of wolves and ravens.

Aldous ran his hand over the carvings, and there was a stirring in him as he touched the wolves. In the furthest abyss of his mind he could hear them howling, and the sound echoed down his spine and found his heart. It thumped in his chest to the moon song of the wolves on the staff. He twirled it in his hands so that the raven side was up, and he inspected the art closely, running a single finger over one of the forbidding birds' forms. The unkindness of ravens joined the wolves in their song, and the ballad of beasts grew louder, as the wings flapped up and the claws ran across ice and snow from the depths of his consciousness to the front of his mind.

Aldous could no longer see the room. Chayse was gone. Ken and Theron both gone. He was in the woods. The trees grew so tall they must have reached clouds, the branches so thick the sky could not be seen. Fireflies shimmered gold and gave the black wood light. It was haunting; it was beautiful. The wolves surrounded him. And the ravens perched on all the branches. They painted the already dim canopy forever black, all but the reflection of the fireflies in their obsidian raven eyes. The wolves came closer. Hundreds of massive wolves. Aldous was not afraid, for they were bowing their heads. He felt powerful, immensely powerful. His heart thumped and thundered in his ears. It was the thudding like the drums of war, and all at once, in perfect unison, the wolves howled and the ravens cawed. It was a thing most divine, but this was no action performed by the God of Light. This was a god altogether more savage and altogether more present.

~

Aldous stood upright, his legs completely stiff and rooted, while his torso and head convulsed madly as he screamed and frothed, his eyes rolled back so that they were completely white. All the while he clung to the staff, holding it with both hands directly out in front of him. One hand on the wolf carvings, the other on the ravens. The veins in his wiry forearms bulged. It was a sight Theron had never seen before in person. He knew it happened, for his mother had told him, but it was a bloody strange thing to bear witness to.

So the boy truly is a wizard.

"What the bloody hell is happening?" Ken asked as a few of the nearby books fell off the shelves and Theron's and Chayse's hair began to blow.

"It is called binding," said Theron calmly, although he spoke loudly enough to be heard over Aldous' grunting and screaming. "When a magic-blooded human takes hold of an imbued object, it becomes bound to them, until they release it from themselves to give to another through a spell, or until they die."

"But you said this staff belongs to your mother, and you speak of her as if she is alive. How, then, can the object bind to the boy?"

"She released it and left it behind."

"And if someone other than the boy were to try…"

"When Chayse touched the staff, it was no more than a piece of wood with elegant carvings. The same would occur if you or I held it, unless you are hiding some secret." Theron looked at Ken inquiringly.

"Is he in pain?" Ken asked.

"I'm not sure, to be honest. We will have to ask the lad when he returns to our world," said Theron, and at that Aldous stopped shaking and lowered the staff—it was not abrupt but gradual.

"Aldous?" Chayse said, waving a hand in front of the wizard's face.

"Chayse," he said, "I was somewhere else." He looked dazed, as if he'd had a bit too much ale.

"Are you in pain?" asked Ken, putting his massive hand on Aldous' shoulder.

"No. I feel… altered."

"How so?" asked Theron.

"I feel... changed." Aldous turned to Theron with a smile. He was drenched in sweat, and faint purple circles had formed beneath his eyes. A strand of his black hair hung in front of his face, right down to the edge of his grin. He looked a bit mad. He looked a bit sinister. "I feel powerful," he finished, and on the tail of those words, he shrieked.

"You squeal like a pig at slaughter," Ken said.

"You pinched me!" Aldous said, and pulled away, touching the spot on his neck that had already begun to turn purple.

So much for powerful, Theron thought, amused.

"What was that for, you mangy brute?" Aldous tried to shove Kendrick in retaliation, but the mountain of a man was unmoved.

"I was just making sure you were still Aldous," said Ken as he ruffled the boy's hair then shoved his head.

"Who else would I be?"

Ken shrugged. "You left your mind, went somewhere else. I just wanted to make sure you were the one who crawled back into your skull and not some... something else."

"Well, I'm me," Aldous said.

"I could tell from the way you shrieked."

Aldous reached out and pinched Ken right in the neck as hard as he could. Ken's eyes went wide. Chayse gasped. Theron laughed. Aldous backed away slowly then turned and ran. Ken gave chase.

"Was this a good idea? Giving him a catalyst?" Chayse whispered to Theron as the other two ran circles round their mother's old study.

"You were the one who decided yesterday to bring him here without consulting me," Theron said.

"And you were the one dead set against it." Chayse paused. "Well, was it? A good idea?"

"I suppose we will find out soon enough." His smile faded.

"Hopefully what became of our mother does not become of Aldous Weaver."

"We can offer him some small protection," Chayse said, lifting something from a black leather box tooled with intricate designs. "The amulet."

"That will protect him from the seekers' eyes only as long as he does not summon his magic," Theron said, taking the silver medallion set with an ancient ruby from his sister's hands. "It will not protect him from the lure of what the magic may make him become."

"We must trust that he will protect himself from that."

"As our mother protected herself?" Theron asked, and was not surprised that Chayse could offer no answer.

"Get off me, you fat bastard!" Aldous said in a tone more than a bit too high-pitched for a boy of his age, which was really a man, but the noise he'd just made was enough reason for the others to continue calling him *boy*.

"Fat? Fat? It is muscle, you little toothpick. Maybe one day when you become half a man you will grow a bit of your own," Ken said to the pinned Aldous as he held him on the ground and pinched him. The boy screamed bloody murder at every pinch.

"I doubt Aldous will have the capacity to travel down the same road as our mother," said Theron. *For if he does travel down that road, I will render him headless before he reaches the end of it.*

～

"You left them! You deserted our children, you devil. You deserted me! For what?" the man roared at the top of the tower in the rain, in the cold, in the dead of the night.

"I told you not to come. I told you to stay," the woman said calmly, her voice faint on the wind of the rising storm.

"And let you walk away with him? With them?" He drew his sword; the rune carvings down the blood groove glowed their magnificent red. "I think not. You will die before I allow that!"

The woman's laughter cracked the sky and summoned lightning and thunder that shattered and roared at the high tower. "You haven't changed, not after all these years—after all I have taught you, you haven't changed. Your arrogance consumes you, husband."

He lunged toward her. "Let us dance one last time, wife."

And so they danced high on that tower under a blood moon as the sky screamed and a great deluge poured down from the heavens, such a great lover's quarrel was that.

CHAPTER EIGHTEEN

～

CAMPFIRE

ldous stared at the glimmering red gemstone in the campfire light. It looked like any piece of jewelry, really, but when he'd put it on three days ago in Theron's mother's secret lair, it had a similar but much more mild effect on him as the staff. He had felt as if his mind and thoughts were not his own, but the sensation had quickly subsided. Theron said that his mother had enchanted the necklace; it was enchanted with a spell that would cloak him from the seekers. As long as he wore the pendant, the seekers could not sniff him out until he himself revealed his magic by summoning it.

"It looks good on you," Chayse said, then gave Aldous a little punch in the arm, as the beyond-drunk Kendrick and Theron roared in laughter at some raunchy tale about one of the hunter's great adventures in womanizing.

"She had enough hair below that I thought she was birthing a full-grown Northman when I took a peek! Thick black right to the navel and halfway down her legs," Theron said in words broken by laughter.

"So what did you do, you vile bastard?" Ken asked, leaning in.

"Well, I was drunk, Ken," said Theron. "I was very drunk and young, you see. It had been five months since I had even seen a woman."

"You, Theron Ward, are a man most foul!" Ken shook his head, tears of merriment swelling in his eyes; his hard-scarred face was red from drunkenness and mirth and mushed up by his ridiculous smile.

"You think?" Aldous said to Chayse, as he managed to get his focus away from the other two.

"Well, it is a bit feminine," she teased.

"I suppose it is." He paused. "There is nothing wrong with a woman who fights and eats like a man," Aldous teased back just as Chayse let out an enormous belch.

Chayse went solemn for a moment, and regret slithered through Aldous. *Perhaps I am not at the tease-back stage yet. Why am I such a fool?* But Chayse relaxed and laughed, a most heavenly sound.

"What was she like?" Aldous asked Chayse, looking at the pendant once more.

"What was who like?" It was not Chayse who responded but Theron; his voice was stern and he sounded completely sober now, despite the fact that he had downed a good liter of ale. "You ask about my mother?"

Aldous cringed and nodded.

Theron scowled, and, as usual, Aldous felt a fool. He wished to be a man, but he still had the curiosity of a child, and no matter how much he chastised himself, he never seemed to learn. Ken would never have blurted a question like that. Would he?

"She is like no other," said Chayse.

"Chayse—" Theron said.

"No, don't 'Chayse' me, Theron. Stop hiding things away.

I thought you had moved past this when we gave Aldous the staff and the gem."

Theron ran a hand through his hair and fell back onto the grass.

Aldous thought he would not speak, that he would simply drift off into drunken sleep.

And then Theron did speak. "If I'm going to tell you about Mother, I'll have to tell you about Father, too," he began. "My father inherited Wardbrook from his father, and he from his, and so on, all the way back until the original Wards were granted these lands by a king long dead now. Generation after generation, the Wards flourished in farming and trade. Four generations ago our family was so filthy rich we just became landowners, and all our further income was provided, and still is, for the most part—except for my modest hunting contracts—by our tenants.

"Father was supposed to marry some woman from some other wealthy family. I think the Stenmires. Yes, he was to marry into the Stenmire family. He was nineteen years young at the time and he had little interest in settling down, even though that was a reasonable age for a gentleman to get married. There was a ball held at the Stenmire estate, where Father first met the girl he was supposed to marry." He paused. "And I really do mean girl. She was all of thirteen. My father was, and still is in some ways, a very intelligent man, and upon their first meeting, Father knew that even though she was just a girl, Lady Stenmire would never grow to be an intelligent woman. Father broke away from his socializing with her in search of drink, which he found, along with my mother. Mother was a guest, you see, at this Stenmire ball, a friend of the older sister who was already married. Mother was tall, full, and mentally mature—brilliant, really. She had some monies—at least, to hear Father tell it, she did—but nothing in the way of the Stenmires." Theron's voice droned;

he did not tell the tale like he did most of his stories—usually they sounded rehearsed, as if they had been told a thousand times. The beginning of this tale was weak at best, and Aldous wondered if that meant it was more or less likely to be true.

"Skipping ahead now," he continued, as if he was aware of what Aldous was noticing, "they eloped. Grandfather Ward, of course, was furious and he threatened to negate Father's inheritance if he did not return and marry the young Lady Stenmire. Father didn't care. He didn't give a damn. He only wanted to be with this brilliant, beautiful woman, a woman who always knew exactly what to say and when to say it. She knew how to push Father ever further, to awaken in him dormant talent. Father had served in the army when he was sixteen until his nineteenth birthday, even though he didn't need to because of his social position, but he always loved adventure. He always wanted to be a character in a story-book. He used to tell Chayse and me. I can see now that Mother helped push him, and mold him into that character. She made him into a hunter. That was what she was, and had been. It was how she knew the older sister Stenmire, for she had fulfilled a contract for her years prior."

"Sorry, but I must interrupt," said Kendrick. "How old was your mother when she met your father? Either she was a young lady of unusual poise and skill to influence him so, or a lady whose years surpassed his own."

"We don't know," said Chayse. "Sorcerers and sorceresses can conceal their age and preserve their bodies with magic."

As soon as she said that, Aldous thought of the Emerald Witch and her dark hair sprinkled with gray. Yet Theron had told him she was young and fresh as dew the first time he saw her.

"The great ones can live for hundreds of years, even changing their appearance. A pointed nose becomes rounded. A rounded chin becomes sharp. Hair changes from gold to brown," Chayse continued. "And trust me, if you had ever had the chance to hear our mother speak, you would think she had already been living for an eternity. Not because of her voice, but because of the things she used it to say. There was always a detached, inhuman logic to her, something acquired beyond the life cycle of the average mortal."

"If they are capable of living that long, multiple lifetimes of ordinary mortals, well then, is it possible that you have siblings you know nothing of?" asked Ken.

"If our father had been a sorcerer, it would be more likely," said Theron. "For a sorceress, when she conceives her first child, her womb enters an irreversible standard life cycle. No one knows why; that is just how it is. Yet it is possible we have siblings running around, just as anyone else may. Likely none are as handsome as I, though." Chayse punched him in the arm. "Ow!" He rubbed the spot and shot her a glare. "Anyway, that doesn't matter. This is not a scientific dialogue. This is the prologue to Chayse and Theron Ward." He scowled. "Do not interrupt it again."

"Sorry, Theron. Continue," said Ken.

"Where was I?"

"Your mother is a hunter. She taught your father to be a hunter," Aldous said, hanging on every word. "Wait... did he know she was a sorceress?"

"I am getting to that," Theron said. "No. He didn't, not right away. When they hunted together, Mother would use sword and bow, until on one of their hunts, four years in. They were nearly overrun by a swarm of fiends, and sword and bow weren't cutting it. So Mother turned them all to cinders, and my father finally had the real answer to the walking stick she always had strapped to her back but never used." Theron yawned. "I do apologize, but my own story is beginning to bore me."

"That is because you're not in it, you ass," Chayse said.

"You are right," Theron said, unashamed. "Well, they survived, obviously. Eventually they returned to Wardbrook. Father was twenty-six years at this point, if I remember what I was told correctly." Theron paused and snickered. "Yes, you must all bear this in mind. The story I now tell you was only told to me once, and it was told to me once by Sir Hakesworth, nearly ten years ago. So all of this is really not exactly certain."

"Wait!" Aldous said. "He told you the story and you asked no question? You never asked for the story to be retold? You heard it once and let it go?"

"They were gone. What does it matter?"

Aldous jumped to his feet. "My father was gone. My mother was gone. But I retold their stories in my mind night after night for the entire time I was as the monastery."

"I am not you and you are not me. Sit," Theron replied.

Aldous sat.

"So why are you telling us this?" Ken asked, then yawned and belched.

"Because I'm drunk and I thought it was important when I started telling it," Theron said, and then asked, "Why am I telling you this?"

"Aldous asked about Mother," said Chayse.

"She is insane, Aldous. Absolutely mad," Theron said. There was no emotion in his tone.

"What?" asked Aldous.

"Not in the beginning, not when Chayse and I were very young," Theron said.

"Wait," said Ken. "What happened to the young Lady Stenmire? And how did your grandfather allow your father to marry your mother and still hand over the inheritance?"

"Were you not just listening to me, Kendrick? I told you that I heard all that hubbub when I was fifteen. It was the same day Mother left us and the first time I got drunk. Grandfather is dead, so I can't ask him, and who in the hell is the young Lady Stenmire?" Theron asked then sat up and had a sip of ale.

This response made Ken look all the more confused, and he also appeared to be wondering why he cared who this Lady Stenmire was. He pulled the jug from Theron and took down a big gulp.

"May I continue?" Theron asked, drunk and frustrated.

"Yes," said Ken. "Please do."

"No more bloody interruptions," Theron said, jabbing his finger into Ken's chest.

"I'm sorry, there are just a lot of plot holes," Ken said.

"Plot holes? What the hell do plot holes in the story of my conception matter? I exist, don't I? And I rule the estate named Wardbrook. My very drunken presence at this camp-fire can fill in your bloody plot holes, Ken."

"All right. I'm sorry," came Ken's toneless, even apology. "I was just trying to picture it, is all. Carry on."

"What was the initial question, Aldous? Quickly, ask it again so I can respond before I fly into a rage," Theron said, and before Aldous could reply, continued. "Chayse, why would you say I should tell the story? *You* tell it, or answer the question, or whatever it is that we are doing here."

Chayse responded with a snore, out cold or at least pretending to be. Either way, Aldous was stuck getting his question somewhat answered by Theron, and as he thought of the question—had he known this would be the response—he would have never asked it in the first place. But it was too late to back out now; he had to get something for his efforts.

"What was your mother like?" he finally asked again, not caring anymore about the answer and wishing he had asked something better, such as how she controlled her power, or even how much power she had.

"She was absent. Always there physically, but mentally and emotionally she was hollow. Father was the same. They spoke of their adventures when we had guests, and I loved listening to that. So did Chayse." Chayse let out another snore, ladylike and delicate, ending in a huffing snort. "Yet when no one from the outside world was around... But they were our parents, and when they left, our massive house became hollow. Chayse and I read and sparred every day; we played and we rode horses. We fought." Theron laughed, then had another sip of ale. "But you asked only about Mother, and so I will answer. She was just a wraith, a strange wraith in the house that gave strange guidance, and did so from a distance. Then one day she was gone."

Aldous felt that must be strange for Theron and Chayse, for their parents to simply be gone. In a twisted way, Aldous was glad that he at least knew his parents were dead. They left him because they left this world. Theron's parents left because... because why?

"That's all you get, Aldous. I'm not sure if that answers your question or not, but I must sleep. Tomorrow will be another long ride." At that, Theron quickly nodded off, Ken not far behind.

Aldous wondered if it was the drink that caused the slurred and immensely blurry narrative, or if Theron just pretended it had. *A distant mother who picked up and left on a whim, a father who did the same, never to see their children again. To completely abandon a life of wealth, to just vanish.* Aldous looked at Chayse sleeping close by. He thought of Theron's assertion that he had asked Hakesworth about it only once. He thought of the tidy telling, as if deeper details did not matter, or perhaps did not exist. He thought the telling scrubbed clean of anything truly important.

~

*To any man who brings the fugitive Kendrick Solomon Kelmoor,
also known as Kendrick the Cold, before His Royal and Exalted
Majesty the King of Brynth for punishment, he shall be awarded
the outlaw's weight in gold. If the outlaw is brought in as a corpse,
the man shall be awarded the outlaw's weight in gold. The fugitive
was last seen fleeing the city of Norburg, allegedly after murdering
his own wife. His list of crimes now stands at: desertion, the murder
of an officer of the king's army, and the murder of his wife, a
citizen of Norburg. Take caution, for he is a man most violent and
most wicked, well versed in all forms of melee combat.*

*Bounty notice circulated throughout Brynth, eight months after the
arrival of the Rata Plaga, written by Count Salvenius and sealed
by the king.*

~

CHAPTER NINETEEN

DUKE DUNCAN OF DENTIN

he Dukedom of Dentin was pleasant, Theron thought, as the four of them slowed their steeds to a trot now that Duncan's keep was in view. It was not a city like Norburg, not even close. They passed villagers in a lush valley, one of the very few green valleys other than Wardbrook Theron had seen in years. A stone keep stood atop a low hill with squat stonewalls, maybe eighteen feet high, but the hill gave them the appearance of being taller. A fine cobbled path wound right up to the front gate of the keep, perhaps a mile and a half in the distance.

A year ago Theron would have stopped at the inn to the left of the road. He would have cleaned himself up from the journey to Dentin, had a shave. He would have taken off his armor and put on fine cloth, combed his hair and tied it tight at the base of his skull. Indeed, a year ago he would have done all that nonsense; he would have played the game.

That was before his home was attacked; it was before he watched his people die. His life was no longer a game. It was time that he stood as what he was, and Theron Ward was a hunter above all else. So he left his sword on his back, he kept his chain mail over his shoulders, and his hair flowed with wild savagery in the wind. He wore his helm, and he did not smile at strangers.

Carts stopped as they passed down the road to the keep. Villagers kept their heads down or stared with fear and respect at the four riders that rode into their land.

$\sim$

They reached the gate to the duke's keep, and only then did Theron remove his helm.

"State your names and your business in the Dukedom of Dentin," said a lazy guard who had just risen to his feet as their party approached.

"I present to you the mighty Theron Ward, renowned hunter and Lord of Wardbrook. The man to his left and the woman to his right are his humble apprentices," said Aldous, with a little less exuberance and a few less titles than Theron would have liked, but it wasn't bad for a first time.

"Fantastic," said the guard, after he gave a yawn. Then he squinted at Ken. "Aren't you a bit old to be an apprentice?"

A second lazy guardsman—one whom no one in the party had noticed because he was lying against the wall just around a corner under the shade of an olive tree—gave a snicker at this. What made it all the more irksome was that he wasn't even looking at Ken, yet he still found his mate's joke to be a laugh.

"Aren't you two a bit useless to not have been reported to the duke?" Ken said, and his tone made it more a statement than a question.

"And who are you, boy?" the guard asked Aldous, ignoring Ken's remark.

"I am Lord Wardbrook's herald and the documenter of his journeys."

"Fantastic," said the guard without any enthusiasm, to which the shaded olive tree guard gave another chuckle. "You're here to see the duke?"

"Yes," Theron said, his patience quickly thinning. *Gate guards, useless bastards puffed up on paltry power.* "We are here under contract of the Duke of Dentin, and time is of the essence, as we are here to deal with your Obour problem."

The guard's eyes went wide at this, and the olive tree man stood up.

"Well, why didn't you say so from the get-go?"

"I thought you would recognize the name Theron Ward and have opened the gate," Theron said, venom dripping from his words.

"We don't recognize much, sir. Do we, Sam?" said the first guard.

"We don't recognize much at all, sir, not much at all," said the one named Sam.

"Ah, a very useful skill for a guardsman, the ability to not recognize much," Theron said to Ken, who gave him a cynical smile.

"Open up!" the first one yelled, and the wooden gate began to creak open.

"I will warn you though, me lords and lady. It ain't an Obour problem no more—it's an Upir problem now. A farm just a few miles south from here was attacked two nights ago. Whole family dead. A friend found 'em this morning."

"Were the bodies burned?" asked Chayse before Theron had the chance.

"No, we gave 'em a proper burial."

"Ah," said Theron. "Now you likely have an Upir problem *and* a ghoul problem."

They passed through the gate into a small courtyard; the stables, the smithy, and the keep were all pressed against the inside of the walls. A large balcony faced into the courtyard on the highest floor of the keep. Three archers stood atop it, peering down at Theron and his band. Several more archers stood in the battlements.

It was a small fort, but well protected, the walls being on a hill as the first line of defense, and should they be breached or taken by an escalade, the invaders would find themselves in a small, but open courtyard, at the mercy of the keep's archers.

They came to the oak doors and Theron did not wait for the guard named Sam to open them, for he was lagging behind. Theron dismounted and opened the doors himself then turned to Sam.

"See our horses to stable. See they are fed and watered." Theron was stern and clear. Whether or not tending to the mounts of the duke's guests was part of Sam's duties meant little to Theron. It also seemed to mean little for Sam, for without argument he shrugged and did as he was told.

The walls were stone, the floors packed dirt, covered in fresh rushes, a pack of hounds sleeping in one corner. The keep of Dentin had homeliness that Salvenius' keep did not possess.

Aldous gave a sigh as they walked into the court. Theron turned to the boy to see that his eyes were shut and he was massaging his temples.

"What ails you, Aldous?" Theron whispered so the duke's man would not hear his words.

"I feel something... I think there is magic here," Aldous whispered back.

"An Upir is a sort of magic," Chayse murmured.

"No, I mean here." Aldous gestured around him at the stone walls. "Right here."

"We will find out soon enough," said Ken.

The thin, mustached, long-faced messenger who had

come to Wardbrook was standing direct center of the court, as if he had been doing so all day. Likely he had.

"Please, do come with me," he said. He gave a long sniff then flared his nostrils and scowled when Theron and the rest got close. This was the first time Theron had smiled since his arrival at Dentin.

They were shown to the duke's study. The room was vast. The ceilings were as tall as those in Wardbrook's library, and the walls were stacked with just as many books. From where Theron stood, the place looked pristine, finely dusted, and everything was in order. In the center of the room, sitting in a reading chair and looking deathly pale, was a young man of perhaps Aldous' age.

"Welcome to Dentin," said the pale young man. "I am Duncan, Duke of Dentin. Please take a seat and make yourselves at home. Tea?"

Theron had heard that the Duke of Dentin was a large man, not far off Count Salvenius in size. Likely this was Duncan the second.

"Do get our guests some tea, Fabius," said the duke as his quick eyes shifted to the thin-mustached man who had summoned Theron from Wardbrook, then shifted back to Theron, Chayse, Aldous, and Ken, not lingering on any of them longer than a moment.

"Thank you for your hospitality," Theron said as he took a seat in a fine armchair, and the others did the same. The study was hot and stuffy with a fire going, yet the duke sat curled up in multiple sheets and furs, despite the season.

"It is I who must thank you, Theron Ward," said the young Duncan as he gave a slight bow of his head. "I have heard many bards sing of your deeds in my halls and in these dark hours that have befallen Dentin. I knew you were the man to return this place to the light." He looked Theron in the eyes. "The past two years have been horrific here. It started with my father's death. A strange and sudden illness overtook him. His last morning he was jovial and enjoying his favorite breakfast dish. Come nightfall he was taken by fever, and by the next morn he was dead. Mother was taken over by a most terrific melancholia, as was I, of course, for I dearly loved my father, but over months and seasons my ailment passed, whereas Mother's only seemed to worsen."

"What symptoms does she suffer?" asked Theron, while the others listened intently to the duke's story. It was important that a hunter always have a good idea of the whole story surrounding a contract, for monsters were drawn to suffering like flies to shit, and although the duke's tale might have nothing to do with the evil they would soon face, more information was never harmful.

"Of course she has the lack in appetite, as has risen again in myself. In private, she question's her faith—she questions the God of Light." The duke whispered that bit, as if he feared anyone would overhear his mother's blasphemy. "She only eats once every two days, perhaps, and when she does, it is very little. She has become skeletal in form, and the servants must clean her. For alone, she does not leave her bed.

"By some fortunate twist of fate, or so I thought, a month past a mysterious woman who claimed to be a healer arrived in town near the same time as the first news of the Obour. She said she could cure my mother's ills, restore her to the way she was before Father's death."

"But she did not?" Theron asked.

"She said…" the duke began, then shuttered.

"What did she say?"

"She said that she needed the blood of the beast, a creature of darkness, a thing of the devil," said the duke, his bagged eyes closed tight.

"Then?"

"I am ashamed to say, but I saw her arrival at the same time as the Obour to be some dark sign, an answer to my prayers in a form most grotesque. I wanted to leave nothing to chance, so I sent for one as skilled as you, to slay the devil and bring me back a vial of its blood. Just a single vial. The mysterious woman said it would be sufficient for her to weave her spell."

Theron stood from his seat at this mention of dark magic. "I am sorry, Your Grace, but we will not aid you in this pursuit of dark magic. Such a spell would likely turn your mother into the manner of thing that I have pledged my life to kill." Theron made for the door, and the others stood as well.

"Please wait, good Theron, please wait," the duke said in a tone most pitiful. "Stay and listen to the rest."

"Very well, sit back down, everyone," said Theron after a moment. He sat, and the others did the same.

"The woman, she left three days past," the duke began. "As we supped, she asked which hunter I sent for. I told her I sent for the best hunter in the land, for I wished to be certain of success. I told her I sent for you, Theron Ward. At the mere mention of your name, the woman went paler than her already most pale complexion, and her wide eyes looked as if they would burst. She stood from the table, and like a wraith she flew from the room with inhuman speed." A tear ran down his cheek; he made no effort to wipe it away. "My men, they searched for her, but to no avail."

"What good is a vial of blood to you now if the woman has fled?" Ken asked.

"No, no, you misunderstand. I have no wish for the blood or the spell. The woman is clearly a villain." The duke huddled beneath his furs, shivering. "I know not who I can trust."

"You can trust me, my good sir," said Theron as Aldous asked, "What did she look like?"

But Theron knew the answer, knew it deep in his gut even before the duke said, "Her hair was black, but not like yours, like slate, like the blackest slate."

Is it luck? Or am I cursed? Do I hunt her, or does she hunt me? She and I are bound, and only in death shall we part.

"Her eyes, emerald green?" asked Ken. "The strangest green you have ever seen?"

The duke's eyes went ever wider.

"You know this woman? And she knows you? What is your relation?" The duke pressed himself against his chair, clearly afraid of his own tale and now afraid of those who sat before him.

"Of course you heard of what happened at Norburg a year past?" asked Theron.

"I know what I have been told, but I don't believe it," said the duke.

"Well, you better start," said Ken.

"We were there," said Aldous.

"The only survivors," said Theron.

"And her as well? The emerald-eyed healer? She was with you?"

"The emerald-eyed *witch*," said Ken. "That devil whore is no healer, Your Grace. And aye, she was there, but she wasn't with us. She was the one who brought Norburg to ruin. She was the rouser of those rats."

"What do you mean?" The duke was shaking hard now, and he waved away Fabius when the mustached man returned to the room with the tea.

"She was controlling them," said Aldous. "Through some hellish sorcery, she was controlling them."

They took a moment to explain the events that had unfolded at Norburg, then about how a small pack of the rats had come to Wardbrook with a seeker, as some sort of assassination attempt.

"Fabius!" the duke yelled after the tale was complete, and in a matter of moments his man appeared back in the door. "I need a drink—something strong, Fabius, something very strong." Fabius disappeared to carry out his orders. "This Emerald Witch, will she strike Dentin? Strike with her swarm of rats? For we are smaller and not as well equipped as Norburg. We have less than a quarter of guardsman that Norburg does. Are we doomed, Theron? Tell me now, are we doomed?"

"Norburg's Count Salvenius was a damned fool, and he was under some spell of the witch's," Theron began. "As I said when we described the events to you, Norburg was betrayed from within, and no one was prepared. What you must do is get the citizens of your townships to come to your keep. You must brace for conflict, for if she was here and she fled, she will return. I don't know when, but she will, and you must be ready." Theron grabbed the duke's shoulders in a firm hold. "When we return from carrying out our initial contract, when the Upir and perhaps a ghoul or two are dead, I want Dentin Keep to be fortified with men ready for a scrap. For if she comes with the entirety of her swarm, there will be slaughter. And if by chance she has some connection to the appearance of this Upir in your midst... Strange that her appearance and the arrival of the Upir coincided..." He waved his hand. "No matter. We will hunt it."

"The previous contract hardly seems a problem now," the duke protested, and reached out as Theron and the others stood.

Theron exchanged a glance with Chayse.

"Your Obour is now certainly an Upir which has feasted, and since you buried the remains of the feast instead of burning the bodies, you now have ghouls as well. If we leave him, then by the time we are done with the rats you will be facing a horde of ghouls. Or worse yet, you will need to face both an army of rats and a horde of ghouls at once." Theron released the duke, and with his party made way for the door. "Fear not, Your Grace—we shall make great haste in our slaughter, and we shall return to aid you in yours."

～

I've blockaded the windows. I've blockaded the door. It has been a week and I am perilously low on water and food. I feel the pangs of hunger and the longing of thirst. It is hard for me to even hold this quill steady. If you find this, whoever you are, then it means they have gotten in; they have gotten in and they have consumed my flesh. They look like the men, women, and children of my village, wretched, nightmarish versions. Their skin has gone gray and their eyes have yellowed. They look dead, but I assure you they are not! Nor are they alive. They seem to exist in some state in between. What frightens me most is the moaning, and I daresay, in the moments of my truest terror, I can hear them talk; they talk to me. They say they are hungry and they beg for my flesh; they beg and moan to eat the flesh from my bones. Yesterday, little Timmy nearly broke through the southern window, nearly squeezed his way through the barricade. I got close and tried to speak with him, to ask him why he was doing this, why he and the other townsfolk begged to consume me. He bit my arm in response. Luminescent forgive me. Oh, Luminescent, please forgive me. I cracked apart his skull with the leg of a chair. He lies dead in my living room. I've boarded the window back up, but they will come through again. I hear a rustling from the living room. My God, there he is, there is little Timmy standing in the doorway to my study, his skull shattered, his gray brains oozing from the chasm... If you are reading this, I have been consumed.

Bloodstained letter found near the mostly consumed corpse of Lord Edgar Alabaster Pote in his estate.

～

CHAPTER TWENTY

TRAIL OF DEAD CRUMBS

The farmhouse was empty. Maybe.

"What if they're hiding?" Aldous asked.

Theron just looked at him.

"What if we get bitten?" Aldous asked, his nerves firing as he stared at the blood-spattered sun sigil, the symbol of the Luminescent hanging above the family's fireplace. *Little protection he gave them—as little protection as he offered my family.*

"By what?" Theron asked.

"By the Upir, or the ghouls," said Ken.

"It will hurt," said Chayse.

"Will we turn into them, is what I mean," said Aldous.

"No. That is mostly a myth. The family turned to ghouls because the Upir sucked them all completely dry," Theron said, and Aldous shuddered. "Not a drop left in them. They must have been sleeping when it came. After a day or two, sometimes three, the Upir's emptied victims rise as ghouls, or minions to the Upir. Their bite can't turn you into anything but their dinner, for ghouls feed only on human flesh."

Theron walked from the small home out into the field. Aldous followed.

"What if we get bitten by the Upir?" he asked.

"I just explained that. Were you not listening?" Theron asked, and stopped by four freshly dug—then un-dug—graves in the ground.

"They just got up and left," Aldous said with a shudder. Of course he had heard stories about Upirs and ghouls and Lycos, and harpies and so on, but even after he'd witnessed the Rata Plaga, he still held the hope that he would never need to see any of the others. That perhaps they didn't truly exist.

"If Upirs drain humans to make ghouls, then what makes a human into an Obour then an Upir?" asked Ken, as he strode over to join them.

"Greater Upirs spill their blood into a fresh human corpse," Theron began as he crouched over a grave and inspected the turned up earth. "Two days old at most." He glanced up. "The blood regenerates the corpse and then it rises as an Obour, eventually becoming an Upir. They're nasty things, Upirs. Greater Upirs even worse. They look like us, completely human, except, of course, when they unsheathe their fangs. Lesser Upirs, on the other hand, are skeletal, with white and purple flesh, and red in the eyes. He will be slow, the one we are hunting, engorged on blood from his recent feeding." Theron paused. "Well, relatively slow, compared to if he were not engorged on blood. The ghoul tracks will lead us to him. After they rise, they go in search of their master."

They followed the tracks for three hours as daylight died. On the near horizon was an abandoned windmill.

"No doubt with a deep, dark cellar full of damp and cobwebs, and for our sakes ghouls and an Upir," Aldous said.

"No doubt," Theron replied with a broad smile.

Aldous sighed.

The fading sun cast a red glow behind the windmill; the wood was rotten and the decay was visible from their hundred paces out. They crouched in the bushes, waiting.

"What are we waiting for?" asked Aldous.

"Do you want to go in there?" asked Theron. "We have no idea how many ghouls the Upir has already risen. If there is a good score of them, I'd rather have the scrap outside than in the tight confines of the windmill."

"So we wait here until they come out for an evening stroll?" asked Ken.

"Who is the hunter here?" Theron snapped. "We wait until they get a smell of our flesh—the ghouls are fresh and they need to eat. They will be mad with hunger. They have found their master and now they are ready to feast."

"What if they aren't in there?" Aldous asked, hoping dearly that this was the case.

Theron did not need to answer, for just as Aldous asked the question, a thing in the figure of a man stepped out from the mill. It had a lit torch in its right hand and a small sickle in the other. Although it held the tools of a man, and was in his form, even at that distance Aldous could tell it was not a man, at least not the traditional sort. The skin was an unnatural gray, and it clung to the bones and muscle as if all water had been pulled from the body.

"Some say that the ghouls can still think," Chayse said softly from behind Aldous. "That they can even reason. But their thoughts and their reasoning only drives them toward the will of their Upir and the consumption of living human flesh." Aldous was not sure if she was trying to break his morale on purpose, but her words had such an effect.

"That must be his family," said Ken, as four more of the gray, hollow-skinned forms came from the mill, pitchforks and cleavers in hand.

"And those must be their neighbors," said Theron as a good deal more came filing out. They looked like a drunken mob ready to string up an oppressive landlord, but without the screaming and shouting, just hungry stares. "Take off their heads. When we're done, we burn them all. Chayse, start us off."

Chayse stood and stepped from the bushes. The entire group of ghouls whipped their faces toward her, scenting her flesh. She raised her bow and pulled an arrow from her quiver, notched it, aimed. Loosed. In a split moment perhaps halfway from Chayse to impact, Aldous thought he saw the arrow split in some sort of silver flash, then curve, and the next instant the head of the torch-bearing ghoul was clean off its shoulders.

"How the bloody hell?" asked Ken.

"Guillotine arrow," said Chayse as she strung another. The ghouls were charging now, just over twenty of them; they were brittle but they were fast. Chayse let fly another, and a second head came off. "The long arrowhead splits at a certain speed, turns into more of a bladed cross," she explained as she drove the spiked end of the bow into the ground and drew her short swords. "This time, Ken," Chayse said, looking back, "if I say I have it under control, then I bloody well have it under control."

Ken said nothing, just gave a nod, and although Aldous knew this was not the place or the time, he felt a pang of jealousy that Chayse and Ken had shared some prior moment that allowed there to be a *this time*.

"Focus on the task," growled Theron as he drew his claymore and charged in, Ken right behind him, his axe and mace ready for work. The ghouls gave their hellish moans, and thrashed wildly with their villager tools tasked with harvesting flesh.

Short staff in hand, shield and short sword on his back, Aldous decided he would take up the rear.

Ken split an incoming pitchfork to splinters with his mace then split its wielder's skull with his axe, right down to the chest. "Come on, then, wizard! Set something ablaze."

Aldous raised his staff and tried to focus on one of the ghouls that was a safe distance from his three companions. He tried to picture the thing bursting into flames. It wasn't working, and, as if the once-human thing could sense Aldous' ill intent, it turned to him, kitchen knife raised, and came scrambling forward. It was a fright up close—not as bad as the rats, but a good fright nonetheless. The thing had been a woman no less than a week ago; now it was a corpse with an uncontrollable hunger, its eyes glazed over with an opaque mist in the pupils, and the whites were stained piss yellow.

It slashed. Aldous blocked with the staff and was shoved back, amazed by the force that the thing had just unleashed. Another fiendishly heavy strike sent Aldous toppling backward onto the ground.

Burn, you fucker, burn.

Aldous aimed the staff uselessly at the ghoul as it in turn raised its knife with both hands above its head, ready to plunge a killing blow. Before it got the chance, the edge of Theron's claymore cleaved its forehead, showering Aldous with skull fragments and a mist of brain juice.

"If you can't bloody well burn them, draw your sword and do what we spent months teaching you, boy," Theron growled as he turned around to evade a cleaver, lop off an arm, and shatter the base of a skull with all his strength behind a pommel blow.

Aldous tossed down the staff and pulled the shield and sword from his back as he sprang to his feet and joined his comrades. *Keep your shield up, block, bash, and cut,* Aldous told himself as he advanced behind Theron. Two grabbed the hunter's focus, but a third slipped by and came at Aldous.

It was a child, no doubt from a poor family on some farm that went hungry every winter, but the hunger he knew then was a romantic hope in comparison to the hunger the ghoul child knew now.

"It is a boy no longer, Aldous!" called Ken from twenty paces away, as if reading Aldous' thoughts. Ken ducked and twirled below the wide strike of a burly ghoul's smithy hammer. Ken kneecapped the ghoul with his mace, and it moaned and fell, not exempt from pain in its un-death.

Aldous looked back at his foe before Ken delivered the smiting blow upon his. The living-dead child brandished a hatchet in pale gray hands, veins black beneath the thin skin. It struck. Aldous blocked, willing his training to take hold, to guide his movement, but it was too hard to strike out against this child that was not a child. It struck again, and he bashed forward with his shield, but the thing had the same freakish strength as the last and was not leveled by the impact. Again it came for him. Aldous back-stepped then lunged forward and drove his short sword through the ghoul's chest. It moaned, and a viscous, coagulated black muck oozed from between its teeth. It kept walking, sliding its small body down the blade, and began driving Aldous backward.

The boy had black hair, like Aldous himself. It slid along the sword right to the hilt, until its face came inches from his, and it snapped its teeth, trying to bite at his flesh. It raised its hatchet again, still impaled to the hilt of Aldous' sword. He smashed the rim of his shield into the thing's face, knocking it back, and then pulled his sword free. The blade cut through the abdomen as he did, and the ghoul stumbled back, its rotten entrails hanging out. It gave a moan and again came forth.

"It will not die, Theron! The fucking thing will not die,"

Aldous screamed, his hands shaking violently as the gutted child advanced, still every bit as hungry as before.

"I told you, take off its head!" Theron called back, his words followed by the whistle of his mighty sword, the crunch of shattering skull, and the splatter of mulched brain.

Aldous gave a shout and charged, almost tripping and falling face first before the ghoul, for his legs wobbled madly with adrenaline. He managed to stay upright, and his training finally kicked in. With his first lash he took off both the ghoul's upraised hatchet-wielding arms at the elbows. Aldous spun, and on the back slash he hacked his sword through the thing's head just under the eyes—almost made it all the way through. Didn't matter, though. It was enough. He slid the blade out, and the ghoul's brains followed.

~

"Good lad! Now carry on," said Kendrick as he caught a glimpse of Aldous getting his first kill out of the way. Pride touched him, for he and the others had taught the boy well.

The ghouls' numbers were dwindling; more than half were ready for the torch. If they were human they would have run, they would have known fear, and perhaps these things did, but they knew hunger a great deal better. So the last of them came just like the first.

Ken hooked a ghoul over the shoulder with the beard of his axe and heaved it close; his mace met its face as he brought it in. He got a good bit of coagulating plasma on his leather for the effort, and another ghoul was ready to stoke the fire.

Ken saw a ghoul getting the drop on Aldous. He headed for it, but it was too close to the wizard, who was over top of a downed ghoul and shrieking as he stabbed like a wild thing into the creature's face.

"Boy!" Ken yelled. Aldous turned, but he was not prepared.

A ghoul closed in on Ken from the right, another from the left. He needed his axe, but Aldous needed it more, so Ken threw it with the honed precession acquired from carrying out such a motion a thousand times. The axe struck Aldous' threat right in crown of the skull. The thing twitched wildly on the ground; it was a threat no longer.

They came at Ken now from the right and the left. He caught the right ghoul's dagger arm by the wrist, and parried the left attacker's crude, rusted sword with a downward blow of his mace. It came off balance for a moment; Ken took the opportunity and bashed it in the head as he swung the other creature off its feet by the wrist. Before it could get to its feet, Chayse was stomping its brains into mush with her iron-heeled boot.

"That's"—Theron plunged his sword through the eye of a legless ghoul crawling aimlessly through the grass—"all of them."

"What about the Upir?" asked Ken.

"He's still sleeping in the mill, no doubt. Perhaps the scent of his new family cooking will wake him," said Chayse.

Theron gave her a disapproving glance.

"A bit grim, Chayse, a bit grim," he said.

"We are monster hunters, brother," she said, her voice strained as she dragged two headless ghouls to join three others, aiming to start the bonfire. "Grim is what we are," she finished with a grin.

They dragged the bodies into a heap; Ken did so two at a time.

"You want to have another try with that staff, oh great Arch Mage Aldous Weaver?" Theron asked when the bodies were well stacked.

Aldous gave him a pitiful look.

"It shouldn't be too hard to get them cooking. Their flesh is paper dry; it should catch flame with ease," Ken said.

Aldous looked a bit sick. He still looked like a new recruit to Ken, and part of him wanted to leave the boy alone. He knew Theron felt the same. But the greater part of them needed Aldous to perform, they needed to push him, they needed him to cross the line. Because he was one of them. They could not leave him behind.

Ken was a killer. Theron and Chayse were killers. Aldous needed to prove he was the same.

"Do it, boy. Swallow the bitter taste and do it," Ken said. "Set them ablaze."

Aldous remained still. The adrenaline from the fight had passed through, and he was pale, staring at the pile of ghouls that mostly looked like humans, gray, mangled, headless humans.

"Norburg was worse, Aldous. You made it through that. Now make it through this so we can get back to Dentin and live through Norburg all over again," said Ken.

"I can't," said Aldous. "Theron, use your oil flask and some tinder. I can't do it."

"Then why did I give you that staff?" said Theron as he stepped up to Aldous' back and spoke down the boy's neck. "So you would have a fancy walking stick? Light the corpses so we can drag out the Upir. So we can kill it and, like Ken said, get back to Dentin and kill some rats."

Ken watched as the boy looked to Chayse, but she did not come to his aid. Not this time. She only crossed her arms and stared at the boy.

"Light it," Theron said, shaking Aldous by the head. "Light it... Light it, light it."

Aldous whirled round and yelled in Theron's face.

"I can't do it! I can't do any of this. I'm not like you. I'm not like Ken."

261

"What if you need to be?" said Ken, his voice cold. Aldous had to perform. Ken couldn't show mercy to the boy now. If he did, it might mean the boy's death later. Or his, or Theron's, or Chayse's. But it wasn't just their lives at stake. It was the lives of all those who might fall prey to the monsters they failed to kill. No longer Kendrick the Cold. Kendrick the Altruistic. He almost snorted. "What if you need to be like Theron? What if you need to be like me?" Ken stepped forward now and closed in on Aldous, surrounding the boy. "Make the choice to be the man you need to be."

"Leave him be," Chayse said. "One of you just get on with it and light the bloody bodies, before they find their mushed-up heads and start walking again."

"No," said Theron, his voice as cold as Ken's, "this is the way it must be. He must stomach this, for in the days to come things are going to get worse, and I want to know we can count on his talent."

"I don't have any talent! I don't want to light it, Theron. I don't want to watch them burn." Aldous' voice was quivering now. "I don't want to see it. I don't want to fucking smell it. I don't want to taste it in the air."

"You've done it once and you've seen it twice. Third time is the charm. Light them up and it will be smooth sailing from here on out. These things are not even human," said Ken.

"Fuck you!" said Aldous, and sniveled.

Ken laughed. Theron gave a chuckle too. This was the way of the pack: when it came to day-to-day life it was love and laughter, when it came to the killing, to surviving, it was savage and cruel, but it was done together.

A sky-splitting wail came from the mill. They all turned.

The Upir exploded from the rotted shingled roof and hit the ground below with the nimbleness of a predatory feline.

"Don't watch, don't watch, my son," his father pleaded, tears running down his face, the torchbearer coming closer.

The boy turned his head away.

"Watch, you must watch. You must know what happens to heretics, to sorcerers," said a cloaked priest as he turned the boy's head to look forward once again.

"Bastard, you bastard," the boy's father wailed at the priest.

"This is the will of the Luminescent. This is the will of God."

"Father!"

"Close your eyes."

The torch ignited the stake. His father screamed, his flesh burned, and the smell crawled into the boy's nose.

"Look. Look, as the heretic burns, or you shall suffer the same fate."

The boy kept his eyes on his father as he burned—not because he feared the priest, but because he wanted to be sure he would remember this day for the rest of his life. He wanted to be sure he remembered the sight of the flames boiling the flesh from his father's bones, the singular smell of charred human, and the taste of the soot that was his forsaken father, for one day he knew this memory would light the fire that would ignite the world.

≈

CHAPTER TWENTY-ONE

UPIR

"If you won't burn the ghouls then you damn well better burn that," said Theron as he dipped his chin to the Upir. What a fiend it was. Naked and white as snow, purple veins bulging beneath its absurdly muscled flesh, belly grotesquely distended from gorging on blood over the days past. It bared its teeth, a mouth full of fangs, red eyes glowing in the dusk. The Upir circled, studying them, obviously no mindless threat. "So stop your sniveling and get ready. Here comes a hell of a fight."

"How do we go about this?" Ken asked, twirling his weapons.

"Circle it. Ken, go right, I'll take left," said Chayse. She notched an arrow and sidestepped slowly, her eyes fixed on the Upir.

"Don't you miss and hit me," said Ken, only half in jest.

"I'll try not to," she said. "Though it would be easy to mistake you for a fiend."

Theron wasted no time on words and went at the thing straight on. He swung from the hip. *Not even close.* The Upir sprang back so quickly it was hard to see, and then swung a clawed hand at Theron. It struck him in the head, but his mighty helm took the blow well. He stood strong, and sent another swing, and again the Upir dodged.

Chayse let fly her arrow.

Ken gaped as the devil caught the projectile midair, then snapped it.

Bloody hell.

He lunged, thinking this would give him a chance to strike. He was wrong.

The Upir spun back round, ducking under Ken's axe, and pirouetted away from his mace. Somehow the creature managed to get round to his back and create a good distance from Theron and Chayse. Ken sensed the fangs coming down for his exposed neck, but there was a bestial cry and the fangs did not come.

Ken spun round to see the boy driving his sword into the Upir's ribs. But the boy was completely lacking battle experience, and left himself completely open to attack. In defense of *him.*

The Upir steeled itself and sent the wizard flying with a heavy forearm strike to the chest. He hit the ground, limp, and did not move again.

Aldous, no.

Ken swung each of his weapons, and missed with both again, but an arrow whistled over his shoulder so damn close he could feel the goose feathers touch his neck. The missile struck the fanged fiend in the chest, making it stumble back.

Theron delivered a heavy downward strike, with no success. Two heavy wounds and the Upir was just as spry as it was at the start of the fray.

"I thought you said it was going to be slow," Ken said to Theron.

The Upir slashed with a claw most vile. Theron rolled under it and sprinted away ten strides, loading his hand crossbow as he did. The creature took pursuit, but Ken hooked it around the arm with his axe, turned it around, and gave it a good bludgeon across the mouth with his mace. Fangs crunched and purple blood sprayed.

"Take a bite out of me now, you fucking bastard," Ken said. The Upir seemed to have a mind to obey the taunt, and opened its devastated mouth wide, growling from the throat and lunging at Ken.

Ken struck twice. The Upir caught each blow by the wrist, and they wrestled. Ken pushed forward, the muscles in his legs snapping into action, as he fought to drive the tangled fiend toward Theron.

Its teeth gnashed closer and closer, and it was as strong as ten men as it pushed against Ken's might. The head of Theron's bolt burst through its eye, sticking right through the back of the skull. It weakened from the shot and Ken pulled his arms free. Chayse re-entered the melee, her short swords piercing the Upir's bloated gut with a double stab, and blood burst from the holes like waterfalls of deep red. Chayse and Ken got painted head to toe, and the Upir screamed.

The fight was yet to leave it, though, and without the extra weight of bloat it only increased in speed, frantic now, desperate to survive. It sprang on Ken, grabbed him with both hands, and, like he was a rag doll, slammed him into the ground. He hit the ground with such force he feared for his spine; the wind sprinted free from his caving lungs. The fiend dug its talons into the boiled leather cuirass that covered his chest and hauled him up, fetid breath fanning his face. Ken's strength had left him with his air, and though he fought, he could not resist a second slam.

Theron came to his aid, and with an immense upward sweep he lopped the Upir's right arm in two. It dropped Ken, took its mutilated limb in hand, and thumped Theron hard across the helm with it, dropping him to a knee. Ken watched from his hands and knees, breathless, unable to speak as Chayse wiped the blood from her eyes and sprang to save her brother.

~

Aldous shook the haze from his head and sat up. He took a breath. It hurt. He saw four figures, fuzzy, indistinct, moving apart, then together, then apart again. An inhuman shrieking filled the air, followed by a thud.

Where am I—

The mission. The ghouls. The Upir—

He blinked and his vision sharpened. Ken was down. Theron was down, and the devil beast was using its own mutilated arm to clobber him.

He glanced toward the distant trees. He could run. While the thing was busy killing his comrades, he could run. To the east. To the north. He could run and he could hide.

He never asked for any of this.

Get up. That is the man who saved you, the man who took you in, the man who has faith in you.

And he, a warrior of such renown, was on the ground before the monster.

What hope did Aldous have?

He should run. The Aldous in the basement of the church would run.

Aldous crawled up onto his hands and knees, the world spinning around him.

Chayse sprang and slashed, got in two good strikes, spraying the thing's blood in wide arcs, drawing the Upir's attention from her brother for the briefest moment. But still it would not fall.

The Upir dropped its arm and lashed with the claws of its remaining hand.

Aldous pushed to his feet, heart pounding, muscles tensing.

Chayse was not quick enough.

The razor talons bit into her mail.

The iron rings split.

Her flesh was exposed.

She hit the ground bleeding.

Chayse.

Theron.

Ken.

And Aldous knew he had never intended to run. He saw the staff of wolves and ravens in the grass. He dove to it, rolling as he took it in his hands. There was no specific intent. No decision. It simply *was*. The power of the staff entered him, became him, and he became it. He could feel its life, and it could drink from his.

The fiend battered Theron back to the ground as he started to rise, and then it turned on Chayse. She was hurt, struggling to rise.

It hurt Chayse and it will kill her.

The wolves howled in his mind and his heart; the ravens cawed in the marrow of his bones and the sinews of his muscle. The wooden staff began to glow. It was hot, burning his flesh, but he did not blister. His shirtsleeves caught flame.

Chayse. Chayse. Chayse. All he thought was her name. All he knew was the need to keep her safe. Keep them all safe.

The Upir turned, sensing danger.

Fire burst from the staff so quickly it was hard to say whether it did at all, or whether the energy of the flame transported from the staff directly into the Upir. The red-orange glow of the flames engulfed it from the inside out. Fire burst from its mouth as it opened on a silent scream. It flailed as it burned, stumbled aimlessly, stumbled to the blood on the ground that had spilt from its eviscerated gut, and, still burning, still screaming, it dropped to its hand and knees and tried to lap it up. The red puddle boiled beneath the writhing, living torch.

Melting to boiling plasma, boiling, burning to ash, it died the truest death.

Aldous heard his name, a distant whisper. Ken. Theron. Chayse. They were calling him, but he did not—could not—answer. He walked to the dying flames in the Upir's remains and put his hand into the fire, the staff still clutched in his other hand. The pain was so fierce Aldous wished to scream and howl, to sever the burning limb. He did none of that, for the flaming hand did not blister, and the fire did not spread. He walked to the hill of ghouls and placed his hand upon it. The fire was hungry, and it climbed the mound of dry flesh with ravenous speed.

He felt the drain, the singular drain he had felt the night he set the chapel ablaze, the first night he had ever used his magic. The mountain of gray meat was burning before him and then it wasn't. He was flying through black clouds, over rotten fields flooded with a sea of rats. She was among them, emerald green, everything so green. And then she turned and looked up and up to the sky. And he felt like she looked into his eyes, into his heart.

Aldous gasped and dropped the staff. The image faded.

"Fucking hell, now that was a good bit of wizardry," Ken said.

Aldous turned to him, then looked back at the fire. *Wizardry.* He was a wizard. He *was* a wizard.

Ken coughed and got to his feet. Theron was up next and rushed to Chayse, reaching her a second before Aldous did. She was standing before they got to her, staring at the bonfire. The wound was not nearly as bad as Aldous had thought; the splintered chain mail had cut her more than the Upir's claws. She was scraped but not gushing, and he thought she would be fine.

She looked in awe at their smoldering enemy and the pile of flaming ghouls.

"Aldous?" she said, the fire glinting in the reflection of her beautiful eyes.

"Aldous indeed," said Theron, the pride abundant in his voice.

"Fucking Aldous indeed!" shouted Ken, as he ran up and shook him by the shoulders. Aldous had never seen the large man so enthusiastic.

They were all looking at him, not the way they looked at a boy. The way they looked at a colleague, a comrade in arms.

He was well and truly one of them.

"You saved us all," Theron said, bowing his head and dragging off his helm. His golden hair was sweat-plastered to his skull. Blood splatter freckled his face in the places the helm had not covered. "Never have I fought an Upir such as that. I truly hope we never cross its creator."

"You would have figured it out without me," Aldous said, truly believing it.

"I really doubt that." Ken laughed, the sound like nails in a bucket. Aldous had rarely heard Ken laugh. He swept Aldous into his massive arms and squeezed. If he hadn't laughed first, and were Theron not ruffling Aldous' hair as if he were a puppy, Aldous might have thought Ken meant to crush the life from him. But it was a hug, and Aldous forgave him in an instant for his earlier hardness. This was the way of the pack.

"What stirred it in you? What gave you the key?" Chayse asked, looking at him in a way he had never seen her look at him before. It made him feel a little uneasy.

"You," Aldous said. "When I saw you fall, when I saw you were wounded... I don't know... I just knew what I had to do, and Theron and Ken, seeing you like that... I could not remain idle."

"Aldous, you truly did save us. I know that you have thought all along that you owe me something for that night in Norburg, but you owe me nothing. You owe none of us anything. Except, of course, an excellent written recounting of my exploits." Theron grinned.

"Perhaps Ken would like to try his hand at writing of our exploits," Aldous said.

"I could try, lad, but I think the task is better suited to you, wizard or no," said Ken.

"I have yet to document a single one of our adventures," Aldous said, looking at the ground.

"It's in your blood," Theron replied, poking him in the chest.

Aldous opened his mouth, closed it, and then he turned to the burning bodies. He even took in a deep breath through his nose, for he wanted to smell it now. He wanted to be sure. Then he thought of Wardbrook, and laughing and eating with his new family. He thought of the chapel, of Father Riker. He thought of his own father, not a sorcerer, just a man. He thought of him burning on that stake, screaming and begging as the fire climbed up his legs. He had stopped when his face began to blister and boil.

Then Aldous thought of the man he needed to become, for never again would he be a victim. Never again would he allow those he cared about to be victims.

~

It doesn't matter how many thousands of troops are on the field; it doesn't matter what they're armed with or what type of mail they're wearing. The side that wins is the side with a few good men. That is all it takes: a few good men can rally a thousand that are of the lesser making, the typical making.

Fighting is won by killers, by good, savage killers, the type of fellows who bend but never break. The type of blokes who walk into the thresher, and before they're out, they become it. If you can't kill with your bare hands, don't ever pick up a sword. Turn around now and become a baker, or a milkmaid.

A speech given by Marshall Theodore Rosehammer to new recruits the day Kendrick the Cold joined the king's army, in the second Norburg battalion, as documented by a scribe of the Honorable Count Salvenius.

~

CHAPTER TWENTY-TWO

KEN'S SPECIALTY

They were back at Dentin just before dawn. The duke had acted on Theron's warning, at least somewhat, for though they were not as ready as Theron would have liked, some preparations were in the making. Although the sun was yet to rise, the villagers were bustling their way toward the keep. Soldiers holding shields bearing the sigil of Dentin—a red fox on a black field—conducted and ordered the villagers to take only the bare necessities of food and water. A column of peasants, some carrying their goods, others dragging foodstuffs and small children in carts, wended along the road. Theron was impressed with how composed the soldiers were; he hoped they kept that composure when they set eyes upon the swarm. Aldous had seen them, a sea of rats, and Theron believed it.

The party spurred their steeds and galloped to the house of Duke Duncan.

The guards recognized them this time, and at a distance.

"Hunters, you have returned. What of the Upir?" asked the one named Sam.

"Dead," said Chayse. "The Upir and the mob of ghouls are

but smoke and ashes." They trotted through the already open gate alongside the column of peasants, and this close, Theron could read terror and panic in their faces.

The order to move to safer ground within the keep's walls had fed their terror.

"Huzzah! The hunters have killed the devil," yelled Sam, fist in the air, but the tired and confused peasants did not take up the cheer. They eyed the group of hunters warily and rushed through the gate.

The duke was right where they had left him, sitting in his chair in the study covered in his blankets, looking more haggard than he had the previous night.

"Mother died last night." His tone was hollow and distant, his expression vacant, for he was lost in his grief.

They sat around him and gave a moment of silence to show their respect.

"The Upir is dead," said Theron. "I do not intend to sound cold, but you must rise, Your Grace, you must rise and address your people. You must tell them what they are soon to face."

"What if you're wrong, Theron?" the duke asked. "I do not doubt your knowledge, but for the sake of joy and happiness, could you be wrong? Must I build fear in my people without proven cause? The rats were a plague that has passed. I see no rats now. Perhaps they will not come."

"They will come," Ken said with a long look at Aldous.

Theron could see in the duke's eyes that they were losing him, that terror and heartbreak would soon render his decisions incomprehensible.

"I could be wrong," Theron said without much conviction. "And for the sake of joy and happiness, I hope I am wrong." Theron shook his head and paused. "But I doubt it. The Emerald Witch wanted you to believe she would save your mother. It was her way into your confidence. Then she would steal your mind, your power, your dukedom. Dentin is a vast and profitable place, perfectly located to reach her tendrils into all of Brynth. Her plan was to do to Dentin what she did to Norburg, to bring your lands to ruin, to establish a firm foothold in Brynth. The Emerald Witch herself is plague. She desires to destroy this nation from the inside."

"But how do you know that as truth?" the duke asked. "It is pure conjecture."

"Logical conjecture," Theron shot back.

There was an overlong silence and the duke looked highly doubtful.

"She will take your women for demonic rites most foul," Aldous blurted.

This statement roused the duke as Theron's had not. "Foreigners taking our women?" he asked. "Why?"

Chayse rolled her eyes, and Theron frowned at her. This was the most life the duke had shown since their arrival. If talk of women was what it took, then talk of women it would be.

"The young ones," said Ken. "That is what she did in Norburg. Took the young ones, but we know not why."

"Yes," Theron said, his tone grim. "I don't as of yet know the method in the devil woman's madness, but she took the young women, and I can only fear for what. Something terrible is being designed in our realm of Brynth, Your Grace, and I am near to certain that your land and its people are set to be destroyed for it."

Tears welled in the duke's eyes at this. "How can we face such monsters? How can we win such a fight? I have but eight knights in my court, forty men-at-arms, and thirty-six archers under my command. If we gather men capable of fighting from the peasantry, we will stand with two hundred, perhaps a few more. How many of the rats do you think shall descend upon us?"

"We saw a sea of rats in Norburg," Theron said.

"A thousand," Ken said grimly.

Neither mentioned Aldous' vision, as if by silent agreement they avoided talk of magic and sorcery.

"Impossible odds." Duncan shook his head. "Impossible odds." He looked to Ken, perhaps sensing the soldier in their midst. "So we are doomed."

"The odds are good enough to fight," Ken said, and stood from his chair, chest out, jaw tight. "You hear me? The odds are bloody good enough. Now stop sniveling, Your Grace—stand up and come outside with us to address your people. Tell them a fight is coming and they don't have a damned choice about it, because it is fight or die."

Fabius, the duke's mustached servant, had remained silent until then, but at the verbal manhandling Kendrick had bestowed upon his lord, he stood and walked toward Ken. Theron watched and let it play out. Chayse was about to speak, but Theron raised a hand for her to stay silent and let Ken be a military man.

"Do you know who you are speaking to, you... you ape, you barbarian?" spewed the fuming Fabius.

The duke said nothing as Ken pressed his chest against Fabius and drove him back a few steps. The fancy opened his mouth to call for the guards, but Ken grabbed his cheeks with one powerful hand and squeezed the man's jaws shut in his grip. The duke looked on, his expression contemplative, as though he was in the midst of making a grave decision.

"What about you? Do you have any idea who you're talking to?" Ken did not yell. He spoke in a hush so all in the room had to strain to listen. "When the king's army smashed into Kallibar, I led my men through the breach, ten to one. Their favor. Didn't matter—me and the lads, we killed them all. The easterners had these magnificent crossbows. They shot a bolt every second for six seconds until the bloody

278

thing needed a reload. Do you know what happened then?" Ken waited for a response. None came. "Do you?" He raised his voice a little.

"No... no, I don't," said Fabius, his voice trembling.

"We just kept marching, heavy armor against a storm of bolts. I looked like a porcupine by the time we got through, but we got through, and their royal streets ran with blood.

"When we finally got to the palace, when Kallibar was a marshland of blood and guts, a red oasis in the endless sands of the far east, I took all the fancies, the ones who did a lot of talking, a lot of begging and offering up women and children so they could walk away, the ones that did no fighting while their people died in the streets, the ones that looked just like you." Ken paused, let go of Fabius' face, and gave him a little slap on the cheek. "I took them. Do you understand?" At that last remark, Ken finally cracked a little smile.

Theron shuddered as he watched the monologue come to an end. He had known Ken for a year. They had lived, trained, and eaten together, and not once did Theron hear the man speak so much, and with such purpose.

"I know who you are," whispered the duke, as if he were addressing a ghost. "I know who you are."

"I bet you do, Your Grace. I bet you do. Lucky for you, I'm on your side. Not so lucky for the rats and the witch. Now get out of that chair and your snuggly sheets and tell your people it's almost time for a fight."

Ken almost had the urge to smile, pleased with his persuasive power over the duke, pleased that he had swayed him to do what he must. They stood, the five of them, on the large balcony on the second floor of the keep that looked out into the outer courtyard. The entire population of Dentin all gathered there shoulder to shoulder.

The duke called for silence, and a trumpeter sounded his horn. The rabble grew quiet and they gazed up at the duke.

"Good people of Dentin," he began. "We have all heard what happened in Norburg. We have all heard of the swarm of rats that brought the capital of Southern Brynth to ruin. The hunters that stand beside me now fought in Norburg and escaped alive. They have just rid us of our Obour turned Upir, and the pack of ghouls that followed it." He held up both hands to attempt to maintain the silence as his audience reacted to the news. Then he continued, "But with this good news comes knowledge most dire."

The rabble began to grumble.

The duke's man, Fabius, bellowed for silence.

"The healer who came from origins unknown to Dentin," the duke began again over the few still doubtful voices, "the one who claimed to have intentions of healing my mother, was no healer, but a sorceress. A witch."

Again the rabble grew restless, fear moving through them like a wave.

"I have been informed that this very harlot of the dark arts was responsible for the fall of Norburg, for she has a control over the rats—"

The crowd cried out, and their voices overwhelmed the duke.

"Hold your tongues," Theron ordered, and the noise died down enough for the duke to continue.

"The plague was a curse of her design. She now intends to turn her evil onslaught upon us."

"You brought this on us!" came a shout from the crowd.

"You invited her here. Offered her shelter and succor!" came another.

"We are losing their sympathies," Theron said in Ken's ear as the duke tried to turn the crowd. "The duke is but a boy..."

"Then intercede," said Ken.

"A fine idea," replied Theron. "I am going to give you an introduction, and then you are going to explain what happens next."

"What? You're the leader, not me," said Ken. He had no intention of leading a military effort. He had had his fill of leading men to the slaughter. "I will fight. I will die fighting. But I will not lead again."

"I'm the leader in the hunt, Ken. We are coming to a great battle. I don't know much about great battles, and I surely don't know much about holding keeps. This is up to you, my friend, Kendrick the Cold, defender of Dentin. "

"This wasn't the deal," Ken said. He was not feeling cold; he was feeling warm, and his palms were sweaty.

"Hold your tongues!" Theron roared again at the crowd of peasants.

In all his military life, Ken had never heard an officer or above command such a booming voice. It came deep from Theron's belly and gave not the slightest crack; it was the voice of a mountain. The courtyard fell silent and Theron's voice echoed in the valley beyond.

"It matters not what you believe," the hunter began. "And it matters less where your duke acquired the news of Dentin's incoming peril or why the witch came here in the first place. Whether you accept it will not change what is to come. If you are cowards, and you run, so be it. But if Dentin falls, wherever you go will crumble soon after. There is no reasoning with this evil. There is no hiding from it. We must stand and fight it. We must stop it here."

"We are farmers, not soldiers!" a voice cried from the mob.

Ken stepped forward at this. "You will damn well be what

you need to be, or you will be watching your families die, shredded by rats before your eyes." There was a murmur from the crowd, but it was weak. "If we work together, if you follow the lead of Theron Ward, we will send the rats to the devil. We will send them with flame on their backs right to hell. We have a fort, we have bows, we shall set traps and fortify the walls with palisades, and, above all, we have tactics. The witch took Norburg from within. She will not be able to take Dentin from without."

The crowd began to calm. They began to listen.

"Your duke says we have two hundred fighting men—two hundred fighting men in a fortress on a hill against a thousand filthy vermin is the best odds I've ever had. This victory is going to be a hand-wrapped gift, as long as you stand and you give these fucking devils a fight!"

There was a few whoops and hurrahs from the duke's knights. Ken looked down at them. They were heavily armored and heavily scarred, a bit old, but they looked to be itching for a fight, a taste of their heroic pasts. At the cries of the knights, the men-at-arms and the archers took up the battle cry. Finally the peasantry joined in as well. Ken grinned at Theron. *All right. So you got an army—time to put them to use.*

~

After meeting with a group of the duke's knights and assigning them the task of gathering weapons for the peasants and breaking the men and older boys into working groups, they returned to the duke's study, cleared a central table, and spread out a map of Dentin. Theron's party, the duke, and three of his knights crowded around.

"Dentin Keep's dungeons—are they underground?" asked Theron.

"No, above ground," said the duke. "The keep has no subterranean level, for it was built on bedrock, hence the low walls. It was impossible to dig a deep enough foundation for high walls. Nor did we need walls higher than we have, given our position atop this hill."

"We are in luck, then," said Ken as he remembered the rumbling ground in Norburg.

Theron smiled and shook Ken by the shoulder. Ken smiled back.

"I fail to see how low walls are good luck," muttered the duke.

"It isn't the walls. It's the bedrock. The rats had tunnels beneath Norburg," said Theron. "They dug their way into the dungeon. If Dentin is on bedrock, they will not be able to come from below. They will need to charge the fortified keep head-on."

"So how do we go about fortifying the keep?" Aldous asked.

"Me and you, boy," said Ken, turning to Aldous. He was careful not to call the boy "wizard," for that would only undermine the confidence they had so recently won, and perhaps even see Aldous confined to the dungeon they had just been discussing. "We shall take every able-bodied villager, man and woman alike, and we shall gather wood from the nearby western ravine. We don't know where the rats will be coming from, but they will likely surround the keep, so we will need to palisade the whole perimeter. Two rows of spikes will be ideal."

"Understood." Aldous nodded.

"What of Theron and I?" asked Chayse. Her asking him for instruction came as great surprise, but Ken gave it. "You and Theron go with the knights and men-at-arms and dig up spike pits round the keep's outer walls, then return to the keep and help dig out a trench beneath the palisades." Ken turned to the knights. "Each of you choose men to send out as scouts." He paused. "Any sappers among you?"

"Aye, I was a sapper in the king's army two decades past, long before I was knighted, but it was my work digging pits and bringing down walls that saw me through the ranks," said a thick, white-whiskered man. He was studying Ken with a curious expression, as though he had a thought he could not quite put into words.

"Very good. Between you and the hunters' expertise, you'll set a good few nasty traps for the fuckers." *Time to set the duke and the fancy Fabius to task.* "Your Grace, you must supervise your servants to get the biggest cauldrons from the kitchens that are still small enough to fit on the fire step. We shall use them to pour boiling oil on the rats as they make attempt to escalade the walls."

"I will not supervise," said the duke. "I will carry the damn cauldrons myself right along with them. This is my keep. These are my walls. My people."

"I hardly think that the duke should—" Fabius began.

"Silence, Fabius!" shouted the duke. "Everyone must do their part—if mine is readying cauldrons, I am more than happy to oblige, and so are you."

"Yes, Your Grace." The fancy bowed his head.

"We're all sorted, then?" asked Ken.

"All sorted," said Theron, and Chayse nodded.

"Ready," affirmed Aldous.

"Aye, let us make this nightmare bleed," said one of the knights, the one who had been studying Ken. He still had a strange and wary expression on his face.

Ken could not help but wonder if it was only a matter of moments before the man pointed a finger and revealed him as Kendrick the Cold instead of Ken the Monster Hunter. But he could not spend overmuch time worrying about that now. The witch and her rats would soon be upon them.

~

"There is no animal quite like the wolf, not in all the world. At least not that I have seen. Sure, there are beasts that are bigger, beasts that are faster, stronger, with sharper teeth and sharper claws, but no creature has the same spirit as the wolf. No creature is so driven by love as the wolf."

"Love?" the boy asked his father, who was puffing on his pipe by the fire, as he stared off into memory, fondling the dagger-sized white fang round his neck.

"Yes, my boy, love. They have a love of life, a fire to persevere that they share only with mankind, and I sometimes wonder if it is greater in the wolf. Once in my travels before I met your mother, three other adventurers and myself came across a small pack of wolf pups. Such beautiful white was their fur. When they saw us, they howled and yelped in fear. Far off in the woods came an answering howl. These pups, you see, my son, they were alone, five of them—they were alone and cold. They were hungry. The sight tugged at my heart. We stayed with the pups, gave them some of our provisions, warmed them by the fire as a man would with a domesticated dog. In the night she came, the wolf mother. Three legs and a bleeding stump."

"What happened?" asked the boy.

"She was a great white wolf, near the size of a horse, fangs like daggers. She must have been caught in a trap when she heard her pups howl. She must have bitten off her own leg, for that is how much she loved them."

~

CHAPTER TWENTY-THREE

THE PACK PREVAILS

*A*ldous and Ken rode at the front of over three hundred villagers toward the ravine, pack horses and carts ready to be loaded with lumber and sent back quickly to the keep, where five of the knights would direct the placement of the palisades.

He could feel the witch's tendrils worming into the edges of his own magic. He could sense her, feel her, and with that awareness came dread.

"Do you think we will win this, Ken?" Aldous asked in a hush, not wanting to alarm the villagers just in case Ken's answer was too honest.

"Even if we do, by the end of it there won't be much left of Dentin," said Ken.

"What if the duke sent a rider to Aldwick? To Mavvern? To Baytown? To the bloody Imperial City?"

"He sent a rider to Baytown," responded Ken. "For it is the closest. It will still take a messenger four days at a breakneck pace and going through three good horses, running them all to death. Then a force would need to be gathered and they would need to march." Ken shook his head. "Best case, we will see the aid of a few hundred men in two weeks. Maybe she won't strike before then—"

"But she will," Aldous said. "Her swarm and her men are close. She is not more than one day as the crow flies."

Aldous realized that for the first time he did not doubt himself. He had seen the Emerald Witch as the Upir and the ghouls burned. And she had seen him.

Ken nodded, not doubting his assertion, and not asking how he knew it for fact. "She was likely planning this since the fall of Norburg," he said. "I reckon the killing will be done before anyone from Baytown gets here."

Aldous did not feel as he had in Norburg, or how he felt when Wardbrook was attacked. He did not have the fear like when they faced the ghouls. He was a wizard; he could control fire. He had done it once and he would do it again. But would it be enough? Would any of their preparations be enough? He did not know.

"Ken?"

"Yeah?"

"If I die, will you do something for me?"

"You won't die, lad, not if I can help it," Ken said.

"I appreciate that, but if I do…"

"If you do, then what?" Ken asked, his tone betraying irritation, a rarity to be sure. Aldous pressed on nonetheless, for he knew it was not that Ken was averse to making a promise, he was averse to confronting the thought of Aldous' death. Aldous knew this because the feeling was mutual. It was mutual with all of them. The thought of losing any member of the pack was a simply sickening prospect.

"There is a man in Aldwick. His name is Morde De'Sang."

"I know that name. The king's lead inquisitor?"

"Yes."

"What of him?"

"I'm sure you know what I am about to ask," said Aldous.

"I'm sure you are right, lad, but it would be better you say it aloud, just in case I have to carry out the deed. I'm thinking you want me to kill him, but what if you want me to bake him a cake?" asked Ken with his particular smile. "I want to be sure I am doing what you said and not what you implied."

Aldous gave a small chuckle. "Will you kill him for me, Ken, if I don't survive this?"

"Is he the man responsible for burning your father, and getting you into that bloody chapel of the Luminescent?"

Aldous thought of the man, tried to imagine his face when he barged into their home with his soldiers. He could not see it, though; he could only remember the name and the pleasure the man had taken in Darcie Weaver's suffering. "Yes," Aldous said.

"Aye, I'll kill him for you. I'll thank him first, but then I'll kill him." Ken reached across and slapped Aldous on the shoulder.

"Thank him? Why the fuck would you thank that bastard?" Aldous turned to Ken, brushing his hand away.

"Well, if he didn't do what he did, then we would have never met. You would have never met Theron Ward." Ken put it simply, and without emotion, as was his way.

"I wish I could have met you all on different terms."

"A world of different terms would never have allowed us to meet. Had your father not come to such a fate, you would still be there with him, rich and happy, with fine young girls swooning to marry you."

Aldous laughed.

"Had I not deserted," Ken continued, "I would still be far out in the east, burning helpless families and crucifying princes. Maybe I would have hung myself by now. The point is, in a world of different terms, we wouldn't be here, we wouldn't be doing what we can to save the innocent lives of Dentin."

Aldous stared at Ken for a long moment. He had a strange talent in delivering fact, a perfect and simple logic that seemed pointless to contest. Besides, Aldous didn't want to contest it.

"When we first met, I was terrified of you, though your hands were chained and your back bloodied. At Wardbrook, I started to think you might have been a good man, a good man who has done evil things, but still a good man." Aldous took a good look at Kendrick the Cold, his etched-stone features and his patchwork of scars across his face. He looked at his scarred arms in his shirtsleeves and his steel muscles beneath his mutilated flesh. This *was* a good man, a good man born into poverty, raised by hunger and loneliness and baptized in blood and slaughter, a man who chose a dark and twisted path for a time, but at the end of it there was a good man.

"What do you think now?" Ken asked. He scratched the back of his head and wouldn't meet Aldous' eyes.

"Now I *know* you're a good man. I know it to be an indisputable fact."

"I need a drink. It is too bloody hot out! Too bloody hot," whined Theron.

"You are soft, brother. The sun has only been up for three hours and you are already complaining," chastised Chayse.

"I am surprised to hear the great Theron Ward complaining so." The gray-mustached knight, who had introduced himself to Theron and Chayse as Sir Elizure Crowle, chuckled.

"I am a gentleman turned hunter, Sir Crowle, not a laborer. I don't have the emotional endurance to be digging like this under the hot sun." Theron stared up into the sky for a moment, and hoped that his travels never took him far south, and certainly never to the deserts in the east.

"Your sister seems to be doing fine," said Sir Crowle.

"My sister is a beast of burden," said Theron as he wiped sweat from his brow. "She has the endurance of a mule when it comes to labor. I sometimes wonder if we are indeed kin. Ah, this heat seems to be jogging my memory." Theron jabbed his shovel into the ground, resting one booted foot atop, and closed his eyes, putting his hands on his temples. "Yes. Yes, I remember... Mother and Father, they were speaking in their chamber... they thought me asleep, but I can see it as clear as day, hear it like the raindrops on a lonely tavern roof."

"Shut your mouth, Theron," said Chayse, as she flicked a load of dirt at him, splattering his clothes.

"They said you were adopted," he continued. "They were deciding whether or not they should ever tell you the truth, that you were raised until the age of five by a small herd of wild donkeys."

Sir Crowle gave a good chortle. "You're a horrible man, Theron Ward, a most horrible man," the knight said good-naturedly.

"He's nothing but a tyrant and a villain, my good knight, I assure you," said Chayse as she shoveled another load of dirt at Theron.

"This is the worst day so far this season—so bloody hot I feel I may begin to hallucinate," Theron said as he crawled from the ditch that he was digging and sat on the edge.

"Have you ever been to the great desert, son? The endless sands of the far east? When the king's army marched on Kallibar, now that was heat." The old knight paused for a moment and looked up at the sky. "Kallibar..." His tone was no longer one of good nature. He dropped his shovel and stared at Theron. "I recognize your man, Theron Ward."

"Do you?" Theron asked, calm and easy. He did not stand from where he sat, but he became all at once ready for potential conflict.

"I'm afraid I do."

"What are you afraid of?"

"He is a fugitive, a deserter, and a murderer." Sir Crowle was as solid as stone now, his face stern and his posture rigid. "There is a bounty on his head in Brynth. You are aware you are keeping company with such a man?"

There was no one close enough to hear their conversation other than Chayse, who remained silent.

"I am." Theron stood and stretched his arms then twisted at the hips, his eyes lazily half shut as he studied Sir Crowle. His mind was not as his body portrayed; his mind was ready for violence.

"I serve the king. I serve the Duke of Dentin and I serve the laws of Brynth," said the knight, who took a step forward now. Chayse looked to Theron; he gave her the slightest shift in his eyes, indicating for her to remain still.

"You serve the church, too? The God of Light?" Theron asked.

"I do." The old knight huffed.

"Well, after you are done capturing or killing Ken, go ahead and do the same to the boy that arrived in my company. He's a sorcerer, a bloody good one at that... scorched your Upir." He had no qualm revealing the lad's secret, for he had every intention of keeping him safe. Besides, when Aldous set the rats alight from the battlements, all would know his secret.

"You are a keeper of fugitives? That in itself is a crime. A crime punishable by death."

"I don't give a damn about your laws. I don't give a damn about the past of Kendrick the Cold, and I don't give a damn about the Church of the Luminescent. The way I see it, right now, is you have two choices." Theron walked away from the pit he had been digging and stood face to face with Sir Crowle. Chayse closed in a few feet behind him.

"And what choices would those be?" said the knight, not backing down an inch.

"The first choice is you keep on the path you are now marching. You attempt to notify your knights and your men-at-arms, and together you try to do in my friends." Theron paused. "If you try that, I will kill you where you stand, and I will throw you in the pit I just dug. Chayse and I will run to find Aldous and Ken. We will flee Dentin and we will kill any of your lads that try to stop us. When we are gone and the rats come, they will swarm over your keep's low walls and they will feast on your women and children." Crowle tried to speak, but Theron held up a hand and took another step so that he stood looking down his nose at the knight.

"That is the first choice, which is the evil choice, the selfish choice. Your second choice is to keep your mouth shut about whom you remember my companion to be, and together we preserve Dentin and we stop the swarm of rats from carrying out any more destruction of our country. When it is done, you can go ahead and keep serving the king and the church, and I will go ahead and continue to protect the weak and the forsaken."

They stood face to face for a while. Chayse moved to stand behind Crowle, at the ready, for if he made a move, then they would kill him and have him buried in that pit before anyone was the wiser.

"I yield," Elizure Crowle finally said. "But not because you threaten my life. And not because you threaten to leave Dentin to its fate. I yield because you protect the weak and forsaken and so while you might kill me to silence me, you would not forsake the women and children behind the walls. For that reason I grant you this reprieve. For now it is better that we work together. When it is done, though, I will bring your lads to justice," he added spitefully.

"I was told that wisdom came with age." Theron smiled. "Listening to you speak, it seems that all you have in your dotage is a greater ignorance. Do as you will."

"I'll find somewhere else to dig," Crowle spat, and walked away.

"Remember, if you but murmur a word of this to your men, you and only you will be responsible for Dentin's fate," Theron said to the knight's back. "We need both Ken and Aldous in order to win this fight." He did not respond, but Theron knew that Crowle was aware of his sincerity.

"Do you think Crowle is a legitimate threat?" Chayse asked Theron when the knight was out of earshot.

"No. He won't be during the assault, at least. If he survives then perhaps he will be, but that is the least of our worries." Theron went back into the pit and took up his spade.

"Will you actually kill the king's men if they try to take Ken and Aldous?" Chayse asked as she, too, began to dig once more.

"I did in Norburg, and I will do it again. I will not ask you to do the same, but if Sir Crowle rouses any of the survivors against my friends, I will put my sword to those that we now work to save."

"That does not seem like something Darcy Weaver would condone," said Chayse.

"Perhaps these friendships have changed me. Perhaps I care now more for the words of the younger Weaver." Theron drove the spade deep into the earth. "For he is present. He is within my current reality, and I do not doubt that the future of Aldous Weaver is a future that must be ensured. When he decided to come with us to Dentin, I knew that our fates, our destinies, will be forged by the unified choices of all four of us."

The spade came down; dirt went over his shoulder. The hole went deeper.

"Together we may stray from goodness, but perhaps that is needed to destroy the greater evils." Theron took a deep breath and exhaled. He stayed in the pit under the hot sun, and together he and Chayse dug. He thought of Darcy Weaver; he thought of goodness. They drove the spikes into the ground, and he thought of the Emerald Witch and he thought of evil. They covered the pit with branches and dirt, and he thought of doing whatever it took to destroy that evil, then he thought of doing one step more to protect the ones he loved.

~

They worked for fourteen hours. Aldous marveled at Ken's resolve. He worked twice as hard as any of the villagers or men-at-arms. He did not break to eat, and he rarely took a sip from his canteen. He drove long, thick logs into the ground and he sharpened them fierce, and so the two rows got done around the whole perimeter of the keep faster than they had expected. Instead of calling it a day, Ken ordered everyone, himself included, to get to work digging the trench around the perimeter of the hill on which Dentin Keep stood.

Some of the men mumbled at this. Ken reminded them that the more work they put in today, the less friends and family they would need to watch die when the fighting got started. That got them digging.

~

When the day was finally done and the sun was well down, Aldous, Ken, Chayse, and Theron all sat together in a cozy chamber that had been assigned to Theron. They wanted to be alone, and so they had brought their bowls from the great hall to sit on the floor before the fire. No one commented when they left. The great hall was overcrowded and those who left made way for those yet to be fed.

They ate a weak stew with weaker ale, for the provisions had been watered down in the expectation of the possibility of a long siege. It was certainly not the food and drink of Wardbrook, but the company was the same, and for Aldous that was all that mattered.

"Ken, this is your doing," said Theron. "You, and you alone, are to thank for the fortification of this keep. It is your doing that saw me out under the hot sun all day laboring like a common peasant."

"Thank you, Theron," Ken said, ignoring the second part of Theron's statement.

"It is true—if we survive this, much of the thanks will be owed to you," said Chayse.

"Not *if*, but *when* we survive this," Aldous said in a stern tone. A tone that he tried for the first time. They all smiled at him and clinked their mugs of ale.

Theron's expression changed and grew somber.

"The old knight, Sir Crowle. He knows who you are, Ken. He told me so as we dug the far ditches."

"Does he, now?" Ken seemed unconcerned.

"He was none too happy," Chayse added.

"What does he plan to do about me?"

"He says he will arrest you after the siege, carry out the king's justice." Theron chuckled.

"To which you said?"

"I told him to carry out the church's retribution at the same time, that he should arrest Aldous also, for he is a wizard."

Aldous spewed ale all over the floor.

"They will do as they must, and we will do as we must," Theron said. "There was no harm in the telling, for all will know soon enough when you are lighting rats on fire from the battlements." Theron laughed, Ken laughed, Chayse laughed, and, although he was a bit uneasy at first, Aldous finally laughed. *Fuck the king, and fuck the church*, he thought. *I am here risking my life for the citizens of a country that has done nothing but wrong to me. If at the end they still see me as a monster, so be it.*

"I had asked Ken earlier whether or not I should conceal my magic in the fight. I suppose now I have my answer."

"You do," said Theron. "The people of Dentin will be glad for your magic when this is over. They will be glad for Kendrick the Cold as well. I made it obvious before that I wished for the two of you to conceal your identities." Theron paused. "In truth, this was out of fear for my own name as well as your safety. I no longer wish for that. You are who you are. Together we will save Dentin and we will seek a king's pardon for you both."

"If the king denies us a pardon?" asked Ken.

"Likely he will. And then the road becomes our home, and we carry on the hunt. We abandon Wardbrook." Theron looked at Ken as he spoke, and then to Aldous. "Together."

"What of the people at Wardbrook you are responsible for?" Chayse asked.

"When their identities are revealed, you and I will become fugitives as well, simply by association. Our land will be taken from us by the king. My people are in his hands now, no matter what."

Aldous felt sad that Theron was forced to make this choice, while at the same time he was glad—no, more than glad—that Theron had chosen him.

"Chayse?" Aldous turned to her, for her desires must be considered as well.

"I agree with Theron," she said after a painfully long and somber silence. "I have only fought by your sides twice, and recently, but it was not the fighting that makes me stand by my brother in this. It is the differences we overcame living together at Wardbrook. We will ride together, realm to realm, and we will follow our destined path. We will banish evil and destroy monsters in every nook and cranny that we find them. Theron is a hunter. I am a hunter. It is more than what we do. It is who we are." Chayse downed the rest of her ale. "The men that hunted with me in Azria were good at their business, but none of them were Theron Ward." Chayse looked to her brother. "I hate to admit it, but none of them were Kendrick the fucking Cold." She reached to Ken and they clanked their mugs.

"Lady Chayse," Ken said, bowing his head.

Then she finally looked to Aldous with something in her eyes that made his heart erupt. "And they would all marvel if they set eyes upon the great wizard, the glorious Aldous Weaver." He held out his mug for a clink, but she leaned in and kissed him on the cheek. Fiery passion ignited in his loins. He let out a sigh and they all laughed, and Ken ruffled his hair.

Aldous had little sleep between thoughts of the coming fight and the recollection of Chayse's warm lips on his cheek. He thought of the battle to come. He thought of the blood and the killing. He thought of Theron or Ken or Chayse dying like his mother had died, like his father had died, and he fought away the images, for he was afraid that he might accidently set the bed on fire.

So he forced his mind to happy thoughts, ridiculous thoughts, thoughts that were years and miles and likely realities away, where he was a great wizard and he and Chayse were married, and Ken and Theron were the uncles to his children.

When sleep finally took him, though, his dreams did not remain as he would have wished. He was running through the ravine near Dentin; he was leaping through bushes and pouncing over fallen trees. He saw them in the valley. The vermin were hungry and they were at the door. The witch was dressed in her finest emerald silk. She smiled at Aldous; she was ready for the dinner party.

The sun wasn't up yet when Aldous heard the hammering on the door to Theron's room a few doors down.

"Wake up, Lord Wardbrook! Riders have been spotted! Wake up! They hold a white flag."

Ken, Theron, Aldous, Chayse, and the duke and his knights stood on the wall above the gate, the defenses' highest point. Ken had not slept well, not well at all. Ever since Norburg he had become a dreamer. Every dream was the same. Every dream was of his wife, his wife-turned-rat eating his child. His wife-turned-rat whom he could not save. He dreamed of a mountain of bodies, a mountain that promised to grow. It was a marvel that a single night could allow him to dream of all that, but it did allow, as it had allowed every night since Norburg. And each time he dreamed, he saw the painting from the count's chamber, the leviathan rising.

The sky was gray that morning, the gray that they had thought had maybe passed, the gray that hid yesterday's smoldering sun, the gray that birthed a cold summer day. Under the tragic sky they came riding, five men on mares as black as coal, great and mighty steeds, muscles glistening with sweat from a hard ride, but not a far one. They came from a camp close by. Their armor was cast from black iron, much like the helm Theron wore from the north. But the metalwork on the riders' was grotesque; the plates were unbalanced and spiked, and covered the riders head to toe, but for small slots for the eyes.

"We bring the demands of the Emerald Queen," roared one of the riders, his faceplate lifted to expose a visage more mangled than Ken's.

"Who is this Emerald Queen?" called back Theron. "We know of no queen. We answer only to the king."

"You know of whom I speak, hunter," said the rider. "She knows you are here."

"What does she want? There was no talk of terms at Norburg, only a massacre."

"Count Salvenius caused that massacre. He denied my queen that which she desired."

"Queen of what?"

"Queen of Brynth, and all shall kneel before her. The Emerald Queen wishes to dine with you, Theron Ward. She extends an invitation for you to join her at her camp. Perhaps you will be offered some opportunity to serve beneath her, and you will not be slaughtered with the rest of Dentin's filth."

"Know this, knight of rats. The only time I'd ever consider serving beneath your queen is if I were to be giving her a good plowing from the bottom, but the Emerald Whore already has enough vermin cocks to see that done."

Well done, Theron Ward. Well done. Ken could not see the fury on the man's face from the distance, but he knew it was there.

"You will dearly regret those words, Theron Ward. I will spit on your gore after the swarm shreds you apart."

"Spit on your own, you rotten bastard." Chayse's words were given a bit more punch by the arrow she shot into the rider's exposed mouth. He fell from his horse and twitched for a bit on the ground, spurting blood up the arrow shaft and onto the grass around him, and then he died.

"Under parlay?" His Grace asked, eyes wide.

"I don't parlay with rats," Chayse said. "Besides, he was offering parlay for Theron alone. There was no mention of letting anyone else live."

"A fine shot," the duke replied, and Ken took that to mean they would see no opposition from him.

The other riders said nothing, but they did not retreat right away. They waited for a few moments, until the men on the battlements shifted with unease, the menace of the black iron knights amplified by their very stillness. Then they lit torches, turned, and trotted some distance before taking to gallop. As they went, they set fire to the fields and houses they passed.

~

"There is only conflict, sweet child. That is the force beneath every-thing, the struggle for control, for power. That is all there is; that is why I teach you how to fight," the mother said to her golden-haired boy.

"Not everything, I am sure," said the boy.

"Everything," said his mother, her voice cold. "Raise your sword."

"Even love is conflict?" asked the boy.

"Especially love."

~

CHAPTER TWENTY-FOUR

HUNTERS' BATTLE

*I*t was night and it was chill. The clouds remained. The burning homes and fields were all but ash.

They heard them before they saw them. The squealing rats came with no torches, no siege engines, no lanterns. They did not light fire arrows and release a volley; they just tramped through the shadows, a black tide under a moonless sky. They squealed and shrieked; they gagged and retched; they snapped their jaws and dragged their claws.

"Not a man fires until my say-so," Theron yelled. "I know you are all afraid. Use that fear, use your animal desire to live, to slaughter these beasts at your door. When we win, and when they all die, every man who fights will be etched into legend as the ones who crushed the plague of Brynth." Theron clanged his pike on the battlements. The archers on the battlements roared and did the same. It was his first full-scale battle, and Theron Ward was afraid. And he was angry. And he accepted that his life, the life he had chosen, had led to this.

Ken was on the southern side of the outer wall, whereas

Theron stood on the northern. He heard Ken shout, "Most of you lads are farmers?"

"Aye!" came the farmers' cry.

"Then none of you are strangers to killing fucking rats! The only difference is their size and the guts you'll be spilling from them as they squeal!"

"Rah!" cried the farmers, and they hammered their pikes ever harder on the walls.

"This fight will be fast, and it will be savage," Theron said, voice ringing down the walls. "They will not strike in waves and they will not tire; they will come as a single great tide of meat! Give them the grinder!" Spittle flew from his mouth, and he could feel the muscles in his neck strain as he formed words to rally the men before they stared into horror, before they made the devils of hell bleed.

"Aldous, give us light!" Theron called up past the court-yard to the keep, where Aldous, Chayse, and the archers were at the ready on the higher position. They would fire over the walls past the pikemen and weaken the further ranks of rats.

A moment passed. Aldous did not produce light.

A second, longer moment passed. Still nothing.

"Aldous?" Ken called up.

"I'm trying to focus!" the wizard cried back, his voice cracking.

Theron could see them now, the rats. The first of them were close enough to be visible in the dark. They entered the trench and crawled out the other side.

"Chayse, give him a rub that will get his fire lit!" Ken yelled, followed by a deep, bestial laugh.

Whether Chayse took Ken's order or not, Theron could not know, but Aldous sent a mass of fire the size of a burning keg into the swarm. It hit them just under a hundred feet away from the trench, and it burst on impact.

"Fire!" Theron yelled, and a susurrus carried as arrow

after arrow arced through the night, hidden by the darkness. The creatures started screaming as they were taken by arrow or fire, and the ones that were caught on fire ran wildly, creating greater visibility on the field. Theron's blood ran cold as he set eyes upon the sheer number of them. When he had said days past that there would be over a thousand, he had been hoping that number was a thousand and one at most. Over two thousand would have been more accurate.

On the wall, whispers passed from man to man: "Sorcerer... demon..."

The smell hit them first, rotting, putrid, like a dead sheep left under the sun. And then the first rat came over the palisade.

"Eyes front, you bastards, and be thankful such a demon is now standing with you!" Theron bellowed as he drove his pike into the rat's throat. It fell into the crevice between the palisades and the wall.

And the escalade began. With immense speed and force, the swarm rushed through the trench, crawling over each other, and ripping themselves apart on the palisades. It did not slow them. They did not care about pain. They did not fear. They did not reason. They were hungry for death and slaughter.

"Oil! Pour the oil!" Ken cried.

The men on the walls tipped the great cauldrons that were heated above small fires. The oil poured into the fissure between the palisades and the wall first, and the shriek of the downed rats could split glass as the smoldering black liquid set their bodies to a bubbling boil. Men close by vomited off the wall as the scent rose to them. From the fissure, the oil ran past the logs of the palisades and seared the feet of those rodent devils in the trench. They squeaked and squealed, but they kept driving forth. Some stuffed their own kin into the hot oil and clambered over the downed bodies to avoid the terrific heat.

"Light it now!" Theron ordered. A man next to him skewered a rat that was climbing the wall. When he withdrew his pike there was a hissing noise from the gaping wound in the fiend's lung. Theron drove his own pike down the throat of a snapping beast closer to himself, and sent it tumbling down.

The torches dropped and lines of fire burst from the base of the wall and ran into the circle of the trench, which burst into flame entirely. The magnitude of what the people of Dentin faced became visible. From all sides they came; the purple and black pustulant carbuncles writhed and glowed on their flesh. Some were naked of fur, wrinkled and pale; others had tufts; more had long, mangled fur like that of an unkempt dog. They all had claws, though, claws and grinding maws. Some hulked, while others were frail and decrepit, but all came forth, the tide of obsidian sick wading up the hill.

Some of the men on the south wall jumped down from their places. They tried to run and hide in the keep.

"Hold! Hold, you scum! Back on this wall, back on the fire step, or I shall drag you back up here myself and throw you over to the horror below!" Theron heard Ken from down the wall and turned just as Ken caught one man by the back of his shirt and threw him back to his place. The others turned, some shaking so hard they could barely walk, and returned to their places at the wall.

Theron caught Ken's eye and nodded, and Ken nodded back.

The circle of fire that surrounded the trench did not slow the rats, but it hurt them. One in three came through fully ablaze and screaming, mostly the shaggy ones. The others popped and steamed, their naked flesh blistering from the heat, but they did not fall and turn and smolder. They kept on. So many impaled themselves on the palisades that some of the spikes splintered and snapped under the weight of the squirming things skewered on them.

More keg-sized balls of fire came hurling from the keep and into the mass beyond the wall. Chunks of meat and limbs flew into the air, ablaze as they did, and Theron silently thanked Aldous, and he silently thanked his mother for the catalyst the boy now used to bring great suffering upon the rats.

~

"Stab them, gut them, burn them!" Ken held a pike at its center in each hand above his head, and he impaled and retracted at a steady pace. His part of the wall was beginning to pile so high with corpses that the rats could touch the top by crawling over their own dead and dying. "If we keep up like this the fuckers will never get over the outer wall. Show them we have fangs; show them we are hounds."

There was a cheer, and the men on the southern wall were rallied by Ken's fury as he impaled the fiends.

Ken stared at four of the knights and a handful of the men-at-arms pushing themselves against the gate as it thudded and buckled from the blows of the vermin beyond. Above on the platform, villagers poured oil and set the things ablaze, but the seemingly endless advance of the rats quickly stomped out the fires on the dead backs.

It was not enough. The gate would not hold.

"Kendrick! The gate is going to give!" cried Sir Crowle.

"If I leave this post, they will come over the wall!" Ken called back as he ran east down the southern wall to slaughter a rat peeking his head over the fire step. For this he threw his pikes into the mass of foes and drew his axe and mace. He splattered five of the men on the step with the creature's blood and brains. "The bodies, you fool! Drag the corpses over to build a mound!"

He waited only long enough to see Sir Crowle nod at him before he turned back to the men fighting at his side. All around them the hail of arrows from the archers above continued to fall. And Aldous continued to send fireballs down to light the rats ablaze.

"Swords and axes!" Ken cried. "We have made an easy escalade for them from their dead. Swords and fucking axes; they are coming up too quickly and too close. Time for a fight!"

The first man on the wall to die got his gut torn open by a putrid claw, and the lads close by screamed and shouted as they hacked the culprit to bits. A second rat emerged and pulled the wounded man into the abyss of rats by his spilt intestines.

"Hold! Do not panic—if you panic, they get through! If they get through, we die!" Ken swung his axe into an oncoming claw and split the assailant's limb apart with a crack of bone and a spray of blood. A mace blow sent it back over the wall and tumbling down its dead kin through the shattered palisade, and into the trench where the rest of its life burned away.

Another man went down on the wall, then another, and a third in quick succession. Ten paces down from Ken, a good-sized breach was beginning to form and the rats were making it through. Three of them leapt down from the fire step and charged the men-at-arms in the courtyard.

"Time to wet your blades, lads!" yelled one of them, and he was the first to die. Gullet torn out by the first rat, he hit the ground, hands on his throat trying to cork the leak. It did him no good.

Ken turned back to the wall and pushed his way to the

breach. The stone fire step had become slippery with blood and guts, so he took his time.

They're through now, and they'll keep making holes. No need to rush, not anymore—just keep killing, nice and steady.

A dying man stumbled into Ken, screaming, "God save us! Luminescent save us all!" as he bumbled wildly, his arm missing, having been chewed and clawed off like it was a piece of jerky. Ken looked him in the eyes a moment; tears rolled down the man's ash- and blood-stained face. "My wife! My wife!" he croaked, the certainty of death in his eyes. Ken used the axe to slit his throat, a mercy, tossed his body into the courtyard, and moved to the widening leak of rats.

Sentiment is long gone.

"Close it up!" he called as he buried the beard of his axe in rodent skull. The rat twitched and Ken smashed the things face apart with his mace. The snout caved in. The jaw ripped off, and then it was just pulverized flesh. *On to the next.*

His calm confidence inspired the nearby troops, and they recovered and hacked their swords and axes madly into the tide. Men went down, but others filled their places. They were frenzied, they were wild, and they were hungry for life. They were rat hounds on the rats; they were mad curs in the pit, purpose and humanity all forgotten. All that remained was the animal violence, the fury only heightened by the growing slaughter. Men vomited and pissed their britches, they screamed and sobbed, but most of all they just kept killing, and killing because they needed to.

"There it is! Fight, you dogs. Fight! Show the devil your spirit. Let him know that his realm is not the only home of demons." They closed the gap, but just as they did another began to form. Ken looked to the north, where he saw Theron surrounded. All the men around him dead, rats to his sides and front, but the hunter only became more deadly in his solitude, for his great claymore swung freely and severed limb and head from body like a farmer scything through the fields.

"Aldous! Chayse! Focus your fire to the north wall. It is falling. It is overrun," Ken called up to the keep.

Aldous released another fireball, this one bigger and faster than the others. A chunk of wall exploded, and with it over a score of rats. Flaming bits of meat soared into the sky then rained down on the next invaders. Flame arrows poured into the burning breach and the screaming rats died by the dozen, but still they came.

Ken leapt from the south wall and charged across the courtyard, ignoring the fights between the men-at-arms and the rats that leaked through the south side. The north side was no longer leaking but gushing.

"Theron! To me!" Ken called to the hunter.

Theron finished a swing then leapt from the north wall, and came to Ken. The horns on his helm dripped with blood, his mail coat shimmered red and black, and the blood groove in his sword drained into the drenched ground below.

"Close ranks! Form a shield wall! Chayse, Aldous! We need you down here."

~

Aldous braced his shoulder against the wall to stay upright, the staff in his hand heavy and consuming. From far away he heard Ken calling for their aid.

"Swords, shields, into the fight!" Chayse said to the archers, who had thus far had remained out of the thresher.

The men roared and followed Chayse from the balconies and battlements back into the keep. Depleted, Aldous forced himself to pick up a shield in his left hand while he kept his staff in his right, leaning his weight on it as he followed the others down the stone steps. They gave a final rallying cry before they burst from the door into the courtyard.

It was frightening from above, but it was not like this. The vantage point had given Aldous confidence; entering the heart of the melee sapped him of that. But Theron, Chayse, and Ken stood fearless, as would he.

The remaining villagers, men-at-arms, and knights closed ranks and formed a shield wall. Aldous found himself within the protected formation. They back-stepped toward the door to the keep. A few archers remained above to give suppressive fire.

A rat took a quarrel and just kept coming unfazed. Aldous squeezed his way to the front of the formation, where a wild Theron pulled the smaller rats one at a time behind the shield wall and then stabbed, and stomped the guts and brains from them. Ken did the same.

"A warming sight, to see you here with us, Aldous!" Theron said, his voice wavering as he repeatedly drove his boot into the face of a twitching man-sized rat, its eyeballs bursting from the obliterated skull on the last stomp.

"Perhaps you shall find this more warming," Aldous said, then he raised his staff over his shield like a spear. *Breath deep, relax, focus. Small bursts.* He visualized a swirling beam of fire, a tight whirlwind of burning death shooting from the staff, and then it was so.

A thin funnel of flame shot from the raven side of the staff, and set three incoming rats to fire. Spears thrust into them from the shield wall. Chayse pushed her way beside Aldous. Halberd in hand, she got to thrusting and hacking right away.

Every time a man fell the formation grew tighter, but for every man that died so did five rats.

"They are thinning!" Ken gave a drubbing blow with his

mace. "Keep at it, they are fucking thinning! We shall fight to the last man, for they will fight to the last rat."

It was easier said than done. The men were far past the point of exhaustion. Some were mortally wounded but kept fighting, kept fighting on fury and hatred alone. Hatred for being eaten alive by rats to be the end of a hard life. A hard life was only justified by a hard death. So the men of Dentin dug deep, past their hearts, and they found that hatred and spite needed to fuel that hard death.

When the storm finally began to calm, there were fewer than three score of them left. It began to calm, but it was not over. The grass of the courtyard was covered, every inch and more, hundreds of dead men and over a thousand dead rats. The formation was broken. The survivors walked around freely, butchering the stragglers and the ones too wounded to fight back.

"We have won! We have repelled the devils! We have won!" roared the old knight, Sir Crowle, thumping Ken on the back. "Well done, my boy. Well done."

The remaining survivors took up the cheer.

"Victory!"

"Dentin is saved!"

"Our women and children are safe."

"She is here," Aldous whispered, feeling the presence of the Emerald Witch like the slide of dank mud oozing along skin. He looked to Theron, but the hunter had already stilled, head cocked, expression dark, as if he, too, sensed her.

"Silence," Theron said, just over a whisper. No one could hear him but Aldous. "Silence, you dogs!"

Where the energy came from for the volume Theron had just found, Aldous did not know, but at his call the cheers broke.

"She is here. And she brings reinforcements. It is not over. Ready yourselves." The hunter took a deep breath. He looked too tired to stand, and he looked too tired to live, never mind keep fighting. Yet his eyes, peering from his mighty horned helm, told a different story than his body. His eyes were those of a beast corncred and looking at death, feral and refusing.

A great thundering vibrated the front gate. Then came a bestial roar, like a bear but greater in sound and higher in pitch. Such a bellow Aldous had never heard.

Ken stepped forth to Theron's side. He too looked exhausted, but at the same time fully composed, ready, and calm. If it was a mask, there was no horror in the world of men or the pits of hell that could crack it. His calm was ice.

The gate cracked, and through it came an arm larger than a man. Again, whatever was beyond gave its roar.

Chayse notched an arrow and stood with Ken and Theron. She was haggard and on the verge of collapse from exhaustion. Her hair was wild and matted with dried blood and pus from her foes. She was still beautiful to Aldous even then.

She looked back at Aldous, unfazed by the second giant fist smashing through the gate.

"Join us, Aldous—come fight with us." Her words were soft and inviting. Aldous was tired, he was drained from his magic, he felt as if he were plastered drunk, and he could hardly stand. He was not sure how much fire he had left within. But he went to them, for there was nowhere else he would want to be but by their sides, and they stood, ready for whatever came through that gate.

A final blow, and the thing splintered through, a colossus, a true behemoth amongst its fallen ilk. It was twice the size of the mighty brute they had fought in the dungeons of Norburg. Its great fists were the size of boulders, and splintered wood protruded from its boil-covered knuckles. Its head was larger than a horse's, and it had a monstrous, overgrown tooth on the lower jaw that pierced the upper lip.

It stood in the shattered gateway, and from the smoke she appeared. The Emerald Witch. She wore a green dress, long and thin, that clung to her form. She trotted in atop a mare the same un-shimmering black as her long, flat hair. Her pale white skin was a lifeless light in the dark reds of gore, the vibrant orange and vermillion of the flames, the blackened sky, and the piles of rats. Her black iron knights were next to materialize from the fog, nine of them, with a score of the last rats. Lastly came the ones that set Aldous' blood to freeze beyond anything they had faced thus far. Five seekers, eyes glowing blue fire, their wide hats shadowing their faces.

They, of all the things that had come this night, were here for *him*.

~

It is a sensation beyond words, beyond art and music, beyond any alchemical substance. Sadly, I am not an artist, nor am I a musician, and I cannot through the medium of a book provide you the reader with any alchemical substances, so words are all I have to help you understand the process of magic. There is a cost, you see, a sort of economy of life and death, a delicate scientific/mathematical balance that must be kept within the self, that must be in an instant understood and controlled, or else the scale will lean too far toward death, and the death shall be your own. Magic is neither altogether a sensation of pleasure nor a sensation of pain; it is rather the feeling of riding the wind of eternity—in a ship or as a bird, it does not matter. What matters is that the mage understands he is riding on nature's force. Riding a magnificent storm, and if the mage does not keep his sail steady, his wings steady, the result will be catastrophic. The forces of the elements are outside; they exist in the world not within the body, and the mage is able to unconsciously connect with the forces, to ride them, to let them set their coarse. The greatest spellcasters can tame the forces. They themselves become the catalyst of nature and they decide how it flows. The pursuit of such control is the most common cause of death for magi—next to burning at the stake, of course.

Phelix Calliban, from his forbidden text An Introduction to the Forces.

~

CHAPTER TWENTY-FIVE

DENTIN'S DEMONS

*K*en stared at the massive beast that had bludgeoned down the fortress' gates with its bare hands, and for the first time in a long time, Kendrick the Cold felt fear, true and pure. If he hadn't already been to hell in the east, he could be damn sure he would see it now.

Before dawn, or before his death, he would know hell.

He would know hell, for there was no question that their meager band of exhausted warriors could not hold against the new threat. There was no hope of saving those women and children they had sworn to protect. Despite all the brave fallen lads who had fought as they pissed themselves in terror, Dentin would fall as Norburg had fallen. The rats would feed.

And Ken's last hope at salvation would drown in the blood-soaked mud.

The thing before them now, the Emerald Witch and those dooming, black iron knights, had Ken believing the whole struggle was for naught.

"Are you afraid, Kendrick?" It was Chayse who asked the question as the final clash neared.

"Yes." He turned to her, expecting to see a sneer and finding only compassion.

"It's all right. I think I have been afraid every day of my life since my parents left us. Use it to fight."

"It was an honor and a privilege knowing you, fighting with you, Lady Chayse," Ken whispered to her.

"And you, Kendrick of Wardbrook," she answered.

The Emerald Witch was a few hundred feet away, smiling.

"Enough," barked Theron. "Don't you two get fucking sentimental, not yet. We kill them like we killed the rest."

Ken turned to Theron. The man was shaking, likely more from exhaustion than anything else, for he alone must have killed over a hundred of the rats. The hunter turned to the remaining men. They stood with their backs pressed up against the keep. Ken thought some of them stayed on their feet only because of those cold stones at their backs.

"Hear me now, men of Dentin. Champions of Dentin, we will win this fight. On this hill, in this courtyard, let us butcher the rest of our nation's enemies." The men stared at him. Theron lifted his claymore, and Ken wondered where he got the strength to raise the thing above his head. "Raise your swords! Raise them! Fear not death, for it has already taken us. Fear not pain, for it has already been suffered! Those are your wives behind us in that keep. Those are your children!" Theron roared. "Let us be the devils before dawn. Let us be savage. Let us be demons."

The men roared a great cry, as mad a sound as the rats. It was fevered and it was deranged, it was the rallying cry of dead men, and it built a magnificent rage in Ken. The bestial screams of Dentin's demons grew, and a thing, years dormant in Ken's breast, began to truly wake. He felt the chill; his spine was frost and his veins were ice.

"Charge!" Ken shouted.

And they charged. They raced one another to the foe. Strategy was gone. This was pack against pack; animal against animal; fangs of iron and steel biting against the plague and the Emerald Witch.

And Kendrick Solomon Kelmoor felt cold once more.

At a hundred paces, Ken watched as the Emerald Witch's eyes rolled back into her skull and her colossus came rushing forward, the remaining rats, the black knights, and the seekers close behind.

A rat leapt through the air at Theron, who was at the head of the charge. He batted it down with his claymore, splitting its chest apart right to the mid-belly, and it hit the ground and added to the thousands of dead on Dentin's earth. With a low-throated growl, the colossus swung a tree-sized arm at Theron. The hunter ducked and rolled, rising—sword outstretched—to impale another rat. Ken pirouetted around the hunter and went head-on at the colossus.

After the mighty beast missed Theron it turned its focus on the others. It brought a fist down on a man, snapping his neck and pulverizing his skull. Ken assessed the beast with a warrior's eye. The head was too high, even the chest was too high, the belly too protected. The tendons at the back of its knee and the unstable joint were less so. So he attacked the beast's knee; he struck the side of the joint hard with his mace. The bone was so dense it was like hitting an iron deposit, and the strike rocked Ken to his core. The mountain of a rat screamed and tried to whirl around to deal with Ken, but his mace had done some damage and the thing was slow.

A blast of fire hit the fiend in the chest, and then Ken saw a blue blast and Aldous was screaming somewhere in the courtyard.

Dammit.

The giant rat screamed as it slapped at the flames on its chest.

Finish it.

It would not be so easy.

Ken sensed movement and turned just in time to deflect an incoming blow from a great sword-wielding, black-armored foe. The enemy swung again, hazy green eyes glowing through the eye slot in his faceplate. Ken blocked, then locked the blade in the beard of his axe and pulled it to his left side. He brought the mace down on the bastard's helm with everything he had. The black iron dented beneath the blow and the knight fell to his knees. Three more quick and powerful blows caved the helm in completely as blood and brain leaked out of the eye slot.

Ken turned to see the colossus put out the fire, swiping at it and shrieking until only a boiling, pulsating burn the size of a man remained on its chest and abdomen. It re-entered the fray, mulching men into sprays of gore and stains on the earth. Ken saw the old knight Sir Crowle then, his white mustache stained black-red with the blood of the blighted fiends. His eyes were mad and he swept a mighty war hammer into one of the black iron knights, knocking him to ground, where a man-at-arms pulled off the enemy's helm and set to repeatedly stabbing him in the mouth and neck with a dagger.

Ken looked around the field for Aldous, and he saw him. The wizard was on his knees, the seekers approaching. The seekers had gained some measure of control over the boy. He went for the seekers surrounding the wizard, but one stepped into his path.

The man was outlandishly tall and lean, with a long face, his eyes an unblinking blue glow. His blade was an eastern-style saber, his movements like a viper as he attacked. Ken deflected two strokes then was bitten by a third. The weapon opened a gash on his chest and he leapt back to create some distance. Ken had seen the seekers fight at Kallibar, and he thought even then that he wished to never do battle with those snakelike warriors. But wishes meant as much as prayers.

～

Theron, back to back with Sir Crowle, took the heads of the foes the old knight had bludgeoned to the ground with his hammer. All but one of the black iron knights were dead. The last one was weaving his way through the rat colossus' legs, slaughtering the men that tried to kill the beast with their pikes.

"You do in the beast hunter, I'll deal with that last swordsman," Sir Crowle yelled to Theron, as he snapped apart the spine of a crawling rat with his hammer.

Theron simply nodded, and together they charged. Theron could hear Aldous yelling. He turned for a moment and caught a glimpse of two seekers holding the boy in place with blue beams of arcane chain extending from their arms. Chayse battled to get to him, her short swords working hard against the attacks of two more seekers.

He took a step toward his sister, but a bloodcurdling scream stopped him in his tracks as the colossus ripped a man in two and spilt the leaking organs into his mouth. He could not ignore his duty, not even to go to his sister. He was Theron Ward, monster hunter, and there was a monster to be killed.

The last of the black iron knights turned and saw Theron and Crowle advancing. He threw off his helm. Hair, snow white, skin pale like the seekers, but he was not a seeker. He was a greater Upir.

He smiled.

No.

Crowle roared as he swung his hammer at the Upir. The fiend dodged the old knight with ease.

Dammit all, damn them all. I'll kill them all.

Theron knew he would not have long, so he made sure he acted quickly. The colossus swung, Theron dodged, ran through the thing's legs, and with a broad sweep of his claymore he swung at the tendons in the back of the creature's ankle from behind. They sounded like roots ripping from the ground as they tore apart. The great rat screamed and fell to a kneel.

Theron planted his claymore in the earth. He pulled his daggers and leapt onto the screaming monster's back. He sank the first dagger deep, then reached up and sank the second, using them to pull himself up as the creature writhed and shrieked.

The colossus reached back with one arm then the other, flapping ineffectually, trying to grab at Theron, but he evaded the monstrous groping claw. He made his way up until he clung to the dagger he had thrust in to the muscle that covered the top of the creature's skull.

Sir Crowle screamed out from below, the sound abruptly going silent.

Out of time.

Theron plunged his knife into the massive creature's eye. It burst apart and sprayed Theron as he stabbed it again and again.

~

Ken was bleeding badly, a slash across his torso, and one on his arm, another on his leg. The bastard was too fast.

The rat colossus roared in agony behind Ken, a sound that could part clouds and shatter mountains.

Chayse screamed, a sound of pain.

Blue streams of light glowed all around the seekers who stood over Aldous.

Finish it now.

The seeker lunged with a stab. Ken dropped his weapons and caught the saber in his gauntlets. They took most of the edge, but his hands still bled. It didn't matter; he pulled the fucker close, and like a beast, like a thing not human at all, Ken sank his teeth into his enemy's throat.

He felt the cartilage crunch. The seeker tried to pull away, and the skin started to rip, the taste of blood filling Ken's mouth. So he kept biting. The hands on the saber released. So he kept biting.

He bit down until teeth hit teeth, and, with his mouth full of human throat, he pulled away. He spat the hunk of flesh to the floor and the seeker fell next to it, convulsing, the blue glow gone from his eyes. Ken picked up the viper's saber and pinned his skull to the ground with it.

He picked up his mace and his axe, and he ran to Chayse and Aldous.

≈

A better world? Peace? Green pastures and food and land for all? Everyone free to do as they desire, as long as no one else is harmed? Please. Don't make me laugh. This world is as it is. We are all but the same scum in the same pond whirled into a chaotic mist by the edge of a child god's stick.

Words of a drunk overheard by another drunk at the Scathing Skeemer.

≈

CHAPTER TWENTY-SIX

TASTE OF VICTORY

*T*heron stabbed the monster in its second eye, the Upir climbing the colossus back behind him, hand over hand, clawed gauntlets digging in the way Theron had used his daggers. All around them smoke and orange flame rose from the corpses, tainting the air.

"The son and daughter of Diana Ward," said the white-haired fiend with a macabre smile, "handed to us along with Dentin. We did not expect this. None of us did,'"

Theron twisted his hand in the stinking, matted fur and held on as the monster screamed and tried to get back to its feet beneath him.

"Nothing has been handed to you," he snarled at the Upir, "and when I have you pinned beneath the point of my blade, you will explain how you dare say my mother's name."

The Upir came at him, fast, faster than anything Theron had ever faced, faster than the Upir they had faced at the windmill. But in the fight, Theron no longer knew fear. He felt possessed by the night's violence; he felt a god of the hunt, and the creature before him was nothing but another trophy.

The Upir slashed. Theron dodged left and lost his footing, his hand ripping away with a clump of bloody fur clutched in his fist. He fell from the beast's back, but managed to land on his feet and roll away from the Upir's clawed gauntlets. He got to his feet and lashed out with his daggers, a whirlwind of combinations, but the fiend was too fast. He deflected and evaded like fog as he drew his own stiletto.

This was a greater Upir, in truth, the predator at the top of the chain, likely alive for centuries. It looked like a cold marble version of a human, but with the fangs of a monster. It bared them now and came at Theron again.

~

By the time Ken got to Chayse, she was cornered, her back pressed against the keep, her face gashed open, her abdomen stained red and wet. She held her short swords, parried and deflected the two seekers that pressed her. She was as pale as they from loss of blood.

Ken hooked his axe on one of the blue-hatted bastard's shoulders and pulled him in to strike with the mace, four repeated blows into the spine leaving the man twitching and convulsing on the ground—a bit of luck Ken needed badly.

Chayse nodded to him as if it were just another day at Wardbrook, as if they were just strolling through the halls, then she locked her short swords in an X as she stopped a downward swing of the seeker's blade.

Ken forced a smile. "Let's kill this bastard."

The seeker blocked Chayse's feint, and Ken flanked him, wrapping his arms in a bear hug from the back, pinning him. He swung back with his left foot, trying to take Ken out at the ankle, but Ken lifted him from the ground and pressed his forehead against the back of the man's skull so he could not head-butt backward. Chayse grabbed her chance and slit open the man's belly, shoveling out his intestines with her second sword. Ken dropped the twitching body like a sack of refuse.

Chayse doubled over, teeth clenched. She raised her head and met Ken's gaze, her eyes bloodshot, and she gritted out the order, "Help my brother. I will release Aldous from the last two seekers and the wizard will finish this fight." And when Ken hesitated, she said, "I have this under control."

He turned to Theron. A black iron knight was on top of him, snow-white hair protruding from his head like spikes. He was pressing his stiletto down as Theron held his own forearms locked at an angle, pushing against the knight's weight.

Theron was losing.

A shriek grabbed Ken's attention, and he glanced over his shoulder to find the Emerald Witch standing by the colossus, her eyes rolled back in her skull, arms upraised, lips moving in a silent chant as the wounded beast responded to its maker's spell and began to rise.

Kill the witch. Kill the fucking witch and this is over.

Ken looked back at Theron, at the point of the blade mere inches from the eye slit of his helm.

"Kill the witch," Theron snarled.

Ken ran at her. *Under a hundred paces.* A rat got in the way. Ken gave it the axe. Theron roared in defiance off to Ken's left.

Hurry, kill her. My friends are dying. Kill her and I can save them. I still have time.

Another rat came at him; its brains shot from its ears as the mace came down. He was feet away now.

Her emerald dress was still clean.

He could taste her fucking blood.

Then it grabbed him, and he was leaving the ground; he was being pulled away.

It turned him around and he faced it, looking into the missing eyes of the colossus, the witch guiding its every movement, for she was its eyes and it was her hands. It engulfed each of Ken's hands in its own and began to pull in opposite directions. Ken felt as if his shoulders were being ripped from the sockets.

His weapons fell. He fought, but the creature was too strong, and the pain of being torn apart was surreal. The bones in his left hand cracked and shattered, and Ken screamed.

The east flashed before him. The bodies on crosses flashed before him, and Ken kept fighting, the muscles of his back screaming.

This is the hell I deserve. The hell I have deserved for a long, long while.

He pulled with everything he had, and he felt a pop in his left wrist. Then he felt the bones snap. Sharp under his flesh. So he began to squirm as he pulled, and the rat kept heaving the other way.

The bone ripped through flesh, dagger sharp. Ken gave one last tremendous tug and his left hand came off. He could no longer feel the pain; he was beyond it; he was burning in hell, but somehow he managed to stay cold. He swung from his still trapped right arm and plunged the jagged bone of his mutilated limb into the creature's already eviscerated eye socket.

∼

Aldous' brain was going to explode. The first time he had been brought to his knees and drained by the seekers at the chapel, there had been no pain. That was because the first time he had not fought. Now he fought, and it hurt.

The noise was the worst of it, a deafening screech, the

sound of mountains splintering apart, of a dragon dragging its claws across marble as it roared. Aldous fought on, for he could see in the faces of the two seekers that had him pinned that they were in the same pain as he. And he would not break.

I am stronger. I am stronger than them.

That singular sensation, the one he had felt when he first took hold of the staff of the ravens and wolves, filled him, and he opened to it, welcoming it.

The pain left him, and he left himself, and he flew above, watching. He saw himself kneeling in the blood-soaked mud, one seeker's blue arcane tether ensnaring him. He saw Chayse as she fought the second remaining seeker. She was hurt; a deep gash in her left shoulder poured blood down her arm, and there was a slash across her cheek, exposing teeth. Her stomach was stabbed deep and oozing blood as she moved to keep up with her enemy. She kept fighting. Somewhere Aldous knew he should feel heartbreak to see her thus, but in truth, he felt nothing.

Theron was screaming. A white-haired, ghostly pale, helmless knight was on top of him. Theron was unarmed. His hands bled as he gripped the descending blade of his pale foe. Slowly it slid through Theron's hands, his gauntlets cut through.

What would you do to save them? a voice asked from within, but it was not his own.

Theron tried to turn his head away, but the horns on his helm allowed him little room to squirm. The blade slid and Theron screamed.

Ken. The scarred man was leaning against a shattered fragment of the wall, the blinded rat colossus close by, writhing in pain. Kendrick was calm. He sat there, the stump of his wrist bleeding as he held the blade of a dagger in the flames of a nearby blazing rat corpse. When it was near red-hot, Ken stuck it to his stump, and he opened his mouth and howled, but still he held it there. The wound steamed; he closed his eyes and dropped the blade.

What would you do? the voice asked again.

Chayse. Her foe was deadly quick—a viper with his daggers, his speed was relentless, but Chayse matched him. Her short swords flashed and danced well with the daggers of her foe. But for every strike of hers, he had an answer, just as she did to his. But she was fading… fading…

The seeker took a chance and pressed in when Chayse made her next attack instead of back-stepping. She could have parried, but if she had he would have retracted and their dance would have continued, a dance she could not hope to master. She didn't parry. Instead she took the seeker's right-hand dagger to the torso. She didn't scream out, only gritted her teeth. Chayse cut off the seeker's other arm at the elbow. He let go of the blade in her belly and stumbled back screaming, staring at his gushing stump.

Chayse. The scream of her name only sounded in Aldous' mind, or whatever space he now inhabited as he observed the battlefield. The dagger was at least nine inches, and it was buried in her to the hilt. Emotion began to rise in him, a molten flow.

She stepped forward and crossed her blades on the armless bastard's throat and slit it to the spine.

Theron could not hold the impending blade any longer, and at the pace of thawing ice under a winter's sun, the pale knight's sword snuck through the vision hole in Theron's helm and bit into his eye. His screams were mad and frantic and his legs kicked like a hanged man's.

Stand, Aldous Weaver.

How? I am dying.

Stand and save Theron. Theron Ward must survive. It was a woman's voice.

How? How, damn you!

Pay the price and he will live.

What fucking price?

Chayse, blood running down her legs from the blade in her gut, still gripped her swords, and with them she stumbled to her brother's aid.

The pale knight stood, and for the first time Aldous realized what he was. For he flared his fangs as he met her swords. She was disarmed in a flash, and then the world seemed to slow.

Theron screamed his sister's name as he sprang to his feet, blood gushing from his gouged socket. He was not fast enough. Not nearly fast enough to save her. The greater Upir's sword did not slow. It did not waver as it parted Chayse's head from her shoulders.

Chayse.

Aldous could feel the heat of the tears burning down the face of his body far below.

Chayse.

Theron howled into the night like the beasts he hunted, the sound chilling and rife with pain. He tore off his helm, caught the stabbing blade of the Upir in the visor of the helmet, and gave a twist. The sword sprang from the Upir's hand and Theron dropped the helm; before it hit the ground he drove his bloody, gauntleted fist into his sister's slayer's face. Then a right and another left landed before the enemy adjusted and avoided the next blow.

Ken's gone. Chayse is gone. Theron yet lives. Save him.

What is the price?

Everything. The price of worlds. A cost far greater than you can comprehend. Now pay it.

Aldous returned to his body, he returned to his pain, the earth screaming in his ears, the pressure devouring and exploding his brain. He returned to it for an instant and then it was gone. The world went silent and his mind became clear. His body pulsed.

He closed his fist around the red gemstone. It pulsed in his hand, a transfusion of power. Slowly, he drew the pendant over his head, the chain catching in his hair as he dragged it free.

The seeker's arcane chains burst. The pale mage collapsed as Aldous stood, and he screamed for a moment before his skull exploded into a mist of blood and brain, and dust of bone.

Then the ravens came—thousands of flaming ravens ascended from the still blazing ring of fire that burned in the trench surrounding the keep. Aldous could feel them, he could see through them, each and every one of them. He could feel their hunger.

The Emerald Witch snapped from her occupation of the colossus rat's mind, and the massive creature collapsed to the ground. Sensing the threat of the infernal ravens, her eyes rolled back yet again, and the corpses of rats on the ground surrounding her began to stir. They stood, some without heads, disemboweled and with severed limbs, but they stood nonetheless and made a shield around the witch. The first raven made contact and set the rat shield ablaze; the second and the third caused it to burst, sending chunks of flaming, pestilent meat flying through the courtyard. As more and more of the rats burst, the witch began to drain. Her skin wrinkled and grayed, but still she raised more of her dead beasts to her aid. The blinded colossus found his way to her, where it swatted aimlessly at the firestorm of ravenous ravens. It screamed as its limbs were set to flame.

Aldous altered his focus and looked through the burning eyes of his flock that swarmed the Upir. He was fast, and avoided one swooping attack after the next, but some found their mark.

~

Never in his life, and never in his darkest dreams, had Theron witnessed such surreal madness. A swarm of burning ravens soared in the sky, and Aldous stood in the center of the courtyard looking upward, his flaming hands outstretched to his sides. Theron had taken refuge beneath the mutilated corpses of his fallen allies from the earlier fight. He watched as the Upir was hit again and again by raven after raven, but his speed was no match for the ephemeral forms of fiery death. His black iron armor began to glow red, and he screamed as it melted to his flesh. The iron bubbled and Theron could smell the bastard searing.

Finish him, be the one to finish him.

He rolled out from beneath the corpses. He saw Chayse, her head fouled and bloody in the offal of the slaughter, as he reached down and grasped Sir Crowle's war hammer.

The Upir was crawling aimlessly to the north wall. To the breach. Theron saw Ken lying there, his left hand gone, his eyes closed. Theron would give him revenge. He would give himself revenge. He would give Chayse, his magnificent Chayse, revenge.

The clouds clanged thunder, and a cold rain began to fall. Too cold for summer. It ran into his empty, throbbing socket and the water mingled with the blood. As the thunder bashed the heavens, the Emerald Witch began to chant; her voice deepened and left her with inhuman volume. The unknown words echoed through the courtyard and mingled with the Upir's screams of pain, the bestial moans of the burning colossus, and the shriek of the hungry ravens.

A green mist crawled over the dead, and the corpses of rat and man alike began to rise. Theron did not fret, for as they did, Aldous' ravens burst them to bits and turned them to ash. The ones that were not consumed by the hellfire, Theron sent back to death with the hammer.

The ravens burst man and rat alike, living and dead. It mattered not; they circled and protected Theron as he stalked his prey.

"Stop your crawling."

The Upir obeyed, for the fight was over, and somehow Theron and the defenders of Dentin had won. The rain had cooled the iron, but it seared deep into the fiend's flesh, right to the bone in his legs. A greater Upir could heal from such wounds, but it would take time, time the creature did not have.

"You still feel pain, Upir?" Theron stomped on one of the corroded legs and the Upir screamed. He screamed just like a man, frantic, afraid. Just like Theron had been screaming as the bastard cut out his eye. Just as his heart had screamed as the bastard took Chayse's head.

"Finish it, hunter," the Upir begged.

"I will, but tell me why you spoke of my mother. Why did you speak of Diana Ward? Where is she?" Theron tried to keep his voice steady; he tried to focus through the pain, like Ken would have done. Like Chayse had done.

A body exploded nearby and smoldering chunks landed at Theron's feet.

"She was one of us," the Upir said, relishing the telling, his words aimed like pointed darts. "She was one of the heads of Leviathan."

"Leviathan?" And when the creature made no answer, Theron swung the heavy war hammer down on a mangled leg.

The Upir wailed.

"One of the higher orders, an order of mages. Powerful. Unstoppable. You cannot stop us. Even your mother could not stop us."

"If she was one of you, why did she try to stop you?"

"She was one of us once," the Upir said, sly now as it faced death.

"Explain."

"She wanted all the power for herself, and that we did not allow. But we are many. Kill me, kill the Emerald Queen, and another head will just grow! Another..."

Theron brought the hammer down on the Upir's skull. He decided if he survived this he would make inquiries, but for now all he had to do was kill. So he brought the hammer down again, and again. He pulverized the fiend's head into nothingness, into the mulch that was fed to dogs, or rats. There would be no recovering from that.

Next was the witch.

When he turned to find her, it was too late. Over the back of the burning colossus he saw her, hunched over and defeated atop her black demonic mare riding off into the darkness, into the storm.

The ravens were gone, as was the green mist. No more of the dead were walking. There was just cold rain in a court-yard of corpses, and Theron Ward alone had his first taste of a real battle, along with his first taste of victory. It was a wretched taste.

～

They sipped on their golden wine, too lavish for the world of men; they feasted upon their otherworldly sweets and most exotic meats, high up there in their tower that pierced the clouds, so high it nearly touched the sun. But despite their great ascension they did not burn; they did not fall back down to earth. Instead, every year, every month and every day, bit by bit, inch by inch higher, they rose. The one with golden hair at times would look over the edge so far down at the world of men, at the children she left behind. She would think of the lover she'd betrayed and remember watching as he fell all the way back down. She smiled at her children; she smiled at her lover, who was strong enough to reach up and touch the new gods. She smiled because she hoped her son would not only be able to touch them, but in his fury, in his fiery heart that was the heart of man, he would be able to wound them, to draw the blood of the divine. Hunter of monsters, hunter of demons, hunter of gods— how high could Theron Ward climb?

～

CHAPTER TWENTY-SEVEN

NEVER ALONE AGAIN

heron took some small rations from Dentin Keep when he left in pursuit of the witch—not much, but enough to get him through the first few days. He found his claymore and he equipped Chayse's bow. He wrapped bandages around his head, covering his empty socket with cloth. The duke's man Fabius had an impressive personal stash of medicinal herbs, all of which the duke gave to Theron, despite Fabius' protests. They helped with the pain, but Theron consumed them sparingly, for they reduced his focus and made him slow. He found a middle ground and took enough to take the edge off while still being able to make good time in his pursuit.

It took him five days to adjust to the change in depth perception that having only a single eye afforded. On the fifth day his sister's bow scored him a fine buck, eight points on him. He ate well that night as he sat alone by a small fire. He thought if Ken had been there they would have nearly eaten half the beast, just the two of them. Aldous would have nibbled and become full and satisfied after a few ounces of the fine meat.

And *Chayse...* A tear formed in his remaining eye while the hollow socket covered in bandages throbbed. *Chayse would have eaten herself sick just to keep up with Ken.*

The tear rolled down his cheek.

The chasm on the other side just ached.

A missing eye was a strange absence. So were missing friends. A missing sister an absence that could not be described. One could carry on alone and one could carry on with just one eye, but one would never be able to see the whole picture.

He looked at his claymore glinting in the firelight as he ran a wet stone across its edge. Methodically, at a smooth, steady pace, no rushing. Not anymore. It didn't matter when he found her—sooner or later, it meant nothing.

What was time, anyway? There was no Wardbrook to go back to, not after this. He was not the same as he had been; he never would be the same again. Darcy Weaver was wrong; his book was wrong. There was no science to goodness— there was only the weak, the evil, and the wrath that evil invoked.

He was Theron Ward no longer; he was only that wrath. It felt like a choice no longer, this pursuit he now took. This hunt consumed him, and it was he. The witch could run to every edge of this world; she could dig a pit to hell or ascend to the heavens. It mattered not, for he would find her and she would know the feeling of prey. She would be a beast cornered and she would fight with everything she had left to carry on another day, another day to the centuries of her wretched existence, but she would not have it.

Theron bit into the venison, just slightly cooked. He liked it bloody.

That fucking witch will bleed, oh, she will bleed and she will suffer. She will understand fear and pain. The end of the world will not be far enough. The day she crossed me, I became her only clock, her only calendar, and for her the sands of time swirl down to the last grain.

He boiled water and placed a generous portion of the medicinal herbs and roots into the small pot. He tossed some into the fire and wafted the smoke into his face as he waited for the water to boil.

He thought of his childhood, before Mother became very strange. He thought of guests in fine clothes with grand stories and the way Father trained with vigor in the courtyard. He touched the red gemstone around his neck, the piece of his mother's jewelry he had given to Aldous. As he stared into the fire and inhaled the smoke, he could see the wizard's ravens again.

Such tremendous power at that young of an age, power grand wizards and arch mages would take two centuries to unlock. It was no small wonder that sorcery was punishable by death, for if every great sorcerer and sorceress of this world united, they would rule indefinitely. Their arrogance and vanity was what preserved the world of man, for they hated each other too much to ever unify, even as they paid lip service to an order of mages. The words of the greater Upir had confirmed that for him.

The water had boiled. Theron inhaled the steam and sipped on the brew, tears rolling down his right cheek into the potent liquid.

"Do you remember what you said to me? What you said when I left?" His mother's voice, taunting him. A memory. A dream.

"Where were you, Mother? If your power is so great, if you are so high above, then why did you not descend to save your daughter? To aid your son?" Theron screamed into the dark sky, into loneliness. His life of reading gave him no answers; philosophy did nothing for his pain, and although the herbs had now fully dulled the ache in his empty socket, they amplified the ache in his being.

What was Darcy Weaver's answer to this? Aldous the son would give a better answer, and that answer was hate. Ken would give a better answer, and that answer was vengeance. Chayse would know the answer, and that answer was the hunt.

"Do you remember, Theron?"

It *was* the voice of his mother, but it was not a memory and it was not his own thoughts. His hand shot to the pendant around his neck. The stone was cool and smooth.

"Mother?"

"Do you remember?"

Theron looked around franticly, then kicked over the pot of boiled roots and medicinal herbs. *I have taken too much.*

"Do you remember?" Mother asked again.

"Chayse is dead…" He fell to his knees and wept. "Because of me, she is dead. Chayse is dead, Mother! I killed your daughter! I killed my friends! What monster am I? What manner of fiend, what devil was I to decide?"

"The day I left, you cursed my name, you cursed it to the abyss, and you said you would forge your own legend with a sword and the will of man. You said that you held the greater power, not I, but you, the mere mortal, would strike fear into the hearts of all dark things, that the name Theron Ward would become myth, the idol of the hunt for time eternal. As you cursed my name I smiled, for on that first day you understood my sacrifice. Your destiny is myth, my son. This is only the beginning of your pain. This is only your first meal of it. You will be buried alive in suffering again and again, and you will rise from the grave."

"We were children!"

"Children who needed hardship."

"Children who needed a mother and a father!"

"To coddle you? To weaken you, more than wealth already did? One day you will thank me."

"You knew the Emerald Witch was coming to Brynth. You knew our paths would cross."

"I did not know, but I hoped."

"How could you hope for such a crossing? Did you know of her intent? Of the plague?"

"Indeed. It was what caused us to go our separate ways."

"Why do you speak to me now? Why tell me this now? Why did you not warn me? Why did you not kill her? You could have killed her before she killed Chayse." Even as he said the words, he knew she would give no answer. Instead he asked, "Do you know what the plague did to this country?"

"Made it stronger."

"For what? For whom?"

"What comes next."

"What comes next?"

There was no answer. She was gone; the voice was gone or the intensity of the high was fading. Regardless, no answer came.

Theron rose early the next morning. Despite the haze of the herbs, the venison had done him good, and as he followed the tracks he chewed on some of the meat he had cooked, salted and cut into thin strips. Nothing was better on the road than being well fed, not stuffed but not starving, enough to keep the muscles going and fight off the brutal depletion that the road often gives.

The clouds were still above, but there was no rain and the temperature was moderate and cool. The Emerald Witch's tracks led north. She did not seem to stop even once. Her shadowy steed had to have been summoned, for any horse not conjured from the arcane realms would have needed to stop by now.

Theron followed the clues she'd left behind. Her steed—although summoned—made hoof prints in the ground, heavy ones at that, and because her route was more or less untraveled, they were all the more obvious. She did not teleport, and so Theron was sure she was drained, that her defense against Aldous' ravens had completely sapped her, and when he found her he knew it would be in some gulch, some black crevice where she we would go to rest and recover or die, whichever came first.

Theron moved at an inhuman pace, a constant jog for three-quarters of each day through hard terrain and open field alike. The ground slowly elevated each day; by the sixth day the air had thinned, but Theron's trained lungs found it to be no concern. He knew he was getting close, he had to be, for the island of Brynth would soon be at an end. The witch had avoided any main road and not passed directly through a single town, no doubt hoping to avoid detection.

For days he had seen not a single human face, but all the while he felt eyes upon him. The owls hooted as he passed beneath their trees in the night, and the wolves stalked nearby, curious and hungry; fear kept them hidden, for the eyes of beasts could decipher predator from prey. He was a beast now; he was like them, hungry and savagely primitive. He passed the threshold of a vast forest and entered open plain, and there he saw humans again, broken shadows of the souls of men, but human still. They walked in their parade, twenty of them, sack hoods and bare backs. They sang their prayers or their hymns as they put the leather of their whips to their own flesh. They bled and they wailed and they sang of doom. Theron Ward smiled at the sign, for he knew doom was close; he knew that soon great sins would be answered for. And he knew that he and his sword would be responsible for the questioning.

~

It was the seventh day when he found it. Her steed's tracks five days old, for it had rained five nights past and the tracks had clearly been left in wet mud to bake under the sun on the following dry days. She would be five days rested now. Some of her power returned, but it would not be enough.

"Here you are," Theron muttered as he stared at the entrance to the cave he was sure she had taken her refuge in; it was less than half a mile away. Revenge was so close, down a steep ravine, across a shallow river and a field of brambles, but it was there. Right there.

The hunter took a deep breath. He kneeled at the top of the gully and took a moment, a final moment to meditate, to accept whatever evils remained of the Emerald Witch within that nearby cave.

Now I am the invader. The tables have turned, and they shall end in this position. He removed his sister's bow from his shoulder and pulled off the quiver. He dug a shallow, wide hole and laid the bow within.

"I dedicate this hunt to you, dear sister. I would not have come this far without you. I dedicate this ravine to you. Chayse's Copse, may all who hunt here forever kill their quarry; may your spirit guide the bows and the spears of all great hunters for eternity."

Theron buried the bow and stuck the arrows in the ground above it. When he was done, he would place the witch's skull in the same pit.

He began his descent down the ravine, slow and steady, no need to hurry, no need to rush. It was a poor hunter's darkest fear, a cornered beast in its lair, and a great hunter's brightest dream, a cornered beast in its lair.

He crossed the river. The water was calm. His heart was calm, angry but calm. He was cold like Kendrick and burning like Aldous; he was ready like Chayse. They weren't with him, but they were. They were his tribe, his family, his pack, and for them, for the first time as much as for himself, he drew his claymore from his back. It squealed, the sound echoing in the ravine, and he smiled. It was the first note in his song of death, and it never got old.

He swept the blade through the brambles, his stroke light and smooth; it stretched the muscles and warmed the veins. Some of the thorns remained, and they nipped at his exposed forearms and drew hot red blood, but it did not hurt; he did not feel. All he felt as he walked closer and closer to the entrance of the cave, as he stared at the torn shreds of emerald fabric on the brambles, was the urge to kill. The need for it, the necessity for the existence of Theron Ward, was the hunt of the most dangerous game. He paused, took his torch and tinder from his pack, and lit the fire.

He stepped forth into the abyss.

~

He dragged them both. When the killing was done he dragged them both, his friends, his brothers; he would drag them home. Home was far, home was gone, but for these men he'd find it again. He would build it again. He was not his father, he was not his mother, and he would never forsake those he loved. Over a mountain of corpses, across a sea of blood, through the winds of screaming spirits, he would drag those brothers home.

Home is nowhere. Home is everywhere when you're not alone.

~

CHAPTER TWENTY-EIGHT

STILL ALIVE

*A*ldous sat in a chair by Ken's bedside, their positions reminiscent of a time in the past. That time in the past, Aldous had not even known Chayse existed. Now he wished he could take her from his thoughts, for she was always there, the pain too raw and fresh.

He looked down at the words he had written and read them aloud to the still unconscious Ken.

"A thousand gods and devils worshiped all the same, entities sought out to deliver us from the darkest truth: that we are naught but beasts, all sentient things that inhabit this world. That we are abandoned by our gods, we are refused by our devils, we are forsaken by mothers and fathers, to hunger for purpose beyond hunger, to beg to be more than the wolf and the raven, more than the cur and the cat, more than the swine and the rat. When the smokescreen of philosophy is blown away, when the mountain of morality crumbles down, all that remains is the methods man heightens to slither to the top of the food chain. The best method is by fire and sword. That is what I have learned from the legendary hunter Theron Ward. My father once told me, 'An honest writer is the most virtuous of heroes; one who lies is the most deplorable of all villains.' If he were still alive I would tell him I have found a paradox, that to write honestly takes a great deal of villainy, that there is nothing more treacherous than the truth.

"What do you think of that, my friend?" he asked after a few moments, not expecting an answer.

"I don't like it," came a grumbling rasp from the bed.

Aldous turned in his chair and saw that Ken's eyes were open, hazy but open.

"You don't like it?" Aldous asked, turning red. He had thought it was pretty bloody good.

"I don't know what a paradox is," Ken began. "But if I did, I doubt it would change how I feel about what you just read to me. I'm not the smartest man, but I'll challenge you in this." Ken coughed and raised his left hand to cover his mouth, but it wasn't there. Just bandages. Aldous felt his eyes go hot with tears for his friend's suffering. It was obvious to Aldous now that Ken had already been awake for some time, maybe a day or two, but he had been given pain-thwarting herbs in tea and was in a stupor, not yet ready to come back to the world. For whatever reason, what Aldous read to him made him decide to come back and deal with this new reality. Aldous held a cup of the medicinal tea in his hand and delicately pressed it to Ken's lips. He had a sip then continued. "Discarded and forsaken we may be, beasts we may be, and all struggles may always come to fire and sword. Fine, I'll agree with you on that, but you're missing the most important bit."

"What would that be?" Aldous asked as he too took a sip from the tea.

"What gives us strength to walk through a world so dark as all that? To fight our bestiality, our abandonment, and the coming violence?"

"Hatred? Anger? Spite?" Aldous said with a snarl.

"Love," Ken said, and at the word Aldous wanted to die, he truly wanted to die. *Love. Chayse.* For Aldous the same word, such a beautiful word, such a horrific word. Ken kept speaking, and Aldous' heart kept bleeding. "The desire to go through it all is for love. I don't know where I am, and the last thing I remember was watching you all die as I burned shut my spouting left stump. Yet somehow I'm alive, and you are alive."

"Chayse is dead." The tears that had formed for Ken fell now for Chayse. "I could have saved her, but I wasn't strong enough. I had to see her die to get the strength to end the fight."

Ken was silent for a moment, pain searing across his face, and it was not pain caused by his lost hand. "And Theron? Is he dead too?"

"No. He dragged us into the keep. I had cast some spell. A massive flock of burning ravens, that's what the duke said. He watched from a window. He was ashamed. He begged for my forgiveness. I don't know for what, though. He said I fell lifeless and Theron dragged us back to the keep. The hunter told the duke if we died, if he came back and we had died, that he would burn the last bit of Dentin to the ground and hang the duke from the ruins." Aldous snickered. "It will be a great relief for the duke to know that you, as well as I, have survived, and because of it so to will he."

"Comes back from where? Where did he go?" Ken asked, sitting up slightly in the bed, as if he was ready to go find Theron, but he fell back quickly, too influenced by the herbs, too groggy, too wounded to do anything.

"The Emerald Witch survived the firestorm. Nothing else in the courtyard did other than her, Theron, yourself, and I."

Ken sighed. "How badly wounded was our fearless leader?"

"There was a greater Upir among them—the bastard cut out Theron's eye." Aldous stumbled on his words, but forced himself to go on. "Chayse sacrificed herself for him, for all of us. When I saw her die—" Aldous turned away, staring out the slitted window to the courtyard below, the courtyard where she had died. Ken said nothing, only waited for him to be ready to go on. At length, he continued, "The storm started after that, I guess. It doesn't matter what happened. Theron is alive, and so was the witch. The duke said Theron took herbs, a bit of food, and went after her. That's all I know."

"How long has it been?" asked Ken.

"Seven days. Seven days that I have sat here and done nothing while my friend hunts a monster."

"Don't you feel any guilt Aldous, you hear me?"

"About…" His voice cracked and he began to cry, softly, like a broken child. "About Chayse?" Aldous asked.

"About anything." Ken stared hard into him. "Whatever happened, whoever died, others lived. We protected the defenseless. We did what was right. No matter what, Chayse Ward was a warrior, violent and brave… and good. She died fighting for those she loved and for those who she deemed worthy to defend. We tried to do the same. We did what we could." Ken sniffed a bit.

"I just wish—"

"It doesn't matter what you wish, boy." Ken's tone was not hard and cold, it was soft and hurt. Aldous looked at him, and the monstrous, scar-faced man was crying, too. Not sobbing. Just a steady stream of tears and a hurt stare into nothingness, into memory. "I wish a lot of things. I spent a long time wishing I'd never been born. I wished I never fought for the bastard, Salvenius, for Brynth and the Luminescent. Fourteen years old, my head was easy to fill with lies, easy to create a surety that everyone in the east was wicked, down to every woman, child, and dog. More than that, I wished I never left. Never deserted."

Ken clenched his teeth hard, and the muscles in his neck and face strained, as if he was trying to stop the flow of tears. "I killed my own wife, boy, brought the plague into our home. Stitching up my bites, she got sick. I went out to get fresh water, I came back and she was turned. I killed her." The tears dripped off his chin onto the bed, and he whispered, "I killed that sweet woman. I ran for years. I ran and I drank. I found Alma. The count's men found me. They killed her too, because of me." Ken turned and looked Aldous in the eyes. "I'm a man that has meant good, my whole life I've meant good. I hope that counts for something."

"It does, Ken, I promise you it does." Aldous placed his hand on his dear friend's shoulder. "Love matters, Ken."

~

"He's awake," Aldous said to the duke to break the half-hour silence that had formed at their end of the table as they ate dinner. The dining hall was packed to capacity with women, children, and the elderly. The duke was a decent man as far as Aldous was concerned. He did what he was capable of; he gave *things* even if he could not give himself. And Aldous found it heartening to see that the duke's health had improved as the days passed. He was stronger now, walking among his people instead of huddling in his chair under a mountain of blankets.

"Kendrick?" asked the duke.

"Yes."

"Thank the God of Light," said the duke, and Aldous felt he meant it. Not just because it protected him from Theron's wrath, but also because he had seen the villain Kendrick the Cold act as a hero, a champion of Dentin.

"If Ken didn't make it, Theron would not have harmed you. You know that, right?"

"He is a fearsome man. I have never seen anyone fight like he. Not ever, and I hope I never shall again, but that is not why I thank the divinity. I am glad your companion is alive. I have heard terrible things of him, yet all I saw was self-sacrifice for helpless strangers. And you, young wizard, you and you alone have shaped my opinion on those of your ilk. Not the Emerald Witch, but *you*, bringer of the ravens and the flame. You will forever be to me and all those in this hall a savior, a protector divine. Grim heroes you may all be, but heroes you are, both those who lived and the one who fell."

Those close by raised their cups in toast. Even Fabius raised his. He was disheveled, his thin mustache was unkempt, and his shirt was stained. He was a better man for it.

Aldous raised his goblet to Chayse... Chayse... He was glad the duke did not say her name. He could not bear to hear her name.

~

Caroline was a country girl, a sweet, boisterous country girl. Mama raised Caroline all alone; she never spoke of Papa, not once, not even his name. Caroline craved excitement, so she left Mama's little abode. On the back of a donkey to Norburg she rode. High hopes and dreams did the country girl hold in her breast; perhaps she would meet a handsome man and together they would nest. A handsome man she met, such a handsome man was he: blond locks like an angel and muscles like a beast. He loved her once and off he went. She prayed that he'd return. When there came a knocking, her high hopes and dreams would learn that at her country home she should have stayed, for the rats they took her.

Where she went she could not say. All she knew was that it was to some foul nest, and soon she would bear children to suckle on her breast.

~

CHAPTER TWENTY-NINE

THE SPAWNING PIT

*T*he green mist shied from the flame of the torch. The witch's hollow was damp, and the walls crawled with viscous pus and other putrid filth that slowly slipped down to the stone floor. The tunnels were numerous, but the choice was clear, for a most hellish sound echoed from one, a distant squealing and the moaning of women… Deep and guttural, heavy and crushed.

"Theron Ward!" The voice of the witch echoed through the tunnels. It whirled the mist and slid the slime.

"Reveal yourself!" Theron roared. Fearful squeals and heavier moans, frantic and in great distress, were his answer.

"Turn back. Leave my home, devil," the Emerald Witch wailed as the hunter descended ever deeper into the dreadful tunnels. The squealing and moaning grew and grew. The green fog thickened and a distinct scent of rotting beef liver burned in his nose. Some strange organic heat began to permeate through his mail and cloak, and moistness thickened the air.

"What are you mustering in the deeps, witch? What foulness causes such stench?" Theron spat, bile rising in his throat. The ungodly moaning became so loud he feared the walls might crumble.

"Leave them be! Don't you harm them, don't you harm my sweetlets!" The witch's voice crackled with woe. "You have taken enough from me. I will leave Brynth. I will abandon the Covenant of the Leviathan if you just let my sweetlets be."

"I know not of what you speak, but I have come for your life, hell specter, and before I leave this cavern I will hear the banshee scream. You killed my sister, slaughtered the innocents of Norburg, and rid Dentin of many sons, fathers, and husbands. You have already chosen the price. I am merely here to collec—"

Even with the torch, the ground was black, so Theron was caught unawares by the pit he fell through. The fall was not far, perhaps only five feet until he hit the fluid. Waist deep, it splashed into his face as he hit the bottom. He kept his balance and kept the torch dry. It remained lit. Part of him wished it hadn't.

The first thing to hit him was the immense power of the odor. *Rotten liver, shit, rats.* He retched and spewed up his meager breakfast.

The next thing that his mind forced itself to accept was the sound. And then the sight of them, a horror he could barely understand.

They tried to talk, to shriek, to beg, to do only the devil knows what, but all that came was a most grotesque and gluttonous groaning. There they were, the young women taken from Norburg. They were women no longer, but rather chained monstrosities, things so revolting, so pathetic that Theron felt his skin crawl, and a cold, sick sweat drenched him head to toe.

They were naked, and pus pulsed from a thousand terrible sores. They had grown more breasts, like the teats of a pig, and their offspring—naked things that looked half rat, half human child, with a layer of flesh still over their eyes— squealed and suckled blindly.

The fluid, the foul-smelling, rotten, liver-scented fluid, Theron then understood was a pool of afterbirth and filth. Again his stomach heaved, but it was dry.

Not in all his years of the hunt, not in his worst nightmares, could he even fathom the blasphemy to man that was that pit.

"Don't harm them. Let them feed, let the sweetlets feed." The witch was close. He could hear her, but he could not see her. The torch reflected on the surface of the fluid and the spawning pit was nearly fully lit, a score of brood mothers, half reclining, and hundreds of the blind child-rats. The witch hid amongst them.

Theron intended to dig her out.

His claymore severed undeveloped spine and skull like nothing. The blind things shrieked, and the first mother howled and wept. Theron did not know if it was in human joy or a mutated distress. It did not matter. Nothing mattered except killing that witch and crawling out of this cruel dream.

When the whelps were cleared, he raised his blade for the mother, possessed by a demon of disgust, mad and frantic. But his haze was broken for just a moment as he looked the forsaken thing in the eyes.

He knew them.

The sweet lass from the inn in Norburg, it was her. The redheaded girl. Caroline was her name. Horror congealed in his gut, but he held his place.

"I will free you, Caroline. I free you from this." The claymore killed quickly.

The other brood mothers sounded a whimpering

symphony of pleas, pleas for release, for the freedom of death.

"I shall emancipate you all." Theron's roar echoed in the pit, and the child-rats yowled in hellish answer.

The witch screamed and sobbed, still hidden, lurking and squiggling somewhere in the cesspool of afterbirth.

"Monster! Devil!" she shouted. "No more I beg you, no more!"

Theron swung his heavy sword side to side. He felt not the fatigue in his arms as he burned with torch and cut with blade, screaming, all the while trying to release some of the fire from the furnace of trauma that burned in his belly.

"I can listen to them sob no longer," wailed the Emerald Witch.

"Then reveal yourself and die." Theron hacked his claymore down atop the skull of another one of the wretched things.

She emerged for an instant before him from behind one of brood mothers. He caught a glimpse of the witch, her long black hair now crusted gray filth, her emerald eyes a muted glow, more the mud on the forest floor than a green canopy overhead. Then she submerged into the pool. The fluid bubbled for a few moments as Theron drew closer, his torch and sword at the ready. *This is where it ends. The hunt has led me here.*

The Emerald Witch broke the surface.

The Plague Witch she had become.

Her flesh grew and swelled before his eyes. Her jaw unhinged and her tongue extended from the mouth, more a tentacle than a tongue, with a hole in the tip. The tentacle dipped into the pool of placenta, blood, and offal. It throbbed as it drank, and the Plague Witch's body grew larger and larger still as it consumed the ooze.

Indeed, this is where it ends, but it is not over yet.

The witch's fingers morphed into tentacles, and her gut and breasts swelled and greened beneath the expanding yellow skin.

The hunter steeled his mind; he steeled his focus and went forth. He was not Theron Ward now, he was the hunter, and all manner of beast and fiend, no matter the realm, was his game.

"This is for my sister, and my friends." He charged forward, slogging through the waist-deep goop, and swung his claymore one-handed, a mad painter of death and violence, the witch the canvas before him. When slashed apart, she would be his greatest masterpiece.

The tentacles on her left hand shot out like hurled spears. The blade met them, and three of them sprayed hot fluid as they tore from the hand. She screamed and her children answered: the blind rats squealed, some swam, and others crawled toward Theron. Hundreds. It did not matter.

Their great mother wept as she flailed at Theron. He back-stepped and set torch and sword to her "sweetlets." Something grabbed him from beneath the surface. And there was a pressure on his mail boot on the shin. He lifted his foot and stomped down, and he felt a fragile skull burst beneath the pressure, the thing's brains and blood now mingled with the birthing ooze of the rat kin.

As he held off the swarm, the witch returned her long tentacle tongue into the liquid and drank. As she did, the severed fingers grew back.

The burn in his muscles was beginning to grind through his rage, his desire to kill, and his desire to survive. He pressed forward, bashing and hacking his way through the useless whelps. One leapt upon his back, then another. They clung to his legs, and although most of them did not even yet have teeth, could not even bite, they weighed him down.

The witch shot out her tentacles; his sword arm was too

heavy with the weight of her litter to sever the attacking limb this time. Tendrils wrapped tight round his sword arm and squeezed so hard he dropped his blade. Then the vile serpentine limbs grabbed him by the legs.

He went under.

Submerged completely.

It went in his eye, in his ruined socket. His mouth. His nose. The taste alone nearly killed him, driving him into hysteria; he struggled madly, but the rat things weighed him down, smothering him, drowning him in the spawning pool.

Stop.

Relax.

The hunter stopped struggling, his prey dragging him closer, closer. He began to rise from the mire of grime by the legs, the tentacles pulling him up. He fought not at all. The rats swam and crawled off him. His feet broke the surface, his body, his head.

Stay limp.

"Momma will squeeze out his blood, my sweetlets! Momma will turn his bones to jelly. Momma will feed you."

Theron's torch had been extinguished when he was submerged, but he could smell the breath of the witch as she spoke. He heard the tongue slithering from the mouth, saliva dripping. It wrapped around his neck slowly, thinking the hunter was no longer a threat.

The prey was wrong.

So certain he was out of the fight, the witch left his arms unrestrained. When he grabbed the tongue the witch tried to tighten it, to crush Theron's throat and end it. He dipped his chin and flexed his mighty neck muscles. The defense held long enough for him to sink his teeth deep into the goopy tendril. The witch made a noise, not a scream, for she could not involve the tongue, just a strangled gargle deep in her throat.

Her grip on his feet loosened and she tried to retract into her mouth. Gauntleted fists grabbed tight and pulled. There was the sound of tearing fibers of flesh, audible over the squealing and moaning of the things still living in the now pitch-black pit. The witch dropped him, but he held fast to her tongue and twisted upright as he hit the fetid fluid, finding his footing.

He kept pulling as he stepped closer. The tendrils tried to grip him, pull him back under, but he tucked his head and widened his stance, and the horrible pain of her ripping tongue stopped the witch from generating any real force. The rat things tried to pile on him, but the hunter would not be stopped, not this close to the kill.

He knew he had reached the mouth when he reached out to grab another fistful of stretched, dangling tongue and instead he hit teeth. So he hit the teeth, gauntleted fist crashing again and again. She flailed but could not slow his blows. Nothing could slow him then.

"Your—"

Theron felt teeth explode, heard them shatter as he delivered the fourth strike, his left hand controlling the witch's head movement by keeping a firm grip on the tongue.

"—fucking—"

Another blow.

"—magic—"

Another, the lower jaw unhinged, tentacles of restraint lost their grip, and the rats collapsed as well. The moaning of the brood mothers turned to a quiet drone.

"—did nothing to stop me!"

Unrestrained, the blows came down now in a flurry.

"Fire and sword!"

He roared into the pulverized face.

"Fire and sword, know that. Know that as you die!"

The witch was likely already dead, for the pit had gone

completely silent, save for the sound of Theron's panting and the dull mashing of his fists into the minced mound of meat.

That was the end of the nightmare of Norburg, the destroyer of Dentin, the end of Brynth's foreign invader. The end of the Emerald Queen, the mother of rats.

That was the real beginning of the legendary hunter Theron Ward: in the north of Brynth, hidden in a cave, waist deep in plagued afterbirth, he was reborn. In that black abyss, the rotten heart of truest terror, he overcame. He conquered his first truly great hunt.

~

"It is an infection of the face, young man, in the empty socket of your eye, no less. Spare yourself the pain of what you ask me to do, for no matter what you will surely die," said the surgeon of the small town.

"If I will surely die then I have nothing to lose. Do as I ask you, a final request, if you will," said the hunter, his voice shaking, his body sweating and the pulsating infection in his hollow socket throbbing.

The surgeon heated the long knife until it was red hot. "Are you sure? I have no sedatives, young man. The pain alone may kill you."

"I am sure. It is not my destiny to die like this. Dig this evil from me with a burning blade," said the hunter.

The surgeon nodded to his helpers and they tied the hunter down. He clenched his teeth around a strap of leather as he tried to prepare his mind for the pain to come. There was no preparing for it; there was no bracing for that.

The infection popped and seared and the hunter screamed. He screamed from his soul, and so loud was the agonizing sound that the whole town shivered at the cry. Fire and sword, the hunter would not die.

~

CHAPTER THIRTY

MOVING ON

*I*t had been two months since Theron Ward had left Dentin in pursuit of the Emerald Witch. Two months that Ken and Aldous remained, helping to put Dentin back together. Ken did what he could with just one arm, and what he could do was more than most men with two.

They had buried Chayse in the woods beneath the trees, her grave marked by a monument of her short swords melted into a hunk of iron that the smithy fashioned. They had buried other bodies, and now they rebuilt houses, and they helped plant crops. If there was a time when the women and children, when the elders and the sickly feared the wizard and Kendrick the Cold, that time was no longer.

They came to be known as great and charitable men, true champions of Dentin. They declined pay from the duke on the grounds that any coin given to them could instead be used for acquiring the needed resources to rebuild the destroyed village. They accepted only a bed to lie upon at night and food to fill their bellies. The work was grueling, and most days Ken could only manage six hours of labor, for his near fatal wounds still needed time to heal—small fractures and damaged muscles on top of his lost hand. Aldous had recovered fully, and he did what he could to put in eight- to ten-hour days, every day. This inspired Dentin's people to work just as hard, and the progress of their work was inspiring.

"I feel good," said Ken one evening to Aldous as they had ale before the fire.

"Yes? Your injuries are healing well, then?"

"The physical ones, yes, but the ones of the soul as well, lad."

Aldous smiled at his friend, then his smile faded. "I still hurt terribly, Ken. I miss Chayse. I miss Theron."

"So do I. So do I."

"Do you think he found her?"

"I know he found her," said Ken. "I know he killed her."

"Is he alive?" Whatever Ken answered, Aldous decided he would believe.

"Aye, he's alive. I need him to be alive."

"Me too." Aldous looked at his ale. "But what if... When do we move on?"

"I don't mind it here," said Ken, then he sipped at his ale and almost smiled.

"Neither do I. Eventually, though... eventually word will reach other cities about who and what we are. They will come for us. If we stay, we endanger the ones we saved, the people that see us as their champions."

"So when do we move on?" Ken asked. To Aldous it sounded like Ken was asking for an instruction, as if he were asking for an order. Aldous took his time to answer, for he was not sure he was ready to be the one making choices.

"In a month," Aldous finally said, his voice stern and full of conviction. Ken nodded. "We work and you recover for another month. In a month the village will be well on its way to being good as new, and… and perhaps Theron will return."

"A good plan, lad." Ken stood abruptly. "I'm off to the sack. I'll see you at breakfast. You're young, Aldous. You're young and you've done a great thing. Off to a good start, I'd say." Ken patted Aldous awkwardly on the shoulder with his stump, for he was holding his ale still with his hand.

Aldous put a light hand on the mutilated limb, and stared into space before him, nodding in appreciation of Ken's words, but thinking of Chayse. Hurting for Chayse, for himself, for the life he would know without her.

Ken left the room and Aldous was alone with his thoughts.

~

Aldous thought of the woman's voice. The one who had spoken to him in the battle, the one that had told him to protect Theron Ward. Who the voice of the woman belonged to, he did not know, yet he felt he had made an obligation to it, an obligation to some divinity to carry out its will. He swore sacrifice, said he would pay any price. Yet he lay in a soft bed, alive and thinking, and there was a chance, a high and terrible probability, in fact, that Theron Ward was dead. If that was so, he had lied to that divine force, a force Aldous was certain had given him the strength to summon the ravens of fire.

He reached absentmindedly, as he had many times in the many weeks that had passed, for the red gemstone around his neck, only to recall it was not there. It had not been there since the battle.

~

They ate breakfast with the duke and Fabius the next morning. So much progress had they made on the townships that the villagers were back to living happily in their own homes. As happily as villagers could be after their land was ravaged and their loved ones taken by a swarm of rats.

That is the nature of things, thought Aldous. *One must find happiness after despair, lest life become nothing more than surviving from one tragedy to the next. The emotions must recover quickly; the good things must be loved whenever they can, for the good things do not stand the storm.*

"Today is the day the church starts to be re-erected," said the duke.

"There are still other houses, a stable and granary to get done," grumbled Ken.

The duke frowned slightly but did not press.

"And you, Aldous? Where shall you be working today?" asked the duke. He did not make direct eye contact; he gave a quick glance from under his brows, his head tilted humbly forward.

"You're a sneaky man, Duncan," said Aldous, and he laughed.

"A sneaky man? I've never suffered such a charge before. What gives you cause to say such a thing?" asked the duke, smiling.

"What good do you believe it will do?" asked Aldous.

"I'm not sure I follow," said the duke.

"I'm sure you do," chimed in Ken, then he tore off a hunk of cheese with his teeth.

The duke sighed. "The church is not wicked. The Luminescent is not wicked."

"I have done wicked things for this not-wicked God, Your Grace. You are a man who chooses to only see the good things, and you are young," said Ken.

"You are right, Ken. I am young, and I do choose to see

the good. I saw four unlikely heroes save my people and my land for no reason other than they felt obligated to protect those too weak to protect themselves. I saw a primordial goodness in you."

"Yet your church would see us burn," said Aldous.

"Not my church. Perhaps the king's church, perhaps the churches in Aldwick, maybe the ones in Baytown and all the others in Brynth. Not mine, though. My church would not see you burn. Neither would my God."

"There is only one Luminescent, is there not?" Ken said, the mockery clear in his tone. Despite the budding argument at the table, no tempers were flaring.

"I believe there to be one Luminescent, yes. He is not a god that would ask for either of you burned, nor is he a god that would accept the king's crusades in the far east."

Fabius stopped eating and stared at the duke for a moment, shocked at these words. Dangerous words.

"That is a false god, a lied god," Duncan continued. "The real God is good."

"God didn't save your people. We did," said Ken. "And if it was part of some design of his for this to have happened in the first place, then if I ever cross him it will come to blood." Ken paused. "Let's just leave it alone."

"Very well, Ken." Duncan turned back to Aldous. "Where will you be working today?" he asked again.

Aldous burst into laughter at the passive maneuverings of the duke. "Incredible. All right." He nodded. "I'll help with the church, but don't expect me to utter a prayer, or start copying out scripture. The last believer that tried that with me... well, he shouldn't have."

Ken just needed one arm to chop wood, and that was what

he had mostly been doing to provide lumber for the home-steads. Stone and brick the duke had to buy from other cities and towns that owned lands with quarries, but Dentin was plentiful with lumber. So Ken chopped away, and every two hours would load a mule cart with the wood and head into the village.

He missed having a left hand, that was certain. He wondered if he would ever be worth a damn in a fight again, and it both hurt and pleased him to think that he wouldn't be. Perhaps this was an excuse to never kill again. Likely it was just that, though, an excuse. If he could split lumber, he could split skulls—that was a fact he had known for a long time. And so he practiced each morning in the hours before dawn.

He brought the lumber to the granary; there was already more than enough. Across the thoroughfare were the people hard at work on the church. Even those villagers who were inclined to sloth were bustling and laboring with great resolve to build the thing.

Fools. The true house of evil is that.

Ken thought of the church in Grimmshire. Suicide was a sin according to the scriptures, yet the father there had assisted in the suicide of his entire surviving flock, then took his own life to spare them and himself from the plague.

Had he lost his miserable faith? Or had he found a higher one?

Ken would never know the answer to that.

He walked the mule and the cart of lumber to the church.

"Have you come to aid us?" asked the duke himself as he hammered a nail into a plank of wood.

In Ken's experience, when nails went into "holy lumber," there was a human hand or foot in between.

"No. You can have the wood, though, Your Grace."

"Thank you," said the panting, sweating Duncan.

Ken growled, turned, and walked away. He heard Aldous laughing as he did.

He was glad Aldous had little enough of an opinion to work on the church. He knew the boy did not all of a sudden become a believer; he was simply being helpful. Ken doubted he would ever be able to do that. He knew strong ideals and unwavering opinions were things that stagnated humanity as a whole. It was the very thing he hated about the church, and it was hypocrisy he saw in himself that he had such an unwavering opinion about it. Regardless, Ken would never forgive and forget the thing that he had become in the name of the God of Light.

～

Ken walked for an hour. He went past the ravine and climbed a hill; it was soon to sundown, and he sat down on the grass. The clouds had lifted, they had lifted some time ago, and it was because of that he knew Theron had succeeded in slaying the witch. It was a childish deduction, it bordered on religious, but at least his belief was in a man. Ken reached into his pack and took out a loaf of stale bread and some roast fowl. He ate as he watched the setting sun, and decided he would sleep there on that hill under the stars. In the morning it would be three months since the battle. Two weeks ago the duke had warned them that he had gotten word that there was some rabbling in Aldwick and the Imperial City that the fugitive Kendrick the Cold and a rogue sorcerer were responsible for the protection of Dentin.

Ken would sleep here this night under the stars, and in the morning he would return to Dentin. Together he and Aldous would go on their way. Where they would go, they were not sure, but they would stick to the plan of Theron and Chayse. They would stick to the path of the hunt.

Kendrick gave a last look to the horizon before he laid down his head. He jerked upright and squinted in the fading light, and for the first time in his life he saw something good on the horizon. His heart pounded and his eyes welled with tears.

Happiness.

～

Hefferus the smith sat in his shop, smoking on a pipe and nursing a pint as he read a book by some bloke by the name of Darcy Weaver, some drivel called The Indisputable Science of Goodness. His wife was highborn and had insisted he learn to read. There was no sense arguing, for she always won.

"This is drivel, a whole lot of drivel. I'm more than halfway through the bloody thing and there hasn't been a single battle, not even the mention of a dragon, or an Upir, or any manner of were-beast! I won't have it, I tell you!" Hefferus tossed the book into the furnace. The fire grew, and he thought he might just forge something small, a dagger perhaps. Before he could start, into his shop walked three men: two of the nastiest lads Hefferus had ever seen, and a lad small in form but with a devil's eyes.

The man in front drew his sword, a silver claymore. He handed it to the smith. The smith looked at the blade and his eyes went wide, for it was of his own forging.

"By God. Theron Ward?"

"Indeed."

"Have you... have you come for something to be forged?"

"Indeed. My claymore, the one you gave my father. I want it larger, heavier. And my friend here"—Theron indicated the mountain of muscle to his left who appeared to only have one hand—"he needs a fist. An iron fist."

The smith smiled his toothless smile and cracked his knuckles. "You've come just at the right moment, lads, for just now I stoked my fire. Sit and tell me of your adventures as I set to work."

～

EPILOGUE

THE PATH

Across the sea, to the northeast, in the mountainous landscape of the Romarian highlands, in a small village in a downtrodden tavern, Vilnous Neta sipped on his ale and chewed on his mutton.

"I've never seen the like," Vilnous began. "A whole pack. Twelve at least. Never have I seen them in a pack. Always they hunt alone. Days most dark are coming, brothers, days most sinister and dark." The man shuttered and swallowed back his ale, then slammed it down and nodded to the barkeep for another.

"How did you escape, Neta?" asked a frail, white-bearded man to the left.

"I wish to never say if you allow me this secret. I am ashamed for running, so very ashamed." Vilnous bowed his head and stared at the ground. He put his mutton aside, his appetite lost.

"You need not be ashamed, brother. Who would not have run in the face of such terror? Romaria has no more great knights, no more hunters of old. There are no more heroes." The white-haired old man slumped in his chair. "What can a man do when his path meets that of the devil but turn and flee, lest he be taken to hell?"

"Or worse, forced to walk the very path of the fiends," said a glum, hooded man to Neta's right. "The Lycans howl in the night, the demons rise from pits of fire, the banshees shriek, and the Upirs and their lords feed. Our lands are cursed."

"The whole of the world is cursed." It was a woman who spoke now, wrinkled and hunched, with a foggy eye, slurping gruel and tapping her long, filthy nails on the table at which she sat while she ate. "Have you not heard of the happenings in Brynth seven months past? A plague of ratmen, not much unlike our Lycans, but in the form of sickly rodents. They destroyed entire cities, a swarm of them." The whole tavern fell silent at this, all but for the sound of the old hag slurping at her gruel. "Yes, it is not just we who are cursed, but the whole of the world."

"Why? What have we done? What has man done to deserve the demons that torture him?" asked Vilnous, not exactly expecting an answer.

"It is a test, a cleansing and a test," said the hag. "Only the strong shall survive." Then she cackled, spitting up a bit of gruel as she did. She turned her foggy eye to the men at the bar, only her foggy eye. The other remained starring down at the gruel. "None of you shall survive it, for you are weak." Again she cackled, more madly now.

"Enough, you old hag," barked the barman. "You're bad for business. What did I tell you about keeping your doom talk to yourself, eh?"

The few others in the tavern grumbled their agreement.

"Do I make you uncomfortable… ladies?" asked the hag.

"Keep to yourself, you old crone, I'm warning you." The barman stepped out from behind his bar.

"Warning me? What will you do? Throw out an old lady

into the cold and the rain? And in these dark times no less, with all manner of beasties and hellions running 'round?"

"I swear I will if you don't bloody well keep to yourself. And quiet down the slurping on your gruel," said the barman as he returned to his post and filled another mug for one of his thirsty patrons.

The door to the tavern opened, and the cold, wet wind blew in with a howl.

The first man to walk through the door was tall and immensely broad in shoulder. He pulled back a black hood. His long blond hair was wet and fell carelessly down to his shoulders. He was handsome—half his face was, at least. His left eye was missing, burn scars replacing it. He had a large sword on his back and a small, strange crossbow on his hip with a quiver of silver bolts. Gold chimes with strange markings dangled from his chain mail and made music as they swayed side to side from the wind coming through the doorway.

The second man to come through was a few inches shorter and more than a few inches wider in the shoulder than the first. He pulled back his hood, revealing a visage more scar than face, one long and particularly deep one running nearly from ear to ear just below his eyes. His hair was shaved down to the scalp and a thick braided beard accentuated the might of his broad jaw and powerful chin. There was an axe at his hip on his right side; his left hand was clenched in a tight fist... a solid iron fist. From his cloak and armor dangled the same strange golden chimes, and in the wind they added to the mindless tune of the first man's.

Last to enter was a young man, wet black hair slicked back off a sharp-featured face, hollow cheeks, a sharp chin, and sharp jaw. He was excessively lean, and there was more murder in his eyes than the first two. He walked with a staff, a most magnificent staff with detailed carvings of wolves and ravens. He did not wear a black cloak like his companions; instead he wore a deep red one with light black mail beneath. On his hip was a short sword and around his neck was a red gemstone, which looked to be in a lady's fashion.

The trio sat at the back of the tavern and said not a word.

"What will you have, travelers?" asked the barman from across the room.

"Ale and a meal," the blond one said, then turned back to his comrades. Normally the barkeep would ask unfamiliar patrons to show their coin before they were served. He did not ask these men, though. He only poured three flagons.

Vilnous Neta had a terrible feeling about these three men. A deep foreboding, a sense of dread that whoever these three were, dark things were close.

"Who are they?" he whispered to the barman.

"I don't know. Friendly strangers, I hope."

"They don't look like friendly strangers," Vilnous said as he took a quick glance back at the men. The one-eyed man with the blond hair locked Vilnous' stare and grinned. It was not a friendly grin. Vilnous had an impulse to stand right then and there and run out the door into the night and the storm, to run from the town and into the woods with all its terrors.

"What brings you to our town, hunters?" asked the hag as she tapped her filthy nails on the rotting wood table.

The dread magnified as Vilnous looked at the three strangers, awaiting their response. They stood back up, and the blond man's great sword scraped and screamed as it left the scabbard. The stout man with the axe and the iron fist cracked his neck side to side. The black-haired younger one snapped his fingers on his left hand and a small ball of fire hovered over his fingertips.

Vilnous cowered along with the other men at the bar, but it was too late to run.

The hag stood from her chair and put down her gruel spoon. Her good eye rolled back into her head; the foggy one remained staring. From outside the tavern, over the thunder and the hammering of the rain, the beasts began to howl.

The End

If you enjoyed Fire and Sword **please leave an online review** to help other readers decide on this book.

∾

Read book 2—Catacombs of Time—now!

Keep reading for a sample of *Catacombs of Time*!

BONUS SAMPLE CHAPTER

CATACOMBS OF TIME

$\mathcal{T}$he moon was red that night. It peeked through the only part of sky not hidden away by the leaden clouds of the manic storm that shifted from bouts of light mist descending from the heavens, to downpours that made it hard to breathe and see. Lightning split the sky, illuminating it momentarily, then leaving it in shadow once more. Thunder resonated, and it was as if the gods themselves were waging war high above with the cannons and arms of the cosmos, and the storm was the fallout of a battle whose combatants were indifferent to the plight of man.

Below the moon and the clouds, where the rain poured down and the lightning threatened destruction, was the University of Villemisère, which had stood in this place for three hundred years, since the time of the first appearance of the Rata Plaga in Brynth. Five stories of lecture halls and laboratories, of studios and dormitories, of mess halls and infirmaries, and long, high-ceilinged corridors with dim lamps dampening the souls of those ambitious youth who braved the years of solitude and anguish that the university promised.

DYLAN DOOSE

The wind blasted against the front doors. They swung ajar and the draft gusted its way through the vast cylindrical atrium, with its dead gray walls that looked black in the gloom, but for the spaces that had a sleepy orange haze cast by weak lamps. The wind whirled around, an invisible tornado that flew up the wooden stairs, worn by so many years of students and professors hurrying between classes, and then turned left down a corridor, scraping away gray flakes of paint as it went. It put out a lamp nearly a second before it reached its dying place in the library, the smallest breeze now, just a whisper of the thing it had been.

Two forms sat hunched forward over a scarred wooden table. They were alone in the library at this late hour and their conversation was deep, carrying their minds to a different place, and so they cared not for the fury that came down from beyond. They did not notice the wind.

"What you are proposing, Gaige… What it is that you are proposing…" Professor Lumire began, his words reverberating in his swaying, saggy cheeks. "It is not science. It is not medicine." Lumire paused again and lit his long wooden pipe, the light from the match painting shadows above the old doctor's wrinkles as he frowned, deep in thought. "Gaige," he said sternly. "You have just this last year finished your schooling, and already you would reject its teachings?"

Gaige scowled at this remark and swiveled uncomfortably in his chair across from Lumire, wondering if his teacher and mentor knew him at all.

"I reject nothing. I wish only to expand my knowledge, to expand all knowledge." Gaige kept his voice calm, but his heart was pounding. He had waited two full years before revealing his thoughts and research to Lumire, and this was not the reaction he had hoped for.

"Expand knowledge, you say?" Lumire leaned across the table, his eyes so wide Gaige thought they might just pop from the old man's skull. "In... in bloody sorcery?" Lumire whispered the last word, and he turned his head to the doors of the library to make sure no one was there.

"Not sorcery. I am a mortal man. My powers will always be that of a mortal man. How far those powers can go, I am not sure. Science will be the answer." Science was his religion, his faith, his occultism. Science was the hope of mankind. "Science is beyond sorcery. What I will come to learn will not even the battlefield between us and those with arcane blood... it will dominate it," Gaige said, his face hovering close to Lumire's above the library table.

He could see every nuance of his mentor's expression, but Lumire could not see his. Gaige always wore his iron-beaked doctor's mask, for that was the identity he preferred over that of a sickly addict. The mask was the face he showed the world and the veil that hid him from view.

Lumire stared at him and Gaige looked away first, offering his mentor that small token of respect. He sat back and took out his steel pipe, then reached a hand to his beaked mask and tampered with a mechanism, opening a slot in the right side. There he inserted the pipe, then closed the two nostrils with a flick of another very small lever. He drew a match, lit it by running it across the side of the iron beak, put the flame to the bowl, and inhaled. His mask was airtight now, so the moon's widow packed into the pipe burned at a rapid pace. Gaige listened to the shush of the cinders as he took in the smoke. He opened the nostrils of his beak, removed the pipe, and held the smoke deep in his lungs.

He exhaled. The smoke of the moon's widow, a plant so potent that even the inhalation of its ground petals' aroma could produce soothing effects, burst from the mask's nostrils.

Lumire's frown dragged the corners of his mouth lower

and deepened the wrinkles that ran down toward his jaw. "We've discussed this—"

"And we are not discussing it again." Gaige shrugged. "I am sick."

Gaige had always been sick. He was born with a leg that was hardly a twisted strip of bone, with cords of stringy muscle that refused to function on all but the most rudimentary level. It was a weak excuse for a limb. Despite this, Gaige was not weak. He now viewed the agonizing limb as an excellent source for experimentation. Through the study of science and medicine and its applications upon himself, Gaige was fighting, and he was winning against the cruelty of his own design, training the leg to be stronger at a cost of ever-increasing pain. Of course there were other side effects, those of the manner of mental phenomena, those of the physical body, and those of a social nature. They were effects he documented but they did not stop his research.

As to the pain… Pain or not, he refused to cut the leg off. He kept it as a reminder of his humanity.

"The populace will see your science as sorcery," Lumire said. "They will see it as playing God. Worse yet, the seekers will put an end to any research. The lord regent will come down with all his wrath upon the university just for association with your name if you continue in this dreadful dabbling!"

Gaige was shattered by disappointment. He had been wrong to come to Lumire, the one person he thought would understand. "Maybe," he said, keeping his tone even, betraying none of his bitter emotion. "Maybe a time will come where the idea is welcomed."

Lumire slammed his hand down hard on the table; the teacups rattled and the warm liquid sloshed over the sides. "My most favored student, you are at times blinded by your own desire to discover! It pushes you into the direction of black space."

With those words, even Gaige's disappointment snuffed like a dying match, and in its place came the certainty that Lumire had never been the true man of science Gaige had believed him to be. He saw before him now only an old, broken man, bowing to convention. And he had no one to blame but himself, for he had seen something that had never been there. "That is a foolish thing to say, professor. For how can a man ever be blinded by a desire for discovery? A man with such a heart can only ever increase his sight."

"No… It is not our right, not our right as men." The professor bowed his head, sadness crawling into his thoughtful frown.

"I have no expectation of your help. I have no expectation that you will work by my side. Only tell me if you have any books in this great library of yours on the curing of curses." Gaige leaned forward, the tip of his beak almost offensively close to his professor's nose. But Gaige wanted to look into his teacher's eyes; he wanted to see in them the lie when Lumire claimed there were no such books.

Gaige extended his arms and panned them around the library. Floor to ceiling, the walls were covered with tight shelves of books. Dim oil lamps hung from outward poles built into the shelves. To reach the highest shelves, a ladder was needed, and a fall that could kill was risked. It was said to be the world's second largest library. The largest belonged to the Imperial City of Brynth, and it held certain archives allowed entry only to his Holy Majesty.

Lumire lifted his tea, the cup in one hand, the saucer in the other, the two rattling together as he trembled.

Gaige stood and turned around. He was dizzy from the moon's widow, and the shelves around him reached up and up into the unknown darkness.

"What about on the highest shelf back there? Or over in the foreign historical documents? Or the untranslated rune writings from Ygdrasst? All I ask for is your guidance. I came to you like a son to his father. Do not tell me that in this vast catacomb of knowledge there is nothing to aid my quest." He turned back to face the professor.

"You are yet to tell me your thoughts on the last book I gave you, Gaige," Lumire said, clearly trying to direct the topic to safer ground. "You are lucky to have the opportunity to read such a book. Three centuries ago almost every copy was burned, along with the author. The lord regent himself gave that book to the university."

"Professor, I have no interest in reading the philosophical musings of some ancient Brynthian, Arthur Weaver. You know the direction my interest lies."

"Now it is you who sound foolish, Gaige. You are hardly more than twenty years and you believe you know everything. Three centuries ago is not ancient. It is but a blink in the cosmic cycle of time. And the man's name was *Darcy* Weaver, not Arthur." Again Lumire shook his head. Gaige tried to speak, but the professor raised his hand. "Enough, Gaige. That will be enough.

"Let me tell you from all my years of experience and of teaching," Lumire continued, "a curse is a curse and cannot be lifted or altered. When one is taken by the plight of ghoulism, they are dead. Lycanthropy... they are dead. Vampirism... dead. Think of your history lessons. Think of Brynth and the Rata Plaga. For certain these plights of sorcery have no cure. Once changed, there is no return." Lumire scowled. "There is no bringing such a soul back. Such curses are final. That is scientific fact, and I must say your aggressive interest in the matter frightens me."

"I did not expect you to react like this," Gaige said as he limped away from the table into the vast, silent brilliance of the library. No one was there to see them, but he was glad the mask concealed his tears all the same.

He had always hated his birth parents' conservative idealism, and now he realized that the father he had chosen, the mentor he had trusted, was just the same. He bought all that the fearmonger sold and he cowered from the devil's domain —and in doing so, bowed down to its dark majesty.

Gaige had never felt so alone. Not even when the parents he had loved, though he hated their ideas, had succumbed to sickness within days of each other. Gaige and his crippled limb had survived, and buried deep in his box of regrets was the fact that he had never told them he loved them, he had only shown them his disdain.

His disappointment in Lumire changed nothing. He would still follow the path he chose, with no support; with the odds against him he would enter the beyond. He would unlock all the secrets he wanted to know. That was his purpose, the one he chose for himself. But his determination did not lessen the pain of his altered perception of his long-time mentor.

When he reached the doors, he looked above them at the tall painting of the lord regent. The frame was old and heavy, the gold marked with the green patina of age. The lord regent stood, long black hair sweeping his shoulders, dark eyes directed such that Gaige felt they were looking straight at him. The fire in those eyes looked like it could set the whole world ablaze. He wore a fine red coat with black epaulets and a glossy black trim on the high collar. Black threads wove an intricate design across the chest and down the abdomen, wolves on one side, ravens on the other, fur and feathers designed to give the impression of licking flames. At the bottom of the canvas were written the words "Insight be my Sword."

As Gaige pushed open the doors, his crippled left leg

ached more than usual, and with every step it screamed all the more. He passed by dark, empty lecture halls. The dim, lonely atmosphere almost swallowed him up.

The clicking of his cane on the marble echoed through the vast space like the ticking of a distant clock.

Read Catacombs of Time now!

ABOUT THE AUTHOR

Dylan Doose is the author of the ongoing Dark Fantasy saga, *Sword & Sorcery.*

Dylan also pens the new Dark Fantasy/Western Horror series, *Red Harvest.*

Fire and Sword was chosen as a Shelf Unbound Notable 100 for 2015 and received an honorable mention from Library Journal.

For info, excerpts, contests and more, join Dylan's Reader Group! www.DylanDooseAuthor.com

photo credit: Shanon Fujioka

For more information:
www.dylandooseauthor.com

Made in the USA
Middletown, DE
09 March 2024

51140884R00223